STRANGER TO THE CROWN

THE HEIRS OF WILLOW NORTH, BOOK 2

MELISSA MCSHANE

Night Harbor Publishing

Cover design by Jay R. Villalobos www.coversbyjuan.com

North sign and shield designed by Erin Dinnell Bjorn

First Printing
10 9 8 7 6 5 4 3 2 1

For my children,
all of whom have influenced my writing in one way or another,
and all of whom are in the pages of my books somewhere

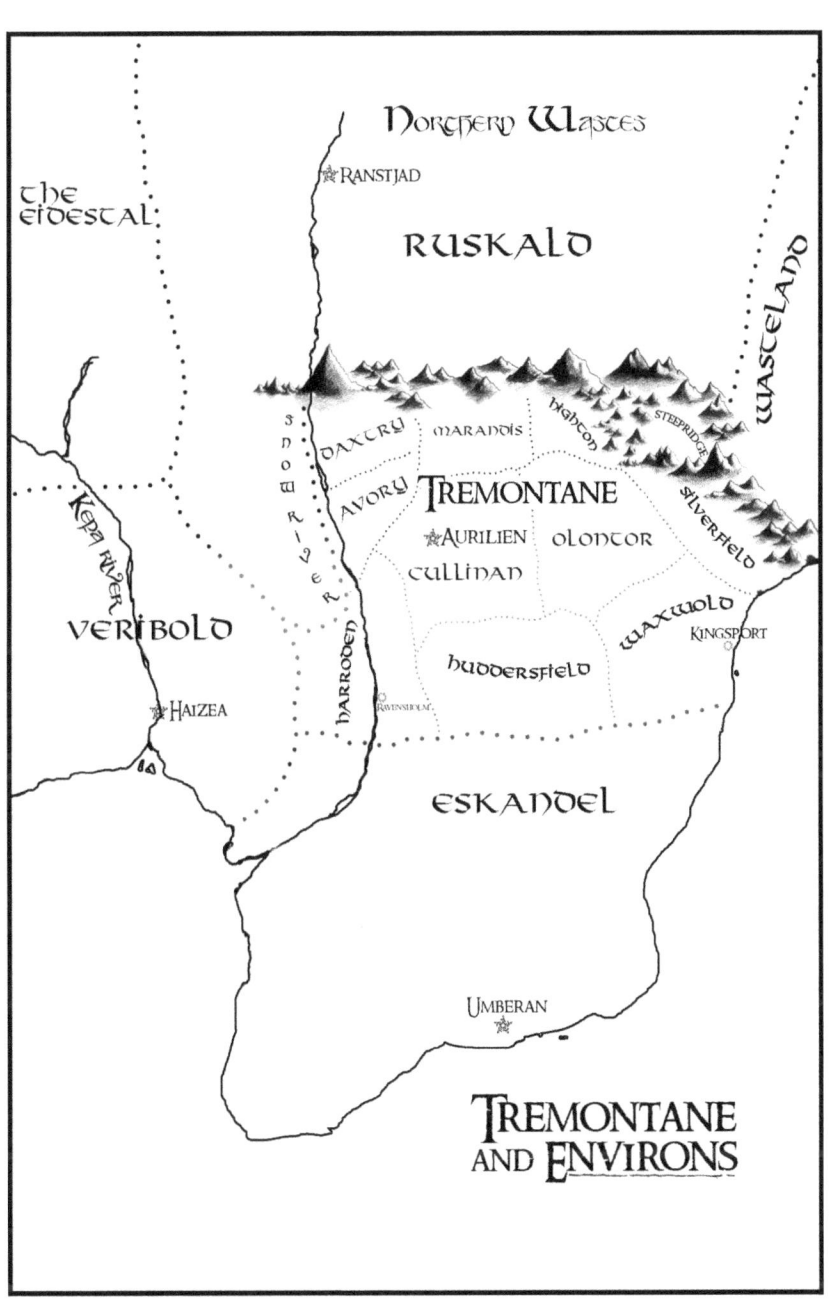

TREMONTANE AND ENVIRONS

orchlight flickered off the floor of the cavern and its rough-hewn stone wall, making a pool of light beyond which lay emptiness. From where Elspeth stood, the space might have been, not deep underground, but open to a starless sky. She tilted her head to look up even though she knew she would see only blackness and the tiny sparkles that filled her vision when she strained to see beyond her mortal limits. If this were an open space, she would feel the motion of the air, brushing her face or tangling her hair, but the air hung heavy with moisture, still and dank. It smelled of mineral-laden water and smoke from the torches and old, old stone.

She shifted her position minutely, her bare feet welcoming the touch of the unfinished stone. It was bumpy and irregular but smoothed by the passage of generations of women's feet. Beside her, water cascaded from a slit in the rock, spraying her with a fine, icy mist that gleamed white in the torchlight. The sodden air clung to Elspeth like a second skin, comforting in its familiarity. She breathed deeply, filling her lungs with damp air, and waited.

Her guide, Tha, held the torch high and gestured to a nearby cabinet that looked like it might have come from someone's sitting room. It had two shelves built into it, and a bar of soap rested in a shallow dish on its top. Nothing could have looked less like it belonged in this rough, ancient place.

Elspeth shed her rose-colored robe, then the black linen shirt and trousers beneath it, and folded them all neatly. She set them on the lower shelf, along with her undershorts, and laid a clean change of underclothing and her hairbrush on the second shelf. The bar of soap was slick in her hand, but she grasped it tightly and, shivering, ducked under the frigid fall of water.

A shock of cold went through her, and she gasped, but her hands had already begun soaping her body. She rubbed soap across her skin and through her thick red hair. Her body tingled with numbness, an exhilarating feeling, and she imagined the freezing water and coarse soap scrubbing away impurities. Nothing in the world could equal that moment.

She handed the soap to Tha and ran her hands over her body, sluicing away the last of the soap like shedding her old skin, rinsing her thick hair until no trace of soap remained. She was numb enough that the water had started to feel warm, sign that she'd taken just long enough under the waterfall. She stepped away from the water's spray and accepted the torch from her guide. The still air chilled her wet body. She shivered again and took a deep breath, exhaling slowly to control the shaking. Her guide was taking her own sweet time getting to the next step of the ritual, and that had better not be because Tha believed she needed to learn patience—

"*Haran approaches the well,*" Tha intoned in a voice deeper than her usual one. She spoke Veriboldan even though Elspeth was by birth Tremontanan. Elspeth suppressed a smile and walked at the fastest pace she could manage that wasn't a run toward the square pool in the distance. The black marble ledge surrounding it gleamed wetly in the light of the torches at three of its corners, and water slapped its edges as if some invisible hand were stirring it. Elspeth imagined she could feel the heat radiating from it, though she knew the water was only lukewarm and just felt warmer by contrast to the freezing cold of the waterfall.

Four women robed in white, their gowns' hems damp from

brushing the wet stone, surrounded the pool. Elspeth set her torch in the one empty holder and crouched to sit on the marble lip of the pool before lowering herself into it. No, *this* was the moment unlike any other, the touch of warm water that felt like gliding into oil, surging up her legs to her waist. Elspeth never felt so perfectly happy as at this point in the ritual.

"*Haran enters the well,*" one of the women, Chie, said, also in Veriboldan. "*She is made clean and washed free of impurities. She is prepared to look on heaven's wisdom.*"

Elspeth dabbled her fingers in the warm water briefly, bidding it farewell, then clambered out of the pool. She took the towel Chie handed her and rubbed herself fiercely. The rough nap of the towel made her tingle as if she were back in the waterfall. Then she handed the towel back to Chie and let the priestesses dress her as if she were a doll, this time in white shirt and trousers under her rose-colored robe. One of them dragged the hairbrush through Elspeth's hair, as gently as she could given the tangle the soap had made it. Elspeth gritted her teeth and made no sound.

When her hair was as straight as human hands could make it, which wasn't very—it would dry in masses of curls and need to be brushed a second time—the woman handed Elspeth her hairbrush, and Tha led the way back across the chamber to the low-ceilinged switchback tunnel. The sound of the waterfall echoed in the tunnel and the stairs beyond, creating the illusion that Elspeth and Tha were surrounded by laughing, mocking voices.

The stone steps underfoot were cool and slick, forcing Elspeth to go slowly. Her skin tingled from the contrast of hot and cold water, a breeze threaded through the steep stairwell, and her legs ached slightly from mounting the steps. She breathed deeply, embracing the sensations. Haran couldn't have undergone this ritual, not on the treeless Eidestal where she'd had her vision of ungoverned heaven, but it still made Elspeth feel close to her spiritual ancestor.

When they reached the top of the stairs, Tha said, still in Veriboldan, "*Those stairs will be the death of me.*"

"*Heaven welcomes your sacrifice,*" Elspeth said, intoning in a pious imitation of the priestess Sela, who was humorless and rigid. It was Sela's response to any complaint from the junior priestesses.

Tha made a rude gesture. "*I don't think heaven cares whether my legs are sore.*"

"*Probably not.*" Elspeth glanced around to be sure no one was watching, then squatted deeply, pressed her hands palm-first against the smooth marble floor of the landing, and stood with her hands still pressed against the floor, stretching out her legs and back. "*I guess heaven welcomes my sacrifice too.*"

"*Next year, you'll take my place,*" Tha said. "*Only eight more months before you take your vows.*"

"*It feels like forever away,*" Elspeth said. She dusted her hands off on her robe, though the floor was clean enough to eat one's supper off. "*I'll see you tomorrow.*"

Tha nodded and walked away down the corridor with its high, slanting roof. Elspeth went the other way, toward the narrow staircase that led to the tiny rooms called cells where attendees to the Irantzen Festival stayed. As she ascended, she passed narrow window slits looking out over Haizea. One of her favorite things about the Festival was the opportunity to see the great city from a bird's perspective. The cells at the top of the temple were almost the highest point in the Jaixante, the royal city within the capital city of Haizea, and Elspeth sometimes did her meditating while looking out her window at the clustered buildings and the green-glass flow of the Kepa River.

Elspeth was out of breath by the time she reached the top of the stairs and the wide hallway whose ceiling rose to a sharp crease. Her cell was fifth from the end. She'd never been given the same one in all the five times she'd attended the Festival, but the cells were identical except for the views one had from the windows.

She let herself in and set her hairbrush on the brass-bound chest beneath the window, then settled herself cross-legged on her pallet and picked up her *toan* jade medallion. The creamy jade pendant, slightly larger than her palm and thick as two fingers' width, was carved with the tiny symbols of meditation rituals. Elspeth ran the silk cord it hung from through her fingers, feeling her skin catch on tiny imperfections in the cord and the bumpy knots that were themselves a focus for meditation.

She closed her eyes and settled into the even breathing that prepared her to meditate. Yesterday, she'd drunk the tea and had a vision. Today, cleansed and made new, she was ready to meditate on the vision and make sense of it in preparation for discussing it with others tomorrow. Her fingers slipped over the smooth, cool, almost soapy surface of the *toan* jade. She had one of her own, but she always left it home on these annual visits. The thought of the hundreds of women who'd used this one before her made her feel connected to her faith and enhanced the experience of the festival.

Her vision had been unremarkable, a memory of walking through the palace in Aurilien as if she were actually there. She'd been to her father Prince Sebastian North's childhood home a handful of times in her life, and in the vision she remembered it better than her waking mind could. As a child, she'd been afraid of the palace because of its patchwork construction, the work of generations of rulers of Tremontane adding to it according to their whim.

Having grown up in the Tremontanan embassy in the shadow of the Jaixante, her standard of architectural perfection was the unified beauty of the Veriboldan city within a city, its white walls and gilded fairy spires that shaded to pale blue and bronze when the afternoon sun sent shadows across it. The palace in Aurilien, by contrast, squatted warm and unwelcoming on its low hill, confusing to her young mind. She'd been afraid for years that someone might come along and build a new wing atop her, trapping her. Even now she was an adult, she never enjoyed the visits to Tremontane.

She relaxed her shoulders, letting her arms hang loose. Her spine was next, that string of pearls threaded on wire that curved softly from the base of her neck. She let her hips relax, wiggled her toes, and let out a deep, warm stream of air from her mouth. The palace. The vision was unremarkable, but in Elspeth's experience, that simply meant she needed to dig deeper.

Her fingers traced the first meditation ritual, the path of awareness. *Wake, and let the inner eye see.* What did the palace mean to her?

Confusion. Distance. Discomfort. It reminded her that she wasn't one thing or another. She'd been raised in Veribold, true, and she understood that culture, but most of the Veriboldans she met—particularly the Veriboldan landholders her father the ambassador most often encountered—treated her with the distant politeness that said she would never be one of them. And yet she never felt at home in Tremontane, which was loud and boisterous and had all sorts of customs she didn't understand. Her cousin Francis had always tried to make Elspeth and her siblings feel at home when they visited, but he was awkward and they never knew what to say to each other.

Elspeth let out another long stream of breath. She hadn't thought of Francis in years, not since his father Landon had died unexpectedly, making him King of Tremontane. It was hard to imagine gawky, ill-spoken Francis as King of anything. Then she felt guilty for the cruel thought. Francis wasn't terribly bright, and he was prone to saying the wrong thing, but he was well-meaning and might make a good King. He couldn't be worse than his father, whom Elspeth hadn't liked. Her father hadn't liked him either, though he wouldn't say bad things about his older brother in Elspeth's presence. Mother would only say "Landon's interests are limited, and that's bad in a King." Elspeth couldn't imagine how her Aunt Veronica, quiet but kind, had ended up married to the loud and uncouth Landon.

She dragged herself back to her meditation. The palace. Her vision had taken her through its corridors, down the Long Gallery with paintings of the Kings and Queens of Tremontane and into the north wing and even to the ancient hall where the Scholia was housed. Maybe there was meaning in the places the vision had taken her. She relived the vision in memory, retracing her steps: antechamber, the Rotunda with its high domed ceiling, the Long Gallery, the Scholia hall, and finally the north wing.

That last had to be her imagination. She'd never been closer to the north wing, where the business of ruling Tremontane happened, than the few short stairs carpeted in North blue that led up to its dark paneled halls and heavy doors. And yet in vision she'd seen offices, and a curved desk big enough to sleep on, and windows looking out over the palace grounds. Elspeth was familiar enough with visions to know they drew from your mind and memory, and couldn't show you things you weren't already familiar with, or at least had seen once before. Maybe she'd been in the north wing as a child and had forgotten it.

A soft rap on the door startled Elspeth out of her meditation. She looked up to see the door swing open and Hien enter the room. The chief priestess looked as somber and as expressionless as always, but Elspeth felt a chill pass through her as if Hien had burst into the room sobbing.

"Elspeth," Hien said, "please follow me."

That Hien spoke to her in Tremontanese chilled her further. Elspeth spoke Veriboldan as well as she did her native tongue—though who was to say which of those was truly native to her?—and she was accustomed to using it in the Irantzen Temple. Hien's use of Tremontanese made Elspeth feel like an outsider in her beloved temple for the first time in five years.

Hien said nothing more as she led the way back down the stairs. Elspeth was desperate to know why Hien had interrupted her meditations, but Hien's silence was the sort that bound someone's tongue, and Elspeth couldn't think what to ask first anyway. Dreadful possibilities presented themselves: something had happened to her family, she'd done something wrong and the Temple was kicking her out, they were rescinding their offer to make Elspeth one of them...she'd started imagining truly absurd possibilities, such as that the King of Veribold wanted to marry her, by the time they reached the foot of the stairs.

Hien took her to one of the little rooms where in normal times, not during the Festival, people would come to receive guidance and counsel from the priestesses. "I will speak with you later," she said in a low voice. "Remember that you are always welcome here."

That made Elspeth truly frantic. Before she could grab Hien by the collar and demand an explanation, the door swung open, and Hien gestured Elspeth inside. The room was unfurnished except for a couple of chairs and a tall vase, half Elspeth's height, filled with decorative striped grass that let off a spicy scent. Elspeth's heart beat faster when she saw her parents waiting for her.

It was a possibility she hadn't considered. Her mother, maybe; Mother attended the Festival occasionally and was friendly with Hien. But Father should not have been allowed in this part of the temple during the Festival—no man was. And yet here he was, standing rather than sitting, with his hands clasped behind his back the way he did when he was about to deliver bad news. Mother sat beside him, her hands resting loosely on her thighs. Her red hair, threaded with gray but otherwise identical to Elspeth's, was a tangled, windblown mess. It reminded Elspeth that there was a world outside the temple. A world that had intruded on her cozy, peaceful sanctuary. That could mean nothing good.

No one spoke at first. Elspeth's gaze roved from her mother's face to her father's. Finally, she couldn't bear it any longer. "What's wrong? Did something happen to my sibs? Or—"

"No, the children are fine," Father said. His handsome face looked ashen, though, as if he'd witnessed things he couldn't bear. "It's your cousin Francis. Influenza. He passed away three days ago."

Guilty relief surged over her. "Oh. That's...I'm sorry to hear that."

Mother glanced up at Father. "There's more," Father said. "Francis died without producing children, and he was Landon's only heir, which means the Crown passes to Landon's siblings."

Shock struck Fiona so hard she tingled as if she'd once again passed through the waterfall. "You're Uncle Landon's next brother. You—does that make you the King?"

Father shook his head. "I renounced my claim to the Crown before you were born. It was—it doesn't matter. The point is, it turns out according to the law I can only make that decision for myself. I can't disinherit my children. It's a safeguard against...well, against situations like these."

He fell silent. Mother took his hand and squeezed it. "Oh, Elspeth," she said. To Elspeth's horror, tears slid down her mother's cheeks.

"I don't understand," Elspeth said, though a horrible suspicion had crept over her. "What are you saying?"

Father swallowed, the least controlled motion she'd ever seen him make. "Elspeth, sweetheart," he said, "you're the Queen of Tremontane."

---

2

*E*lspeth stared at them both. Then a laugh bubbled out of her, unstoppable and painful. "That's so funny I don't even mind that you interrupted the Festival for your joke. Who is it really? Aunt Emily?"

Her parents exchanged glances. Mother rose and came toward her with her arms outstretched. "I'm so sorry," she whispered.

Elspeth jerked away from her. "Stop it," she demanded, her voice so harsh she sounded like a stranger to herself. "Stop. This isn't funny anymore. I can't be Queen. It's a lie."

"I wish it was," Father said. He looked like he wanted to be sick. "Damn that idiot Francis for not marrying immediately. But *no*, he didn't want to choose, didn't want to be tied down—"

"Sebastian, don't," Mother said. "There's no sense blaming the dead. Or blaming Veronica for only having one child, or Landon for not divorcing Veronica when she couldn't have more than one child... none of that does anything but make it worse."

Father turned his back on Elspeth. She knew he was trying to spare her his emotional reaction, but it felt like a slap to the face. "What am I supposed to do?" she exclaimed. "How do I get out of this?"

"You can't," Mother said. "We've been over this with a handful of Tremontanan law-speakers and a couple of Veriboldan ones all night, ever since the word came. Of the four North children of Landon's generation, your father is the only one alive who's still a North after Emily adopted out fifteen years ago. The line of succession is clear. The only alternatives are for you to abdicate in favor of one of your siblings or for the succession to pass from the Norths entirely. If you did the first, well, none of your sibs are adults yet, and that would be a nightmare of a different sort."

"So let some other family take the Crown. The Norths have ruled for a century—that's long enough."

"That would mean civil war," Father said, not turning around. "There are at least three families who consider themselves to have a good claim to the Crown and would be willing to go to war over it."

"I don't care. I *can't* be Queen, Father! It's not even about what I want. I have no experience, no training—I'm practically Veriboldan, not Tremontanan!"

It was entirely about what she wanted. In eight months, she would become an Irantzen priestess and embark upon a life of holiness and worship. She'd wanted it for five years, had studied and meditated and prayed for it. And now some stupid accident of birth meant losing all that. Her chest ached as if it were bound with iron bands.

"You're not saying anything we haven't thought of," Mother said. "We thought—your grandmother Genevieve thought—we'd taken steps to prevent this ever happening." She laughed, a sound as harsh as the one Elspeth had made. "Genevieve is probably raging through heaven right now, browbeating Francis and Landon both."

"I don't understand."

"It doesn't matter," Father said, casting a quelling glance at Mother. "What matters is that there truly is nothing any of us can do to stop this. You're to leave for Aurilien immediately."

And *that* felt like a punch to the stomach. Shaking, Elspeth said, "But the Festival—"

Mother shook her head. "Immediately."

Tears welled up in Elspeth's eyes, and this time she let her mother hold her. Sobbing, she choked out, "Go alone? I barely know anyone there, I don't know what I'm doing...this is so *unfair*."

"Fairness doesn't matter when it comes to the fate of nations." Father put his arms around her and Mother both. "You're intelligent, you're quick to learn, and you don't intimidate easily. You understand diplomacy and you're familiar with Tremontane's relations with Veribold, if nothing else. The rest will come with time."

"It will be all right," Mother said, pressing her forehead against Elspeth's. "They won't expect you to be perfect. You'll have the Queen's Council, and your Aunt Veronica, and I think Merete Alderly is still palace housekeeper—you know her well."

The tears fell fast enough to choke any response Elspeth might make. She shook her head and managed, "It won't be enough."

"Stop it," Father said. "This is not how we raised you. I don't expect you to be happy at losing your whole life. But you know facing a challenge is harder when you dwell on what you can't have." He sighed. "I would give anything to be able to reclaim my right to the Crown and spare you this."

Elspeth shuddered, wiped her eyes, and drew a deep breath. "Immediately doesn't mean in my festival clothes, does it?"

"It means tomorrow morning," Mother said, "and if Tremontane doesn't like it, there's nothing they can do to chastise the Queen." She smiled crookedly and wiped away her own tears. "Do you want to tell Hien, or should I?"

"No, I will. I want—" How to tell her religious superior that Elspeth would now never be one of the sisterhood? The thought made her heart freeze and crack again. "Will you wait for me? I don't want to go home alone."

Father squeezed her hand. "We'll be here."

To Elspeth's surprise, Hien waited in the passage outside the little room. "Let us walk," she said. Elspeth fell into step beside her.

"It is disaster, I think," Hien said after a few paces. "The look on Fiona's face was enough to tell me that, and to convince me to allow the ambassador into the Temple at this time."

"Disaster. That's an excellent word for it." Elspeth wiped away the last traces of tears. Hien was observant and insightful, but she was also polite and would never draw attention to Elspeth's emotional state. "Hien, I am desperately in need of advice. Thanks to Tremontanan inheritance law, I am...I'm now Queen of Tremontane."

Hien came to a complete stop in the middle of the hall. "That is the last thing I expected you to say."

"It's the last thing I expected my parents to tell me. Hien, what do I do? I'm not a politician, I'm a priestess in training! Everything in me cries out against this. But Mother and Father tell me there's no way out of it, not without making the situation ten thousand times worse."

"That is indeed a disaster." Hien regarded her with dark, inscrutable eyes. "It is not the life you planned for. I imagine most who rule nations have some idea, early on, that such is their destiny. So it is also a life you come to unprepared." She tilted her head, giving her the appearance of an inquisitive raven. "And yet I think you will find yourself better prepared than you think."

"How is that possible? Francis had all those lessons while he was growing up. I barely understand how the *Veriboldan* government works, and that's only because Mihn dragged me through his own instruction."

Hien shrugged and walked on, forcing Elspeth to trot to keep up with her. "Two things the ruler of a nation needs—or perhaps I should say two types of thing. One is a knowledge of the specifics of her responsibility. Laws, customs, expectations. That, anyone can learn. But the other is more subtle. A ruler must have qualities underlying that knowledge. Wisdom. Understanding. Confidence. Compassion. You know in Veribold the King or Queen must master five such qualities. It is not so explicit in Tremontane, but I think the two are not so different."

"I don't know that I have any of those things."

"And now you are fishing for compliments." Hien smiled at her sideways, and Elspeth blushed. She had spoken without thinking how her words would sound, and she *wasn't* fishing for compliments, though she felt shaky and off-balance enough they would be welcome.

"You were prepared to accept the priesthood," Hien went on. "That requires discipline, dedication, and patience. But the Irantzen Temple is not the only place one might use such skills. You are good at listening and you demonstrate insight in understanding the visions heaven grants. Again, these are skills you might turn to any occupation."

Her mention of visions reminded Elspeth of the one she had had of the palace. The meaning seemed clear now, particularly when Elspeth remembered how she'd been drawn to the north wing. She was too experienced in her religion to be overcome by the thought that heaven might have a message for her, but it still shook her. "It means giving up my whole life," she said. "I don't think I should be expected to be happy about that."

"You would not be human if you were," Hien said. She took Elspeth's hand and patted it, a gesture of such sympathy tears came to Elspeth's eyes again. "We all of us will mourn your loss. You would have made us stronger."

"If I can return for the Festival someday, I will," Elspeth said. Her heart still ached, but the pain was growing numb and distant. She wasn't totally unprepared. "At least I speak the language. And I know the Proxy and his son, so I won't be completely alone." The Veri-boldan ambassador, Elizdo of the Arhainen, wasn't someone she counted as friendly—she didn't think he approved of her—but his son Mihn was one of her closest friends, and she hadn't seen him in the two years since his father took the posting as Proxy of Veribold.

"You will not lose your faith just because you are in a foreign country. We all believe in the same heaven." Hien reached around her neck and pulled her *toan* jade from within her wraparound shirt. "Take this with you."

"That's an heirloom—I can't accept!" Elspeth managed not to put her hands behind her like a child trying not to snatch forbidden pastries.

"The *toan* jade gathers memories as it is touched by many hands,"

Hien said. "This one is not the first I was given, and it is not the oldest. But it has seen much use, and I think knowing its heritage will give you strength. And it amuses me to think it has ended up in the hands of a Queen. Very few *toan* jades can boast such a genealogy." She took Elspeth's hand and pressed the medallion into her palm. Elspeth's fingers curled automatically around it.

"All right, but I want you to take mine," she said. "It will need a home."

"That satisfies me." Hien stopped again, and Elspeth realized they had made the entire circuit of the hall, which ran the circumference of the Temple, and ended up outside the room where her parents waited. "Elspeth," Hien said, "I leave you my blessing. Remember this place when you find yourself in despair, and let your memories anchor you to what is true." She pressed her first two fingertips against the center of Elspeth's forehead. Then she said, "Farewell— and I hope we meet again someday."

Elspeth bowed, the low bow the priestesses gave to their superiors, and watched Hien walk away. Then she opened the door and said, "I'm ready. Let's go home." That it wouldn't be home much longer was something she chose not to dwell on.

SHE SHOULD HAVE CHANGED INTO HER EVERYDAY CLOTHES BEFORE leaving the Temple, but the revelation of her new status had left her feeling weak and unable to face even the smallest things, like the reminder that she was leaving her true destiny behind forever. So she had to ignore the looks the passersby gave her as she and her parents walked the concrete paths of the Jaixante to the bridge linking the island to the western shore.

A brisk wind, chilly and scented with rain, tangled her hair as it did her mother's. Winter in Veribold was milder than in Tremontane, or so she'd heard; she'd never visited Aurilien except in summer. But the wind was still cold enough to make her wish for a cloak. She clenched her fists and refused to shiver. It wasn't much of a walk, even if she was barefoot, and if she could endure being Queen, she could endure a little discomfort.

She couldn't bear to look at the familiar tall buildings like sheer white cliffs pierced high above by round windows. Was the Queen of Tremontane considered worthy to visit the Jaixante? Veriboldan landholders, the equivalent of Tremontanan nobles, saw themselves as superior to everyone else, and except for the Festival and the Election, nobody not Veriboldan could live there. Of course, Landon and Francis had never come to Veribold, even for a state visit, so it was a question with no answer.

No wheeled vehicles or animals were allowed in the Jaixante, so the three of them crossed the bridge on foot. A carriage waited there to take them back to the embassy. Elspeth settled into one corner of the carriage and rubbed the sole of her bare foot on the smooth linen of her trouser leg. She was grateful her parents didn't feel like talking. She'd get enough of that when they reached home—

"Do my sibs know?" she asked.

Father shook his head. "When we got the message, we immediately set about looking for an alternative. We came for you as soon as we knew it was hopeless. We'll have to discuss it when we arrive. They're your heirs now, and that changes everything for them as well."

So they would be innocently thrilled to see their sister home early. They were young enough not to immediately consider what that might mean, though James was fourteen and maybe it would occur to him how odd it was that Elspeth had never come home from the Festival early before. Maybe they'd think the prospect of being the heirs to the Crown of Tremontane was exciting and not soul-crushing the way she did.

She glanced at her mother, who was looking out the window and had Father's hand clasped in hers. She'd lost two babies between Elspeth and James, babies who would be adults now. If only—but that was cruel, wishing things had been otherwise just so Elspeth didn't have to take up this burden. This was a terrible tragedy, but it was no one's fault, and Elspeth decided to face it like a woman and not like a sniveling child whining about fairness.

The embassy, with its typically Veriboldan tiered roof and small scattered round windows, was home even though Father always told them not to get used to it, that his ambassadorship might end at any time. But he'd always said that with a twinkle in his eye, and Elspeth had guessed from things she'd overheard her parents saying that the position was not one Father would be forced to retire from. It made her wonder what had passed between her grandmother Queen Genevieve and her parents. Genevieve had died when Elspeth was only two, and she had no memory of the formidable woman, but she knew Father and Mother had disliked her, part of why their family had settled so far from Tremontane.

She descended from the carriage and followed her parents up the steps and into the cool dimness of the front hall. "Let's go to the drawing room," Father said. To the attaché in forest green and walnut brown who poked her head out of one of the side rooms, he said, "Find my children and bring them to join us. They should be in the schoolroom, this time of day."

In the schoolroom. Such an ordinary pastime for this extraordinary day. Elspeth doubted they'd go back to lessons after this. She couldn't imagine focusing on education once they knew... sweet heaven, they were royalty for true now. They'd always been princes and princesses, but Father and Mother hadn't traded on those titles in Veribold, hadn't encouraged their children to think along those lines. A little of her pain disappeared as she let go the tiny resentment she'd felt of her father for not preparing her for this possibility. He genuinely had believed his children wouldn't inherit.

They never used the drawing room except for family meetings like this one, so Elspeth's memories of it were all tense and strained. Even the good memories—like when her parents told her she would have a baby brother after all those years of being the only child— were heavy with portent. And now her sibs would have one more ponderous memory to add to their collections.

She took her seat on the Tremontanan-style couch under the

round window that looked out over the back garden. The entire room was a little piece of Tremontane in Veribold, decorated that way by the ambassador before Father and left untouched by her parents, as if they, too, knew it wouldn't be used much. All the public spaces of the embassy, the ones where the ambassador hosted events, were in a Veriboldan style, and Elspeth felt more comfortable there. The thought that she would spend the rest of her life in an alien world made tears rise, which she ruthlessly dashed away. That was the kind of soppy, self-indulgent thinking that would make it impossible for her to take on her new role fully.

Mother and Father sat on the couch adjacent to hers. No one spoke. Elspeth took a deep breath and welcomed the scent of cinnamon that filled her. It was the one touch of Veribold permitted here, because her mother loved the typically Veriboldan smell. Everything else, from the vases filled with jasmine and roses whose scents fought with the cinnamon to the plain rugs with their thick naps, spoke of a country far to the east, dry and cold instead of humid and warm. And she was doing it again. She inhaled the mingled sweet and spicy scents and tried to think of nothing at all.

Running footsteps, and the distant sounds of argument, made Elspeth clench her hands. Such commonplace sounds—Ian and Sariah never walked anywhere if they could run instead, and never ran unless they could make it a race. Soon the twelve-year-old twins appeared in the doorway, gasping for breath and shoving each other amiably.

"I win," Sariah said.

"You wish," Ian said. "You even had a head start and I still beat you."

"If 'beat you' means 'touched the door last,' then sure."

"Ian. Sariah," Mother said sharply, "enough. Sit."

The twins' identical blue eyes focused on their mother. Immediately their joking expressions faded. "Are we in trouble?" Sariah asked.

"No," Father said. "Sit down. Where's James?"

"I'm here," James said, his lanky frame filling the doorway. At fourteen he was as tall as his father, who wasn't short, and Elspeth was certain he wasn't finished growing. He looked from Father to Elspeth, and his face grew grim. "Something's wrong."

"Just have a seat," Father said.

James did so, dropping into a chair next to Elspeth's couch. None of the children had sat next to her, even though the couch was long enough to fit at least one more person. She wondered if they could sense the despair that must surely be coming off her in waves.

"The festival's not over yet," James said. He sat up suddenly and leaned forward. "What's wrong? El, they didn't kick you out, did they?"

Elspeth shook her head. Her clenched hands were shaking. Telling the others felt so much harder than telling Hien. She looked at her father, pleading silently with him to do the dirty work.

"You all remember your cousin Francis," Father said. Ian shrugged. Sariah nodded. Well, they would have been six or seven the last time the family had visited Aurilien. "He passed away three days ago. He didn't have any children or even a Consort, so someone else in his family has to be the new ruler of Tremontane. Ordinarily, that would have been me—"

Sariah gasped. Father held up a hand. "Part of the agreement that made me ambassador to Veribold was that I could never become King. I won't go into the details. The important thing is that my agreement doesn't affect your ability to inherit. And because of that, Elspeth...is now the Queen of Tremontane."

Sariah gasped again. Ian's mouth fell open. James sat back in his seat as heavily as if he'd been shoved. "You can't be serious," he said. "That's...people have to be prepared to rule a country. Elspeth isn't... she just can't. She already has a life."

"There's nothing we can do about it, short of instigating civil war," Mother said. "It's nothing any of us wanted for her, but it's how things are." Tears trickled unchecked down her face again.

"The reason this matters to you," Father said, "aside from how it affects your sister, is that all of you are now Elspeth's heirs. Until

Elspeth marries and has children of her own, any one of you might end up in her position."

"We're not moving back to Tremontane, are we?" Sariah exclaimed. Her face was alight with hope. Sariah had loved their visits to the home country as much as Elspeth had disliked them.

"No, I'm still the ambassador," Father said, "but your lessons will be different from now on. It's unlikely anything will happen to Elspeth, but after this, I'm inclined not to leave you as unprepared as she is."

Irritation flared up inside Elspeth. True, it was nothing she hadn't thought herself, but Father had made it sound like she was some missish schoolgirl, with no experience of the world and vulnerable to any disaster that might strike. "I'll be fine," she said. "I can learn whatever I have to, and Hien reminded me I have all sorts of skills a Queen might need."

Father looked surprised. Then he smiled, an expression that relieved Elspeth's heart. "Of course you will. We shouldn't treat this like a death sentence."

"And it's not as if we don't visit Tremontane," Mother said. "We just have more incentive to do so now."

Elspeth unclenched her fists and smoothed the surface of her robe. She'd forgotten she was still dressed like an attendee to the Irantzen Festival. "You said I have to leave tomorrow morning."

"We'll need to arrange for an honor guard," Father said, "but...yes. I imagine things have been thrown into chaos after Francis's unexpected death, so they'll want you there as soon as possible. It's a week-long trip by carriage, since they don't want the Queen traveling like a horse messenger. I'm sorry we have to hustle you off, sweetheart. I wish Holt were..." He closed his mouth into a thin line.

Elspeth nodded. "It's all right. I want to get this over with as soon as possible." She knew what he'd meant to say, and wished as heartily as he did that the family manservant Holt were still alive. Having him at her back in Tremontane would make things so much easier.

James rose and put his arms around her, hugging tightly. "You can do this," he murmured in her ear. "I've never known anyone as determined as you."

"You mean 'stubborn,'" Elspeth whispered back.

"Yes, I do." He released her and tugged on a lock of her still-messy hair.

Ian still looked stunned. "What, the famous silver tongue is silent?" Elspeth teased.

"If I could talk you a way out of this, I'd do that," he replied. "What did Hien say?"

"That it was a challenge I could face."

He stood, bringing Sariah with him. "That's not what I meant."

She'd successfully avoided thinking about the loss of her dream until that moment. "It's not what anyone wanted for me," she said, her throat closing up around her words, "but sometimes that's what happens."

Sariah plunged forward and threw her arms around Elspeth's waist. "I wish it was me," she said. "I mean, because I know you hate Aurilien. I wouldn't be Queen if you paid me."

"Maybe I'll love it now I have to live there," Elspeth said.

Sariah gave her a skeptical look. Elspeth shrugged. The memory of her vision, contrary to sense, had gotten stronger the further she got from it. That palace...she managed not to shudder.

"I'm going to change my clothes," she said, rising from the couch, "and then...I guess I should pack, though I don't know how much of my wardrobe is suitable for royalty."

Mother covered her mouth with her hand to hold back a choked sob. "Sorry," she said. "That was overly dramatic."

"It's all right," Elspeth said. She managed a lopsided smile. "Just think. A year from now, we can look back on this moment and laugh at how despondent we all were."

"I hope that's true," Father said.

3

———————

$\mathcal{E}$lspeth had never seen snow before. The Aurilien she remembered was a city drenched in summer sunlight, hot and dry like a baker's oven. Now fat white flakes whirled around the carriage, blocking her view of anything more than a foot from it, which meant the entire city. Between that and the low hooting wail of the storm, broken only by the endless rattle of the wheels over the cobblestones, she felt cocooned within the carriage, wrapped in a soft white blanket and free from responsibilities. It was an illusion, but one she welcomed after seven days on the road.

She shivered. That soft white blanket wasn't a warm one, and the hot brick they'd put at her feet at the last stop had long since gone cold. She hoped they would arrive at the palace soon, and laughed at herself for being eager to see that monstrosity. She had to laugh if she didn't want to go out of her mind with anticipatory dread.

The journey had started well enough. The honor guard Father had assembled was mainly men and women from the ambassador's household, all of whom she knew. They didn't always remember to call her "your Majesty," which was fine by Elspeth, but they showed her more respect than they had when she was just the ambassador's daughter, and it left her on edge. Still, she could bear that if she had to. Which she did.

But the second day, they were joined by a group of...Elspeth didn't know what to call them. Not servants, but not peers. She went with "attachés" because they reminded her of those members of her father's household who were on the diplomatic fast track to being ambassadors themselves one day. They'd followed the messenger who'd come so swiftly with the news that Elspeth's life was over, and immediately took command of Elspeth's retinue. And everything had changed.

The second night, when Elspeth had tried to leave her carriage to go into the inn they'd selected, Miss Jones White had said, "Not yet, your Majesty, permit them to establish that this location is secure," and had made her wait in the carriage for fifteen minutes before escorting her inside and up remarkably quiet stairs to a room on the third floor.

Elspeth hadn't found out until the next morning that "secure" meant her attachés had evicted everyone else from the inn for the night. When she protested, Mister Dyer had said, "This is standard procedure, your Majesty. They were well compensated for the inconvenience." Elspeth had fumed silently, but Jones White and Dyer both had the air of people who never lost an argument, even with their Queen. And if it was standard procedure, should she disrupt that and insist on doing things her way? She didn't want to be an entitled snob...though it sounded like all her options ended there.

The following day, Jones White had climbed into the carriage with her and said, "Now, your Majesty, I understand you're unfamiliar with Tremontanan society. With your permission, I will instruct you in the behaviors expected of the noble class."

Jones White's air of superiority irritated Elspeth, but she was grateful for the help. So she endured four hours of Jones White telling her the difference between a Count and a Baron and the rules of a formal supper and what would be expected of her at a state reception until she was dizzy and exhausted.

After a stop for dinner, Elspeth was dismayed to see Jones White approaching the carriage, clearly intent on another marathon session. "Miss Jones White," she'd said, "I think I need time to absorb everything you told me this morning."

"Your Majesty," the woman had responded, with a frown that reminded Elspeth of the easily-annoyed priestess Sela, "we have only five and a half days to prepare you for your new role. We cannot lose any time."

The image of herself as a basin into which Jones White intended to pour knowledge amused, then irked Elspeth. "I don't think anyone expects me to be perfect immediately," she'd said, "and I think the Queen can be excused a mistake or two. You'll ride with Mister Dyer and Mister Hawsey this afternoon, and we will resume instruction tomorrow."

To her surprise, Jones White had bowed and said, "Very well, your Majesty." She sounded disapproving, but Elspeth had realized she didn't have to care. She'd settled into her carriage feeling as if she'd won a battle—and that maybe she could manage to be Queen, after all.

It had set the pattern for the rest of the trip: relentless instruction in the morning, riding alone in the afternoon, supper in whatever inn had been cleared for her convenience. Every day had brought them farther into the uplands, the great plains that lay between the Kepa Valley and the hills of western Tremontane. Every day had been gradually colder, with the occasional rainstorms becoming slushy and frigid. The first hot brick had appeared on the fifth day, and Elspeth had welcomed it, as well as the heavy velvet-lined cloak one of her attachés had found for her. She'd never felt so cold.

The storm had loomed on the horizon that morning, and Elspeth had heard her attachés discussing it after breakfast, whether they should push on for Aurilien, which was only a few hours' drive away, or wait for the storm to pass. Elspeth had drifted over to join them and felt her usual discomfort at how their conversation broke off when she neared. "Is it safe to travel?" she'd asked.

"It is your Majesty's comfort we are concerned with," Hawsey had said.

"I'll be more comfortable when the journey's over," Elspeth pointed out. "If I can make a request, I'd like us to move on."

They all bowed immediately. "Of course," Dyer had said, and that was that. Now Elspeth huddled into her cloak and watched the snowflakes swirl. She hadn't thought how the drivers in her little procession would feel about driving through the storm, and guilt swelled inside her. The drivers, the horses pulling the carriages, the outriders on their horses...she should have considered their needs before she let her impatience with the journey make a decision that benefited only her.

She wrapped her hands more tightly in the folds of her cloak and sighed. She'd been Queen for seven days and already she'd made mistakes. There would no doubt be times when she would have to inconvenience others for the good of the country, but this wasn't one of them.

She ran back over some of what Jones White had instructed her in. She hadn't realized at first how ultimately useless most of it was. "Useless" was probably too strong a word, because if she needed to know how to open a ball, or what the order of precedence in dining was, she was thoroughly prepared. But Jones White hadn't told her anything about the Council, or how to understand the law, or anything, really, that would help her rule a country. The closer they drew to the palace, the more nervous Elspeth became. Not addressing a Count properly was just embarrassing. Not knowing how to draft a law could be disastrous.

The sound of the carriage wheels changed, became higher-pitched, and the jouncing motion grew stronger. Elspeth clung to the edge of the seat so she wouldn't be bounced off. Her nerves, already on edge, tightened to the breaking point. She made herself breathe the way she would if she were meditating, in through the nose, out through the mouth. Being anxious wouldn't solve anything, and might make things worse.

She took hold of the *toan* jade, which hung around her neck beneath her shirt. Even with the fabric between it and the skin of her palm, it comforted her. It had seen so many lives and was about to embark on a new one. *Toan* jades weren't more sacred because of their heritage, but knowing this had been Hien's soothed her as much as her calming breathing did. Whatever came next, she would endure.

The carriage came to a halt. Elspeth waited. That had been another thing she'd learned: the attachés insisted the Queen not open any doors for herself. Elspeth had silently grumbled about the Queen not being a helpless child, but had acquiesced. It wasn't as if she knew where to go, anyway. And the storm still raged outside the window, its howl audible now that the carriage wheels didn't drown it out. Elspeth had no intention of stepping out into it until she knew where she was going.

The door opened. "Your Majesty," Hawsey said. He extended a hand to her, and Elspeth accepted his help down, grateful for it when her foot slipped on the iced-over step. She tugged her hood low over her forehead and hurried with him up the long flight of black marble stairs she remembered well, leading to the great palace doors, which at the moment stood open, shedding a bright light into the storm.

Then she was inside, and the doors shut on the howl of the storm, filling Elspeth's ears with a high-pitched ringing sound. She pushed back her hood and surveyed the room. There was the iron staircase spiraling off into the upper stories of the palace, there were the doors of varying sizes, some open, some shut, that led off into heaven knew where. She'd only ever used the biggest doorway, the one that opened on the wide hall that ended at the Rotunda.

Aside from the attachés, there were only a few people in the antechamber. Some of them wore ordinary shirts and trousers in a Tremontanan style. Others were dressed more formally, in high-waisted gowns with straight skirts or frock coats and waistcoats and cravats like her attachés wore. Most of them looked like they'd been on their way somewhere else. All of them were bowing or curtseying. To her.

"Ah...thank you for your welcome," she said, hoping that would stop them bowing. It did, though it didn't send them hurrying on their way. They all stared at her as if expecting her to do something obviously regal. Elspeth turned to Dyer, who had come in immediately behind her. "I would like to rest after my journey," she told him. There. That hadn't sounded nervous or insecure at all.

"Of course, your Majesty," Dyer replied. "Your servants will be waiting on your arrival. If you'll allow me?"

She didn't know what that meant, but after he took a few steps and turned his head to look back at her, she guessed he meant to show her to...somewhere. Her servants, possibly. If he cared anything for her comfort, as he kept claiming, a bedchamber might be forthcoming. She felt unexpectedly weary for having done nothing more than jounce around inside a well-appointed, if cold, carriage for four hours.

She followed Dyer from the antechamber down the long, wide hall to the Rotunda. No one followed them, not even the other attachés. Elspeth risked a glance over her shoulder and saw everyone was still watching her, though they immediately pretended otherwise. "Mister Dyer," she said, prompting him to stop and bow. "No, please don't—I was just wondering how the...my servants are paid. The drivers, and the guards, I mean."

"That is not something your Majesty needs to be concerned with," Dyer said.

His tone of voice, that dismissive, uncaring sound that said he was growing tired of his royal charge's ignorance, dispelled Elspeth's awkward embarrassment. "Mister Dyer, what I do and do not concern myself with is not your responsibility," she snapped. "I would like to see that those men and women receive a bonus for traveling through the storm. Is that something you can bring yourself to do, or should I find someone more willing to obey his Queen's instructions?"

Dyer's eyes widened. "Ah...no, your Majesty, I would be happy to see to it. Please excuse my lack of understanding. Of course you are entitled to ask whatever questions you see fit."

"Thank you, Mister Dyer, for handling this matter." Elspeth strode off toward the Rotunda, not waiting for Dyer. There was a lesson Jones White couldn't teach her: *don't let anyone think they can walk over you, Elspeth.* That was a good lesson for anyone, not just Queens.

She stopped briefly in the Rotunda, ignoring Dyer's tiny motions of impatience, to look far, far up at the domed ceiling. Murals of Edmund Valant, last of the Valant Kings, adorned the dome, all of them making him look like a larger-than-life hero instead of the indolent wastrel he'd actually been. Why Willow North hadn't had them painted over when she took the Crown was a mystery, but Elspeth wondered if it hadn't been to show how much stronger Willow was than her predecessor. Or maybe Willow had thought they were funny. She glanced at Dyer, who was practically hopping in his anxiety to, she thought, pass her off to someone else, and decided not to torment him further.

The path to the east wing, where the royal family lived, led up and down flights of stairs and through hallways and chambers and past windows looking out on inaccessible courtyards. As usual, Elspeth was lost before they'd taken two turnings. She quashed the nervousness she always felt when she was in the palace and stuck close to Dyer, who showed no sign of awareness of her emotional state. His steps slowed when they were in a particularly narrow corridor, one made narrower by the heavy oak paneling stained walnut-black, and Elspeth bit back a cry of fear when he came to a complete stop. If Dyer was lost...did it make more sense for them to proceed forward in hopes of finding somewhere familiar, or should they retrace their steps and pray to heaven the palace hadn't rearranged itself in the meantime?

"Off that way is the shortest route to the north wing, your Majesty," Dyer said, pointing. Elspeth hadn't even realized there was an opening there, what with the paneling and the poor lighting. "We will arrange for you to meet your staff in the morning. Then you are scheduled to meet with your Council afterward."

"I'm looking forward to it," Elspeth lied. They were moving quickly, if she was supposed to have her first Council meeting almost immediately. She would have preferred having a day or so to familiarize herself with the palace and the people she had responsibility for, but probably there was business that wouldn't wait. A lot of business, the way her luck was running.

Another few minutes' walk brought them to a corridor that, thankfully, Elspeth recognized: the broad, well-lit hall leading to the east wing door. She managed not to run to where two armed and armored men wearing North colors of dark blue and silver stood at attention in front of it. Dyer took a few rapid steps to put himself in front of her and said, a little breathlessly, "Her Majesty, Queen Elspeth North."

The soldiers bowed, though not as deeply as the people in the antechamber had. Elspeth suspected they didn't want to put themselves in a position where they couldn't defend her. She had soldiers willing to defend her with their lives. Soldiers, and attachés, and staff...she needed to get away from here before she started laughing and mortally insulted them.

She said, "Thank you," feeling stupid and ignorant for not knowing how to acknowledge their obeisance. One of the men stepped back and opened the door for her with another bow.

"Would you like me to accompany you?" Dyer said.

"I...don't know. Has my aunt been told of my arrival?"

Dyer nodded. "We sent a messenger ahead."

"Then I think I'd prefer to meet her in private." She managed not to add *if you don't mind*.

Dyer bowed. "As you wish. I will see you in the morning, your Majesty." He turned and walked away before Elspeth had time to respond. That was just as well, because she still wasn't sure what kind of response was appropriate.

She smiled at the soldiers, who regarded her dispassionately. She was used to the soldiers attached to the embassy, who were always properly turned out but never failed to have a smile or a wave for the ambassador's children. But these were the Queen's guards, and maybe the knowledge that they could be executed if they let anything happen to her made them disinclined to be friendly. She stepped inside the door and let it close behind her.

The hall was as she remembered it from her last visit, though what she couldn't remember was how long ago that was...four years, or five? Five, because she had been to her first Irantzen Festival the winter before that summer visit. The walls were still painted a rich cream above the half-paneling in white oak stained burgundy, the strip of ruddy brown carpet still felt slick underfoot, the lights hanging from the ceiling were still dull. They were Devices, not lanterns, and gave off a steady glow, but they gave Elspeth the impression that no one could be bothered to clean the glass.

She walked slowly down the hall, keeping close to the center from some remembered warning from years ago that the creamy walls smudged easily. She'd always felt that was an invitation for her to rub dirty fingers all over them. The smell of roast beef and cooked vegetables came to her nose, rousing her appetite. Lovely. She'd interrupted her aunt's dinner. One more person the Queen had inconvenienced today.

The hallway ended at the great east wing sitting room. A fire roared in the enormous hearth of smooth river stones, around which were drawn up heavy wooden chairs drowning in fat cushions of sage green silk and satin. That was new. Aunt Veronica must have redecorated, though Elspeth hadn't realized her aunt liked Ruskalder fashions.

She took another step toward the fire. She could feel its heat from where she stood, and for the first time in days, she felt warm. Then someone stood up from a chair near the fire, someone who moved as if she had to think about each limb unfolding, and turned to face Elspeth. She wore an unadorned black muslin gown with a narrow skirt and long sleeves, the black ribbon of its waistband just beneath her breasts, and her dark blonde hair was pulled back from her face so tightly it made her features look stiff. If Elspeth was warm, the woman must have been roasting.

Elspeth took a few more steps. "Aunt Veronica," she said.

Veronica came around the chair and walked toward Elspeth. "Elspeth," she said.

Her voice sounded so different. Elspeth was used to her aunt's

31

diffidence, her quiet calmness, but now she sounded close to breaking. Elspeth had forgotten there was one person Francis's death had devastated more than Elspeth. With tears in her eyes, she stretched out her arms to Veronica and said, "I'm so sorry, Aunt Veronica. This must be a nightmare."

Veronica nodded and hugged her niece. "It was so sudden," she said in that strange, tense voice. "One day, he had a mild cough, and two days later he was delirious and feverish, and then..." She hugged Elspeth more tightly. "None of this is anything we expected. I thought...but it doesn't matter now, does it?"

"I suppose not." Elspeth released her, and they looked at each other in silence. Veronica's eyes were dark-circled, and her lips trembled as if she hadn't gotten enough sleep for far too long.

"Dinner's ready, if you would like to eat with me," Veronica finally said. "It's not much—I'm afraid my appetite is gone. But Cook insists on feeding me..."

"I'd like that. Thank you." Elspeth hadn't thought about how Veronica must feel, all alone in the east wing, and her heart ached for her.

They went, not to the formal dining room, but to Veronica's suite, where the small table in the sitting room had been set. Two places, so someone had warned the cook. When Elspeth and Veronica had taken their seats, the door opened, and a servant in North colors entered bearing a covered tray that turned out to contain the roast and vegetables Elspeth had smelled. The woman served them both in silence, and then Elspeth picked up her knife and fork. "It smells delicious."

"I can't tell. Everything tastes like ash. But I don't want to make this a depressing meal. How is your family?"

"They're all well." Elspeth took a bite. "They'll come for a visit sometime, when things aren't quite so busy. Winter is full of diplomatic events, in Veribold."

"That would be nice." Veronica pushed her food around her plate. Elspeth wished she could order her aunt to eat; the woman was already too thin. She took another bite. The food really was excellent.

"I had them make your old room ready," Veronica said. "If you want to choose different rooms, you're welcome to, but I thought you might like the comfort of something familiar for tonight at least."

"Thank you, I do. And my rooms are fine." She didn't much care what room she slept in, had never grown attached to the suite she usually had on the few occasions she'd visited, and was more worried about not disrupting her aunt's life too much. Maybe the Queen could make those kind of demands, but Elspeth North wasn't so carelessly cruel.

"Am I supposed to meet the servants?" she went on. "I don't..." She dropped her knife and fork on the plate, making the gravy splatter on the tablecloth. "Aunt Veronica, what am I supposed to do? I don't know anything!"

Veronica took Elspeth's hand. It felt like having a thin, light-boned bird perch on her fingers. "You'll figure it out," she said. "You're the... the Queen now. They'll make allowances."

"Yes, but I should at least try to meet people halfway, don't you think? I need your help. I had Miss Jones White filling me with etiquette and protocol all the way from Haizea to Aurilien, but it's not enough."

Veronica's thin cheeks were tinged pink. She took up her utensils and took a few small bites. "I'll do what I can," she said, "but I don't know anything about ruling a country. You'll have to depend on your Council for that."

"I don't know anything about them, except that there are seven councilors plus three of the ruling lords. The ruling lords serve a term of five years and take turns at it. The councilors serve terms of six years, but they can be reinstated when their term is up. I only know that because Lord Harrington has been head of Foreign Affairs for...well, since I can remember. If I had some paper, I could maybe remember what all the Council positions are. But that's it. It's not enough to make a difference!"

"It's their job to ease your burdens, or at least, that's what Landon always said." Veronica was eating more steadily now, though she didn't drink any of her wine. Elspeth wasn't used to alcohol, but she sipped from her glass, reasoning it was something a Queen ought to be familiar with. She hoped it was an acquired taste, because it was nothing she would have drunk voluntarily, especially if there was a good rich fruit juice available.

"I just don't want to seem stupid," she said. "If I'm going to be ignorant, I'd at least like to know what questions to ask."

"Then you should probably ask them to talk," Veronica said. "Have them explain their departments. Landon used to say, if they confused him, he would just nod wisely and let them keep talking until it made sense." She smiled, surprising Elspeth. "For Landon, they might have talked a long time."

Elspeth snorted laughter, then covered her mouth to hold it back. "Sorry."

"It's all right. I admit I'm tired of grieving. I wish I was at the stage where I could feel justified in living again." Veronica pushed her plate away; it was mostly empty. "This is a terrible state to be in, this...*emptiness*, where I forget Francis is gone and then it all comes back to hit me in the stomach. But time passes, and the pain is lessened. I'm almost glad you weren't friends. You won't suffer as I do."

Uncomfortable, Elspeth said, "Oh, but I think we were friends."

"Not close ones. How could you be, when you never saw each other? It's all right. Don't feel bad that you're not grieving. It doesn't bother me."

"I was afraid you'd feel I wasn't properly respectful," Elspeth said.

"I'm not so foolish as to demand other people suffer to validate my pain." Veronica leaned back and sighed. "Francis is gone. He was buried four days ago. Life goes on."

"I'm sorry I wasn't here for the funeral." She'd never imagined having this frank a conversation with her aunt, but then the last time she'd been in Aurilien, she'd only barely been an adult, and they hadn't had anything in common.

"It's all right," Veronica repeated. "I think it's better you begin your reign without that cloud hanging over you." She looked away, and added, "If you want me to leave—"

"No, I—wait, you mean, leave the palace?" Veronica gave the

tiniest nod. "Sweet heaven, of course not! This is your home! And I need your support. I hope nobody suggested you should go, because I would have to...I don't know. Do something horrible to them."

Veronica smiled, more widely this time. "Like what?"

"I'm the Queen," Elspeth said. "I'd think of something."

4

_____

The rustle of curtains being drawn back startled Elspeth out of a dream that dissolved upon waking. She sat up, shielding her eyes against the bright sunlight. It was as if yesterday's storm had never happened.

A woman wearing plain gray trousers and a white collarless shirt stood at the window. She wore a strange garment over her shirt, something between an old-fashioned doublet and a belted vest, in North colors. She bowed to Elspeth, making the vest bunch up over her stomach. "Good morning, your Majesty," she said. Her accent was strange, not that of the upper-class Aurilien nobles and not the drawl of northwestern Tremontane, which were the only two accents Elspeth had heard often. "Happen you'd like breakfast now?"

"Ah...all right, I suppose so," Elspeth said. She wished she knew what time it was. Early, certainly, and maybe it didn't matter the exact time, since Dyer had made it sound like her schedule was dictated by other people, but she might feel less disoriented. "What time is it?"

"Seven o'clock, your Majesty. It's when his Majesty always rose. Happen you'd prefer..." The woman bowed again. "We didn't know what your Majesty wanted. I apologize if we chose wrong."

"No, it's fine. Could I have a couple of poached eggs on toast, and maybe a glass of orange juice?"

The woman looked taken aback. "Don't know if we have orange juice, this time of year, but I'll ask. Your Majesty doesn't want ham, or bacon?"

Greasy meat first thing in the morning had never appealed to Elspeth. "No, thank you. Just the eggs."

When the woman had bowed herself out, Elspeth climbed out of bed and crossed the soft carpet to the dressing room. Her clothes had mysteriously appeared there the previous evening, neatly hung on rails or folded into dresser drawers. The few things she owned made the room seem even more cavernous. No doubt the Queen needed more of a wardrobe than Elspeth North the ambassador's daughter did. Another thing she didn't know how to get. She removed her dressing gown from the peg on the back of the door and put it on. She still felt far too cold, particularly in her bare feet.

She went back to the fireplace and regarded the...thing...in the hearth. It was a brass box three feet on a side, with a lid that could be propped open. Inside, glowing coils and spiked wheels and masses and masses of copper wire filled the box to bursting. Elspeth regarded the mysterious contents for a few minutes. This Device hadn't been there the last time Elspeth had used this room. Someone had bricked over the fireplace and put the Device where the andirons had been. She guessed the Device was to heat the room somehow, but she had no idea how to turn it on.

She turned as the bedroom door opened and the woman entered, carrying a carved wooden tray with four short legs at its corners. She stopped halfway through the door when she saw Elspeth, clearly startled. "Did you...his Majesty always took breakfast in bed," she said, her voice faint.

That struck Elspeth as decadent and awkward, but she felt she'd already shocked the woman enough for one day. "I was cold," she said, hopping back into the tall bed. Somewhere, there was a little stepstool to assist in climbing into the bed, but Elspeth hadn't found it last night and had to resort to springing up with her hands shoving off the mattresses.

"You didn't—" The woman shut her mouth and carefully rested her tray on the bed next to Elspeth. "Do you know how to work the Device, your Majesty?"

"I don't. Could you show me?" An irritated thought about why this woman had clearly assumed Elspeth *wanted* to sleep in an ice cave flashed through Elspeth's mind. She watched curiously as the woman flipped up a hatch at the back of the brass box that Elspeth hadn't even seen and pressed a wooden button a little bigger than the tip of her thumb. Something went *click*, and the box emitted a low hum Elspeth found pleasant.

"It will warm up soon, your Majesty, and I'm sorry we didn't think to turn it on last night." The woman bowed and turned to leave.

"Wait," Elspeth said. "What's your name?"

"Gloria, your Majesty."

"And you're a...household servant?"

Gloria smiled proudly. "I have the care of your Majesty's rooms. Mistress Alderly chose me particularly."

"You must be very good to earn Merete's trust. What other servants are there in the east wing, Gloria?"

Gloria's brow furrowed. "There are two maids at your service day and night—I mean, I'm the day, and Shirley is the night. Then two for the Dowager Consort. The servants who clean the public rooms—I mean the ones not yours and the Dowager Consort's. The cook and her assistants. Milady the Dowager Consort has two maids to help her dress and manage her wardrobe. And there's the soldiers, but I'm not sure that's what you meant."

"No, that's good. Thank you. I'm afraid there's a lot I don't know."

"Oh, you'll learn it all soon enough!" Gloria blushed. "I beg pardon for my informality, your Majesty. Certain sure I didn't mean anything by it."

"It's all right, Gloria. Don't feel you have to be perfectly correct all the time." Elspeth sighed and picked up a piece of toast. The poached egg had a light sauce drizzled over it that smelled slightly of lemon and tasted delicious. Gloria bowed again and shut the door behind her. How many servants was that? Seven, plus however many servants it took to keep the east wing clean and the cook's assistants? And that was just for her household. She probably needed a personal maid, once that expanded wardrobe appeared.

There was no juice, but there was a pot of chocolate and a pitcher of fresh cream, and Elspeth poured a liberal helping of each into a cup, stirred, and drank in pleasure. Expecting oranges in winter in Tremontane was a little extreme, come to think on it. She squelched the thought that she might be able to demand it. She wasn't going to be an entitled snob just because she was the Queen.

Fed, and warm now that the Device was running, she pulled the bell rope hanging near the head of the bed and waited for Gloria to appear. "I don't suppose you know when I'm supposed to be in the north wing?" she asked.

Gloria hefted the tray and shook her head. "I'm sorry, your Majesty, I don't. But I think Mister Dyer is waiting on you in the sitting room. Should I ask him?"

"No, I'll ask him myself."

She waited for Gloria to leave, then returned to the dressing room and quickly changed into comfortable trousers and the warmest shirt she could find. She examined herself in the full-length mirror as she brushed her hair. The dryness of the air made it feel bushy, but there wasn't anything she could do about that. Nor could she do anything about her clothes. Well, she'd been born in Veribold, had lived her whole life there, and it wasn't as if her parents had imported Tremontanan clothing just so their children wouldn't look like Veriboldan natives. She slid her ankle boots over her feet and stamped a couple of times, more to comfort herself than to make the boots fit properly. Maybe a new wardrobe was more important than she'd thought.

Dyer was, in fact, waiting in the east wing drawing room, standing before the blazing fire with his hands clasped behind his back. Elspeth wondered briefly why that hearth hadn't been filled in and replaced with a Device. Whatever the reason, she was grateful for it.

She had no idea how efficient Devices were, but there was something about an actual fire that warmed her more deeply than any brass box.

"Your Majesty," Dyer said. "I apologize for not having explained today's schedule last night. You were expected in the north wing ten minutes ago."

Embarrassment swept over her. One more thing she'd done wrong. Then she felt angry with herself for letting Dyer get to her. "Yes, that would have been good to know," she said. "Who decides the schedule?"

Dyer raised an eyebrow. "Why, your secretary, of course. Miss Simkins is very well organized. If you'll come with me, I'll introduce you."

She had a secretary? It made sense, though Elspeth wasn't sure she wanted to give control of her life over to anyone, however well organized.

She followed Dyer through the halls, doing her best to memorize the path and not cringing at the narrow, dark hall that had unnerved her the day before. Soon enough, they arrived at the short flight of stairs leading to the north wing. The steps looked worn, but the North blue carpet and stair-rods were new. Elspeth entertained an idle thought about the wisdom of covering over something that might need to be replaced, told herself it wasn't her business, then remembered it might actually be her business. If it was, it was so far down the list of what she had to deal with it might as well not matter.

The north wing was all dark wood paneling and heavy, ponderous doors with oversized brass knobs. It weighed on Elspeth as she passed through its halls. She couldn't help feeling judged by this place that had seen so many sovereigns, not just her ancestors but Valants and Cammertons and all those kings and queens who'd lived so long ago they didn't have surnames. All those people down to Elspeth North, uncertain ruler of a country that hadn't expected her and might not even want her. It was enough to make her want to flee.

Men and women passed them in the halls. None of them bowed or even made eye contact. It reassured Elspeth, even though she knew it was only that they didn't know to recognize her. Soon enough, that would change.

They came to an open space like a miniature Rotunda, though without the domed roof. A semicircular desk filled half the space, attended by a frazzled-looking man who sorted through piles of papers. "Dyer, you—" he began before looking up and seeing Elspeth. "Is this my replacement?"

"Your Majesty," Dyer said, leaning heavily on those two words, "this is Edrick Branton. He manages the departments and coordinates with Miss Simkins to organize your schedule. Branton, you ought to rise for her Majesty."

Branton shot to his feet. "My apologies, your Majesty, I had no idea—please forgive my rudeness—"

"It's all right," Elspeth said, feeling uncomfortable. That was two people who'd been afraid she'd take serious offense at their lack of manners. She hadn't thought Francis, or even Landon, the type to punish people for simple mistakes. "You manage the departments? I thought that was what the Council members were for."

"Oh, no, your Majesty, I mean, yes, the Council members are responsible for their departments," Branton said, "but when they make decisions or have things the Queen must sign off on, that comes to me, and then Miss Simkins and I arrange for you to receive them. At a convenient time for you, of course."

"I see." So Branton and the mysterious but well organized Miss Simkins had complete control over what Elspeth would or would not see? That struck her as a lot of power for two people who didn't have official government positions. "I'd like to meet Miss Simkins now, if you don't mind." That had slipped out accidentally. Elspeth inwardly groaned.

"Certainly." Dyer gave Branton a glare Elspeth was sure she wasn't supposed to have witnessed and led her past the desk and down another ponderously paneled hallway. The door he opened, however, led to a room that was blindingly bright by comparison. The half-paneled walls were a bright cherrywood below and a pale ivory above, and floor to ceiling windows of fine, thin glass, very modern, filled one wall—the east wall, Elspeth realized, because the rising sun was visible through them. It was so cheerful she relaxed immediately.

Bookcases stuffed full of papers and untidy leather-bound books lined the south wall, with framed maps of Tremontane and the northern continent hanging above them. A desk positioned to catch the full morning sunlight took up most of the eastern end of the room. More books, papers, cups holding pens, and a rack with pots of ink cluttered its top, which was barely visible. Elspeth walked around to look at it more closely. She counted twelve drawers of various sizes, two of them with keyholes, all of them carved with ornate abstract designs. A chair was pulled away from the desk as if inviting her to sit.

"This was King Francis's office," Dyer said. "You are of course free to choose a different room, but you will naturally want to familiarize yourself with the business pending your approval."

Elspeth looked up at him, stunned. "You mean this...mess?" she said, aghast.

Dyer smiled politely. "I am afraid King Francis's illness meant much was left undone. The Council, however, knows what needs to be addressed, and I am sure they will be happy to assist."

Elspeth sank into the chair. From that angle, the mess looked worse. She tried one of the drawers with a keyhole and discovered it was locked.

"Top center drawer, your Majesty," Dyer prompted.

The top center drawer was more cluttered even than the desktop, but a small ring of keys lay where anyone might walk off with it. Elspeth tried a few keys until she found the right one. The drawer was empty. Disappointed, she closed it without locking it and put the keys into her pocket.

"If you pull the cord behind you, it will summon Miss Simkins." Dyer pointed. Elspeth leaned back, grasped the cord, and pulled. She couldn't stop staring at the desk. This was going to take a lot more than assistance from the Council to fix.

The door opened behind Dyer, and a short, round woman entered. She appeared to be in her forties, with the first hints of gray showing in her brown hair, and she walked with short, precise steps that made her seem to be bobbing. Spectacles attached to a long ribbon perched on her nose, with the ribbon fixed with a silver pin to her starched white shirt. A fat brass pocket watch attached to a long chain hung at her right hip. The hem of her long black circle skirt brushed the ground, concealing her shoes. She held a large book bound in white leather in the crook of her left arm. When she drew near the desk, she curtseyed. "Your Majesty, I am Desdemona Simkins, your secretary. I look forward to serving you."

"Thank you, Miss Simkins. I know I will depend on your assistance," Elspeth said, feeling like a prig. Depend on your assistance. She might as well have asked the woman to spoon-feed her.

"I have your Majesty's schedule for the day, if now is convenient." Simkins opened the book and looked at Elspeth expectantly.

"Oh," Elspeth said. "Um...Mister Dyer, you are excused. Thank you."

Dyer looked disappointed, but concealed it well. He bowed himself out. The instant the door was closed, Simkins said, "Your Majesty is to meet with your Council at nine-thirty. Dinner is served in the east wing promptly at noon. At one o'clock you are to meet with the master of ceremonies to plan your coronation. At three-thirty—"

"Wait," Elspeth said. "My coronation? Aren't I already Queen?"

"Yes, your Majesty, but there is a formal ceremony," Simkins said. She sounded irritated at being interrupted. "The formal introduction of the staff is scheduled for three-thirty. Between four o'clock and six o'clock you have a meeting with the head of Internal Affairs. I believe the subject is—this." She indicated the desk. "Supper is at six-thirty, and you have no other meetings or ceremonies after that." She shut the book with a snap. "That is not usually the case, but I believed it sensible not to schedule too many things at first."

"Thank you," Elspeth said, feeling faint. If this was not too many things... "I'll need time to go over...this...if I'm to have a meeting about it this afternoon."

"I believe you will have time between the Council meeting and dinner, and just before the staff is introduced." Simkins drew herself up to her full height, which wasn't very. "Does your Majesty have any instructions for me?"

"Um...no. Not right now. Thank you. No, wait!" She felt even more foolish. "What *time* is it?"

Simkins looked at her. For a moment, something like sympathy crossed her face. "It is 8:42 exactly," she said, looking at her watch. "Does your Majesty not have a timepiece?"

"I don't. Could you find me one? Or find someone who could find me one?"

"It would be my pleasure, your Majesty." Simkins curtseyed again and left the room.

Elspeth sagged deeper into the chair. It had no cushion and its seat felt hard and smooth, making Elspeth wonder how many people had sat in it over the years. It would take some getting used to.

She flicked through the drawers. Most of them were as cluttered as the desk. Finally, she couldn't stand it any longer. She removed the ink stand and the pen cups, setting them on the floor where they couldn't be knocked over. Next, she made stacks of the books piled on the desk and moved those to the floor as well. She thought about putting them on one of the bookcases, but even if those shelves hadn't been entirely full, the books on the desk might be there for a reason, and she didn't want to mix them in with all the others.

Removing all that made the desk look...well, it was still far too cluttered, but it felt manageable. She picked up a sheet of paper and glanced over it. It was a report on crop yields in Barony Avory. She hadn't thought the ruler of Tremontane would be concerned about that level of detail, and she had to set the paper down and do some meditative breathing to calm herself. She didn't want to give up before she'd even begun, but this was worrying. Time enough to deal with it when she'd met with the Council.

She'd made several small piles of papers by the time someone knocked on her door. "Your Majesty," he said in response to her invitation to enter, "I was sent to bring you this."

He came forward and handed her a watch the size of a turnip, made of solid silver. Its case was matte-bright from hundreds of hair-fine scratches, suggesting it had been well-used over the years. Elspeth turned it over in her hands, marveling at how smoothly its hands moved. Then she registered the time, and squeaked in dismay. "Stop!" she called to the man, who was almost out the door. "I need to be at the Council chamber in two minutes. Can you direct me there?"

The man blanched, and Elspeth realized he wasn't much more than sixteen. Probably he was a low-level errand runner, not someone accustomed to speaking to his Queen. "I—your Majesty, maybe—"

Impatience swept over her. "Do you or do you not know the way to the Council chamber?" she demanded.

The young man nodded, ruddy and inarticulate.

"Then you will take me there at once. I realize it's not your usual duties, but I don't have time to find someone else. Please, lead the way."

The young man nodded again and held the door for her. Elspeth swept past, then stopped for him to precede her. She didn't bother trying to keep track of the turnings, and the young man moved too quickly for that in any case. He led her up a ramp carpeted in red and opened the door at its top for her. "Your Majesty," he whispered, and made his retreat.

Elspeth resisted the urge to check her watch again. If she was late, there was nothing she could do about it now. She pushed the door open wider and stepped through.

5

The windowless room was lit entirely by Devices shaped to look like oil lamps. Elspeth was starting to draw all sorts of conclusions about Tremontane from its Devices, most specifically that somebody in the palace wanted to cling to the past while embracing the future. Brightly woven banners hung on the walls between the Device lamps, tapestries representing the eleven provinces, the triple peaks of Tremontane, and the blue and silver panther of the house of North. They cheered the room considerably.

An enormous round table occupied the center of the room. Its top was a round cross-section of a tree so large Elspeth couldn't imagine how it had looked when it was alive, let alone where it might have come from. She also couldn't imagine how they'd gotten the table into the room in one piece, because it was too large to fit through the door she'd entered by and might be too large for the second door on the far side of the room. It was a deep, rich brown with black rings circling its center, and although the bark had been removed, cracks still radiated from the edges across the grain, some of them deep enough for her to fit her hand into. It gleamed with polish bright enough to reflect, however imperfectly, the ten people around it who'd risen when she entered.

Elspeth's gaze swept the room, not coming to rest on any one person. They all stared back at her in silence. She didn't know what she was supposed to do. Etiquette according to Jones White said that the Queen was never introduced to anyone, that others should be introduced to her, but there wasn't anyone to do the introductions, and maybe the rules were different for the Council, some of whom were lords and ladies themselves.

Her eye fell on the one empty chair in the room. It was ornate enough almost to be a throne, and sat pushed a little way back from the table as if waiting for someone to sit. *Yes, you idiot, it's waiting for you.* Elspeth walked around the table, drew the not-a-throne back, and took her seat. It moved smoothly over the wooden floor, and she was able to pull it in easily.

"Please be seated," she said. Her voice didn't shake or squeak, her hands weren't trembling, and she felt her confidence return.

The people all sat. Silence returned, broken only by a cough from someone who might be the oldest person there, with wispy white hair floating around his bald head and a liver-spotted, wrinkled face. So no one wanted to speak first. Maybe it really was her job, after all.

"Thank you for coming," she said. It was a nice, banal opening, even if it did imply that she'd arranged this meeting instead of being directed to it like a child. "I know this tragedy has put us all in a difficult situation. I'm sure you're aware I never realized I would become Queen, but I hope to rule justly and wisely. And I know all of you will do your part to assist me."

Some nods, a few shiftings of position, another cough from the old man. "You all know who I am," Elspeth went on, "but I can't say the same for you. I would like you each to introduce yourselves and your role on the Council. Then we can discuss whatever is on the agenda." She knew enough to know agendas were the sort of thing Councils had, but none of her oh-so-helpful staff had given her one. She hoped she hadn't just made the kind of mistake that would make her look foolish.

The woman immediately on her right stood. "Teresa Quinn,

Countess of Waxwold," she said. She was young, probably no older than Elspeth, and pretty, with nut-brown hair and eyes to match. She had her hands clasped nervously in front of her. Instead of shirt and trousers, she wore a high-waisted muslin gown with long sleeves and a gold brooch shaped like a leaping wolf pinned at one shoulder. She hesitated as if considering something else to say, but sat down in silence. Elspeth, looking at her, felt so out of place she wanted to flee. Why hadn't anyone said there was a dress code?

The man beyond her was up before Teresa Quinn's bottom touched her seat. "Duncan Faraday," he said. "Head of Internal Affairs."

Elspeth remembered she had a meeting with him that afternoon. He, too, was dressed more formally than Elspeth, though he'd left off the frock coat that should have gone with his waistcoat and wore no cravat. He seemed young to be the head of a department, or whatever it was the heads were in charge of, not in his thirties yet, but his expression was hard and unfriendly, his dark blue eyes stony. Elspeth's hope that they might be able to get along died.

She focused on remembering names to go with faces and positions. General Griffin Beckett looked like someone you would put in charge of Defense, with his stern demeanor and stocky build, almost a defensive wall himself; Junia Hardison of Transportation looked like she wished she were somewhere else; Annis Wilde, the Baroness of Marandis, looked like she wanted to be anywhere but where Hardison was. The elderly man was Simon Heath, Count of Huddersfield, and he greeted her with a smile and a friendly nod that cheered her. Both Hardison and Lady Wilde were dressed informally, relieving Elspeth's mind. So she hadn't completely made a fool of herself.

One face she knew already, and for the first time in her life she was happy to see it. "Welcome to Aurilien, your Majesty," Felix Harrington said.

"Thank you for your welcome, Lord Harrington," Elspeth replied. The head of Foreign Affairs had been a familiar sight whenever

Elspeth's family had visited Aurilien, and while Elspeth had never been anything to her father's putative superior but a precocious child, he was still someone she knew.

The introductions went on. Lady Serena d'Arden, head of Commerce, was an attractive woman a few years older than Elspeth. So much for her theories on how old you had to be to have this job. Lady Jessalyn Beaumont was in charge of Agriculture and looked exactly the way someone with charge over crops and livestock ought to look, in Elspeth's opinion, with her windblown, frizzy hair and ruddy complexion as if she spent a lot of time outdoors. The head of Finance, Julius Caxton, had a round, cheerful face, but his eyes were cold and calculating and made Elspeth nervous.

"Thank you all," Elspeth said when Caxton had made his introduction and sat down. "Now, I apologize for my lack of information, and I hope you will all bear with me as I learn. How does a typical Council meeting proceed?"

No one spoke at first, and nobody seemed interested in meeting anyone else's eyes. After a pause that felt to Elspeth to go on for at least two years, Faraday said, "It's the Queen's duty to present those matters she wants the Council to deliberate on, or vote on." He leaned back in his chair as if, having delivered this ultimatum, there were nothing more to say.

Elspeth quailed inside. Faraday hadn't been overtly hostile or even rude, but his whole demeanor was that of a man who'd already decided she was a failure. She firmed up her chin and said, "Thank you, Mister Faraday. I arrived in Aurilien yesterday and there's been no time this morning for me to make any such decisions. But you all know the state of the Council at my cousin's death. Are there any matters of business you were...deliberating on when he became ill?"

More silence. Elspeth's feelings of inadequacy turned into frustration. Yes, she was completely unprepared for this role, but surely these people more than anyone else cared that she not remain that way? "You mean," she said, unable to keep that frustration from touching her voice, "the Council wasn't doing *anything* before Francis's death?"

That got a reaction. Lady Wilde sat up straighter, as did Caxton. "Are you suggesting we didn't do our duty?" the elderly Lord Heath demanded.

"I have no idea," Elspeth shot back. "I wasn't here. I only know what you tell me."

"You are entirely correct, your Majesty," Lord Harrington said in a soothing tone of voice that placated Elspeth rather than infuriating her. "I think we were all simply working out what details you need to know. Foreign Affairs sent a report to his late Majesty on our diplomatic presence in Ruskald and the need to assign more soldiers to the embassy there."

"Is something wrong with our relations with Ruskald?" Elspeth gratefully clung to the lifeline Lord Harrington threw her.

"Something is always wrong with our Ruskalder relations, your Majesty," Lord Harrington said with a rueful smile. "But in this case, it's a matter of cultural differences. The Ruskalder see a show of military strength as a mark of Tremontane's power. Our ambassador sent word that the Ruskalder have been making dominance plays over the last few months. An increased military presence will calm that situation."

"I see. Thank you, Lord Harrington. General Beckett, is that something Defense should handle?"

Beckett looked startled at being addressed. "I, ah, yes, your Majesty. With your permission, my people will work with Foreign Affairs to make this right."

"Certainly." The knot of tension at the base of her neck loosened. She'd done something right! "Is there anything else?"

Hardison leaned forward. "There's the matter of my replacement," she said. Her voice was gruff, deeper than Beckett's and more quavering than Lord Heath's.

"Your...replacement?"

"My term is up in a week, your Majesty. I've sent my recommendations for my successor to your office."

Elspeth thought of all the papers she hadn't yet looked at. Her momentary feelings of success faded. "I'll look at them as soon as possible. Is that a decision the Council votes on?"

Hardison's lip curled slightly. "It's tradition that your Majesty presents your chosen candidate for a Council vote."

Elspeth chose not to address the hidden rudeness. "Thank you, Miss...Mistress?"

"Miss," Hardison said. She leaned back in her chair and rested her interlaced fingers on the table. Beside her, Lady Wilde sneered openly at Hardison. Maybe it was for the best that Hardison was leaving.

"I haven't gotten a response to my report on provincial taxation," Caxton said. The round little man eyed Elspeth as if he blamed her for Francis's shortcomings. "We need approval for more tax collectors. We need more auditors. And there are budget shortfalls to address."

It was like being pelted with gravel, one little thing after another. "I'll find that report immediately," Elspeth assured him.

"The taxation report should come to the Council," Faraday said. "Financial matters are voted on rather than determined solely by the Queen."

He still sounded as disapproving as a tutor chastising her for poor penmanship. Elspeth said, "Thank you, Mister Faraday. I appreciate your patience as I learn." She'd hoped the sideways criticism would soften his attitude, but if anything, his demeanor grew harder. "Mister Caxton, have you sent this report to every member of the Council?"

Caxton reddened. "No, your Majesty. King Francis always made the decision as to what to bring to our attention."

"Well, I realize I'm new to this, but that seems to have potential for abuse. I'd like your office to make copies for everyone to study before we meet again—how often does the Council meet?" There, that had sounded decisive and not at all as if she was desperately putting off something she didn't understand. She'd always been terrible at mathematics, and finance sounded even more complicated.

"Weekly, unless urgent matters arise," Faraday said.

"Then a week from today. That should give everyone plenty of time to become familiar with the subject." It might be enough time for her to learn to fake her understanding.

Thinking that reminded her of something else. "Lady Beaumont, I saw a report on crop yields on my desk. Is there something I'm supposed to do with that?"

Lady Beaumont didn't stir from her relaxed position. "It's for your information, your Majesty. King Francis always wanted to stay informed about the country."

"I see." Francis had been dumber than she'd thought if his idea of staying informed was to be inundated with minutiae. Lady Beaumont's lazy smile told Elspeth she knew how foolish Francis had been and that she fully intended to go on swamping Elspeth, believing she was too polite or too ignorant to protest. Elspeth had seen that smile on Sela many times; the priestess loved burdening the juniors and the aspirants with things they had no power to resist. Well, Elspeth no longer had to put up with that.

"I agree it's important for me to know what's going on," she continued, "but the point of having a head of Agriculture is to have someone who understands her...her charge who can pass that understanding on. I'm sure you know better than I do what those crop yield reports mean. So in future, I'd like you to summarize that information and present it to me as a single document. Oh, and if you could include comparison figures, such as the difference in, say, crop yields from one year to the next, that would be excellent."

The smile fell away from Lady Beaumont's face. Elspeth saw Lady Quinn conceal a smile. "Very well, your Majesty," Lady Beaumont said. She didn't sound nearly so self-satisfied as before.

"Anything else?" Elspeth asked. This time, the silence that fell wasn't quite so uncomfortable, as everyone was able to meet her eyes. "Then, to summarize, General Beckett and Lord Harrington will work together to bolster our military presence in Ruskald, I will make a decision on Miss Hardison's replacement, Mister Caxton will arrange for his report to go to each of you for deliberation next week, and Lady Beaumont, I expect to see that summary sometime before our next meeting. In case there's anything we need to address then." Elspeth couldn't help needling the woman. It was probably unbecoming in a Queen, but she was still on edge and having trouble controlling herself.

She rose, and the councilors rose with her. "Thank you, ladies and gentlemen, I'm grateful for your service to the Crown. Mister Faraday, I will see you this afternoon." That was not a meeting she looked forward to, but maybe she could convince the formidable Internal Affairs head that she wasn't a total loss. Unlikely, but there was always a chance.

She found her office again by way of following some of her councilors back to the north wing, pretending that wasn't what she was doing. The office was starting to feel like a haven despite the glowering presence of the Papers, as she'd come to think of them. They certainly felt like they had a life of their own and delighted in making her miserable.

She discovered in sorting the Papers that a third of them were agricultural reports. She happily dumped those in the fire, which was an actual fire and not a Device. No amount of searching turned up the financial report Caxton had referred to, though, and Elspeth had almost nerved herself up to start searching the bookshelves when someone knocked on the door. It was Simkins. "Your Majesty," she said with a disapproving frown, "dinner was served five minutes ago."

"Oh!" Elspeth pulled out her watch. "I was caught up in all this. I don't suppose someone could bring me something? I'm not terribly hungry."

Simkins' disapproving frown deepened. "King Francis always insisted on a leisurely noon meal. It is important you not neglect your needs."

"Oh." Elspeth's mind went to the cook in the east wing, and how disappointed she would be if Elspeth didn't appreciate her hard work. She dusted off her hands and rose from her seat. "I...need someone to show me the way back to the east wing."

Simkins' eyebrows went up. "I beg your pardon, your Majesty?"

Elspeth's cheeks heated up. "I always used to get lost in this place. It's confusing. I'm sure eventually I'll know my way around, but for now..."

"I see." Simkins didn't sound as if she did, but she refrained from any more comment. "I would be happy to show you the way."

They walked in silence through the halls. Elspeth was desperately engaged in memorizing turns and taking note of unusual paint colors when Simkins said, "Would your Majesty prefer I bring the day's schedule in the morning, or the evening before?"

"What? Oh. What did Francis do?"

"He chose to receive his schedule the evening before." Simkins sounded more disapproving than ever. Elspeth wasn't sure what difference it made, except that if she had the schedule in the evening, that would give her more time to fret over what it contained.

"I think I'd rather have it in the morning. Make a fresh start."

Simkins nodded. "Very well, your Majesty." The look she directed at Elspeth was almost friendly.

At the door to the east wing, Elspeth impulsively said, "Would you like to eat with me? I'm not sure if Aunt Veronica is here."

Simkins' eyes widened and her mouth fell open slightly. "*Eat with...*" She regained her composure and said, "That is an honor, your Majesty, but I'm afraid I have other duties."

"I understand." Elspeth didn't particularly want to share a meal with the stern Simkins, but the thought of eating alone in the east wing dining room, at its table large enough to seat thirty, unnerved her. She entered the east wing and slumped toward the dining room. She'd never felt so alone in her life.

Veronica wasn't there. Fortunately, the dining room was empty and cold, and Elspeth followed her nose to her own sitting room, where she found her meal waiting for her: tomato bisque, a few pieces of roast chicken, and half a small loaf of nutty brown bread. She'd half expected the kind of hearty, overblown, multi-course meal Landon had been fond of, and half expected one of Francis's favorite thin broths accompanied by steamed vegetables. This said someone in the kitchen remembered what she liked even though she'd so rarely visited, and it cheered her tremendously.

She ate without rushing and was still done by 12:35, according to her lovely watch. Steeling herself, she headed back to the north wing and managed to find her way there without a single wrong turn. This cheered her further, and she was able to face the Papers for a few minutes and make more progress before one o'clock, when another knock on her door heralded Simkins' entrance. "Aldous Dane to see you," she said.

Elspeth, conscious that her hair was a frizzy mess, straightened in her seat and raked her fingers through her hair a few times. "Show him in," she said.

Aldous Dane was the oldest, frailest man she had ever seen. He moved as if he was afraid his bones might fracture from an incautious impact with the floor. His stooped shoulders were broad, though, and he had a head of thick white hair, both of which suggested he'd been hale and powerful in his youth. Elspeth rose automatically when he entered. "Mister Dane, welcome," she said.

Half a second's casting about reminded her there was only one chair in the room. "Miss Simkins, please bring a chair for Mister Dane," she said. Simkins looked like she didn't think fetching things was in her job description, but she brought a chair and set it before the desk. Dane sank cautiously into it.

"Well," he said. "You're not what I expected, Your Majesty."

His voice was much heartier than the rest of him, and his frank, appraising gaze was that of a much younger man. "What did you expect?" Elspeth asked impulsively.

"Honestly? A timid mouse who barely spoke Tremontanese," Dane replied. "All anyone knew of you was that you were raised Veriboldan and intended to become a priestess. That implies so much. But you seem to be doing all right."

Elspeth smiled. "I'm not sure how true that is, but I'm determined to see this through."

"Good attitude." Dane leaned back in his chair and said, "I'm here to plan your coronation, as you know. May I ask what you had in mind?"

"I didn't have anything in mind. I didn't even know I had to be crowned. I thought I just...became Queen."

"It's true you're the Queen regardless of ceremony, but the official investiture is to make explicit the link between you and your country and your people. There are a number of different coronation rituals, each designed to fit the needs of the ruler. My estimation is you'll want something that isn't showy, but makes it clear you have a right to the Crown, what with the nature of your accession."

"I'd like that. I don't really want anything huge or dramatic. And —as soon as possible."

"You can leave that to me," Dane said. "Then all you and I need to discuss is who will crown you."

Elspeth blinked. "I thought you did that."

Dane laughed, but not in a cruel way. "No, that would be inappropriate. Usually it's another member of your family."

"Oh. I suppose that means my Aunt Veronica. Is that all right?"

"If you think it wouldn't be difficult for her. She crowned King Francis, after all."

"I hadn't thought about that. Could my father...my family might come for the coronation."

Dane frowned. "The implications of Prince Sebastian crowning his daughter are fraught. It might raise questions of your legitimacy, as people start asking why he isn't King instead."

"I see." Elspeth sighed. "I really think it should be Aunt Veronica, but I'll ask her and give her the choice."

"Very wise." Dane shifted in his seat. "Have you given any thought to a Consort?"

"What? No! I've only been Queen for eight days, Mister Dane. I haven't even met anyone who could fill that role!"

"You should begin thinking about it," Dane said, not disturbed by her outburst. "With King Francis dying without an heir of the body, people can't help speculating about when you will perpetuate the line."

It hit her like a slap to the face. With everything else that had happened, marrying and having children was far from her mind. Dane's words sent her heart thudding against her ribs. Marrying had never been part of her plan, certainly not since she'd entered into her apprenticeship at the Irantzen Temple. That had to change. But marrying—no, encountering men she might marry and choosing between them—the enormity of the task made her brain shut down.

"I'll think about it," she said, wondering who she could even ask about where she might meet eligible men.

"Very good, your Majesty." Dane stiffly got to his feet. "I will send information about what you will need to do for the coronation. Most of the details, you can leave to me."

More Papers to read. Elspeth suppressed a sigh. "Thank you, Mister Dane."

Dane took a few steps toward the door. "You know," he said, "you remind me very much of Queen Willow. She, too, came to this position unprepared. And she made it her own. I think you'll do very well."

"You knew Queen Willow?" He was certainly old enough for that to be possible.

"I was born in the early years of her reign. My father was master of ceremonies when she was crowned. He always said she had no appreciation for tradition, but he said it with grudging pride, as if her lack of understanding was a strength." Dane smiled reflectively. "If you remember why you took on this challenge, what motivates you, you'll retain the strength you will need when things are difficult. Don't hesitate to ask for help."

"Thank you," Elspeth repeated. She shut the door behind him and leaned against it, her forehead pressed to the wood. Why had she taken on this challenge? Because she didn't want Tremontane to fall into disaster. Why that mattered to her, she had no idea, because it wasn't as if she felt any loyalty to the country.

She remembered the great round table in the Council chamber. Willow North had stood before it, faced down recalcitrant councilors and bent them to her will. Elspeth wasn't nearly so forceful. But she wasn't weak, either, and she was determined to see this through. She did wonder what kind of priestesses they had in Tremontane that anyone would believe one to be shy and retiring. Well, if that was the only misconception she had to straighten out, things wouldn't be as bad as she feared.

6

She tackled the Papers more energetically than before, and by 3:15 had, not a clear desk, but one on which the Papers were neatly stacked. It was only a start, because she hadn't yet dug into the drawers, some of which were crammed so full they couldn't close properly, but it was a good start.

The introduction of the staff went more quickly than she'd anticipated. Almost everyone who worked in the palace assembled in the Rotunda for the ceremony, which consisted of the palace housekeeper, Merete Alderly, gesturing people forward and reciting their names. It was rapid enough Elspeth guessed it truly was a formality and she wasn't expected to remember everyone. Aside from a warm welcome from Merete, whom Elspeth knew from previous visits, Elspeth's polite nods were enough to satisfy the staff. She resolved to track down Merete later and ask her a slew of questions, including the one about her wardrobe.

At four o'clock, she sat behind her desk twiddling a pen and hoping that wasn't too nervous a gesture. Aside from Simkins' implication that the Papers were the subject of the meeting with Faraday, Elspeth had no idea what to expect. She hoped he wouldn't be so antagonistic they didn't accomplish anything.

There was Simkins' distinctive knock, *tap-tap, tap*, light and yet forceful. The door eased open. "Mister Faraday," Simkins said, ushering the head of Internal Affairs in. Elspeth remembered in time not to stand in response to his entrance.

"Mister Faraday, thank you for joining me. Won't you have a seat?" she said. She was determined on politeness until he forced the issue.

Faraday sat, more easily than Dane had, with a contained energy that looked to Elspeth like impatience. Maybe, if he wanted to be elsewhere just as much as Elspeth, they could make this quick.

"Your Majesty," he said. "Where did you put all the paperwork?"

It was the kind of question that suggested he knew what she'd done with it and was ready to be upset. "Most of it is still here," she said. "I just organized it. Some of it I was able to give to Mister Branton to pass on to others. And some of it, I burned."

Faraday's eyes widened. "You *burned* important government paperwork?"

"It wasn't important. It was those agriculture reports Lady Beaumont sent. I figured they were redundant because she's going to submit a summary report next week."

"Your Majesty," Faraday said, his expression harder than before, "I shouldn't have to point out that you are extremely new to your position and cannot possibly be capable of determining what is important and what isn't. Burning documentation, particularly documentation you don't understand, is careless."

Elspeth's cheeks warmed with embarrassment. "It's not hard to understand that Lady Beaumont wanted me overwhelmed with information. If it was important, she would have brought it to the Council."

A muscle in Faraday's jaw twitched. "Nevertheless, your Majesty, I would prefer if you asked for advice before making summary judgments. I would be happy to assist." He didn't look happy.

"Mister Faraday," Elspeth said, "I'm not too proud to admit I could use your help. I would like us to work together."

Faraday nodded curtly. "You seem to have made great progress," he said. "What else did you find?"

"What looked like several weeks' worth of daily schedules." Which she had also burned. "Reports from different...what do you call the areas of government the Council members are in charge of?"

"Departments, your Majesty."

"Then—reports from different departments." She didn't mention how few those were. That might mean the department heads were doing their jobs properly. "And a number of requests from the ruling lords and ladies, asking that the Queen pass judgment on certain matters. I wasn't sure what to do with them." She tapped a stack of papers, the largest one.

"Those come under the responsibility of Internal Affairs. I'll deal with them." He held out a hand for the papers. Elspeth hesitated.

"I appreciate your assistance, Mister Faraday, but these were addressed to me—well, to Francis, most of them, but to the King or Queen. Shouldn't I give them my personal attention?"

"My department will assess the requests and return the ones that really do need the Queen's attention. It frees you to deal with other things." Faraday's hand hadn't wavered. Elspeth gave him the stack of paper.

"What I didn't find," she said, "are Mister Caxton's financial reports. I don't suppose you know anything about Francis's filing system?"

Faraday's dark expression grew momentarily more sour. "His Majesty was...not good at organization," he said. "He depended heavily on his secretary to keep track of things. Miss Simkins might know where the financial reports are."

"I'll ask her."

An awkward silence fell. Elspeth hoped it meant Faraday considered the meeting over. But he continued to sit, tapping the sheaf of papers against the palm of one hand, his gaze focused on her. Uncomfortable, Elspeth finally said, "Mister Faraday, could I ask your advice?" She didn't particularly want to put herself in his debt, but for all he was rude and dismissive, he also wasn't servile, and he might be the only person willing to be honest with her.

Faraday nodded.

"How do I know where the balance lies? I don't want to speak ill of the dead, but from what I've learned in clearing his desk, Francis swung wildly between being too involved in the details of running the country and being not nearly involved enough. I don't think he's a good example for me to model my behavior on. But I don't know anything about ruling a country, so I need *something* to guide me. What have others in my position done?"

To her surprise, Faraday seemed taken aback by this question. His stern demeanor relaxed slightly. "It's been a hundred years since there was anyone in your position. And Willow North was prepared to rule by everything she did to reclaim the Crown from Terence Valant. But she wasn't any more or less educated on the details of ruling than you are, though it was to her advantage that she invented the Council and was in a position to tell her councilors what their responsibilities would be."

"So are there...I don't know. Books? Teachers? I mean to learn to do this job, Mister Faraday."

"Internal Affairs stands ready to support you. You can bring anything you don't understand to me or my aides."

It was so unexpectedly helpful Elspeth was surprised again. Faraday didn't look any more friendly, but he seemed sincere. "That's...I appreciate that. But I'd like more than to pass the decisions off to someone else. I'd like an explanation of why things work the way they do."

Faraday frowned. "I'm sure that's possible. But it will impose a heavier burden on my department."

"One that will ease as I gain in understanding."

Faraday nodded again. "I suppose that's true. Very well. Someone will bring you the items from this—" He waved the sheaf of papers —"that require your signature, and will collect any more that come to you in the meantime."

"Thank you, Mister Faraday." She wished she didn't feel quite so uneasy at simply handing off important documents to him, but the point of having councilors was to do just that. She rose, and Faraday followed suit. Impulsively, she said, "You don't approve of me, do you."

Faraday raised a single eyebrow, a gesture that made him look even more annoyed. "It's not my place to approve or disapprove of my Queen."

"But you don't."

"I apologize if I have given offense." Faraday's expression was now bland and uncommunicative.

"No. I understand I'm not the Queen you might have wanted. I just hope you'll give me a chance to prove myself."

Faraday bowed, not very deeply. "I'm sure you will do very well," he said, and let himself out before Elspeth could do more than draw a single outraged breath. The *nerve* of that man...! Well, she'd show him. She didn't like him, didn't really feel she needed him to like her, but she'd be damned if she'd give him any more reasons to look down on her.

She flung herself back into her chair and yanked open the first drawer, which stuck. Muttering angrily to herself, she emptied its contents onto the now mostly clean desktop and sorted through them. *I'm sure you will do very well.* How dare he patronize her!

She managed to clean and reorganize three of the twelve drawers —the smallest ones, but still—before Simkins knocked on her door at six o'clock. "Your Majesty will wish to dress for supper," she said.

"No, Miss Simkins, my Majesty would very much not like to dress for supper," Elspeth said. Immediately she felt bad about letting her foul temper strike an innocent person. "That is—I'm sorry, Miss Simkins. Is dressing for supper mandatory when it's just me and Aunt Veronica?"

"My apologies, your Majesty. I thought you knew. Twice weekly, when you have no other commitments, you are scheduled to dine with members of your Council. It is a formal affair."

And she didn't have any formal Tremontanan garments. "Who is it tonight?" *Please don't say Mister Faraday, please don't say Mister Faraday—*

"Lady Serena d'Arden and Lord Felix Harrington," Simkins said. "Supper will be served at six-thirty in the east wing."

That wouldn't be so bad. "All right. Thanks for the reminder." She shut the final drawer and left the office, passing a servant in rough clothes whose likely job was cleaning and putting the fire out for the night. She nodded politely, and the servant ducked his head and hurried past her. It was hard to believe the Queen couldn't even be polite without embarrassing someone.

Back in her suite, she sorted through her few clothes and settled on a Veriboldan silk robe over black linen shirt and trousers, something she might have worn to an embassy gala. The robe was North blue embroidered with silver cats, and putting it on comforted her. Lord Harrington would understand that she didn't mean any offense by not dressing in the Tremontanan style, and Lady d'Arden...well, Elspeth didn't know the first thing about her, but hopefully she had the good manners of a noblewoman and wouldn't comment. She settled her *toan* jade atop her shirt and briefly ran her fingers over its smooth surface, a reassurance that not everything about her had changed.

When she arrived in the drawing room, Veronica and the two councilors were already there, seated near the fire. They all rose when she entered. That was going to take some getting used to. "Good evening," Elspeth said. "Thank you for coming."

"Thank you for inviting us when you're probably overwhelmed by everything else," Lady d'Arden said with a smile. "I hope we're not a burden."

"No, of course not," Elspeth said. "Shall we eat?"

She almost took the seat she was used to from all those earlier visits instead of the chair at the head of the table, which Lord Harrington held for her. Nobody noticed her near misstep, but she blushed anyway. To cover her embarrassment, while the soup course was being served, she asked Lady d'Arden, "How long have you been on the Council?"

"Just a year, your Majesty," Lady d'Arden said. "Before that I ran my own business—well, string of businesses. I was an importer of chocolate as well as the owner of a number of chocolate- and coffee-houses."

"I love chocolate," Elspeth said. "And that sounds so interesting. What made you take the position on the Council?"

"I was recommended by my predecessor. And much as I loved the autonomy, I had to admit I could do more for the country serving on the Council." She sipped the creamy white soup at her place.

"I haven't found Miss Hardison's recommendations for her successor yet. I'm afraid the royal desk was a little cluttered." Immediately Elspeth wondered if they would hear that as a sideways jab at Francis's skills, and forged ahead with, "Is there some way I can meet with those people? I'd like to have a more personal interaction with them, if one of them is to be a councilor."

"I'm sure Miss Simkins can arrange it," Lord Harrington said. "She's an excellent assistant. She was a Foreign Affairs attaché before taking the position as royal secretary."

Elspeth took a spoonful of soup. So delicious. "Then you must know her—or is that wrong? I don't know how your department works aside from what you do in Veribold."

"I don't have personal contact with everyone, no—it's too large a department for that. But it's true I know Miss Simkins. In fact, I recommended her for her current position."

"She must be highly qualified, then. I know she's extremely efficient."

Lord Harrington nodded. "And how is your family, your Majesty?"

"Very well, thank you." A memory of how they'd all looked the morning she left passed swiftly through her mind, and a lump rose in her throat. "I would like them to be here for the coronation, but that's probably not possible."

"I'm sure you left many friends behind in Veribold," Lady d'Arden said with a look of sympathy that made Elspeth's throat tighten more. "You've led such an interesting life."

"Not really," Elspeth said, swallowing. "I mean, it's true Veribold is different from Tremontane, but the things I did weren't all that unusual. I had tutors and went to parties and made friends."

"And had a religious life," Lord Harrington said. "Tremontane worships very differently."

"Really? I didn't know. In what ways?" Elspeth had assumed that, with both countries sharing the same fundamental beliefs, the way they expressed those beliefs would also be similar.

"Well, we have nothing like the Irantzen Temple," Lord Harrington said with a smile. "And no one here is ordained to lead in worship. Anyone might officiate at a wedding, or creating a family bond, so long as they have a bond of their own. Most Tremontanans would find your desire to become a priestess incomprehensible."

That made Elspeth feel uncomfortable, as if there was something shameful about the desires of her heart. "I suppose I always thought Uncle Landon led the Midsummer rites because being King gave him special...I don't know. A connection to the people?"

"No, that's just tradition. Anyone could do it, but it's an honor accorded the King. And you, now."

The uncomfortable feeling increased. How could these people be so casual about their religious observances? If just anyone could officiate, that made the rites less special, less intimate. "So, you don't have any people who are drawn to worship? No one who cares for the bethels or mediates religious disputes?"

Lord Harrington shook his head. "There are those who care more about religion than others, yes, but they aren't given any special respect except what they earn. That is, the fact of dedicating part of their lives to heaven doesn't itself make them special."

It felt like an insult, but his calm tone and placid demeanor gave her no reason to call him on it. "That's very different."

"What would you have done as a priestess?" Lady d'Arden asked.

Elspeth leaned back for the servants to remove her soup bowl and set in front of her poached fish with a side of asparagus drenched in butter and melted cheese. "Officiated at weddings and funerals. Listened to people with problems and guided them to understanding. Helped others during the Irantzen Festival. But mostly it meant prayer and meditation to bring me closer to heaven." She touched the *toan* jade. "That, at least, is something I can still do."

"Yes, you shouldn't have to give up your faith just because you're in Tremontane," Lady d'Arden said with a smile. "Maybe you'll find similarities between the two."

Elspeth smiled back. "It's true that I miss my home," she said, "but I hope to make a home here as well."

"You certainly look like a piece of Veribold dropped into the palace," Lord Harrington said, gesturing at Elspeth's clothing. The humor in his eyes made Elspeth laugh.

"I'll need a new wardrobe, true," she said. "Though maybe I can bring some Veriboldan influences into Tremontane. New fashions— these are so comfortable. And I wouldn't mind encouraging the cook to learn Veriboldan cuisine."

"I've never had Veriboldan food," Veronica said in her quiet, pale voice. "Is it true they put fish sauce on everything?"

"They do like *ang dieh*, yes, but it's really only for beef. It tastes better than it smells. Though it is one of those foods where you have to wonder who first had the idea to try it. It's not an obvious condiment." Elspeth took a bite of fish and again had to swallow past the lump in her throat, it smelled so much like *ang dieh*. She needed to control herself so these people didn't think she was overly emotional.

They ate in silence for a few minutes, paying homage to the cook's genius. When the fish course was removed, Lord Harrington said, "Do you know when your coronation will be held, your Majesty?"

"Mister Dane said it would be as soon as possible, but he didn't say what that meant. I hope soon. I'd like to get it over with."

"I imagine having all those people staring at you would be over- whelming," Lady d'Arden said sympathetically.

That aspect of the ceremony hadn't occurred to Elspeth. "I was actually thinking it would make me feel more legitimate. Right now I feel as if I'm waiting for a storm looming on the horizon. It might be a deluge, or it might be a scattering of drops, and I won't know until it gets here what to expect."

"Very poetical." Lady d'Arden accepted the tender slice of pork loin the servant placed in front of her. "I think I understand. You don't know enough yet to even know what's expected of you, is that right, your Majesty?"

"That's it exactly. The coronation feels symbolic of that." Elspeth didn't much care for pork, but she ate a few bites to be polite. It was delicious, for pork.

"We of the Council will do whatever it takes to ensure Tremontane's government is secure," Lord Harrington said. He, by contrast, had tucked into his pork loin like it was the best meal he'd had all week. "So of course we will all support your Majesty as you gain confidence."

"I appreciate that, Lord Harrington." She picked at her meal a little longer until the plate was removed and replaced by tossed green vegetables in a light vinaigrette. That was more to her taste. "And speaking of gaining confidence, I thought I should become more familiar with the legal obligations of the Queen. Is that written down anywhere?"

"You might ask the Royal Librarian," Lord Harrington said. "The Library is housed in the old Scholia chambers."

"*Old* Scholia chambers?"

"The Scholia has grown so much over the last century, it's outgrown the rooms Kerish North chose for it. The Magister of the Scholia recently applied to the Crown for new quarters in a separate building. King Francis gave them Crown holdings in County Cullinan."

Elspeth knew almost nothing about the Scholia except that it was the oldest educational institution in the country. "That sounds very reasonable, though I thought the Scholia was independent of the Crown."

"No, it's funded by the Crown in exchange for providing Scholia-trained Masters to serve throughout the government. And, of course, there's the research into Devisery—the Scholia is still preeminent in that respect. But the Library remains in the palace. Nobody wanted to take on the enormous task of moving all those books."

Devisery was another thing Elspeth knew little of. She resolved not to let her lack of knowledge overwhelm her. "The Library is in the old part of the palace, right? I think I remember where it is. Though maybe I need a guide—I'm constantly in fear of being lost in this place."

"We could assign you someone with a map and a compass," Lord Harrington said with a twinkle in his eye.

Elspeth laughed at the mental image of herself with a walking stick, traversing the halls of the palace as if walking through the hills outside Haizea. "I don't think it's quite that bad, but you're not far off."

They finished the meal with chocolate and a selection of tiny cakes, bite-sized, that Elspeth ate far too many of. Then she walked with her guests to the door of the east wing and bade them goodbye. Veronica waited in the drawing room, staring into the fire. "That wasn't so bad," Elspeth said, half to herself.

"Most people here want you to succeed," Veronica said.

Startled, Elspeth said, "Why only most people? Who wants me to fail?"

Veronica shrugged. "I don't know. I just know that there were those who encouraged Francis to depend on them so they could increase their personal power. You should watch out for that."

Faraday's sour expression, the disdain in his eyes, came to mind. "You're right. I will. Thank you."

Veronica shrugged again. "I think you have a chance at becoming a good Queen. Maybe even a great one. You're sharper than poor Francis—I loved my son, but he had his failings. And you're less self-centered a Queen than Landon, heaven keep his soul."

That Veronica could be that frank about her own husband and child stunned Elspeth into silence. When she recovered, she said, "I'm sure they weren't bad Kings."

"Are you? I'm not," Veronica said. "When you have time, go for a ride in the Park. See what you think." She turned and left the room before Elspeth could ask her to explain. What was the Park? *Where* was the Park? One more thing she didn't know.

She returned to her rooms and wearily undressed. It was too late to find Merete and ask her about getting a new wardrobe—that would have to wait for morning. She snuggled into her warmest nightgown and pulled on her dressing gown, shivering in her bare feet. Tremontane was just too damn cold, that was all.

When she returned to her bedroom, a strange woman was busy turning down the bedcovers. She was dressed in the same uniform Gloria had worn and bowed deeply to Elspeth. "Your Majesty, my name is Shirley," she said. "If you need anything during the night, pull the bell rope and I'll come immediately."

Elspeth said, "But—" and then shut her mouth. This woman— she wasn't even a young woman, more like middle-fifties—was going to stay up all night on the off chance Elspeth might want a drink or something at midnight? And yet it would probably offend her if Elspeth told her not to bother. All the servants she'd met had acted like it was a huge honor to serve their Queen. Maybe it was, and Elspeth just didn't understand the magnitude of her role.

"Thank you," she said instead. "Could you get me a glass of water? And then—" it was early, but Elspeth felt exhausted— "I think I'll turn in."

Shirley didn't bat an eyelash at her mistress's no doubt odd request. "Of course, your Majesty."

Elspeth took the time while Shirley was gone to use the water closet and find the bed stool. It turned out to have been tucked away in a corner of the dressing room, where it folded flat against the wall. Elspeth unfolded it and positioned it where she could reach it easily. She'd never seen the point of these beds raised so high off the ground. Maybe she could request a normal one. They certainly wouldn't be on board with her sleeping on a Veriboldan pallet, however comfortable that might be.

She accepted her glass of water from Shirley, drank half of it, and set the half-full glass on the bedside table. "Good night," she said, receiving another bow from Shirley, and turned out the light. She had to admit light Devices were useful, no oil to spill, no flickering to strain the eyes. Reading in bed would be so pleasant. Maybe the Royal Librarian could provide her with something to read for pleasure as well.

She settled in on her many soft pillows and stared into the darkness. Her first day as Queen, at least her first official day. It had gone on forever. Hopefully the days would get easier as time passed and she grew more confident. She suppressed the thought that it was going to be many days before that happened.

Tiredness caught up to her, and she drifted off to sleep. Her last thought before her eyes closed was that not a single person that day had called her by her first name.

7

---

*T*hanks to her early night, Elspeth rose early the following morning. Instead of getting up immediately, she lay staring at the ceiling and going over plans for the day. Talk to Merete. Find the recommendations Hardison had made for the new head of Transportation. All that on top of whatever Simkins had arranged. The idea of an hour for dinner made sense now, if that was the only way to get private time. On the other hand, it was a terrible idea if it ate into what little time she had to do her duties. Something to consider as she became used to her new role.

She climbed down from the bed and hurriedly dressed in her favorite clothes. If she was going to be busy all day, she intended to be comfortable. Then she yanked the bell rope and used the water closet while she waited for Gloria to arrive. It took Gloria only one minute, by the lovely silver watch, to respond to Elspeth's summons, and Elspeth was still in the water closet. She finished her business and emerged, saying, "Is it too early for breakfast?"

"No, your Majesty, whatever you want," Gloria said with a bow.

"The same as yesterday, and please have them serve it in my sitting room. And would you ask Mistress Alderly to join me? I mean, not to eat with me, she's probably already eaten, but I have some questions for her."

Gloria bobbed another bow and vanished out the door. Elspeth started making her bed, something she always did at home, then realized it was probably one of Gloria's duties and it would embarrass the young woman if the Queen did it for her. She might even take it as a criticism. Elspeth messed up the blankets, just in case. It had never occurred to her that the Queen might need to worry about not giving offense to her underlings. Maybe most rulers didn't, and she was just odd for not having been raised to this rank.

She sat patiently in the sitting room until the food arrived, more poached eggs on toast, more chocolate, and to her pleased surprise, a glass of orange juice. Someone had strained the pulpy bits out, which was a disappointment as they were Elspeth's favorite thing about the juice, but it was still orange juice, and Elspeth sipped it slowly, making it last in case there was only one glass forthcoming.

She examined her sitting room while she ate. It had been assigned to her when she was five, on her first visit to Aurilien, and she hadn't liked it much at the time. For one thing, it was rather somber, not at all a child's room, done in grays and browns with a heavy, bulky wallpaper whose abstract print made Elspeth think of headless tigers. Now, the disturbing image didn't bother her, but she couldn't imagine wanting to spend much time here. Which, if her schedule persisted as busy as yesterday, wouldn't be an issue.

She chewed thoughtfully as she stared into the fireplace, which had not been turned into a Device. Dark wooden pillars coordinating with the wallpaper propped up a heavy mantel that looked like it was about to topple off the wall and take a chunk of the masonry with it. Maybe she should change rooms, after all. They couldn't all be this bleak. And it would be less difficult than remodeling.

Someone knocked on the door, and whoever it was opened it without waiting for a response. "Good morning, your Majesty," Merete Alderly said with her usual cheery smile. Merete had been the palace housekeeper—such a tame word to describe the woman who effectively ran the palace—since Elspeth had been small.

Elspeth and her siblings adored her, and she had treated them like her own children, firmly but lovingly explaining what they were and weren't allowed to do, encouraging them to play games in the parts of the east wing not in general use, sneaking them treats and then pretending she didn't know where the treats had come from. Elspeth had hoped that Merete, at least, would call her Elspeth, but it seemed that was too informal even for their long relationship.

"Good morning, Merete. Please sit. Do you want some chocolate? They've given me more than I can drink."

"Thank you anyway, no. Is there something I can help you with?"

"I hope so." Elspeth finished her chocolate and pushed the pot away. "I need clothes. And probably someone to take care of them, and help me dress in formal wear...I feel so at a loss."

"Do you mean you don't have any Tremontanan clothes?" Merete sounded startled.

"Why would I? I never needed them before." Elspeth hoped that hadn't come out too defensive.

"I suppose that makes sense." Merete nodded. "If you'll allow me, your Majesty, I will send you a seamstress who can assemble a wardrobe for you. She's reliable and I know she will be thrilled to help you. And I can arrange for you to interview a number of ladies for your personal maid, or maids, if you like."

"Just one for now, I think. Thank you so much. And—oh. I think I need a gown for my coronation, and that might be very soon."

Merete smiled again. "Not to worry. The woman I have in mind is used to working to deadline. Though if you can provide her with that deadline, that would be best."

Some of the weight Elspeth had been carrying fell away. "You don't know how relieved that makes me."

"You must be struggling. It's unfortunate your family can't be here to support you."

"I miss them so much." Elspeth blinked away tears. "But it's not so bad. There are so many people ready to help me, I feel I shouldn't complain."

"Well, please call on me if you need anything." Merete raised her hand as if she wanted to pat Elspeth's shoulder but then thought better of it. Elspeth's light, floating feeling subsided a little at the reminder of how much distance there now was between her and her friend.

She arranged for the seamstress and the candidates for lady's maid to come to the east wing at twelve-thirty. Elspeth was sure she didn't need a full hour for dinner, and she was just as sure Simkins wouldn't have thought to leave room for any non-governmental activities on the dreaded schedule.

By the time Merete left, it was almost eight-thirty, and Elspeth felt energized and ready to tackle the new day. She again found her way to the north wing without help, which cheered her further, nodded politely to Branton and pretended not to notice his embarrassment at encountering her, and let herself into Francis's—her office without meeting anyone who might have a demand of her. No Council meeting for a week...this day might actually be pleasant.

She seated herself behind the desk just as the door swung open. "I beg your pardon, your Majesty, I didn't realize you were here," Simkins said. Her expression was more forbidding than usual, and it dampened some of Elspeth's cheer. "I have the day's schedule."

"All right, I'm ready to hear it," Elspeth said with a smile.

Simkins eyed her suspiciously, as if cheerfulness might be contagious and it was an illness she'd rather not contract. "Nine o'clock, meeting with the architects building the pavilion in the royal gardens. Nine-thirty, initial consultation with the artist commissioned to paint your portrait for the Long Gallery. Ten o'clock, high court—that is at the Justiciary, and you will require an honor guard to escort you there. Twelve o'clock, dinner in—"

"Wait," Elspeth said. "What is high court?"

Simkins' lips pursed in annoyance at being interrupted. "You will sit in judgment over the cases sent up from the provinces. There is an agenda waiting for you at the Justiciary."

"I can't do that! I know nothing about the law—how am I supposed to judge fairly?" Sick dread rose up inside her, turning the poached eggs to acid soup.

"Your Majesty," Simkins said, her voice heavy with rebuke, "it is your duty to provide justice to the citizens under your care. If you wish, a law-speaker or criminal questioner may assist you."

"Yes. Please. Someone who knows the law." A law-speaker would know the details of the law, and a questioner would have experience arguing the law in front of a court. Either would suffice. She didn't care if she was passing off the duty on someone else. The thought of holding someone's life in her hands, of judging wrongly, terrified her.

"As I was saying. Twelve o'clock, dinner in the east wing. From one o'clock to three o'clock you are scheduled to meet with the candidates for the new head of the Transportation department."

"I don't even know who they are. I couldn't find the list."

"That is because King Francis gave it to me. I arranged to have them attend on you so you might make a decision to present the Council. At 3:15 you are to meet with the Magister of the Scholia on a matter to do with its removal from the palace. And from five o'clock to six you will meet again with the master of ceremonies in regards to your coronation. It has been scheduled for noon, three days from today."

"That seems fast."

"I am sure if your Majesty wishes, the date can be changed."

"Oh, no, that wasn't a criticism! I'd like it to happen as quickly as possible."

Simkins' cross expression relaxed slightly. "If you will follow me, I will escort you to the small audience chamber."

"Why—oh, for meeting the architects. They can't come here?"

"It would be inappropriate to allow workmen into the north wing." Simkins said "workmen" the way someone else might have said "termites." "And I believe you will come to appreciate the privacy of your office."

"That...makes sense." To her surprise, it did. Maybe Simkins wasn't addicted to formality at the cost of good sense, after all.

She endured the meeting with the architects, who had been commissioned by Francis to build some monstrosity in the royal gardens. Elspeth hadn't ever seen the gardens, as her parents had always seen them as Landon's private space, but she couldn't imagine they needed a pavilion of the size Francis had proposed. At first, she thought about just approving everything Francis had requested. Then her good sense took over. She didn't want to invalidate all the work the architects had done, but *she* would be the one who had to live with it. She asked the architects to return in a week so she could evaluate their plans and compare them to the garden site Francis had chosen. They were surprisingly calm about it, and Elspeth left that meeting feeling she had done something right.

The meeting with the portrait painter went less smoothly, though by the end Elspeth felt strangely comforted that someone in the palace didn't give a damn about her title. The painter was the sort of artist who cared more for her art than anything else, and she flatly refused to paint Elspeth until she "clothed herself in proper attire the way heaven demanded Tremontane's ruler do." Simkins was ruddy with suppressed indignation, Elspeth was quietly amused, and in the end they all agreed the artist would return in five days.

Elspeth was amused enough to forget how much she dreaded the approach of ten o'clock, but when a trio of soldiers fully kitted out in Tremontanan walnut brown and forest green appeared at her office door, dread returned full force. She let them surround her as they took her through the palace down a long hall she'd never used before, down and down until she was sure they were underground. She'd never realized the Justiciary connected to the palace; she'd expected they would go outside and around to the tall doors in its flat façade adorned with bas relief carvings of the lost gods. But their path led through a few more narrow corridors until they reached a metal door that squealed painfully when one of the guards opened it.

Beyond was a high-ceilinged room with a rectangular dais at one end and dozens of wooden chairs, not comfortable-looking, filling the opposite side. A balcony with more chairs overhung the room on three sides. A white marble desk big enough to seat three took up most of the space on the dais, and there were, in fact, three chairs behind it, chairs that looked more comfortable than the others in the room. To Elspeth's horror, every seat at ground level was occupied, and the balcony was full, with two people leaning on the balcony rail.

The guard at the head of her procession stopped so abruptly Elspeth almost ran into him. "All rise for her Majesty, Queen Elspeth North," he said in a voice that boomed through the chamber. Everyone stood, though the two at the balcony rail did so without haste. All of them stared at Elspeth. She stared back, once more at a loss.

"The judge's desk, your Majesty," one of the guards prompted. Elspeth jumped as if goosed and hurried to take a seat at the marble desk. She could see no difference between the three seats and decided it didn't matter which one she took. She sat in the center seat, which was quite comfortable, and folded her hands in her lap.

A man dressed in law-speaker's robes emerged from an almost invisible door at the far end of the dais. He was followed by Faraday, also in law-speaker's robes and looking cranky as ever. Elspeth's heart plummeted.

The first man approached Elspeth and handed her a sheet of paper covered in very neat handwriting. "The docket, your Majesty," he whispered. Faraday took a seat next to Elspeth and scooted the chair to where he could speak to her without whispering.

"You read the first line aloud, and the guards will escort in the involved parties," he said in a low voice. "They will present their case, and then I will tell you how to rule."

Elspeth nodded, too grateful to have help to be angry at his usurpation of her responsibility. "The case of Emberlin Arnot and Ganden Thorp," she read in a clear voice that didn't tremble at all.

Doors at the back of the room opened, and guards marched in, flanking an elderly woman dressed in what had to be her best clothes, though they weren't fancy, and a middle-aged man with a receding hairline and the beginnings of a paunch. They were followed by a couple of men in matching coats bearing some insignia Elspeth couldn't make out.

The little group approached along an aisle dividing the chairs in half and halted in the open space between the chairs and the desk.

The woman stood proudly, but her hands were clenched, and Elspeth guessed she was actually extremely nervous. The middle-aged man by her side looked as if his stomach was bothering him as much as Elspeth's was her. The other men looked like they wanted to be anywhere but where they were.

Two men in questioner's scarlet robes rose from the front row of chairs. "Your Majesty, a judgment," the man on the left said. "Mister Thorp protests the removal of the Merchants' Guild seal from his store. The Count of Olontor deemed the matter one demanding the attention of the Crown."

"The Merchants' Guild is free to award its seal wherever it wants," Faraday said. "That's not a matter for the Crown. It's barely a matter for a provincial lord."

"Your Majesty, may I speak?" the middle-aged man asked, stepping forward. The old lady cast a nervous glance at him, then returned to staring at Elspeth.

"Go ahead," Elspeth said, after waiting half a breath to see if Faraday would overrule her.

"I sell sundries," the man said. "Have done for fifteen years. Been a member of the Merchants' Guild all that time. But a year ago my neighbor, Mistress Arnot, she comes to me and says as she's taken up soapmaking and would I be willing to sell them in my store? And I says, why not? They're just little things, your Majesty. Soaps in the shape of flowers and bees and the like." He cleared his throat. "But now the Guild is saying they want my Guild seal back on account of Mistress Arnot not being a Guild member. That means business will go down 'cause of people wanting the Guild stamp on their wares. I say it ain't fair."

"But that—" one of the men wearing a coat began. The nearest guard glared at him. "I mean, begging your pardon, your Majesty, but may I speak?"

Elspeth nodded.

"I'm Erik Danvers of the Merchants' Guild," the man said, "and we haven't demanded anything but what we expect of all our members. Guild fees are reasonable and help protect the public against shoddy workmanship. If Mistress Arnot will pay the fee, there's no problem."

"But I can't afford it!" the elderly woman cried out, undeterred by the guard's glare.

The questioner on the right said, "The case is simple. The Merchants' Guild agreed to abide by the Crown's decision because that decision will set policy for the future. Your Majesty, we ask that you deliver justice."

"It's a clear cut case," Faraday murmured in her ear. "The law says all guilds are free to assess fees and award their seal of approval according to their own guidelines. We rule in favor of the Merchants' Guild."

Elspeth looked at each of the plaintiffs in turn. "Does the Merchants' Guild have control over *every* item made in Tremontane?" she asked.

Beside her, Faraday went rigid. The two Merchants' Guild representatives exchanged glances. "Ah...over anything sold under the Merchants' Guild seal, yes. The seal means quality we vouch for."

"But if I decided to sell cakes to my neighbors, you wouldn't control that, would you?"

The two men looked as if the possibility of the Queen of Tremontane selling anything out her back door had never occurred to them. "The quality of those cakes—" one said, then shut up.

"I understand. The point is, the Merchants' Guild doesn't have the resources to monitor every sale that happens. Sellers benefit from the relationship with the Guild, and I imagine so do buyers." Elspeth turned to the old woman. "Is there a reason you have to sell your soaps in a shop, Mistress Arnot?"

The old woman's face went white. "Your Majesty," she said faintly. "I...suppose not?"

"If you can't afford the Merchants' Guild fees, I imagine that means you don't make much off those sales. Your neighbors probably know what you can do and appreciate your wares. You'd likely do well selling to them directly. I'm sure you have strong young grandchildren to help with moving your product."

Elspeth turned her gaze on the middle-aged man. "And Mister Thorp. What made you decide to sell Mistress Arnot's soaps in your shop?"

Thorp firmed up his chin. "I like her soaps, and she's an old friend. It's certainly not for the profit."

"So you'd be just as happy if she was successful without needing your support?"

"Of course."

Elspeth didn't dare look at Faraday, who hadn't moved since she began talking. "I don't think this is a case for the Crown at all," she said. "Gentlemen of the Guild. If Mistress Arnot removes her soaps from Mister Thorp's shop, would you allow him to keep his Guild seal?"

"Of course, your Majesty," Danvers said. "But Mistress Arnot—"

"Mister Faraday," Elspeth said, turning to the statue beside her. "Does the law permit a guild to extort fees in exchange for membership? That is, are people required to join a guild to ply their trade?"

Faraday said, through clenched jaw, "No, your Majesty. Guild membership is meant to be a benefit, not a weapon."

"Mister Danvers," Elspeth said, "your ambition is laudatory, and I choose to believe you want to help Mistress Arnot rather than harass her. But if she decides to sell her goods on her own, that is her business and none of yours. I think, though, that we can resolve this amicably. Don't you?"

She smiled at Danvers, who looked like he'd been struck by lightning. His companion said, "Yes, your Majesty, the Guild is satisfied."

"What about you, Mister Thorp? Mistress Arnot?"

"Yes, your Majesty," Thorp said. The old woman just nodded.

"Then—I think that's all. You're excused." Elspeth looked at the paper in front of her. "The case—"

Faraday put his palm flat on the paper, covering the next line. "Your Majesty, that was completely irresponsible," he said in a low, harsh whisper. "I am an accredited law-speaker, and you are supposed to listen to my advice when it comes to legal matters!"

Elspeth met his gaze unflinchingly. "Mister Faraday," she said, "I don't know much about the laws of Tremontane. But I do know how people think. I chose to use a little common sense rather than apply the law like a side-ball bat. And now everyone is happy, except maybe that Mister Danvers, who I think must have the soul of a miser if he wants to wring profit out of an old lady who just wants to make a little extra money."

"And what if your common sense violates the law?"

"If it does, then maybe the law is wrong."

"That is *not* something you're competent to judge!"

"*Mister Faraday*," Elspeth said, "I am, for good or ill, your Queen, and you will treat me with respect. I promised to heed your advice, and I will listen to you when you tell me what the law is. But I am the one whose name is on these judgments, and if I think I need to intervene more directly, I will do so. If you have a problem with this, find me another law-speaker who won't."

They glared at each other. Righteous fury filled Elspeth. She was the Queen, damn it, and she was not going to let this self-involved, self-righteous git ride roughshod over her.

Faraday's lips thinned in anger. "Your Majesty," he finally said, "you are correct. It is your duty and your responsibility, not mine. Shall we continue?"

She was still ready to murder him, especially since he hadn't apologized, but she nodded curtly and read off the next case. As she waited for the people involved to approach the desk, she wondered how much of that fight had been audible. Not much, given that the audience didn't have that avid look people got when a public brawl was imminent.

Her anger drained away, leaving her feeling—not guilty, it wasn't her fault, but cold and uncomfortable. Faraday seemed intent on controlling her, and she wished she knew why. If he'd had as much influence over Francis as he tried to have over her, he might be used to pulling the monarch's strings. That wasn't power anyone might easily give up. Well, if he tried pulling her strings, he was going to get a surprise. Elspeth North might be Queen in name only, but that wasn't going to last.

8

$\mathcal{A}$t ten 'til twelve, the final case was over. Faraday was off his seat and headed for the door almost before Elspeth had dismissed the guards. She stood, stretched, and with her escort went to, not the north wing, but the east wing for dinner. The Tremontane soldiers traded silent stares with the east wing guards in North colors, making Elspeth wonder how much rivalry there was between the two groups. What determined which guards went where, for that matter.

After her meal, she met with Catherine Elwes, the seamstress, who turned out to be a lovely woman with long, agile fingers and a pleasant smile. Elspeth liked her immediately. They had a short conversation about Elspeth's favorite colors, and Catherine had measured her with a long tape that whipped around Elspeth as if it had a life of its own, and it all left Elspeth feeling calmer than she had in days.

The meeting with her prospective lady's maids went less well. Elspeth knew it was to be expected, but the fact that none of the women Merete introduced to her were willing to meet her eyes made Elspeth uncomfortable with all of them. Finally, she exclaimed, "Am I a monster, then?" and picked the one woman who giggled, a girl named Honey who was barely an adult. To Merete's warning comment that Honey wasn't likely to know everything a Queen's maid ought to know, Elspeth said, "She can learn with me. And you must trust her, or you wouldn't have recommended her." Merete had to agree.

Elspeth returned to the north wing feeling more cheerful, a feeling that evaporated when she saw Simkins waiting for her outside her office. "The small audience chamber, your Majesty, where you will meet the candidates for head of Transportation."

The small audience chamber was thirty feet long, inspiring Elspeth to wonder what the large audience chamber looked like. Its parquet wooden floor absorbed Elspeth's steps, making her sound like a cat pacing after a mouse. The ceiling, strangely low by comparison to the room's length, was covered with thousands of little copper plates like overlapping scales and made Elspeth think of snakes' bellies and dragons' hides. The lamp Device lights reflected off the copper plates in ripples, like the sun striking the Kepa River in Haizea, but warm rather than glass-cold. She wished there were a graceful way for the Queen to lie on the wooden floor gazing up at the ripples.

The unusual room contained nothing but a single wooden chair without cushions, heavily carved with the triple peaks of Tremontane atop its back. Elspeth didn't like the idea of forcing everyone else to stand, but there wasn't anything she could do about it.

Simkins disappeared through the far door, which was plain and short, no taller than six feet, which meant at least a few people would have to duck to enter. Elspeth settled herself in the chair and waited.

Presently, the door opened, and Simkins ushered in the first candidate. "Mistress Annabel Jersey," Simkins said.

Annabel Jersey was a stolid-looking woman in her fifties, with her light brown hair pulled sharply back from her face. She wore workman's clothes, coarse trousers and heavy boots and a white woven shirt, so when a patrician accent escaped her lips with her "Good afternoon, your Majesty," Elspeth felt embarrassed about the assumptions she'd made.

"Good afternoon, Mistress Jersey," she said. "Would you tell me your qualifications to head the Transportation department?"

"I was employed on the message route for ten years," Jersey said. "Five of those years I was in charge of the route from Olontor to Silverfield. I'm familiar with the system and I understand the needs of the post riders."

A promising start. "So would you say Tremontane needs to improve its post routes?"

"Not at all, your Majesty. Tremontane is superior to Eskandel and Veribold already."

Not really what I asked, but all right. Elspeth leaned forward. "Mistress Jersey," she said, "if I needed to get a message from Aurilien to, say, Haizea, what would be the best method?"

"Post horse from Aurilien to Ravensholm, then runner to the border at Westholm," Jersey said promptly. "Hand off to a runner on the Haizea route. It should take no more than three days for a message to reach Haizea."

"I see," Elspeth said. "Thank you, Mistress Jersey, it's been a pleasure speaking with you."

Jersey looked a little taken aback—the whole interaction had lasted less than five minutes—but she bowed and let herself out. Shortly afterward, Simkins opened the door again, saying, "Miss Penelope Dawes, your Majesty."

Elspeth interviewed five candidates, all of whom, for some reason, were female. That probably said something about Hardison. They were all well-spoken, intelligent, experienced women, but Elspeth didn't warm to any of them. And all of them answered her question in the same way.

Her rapid-fire interviewing technique meant she was done before two o'clock. "Tell me again what meeting I have at 3:15," she asked Simkins when the last candidate was gone.

"The Magister of the Scholia," Simkins said. "Him, you may see in your office."

"Actually, no," Elspeth said. "I'm going to visit the Royal Library. Please send him to meet me there—I'm sure he knows the way." She left Simkins sputtering in her wake and hurried to the north wing, where she hoped to find a guide. The Royal Library was definitely not something she felt comfortable finding on her own.

Her guide was a page dressed in North livery, not Tremontane colors—that was a question that had started to bother her—who for a miracle didn't seem overawed by her Queen. She was even willing to answer questions. "The Scholia's far too big now, miss—I mean your Majesty," she said. "You'll see when we get there. Used to be mostly Devisers, but now it's all manner of scholarly subjects, mathematics and geography and rhetoric and the like. There was talk of making it two Scholias like they have so many of in Eskandel, one for scholarly stuff and one for Devices, but they decided not to. Wish *I* could be a Deviser, but I can't sense source." She said the last more cheerfully than Elspeth thought the girl's dashed dreams warranted.

The door to the Library looked more like a broom closet than the door to the largest library in Tremontane. Elspeth's guide opened it for her and bowed her in. Elspeth stopped inside. The high ceiling swallowed the light from the narrow windows, filling its farthest corners with clots of darkness like spilled ink. Plain wooden desks with Device lamps mounted on frames above them stood in three rows at the center of the room, and a couple of low cabinets leaned against the far wall. That was all the furniture there was. "But— where are the books?"

"This is just the Scholia, or used to be," the girl said. "The Library is this way."

Elspeth followed her to an enormous double door, one with ornate brass hinges shaped like oak leaves and matching latches. It definitely looked as if something magnificent lay beyond it. The few people in the room paid them no attention; most of them were seated at desks, reading, and there was a woman at the far end of the room taking something out of one of the cabinets that looked tacked on to the rough stone walls. Elspeth shivered with cold. *This* was a room that needed half a dozen brass Device boxes.

Her guide pushed on half of the door, which swung open soundlessly. Elspeth walked through and found herself on a stone landing high above a vast room that rivaled much of the Jaixante in size, though not in quality of craftsmanship. What she could see of the floor was irregularly paved with stones of random sizes, the windows were high and small and didn't let a lot of light in, and it was even colder than the Scholia room.

But what mattered were the books.

Bookcases taller than Elspeth could reach filled the room, some backed against the walls, others standing free, making aisles that turned the room into a maze. Every shelf was full of books, some bound in ancient leather, newer ones in buckram of all colors. It reminded her of the small library in the embassy, though that was old and rarely used and this was clearly a working library, with hand-lettered signs indicating what books might be found where and books stacked on small tables at the end of rows, ready to be shelved. The heady scent of leather and glue filled the air.

Awestruck, Elspeth made her careful way down the stone steps, aware that only a slim rail prevented her from falling, possibly to her death. Her guide had disappeared, but Elspeth didn't mind; she'd already made up her mind to live here forever. She took a few steps and stopped to look at the books. One of them had a cherry-red binding that drew her eye. She pulled it off the shelf and opened it; it was one of the new books, the ones printed with movable type instead of engraved plates. Fascinating.

"Excuse me," a voice said. "Excuse me. Are you a student?"

Elspeth turned. A tall, slim young man approached her along one aisle. He wore a black robe with a red stole and carried a couple of books under one arm. His skin was as dark as a Veriboldan's, but his accent was that of northwestern Tremontane. "I'm afraid if you're not a student, I have to ask you to leave," he said. "It's just temporary while we make the transition from the palace to near Knightsbury."

"I'm not a student," Elspeth said. "I—" For a second, she thought about concealing her identity, but that would almost certainly get her kicked out. "I'm Elspeth North. The Queen."

The young man's eyes widened. "Your Majesty," he said, but

without the awe-filled reverence that characterized almost every interaction she'd had in Aurilien. "What brings you to the Library?"

"Are you a librarian?"

The man smiled. "Martin Keswick, your Majesty. Master of the Scholia and assistant librarian, for my sins."

"Why 'for your sins'?"

Keswick juggled the books from one arm to another. "Oh...I came to the Scholia as a student of law, but discovered I cared more for books, and the organization of books, and the acquisition of books, and everything else to do with books, than I did for the law. So here I am. Isn't it beautiful?"

"It is. It looks like you might have every book in the world."

"We almost do. At least, the ones written in Tremontanese. We also have a sizable Eskandelic collection, and Master Coll Trapane—she's the head Librarian—is deeply interested in expanding our Veriboldan holdings."

"I'd love to see those. I was raised in Veribold."

"Certainly. Though...it really should be some other time. Things are quite busy at the moment."

Elspeth looked around at the silent, empty Library. "Are they?"

"Well, not at this *exact* moment, but...well, let me show you something."

Keswick led the way through the aisles until he came to a shelf near the back tall enough to hold the oversized folios stored there. He carefully removed a book and held it out to her. "Don't touch it, you're not wearing gloves. I'll turn the pages."

Elspeth caught her breath. The pages of the folio were alive with color, the pictures exquisitely drawn. "It's called *Wonders of Eskandel*," Keswick said. "We only acquired it a few days ago. It's hundreds of years old and yet it looks like new—amazing, right?"

"It's so beautiful," Elspeth breathed. "Thank you for showing me."

"Well, it's technically yours," Keswick said.

At Elspeth's astonished look, he said, "This is the *Royal* Library, your Majesty. The Crown paid for every single one of these books. So if anyone's the owner, you are."

It was the most beautiful thing she'd heard all week. Granted, no one was likely to let her walk out with anything she pleased—or was she wrong about that? "I'm honored," she said. "You librarians have done amazing work."

"Thank you. Now, let me escort you—"

"No, wait, Master Keswick." Elspeth remembered why she was here. "You may be ideally suited to help me. I need a book. I understand you're in turmoil, but this really is urgent or I wouldn't ask."

"If it's urgent, Master Coll Trapane will have to understand," Keswick said. "How can I help?"

"I need something that summarizes the Queen's duties under law. I'm not a law-speaker, so it needs to be something basic, without a lot of specialized language. You said you were a law student; do you know of anything like that?"

"Huh." Keswick gazed into the distance as if he could read Elspeth's answer on the air. "I think so. Would a beginner's text on government structure work?"

"That sounds ideal, yes."

"Come with me."

The book he found for her was bound in flaking black leather, but it wasn't huge or heavy and the pages were comfortably thick. Elspeth glanced over the first few pages. "This will be perfect, thank you. Do I need to sign something—I am allowed to take it with me, right? Or do I have to read it here?"

"Like I said, your Majesty, it's your book," Keswick said with a grin, "but we'll make note that you have it, in case someone else comes looking for it."

The stairs were steeper than Elspeth had realized, going down, and she was out of breath when she reached the top. Keswick wasn't winded at all. "You must get plenty of exercise, going up and down all day," she said.

"Oh, I was a post runner when I was young, before I came to the Scholia," Keswick said, "so those stairs are nothing." He led her to the back wall, where the woman at the cabinet eyed them, but said nothing.

"A post runner? That sounds interesting. What route?"

"Back east, at first. I spent a year in Barony Steepridge before they decided that route was unnecessary, then the road between Magrette and Lionsmark in Barony Silverfield. Then they turned that into a post horse route, and I came to County Cullinan and became a private message runner in Treston. It was interesting. I met all sorts of people."

"Really," Elspeth mused. "Can I ask you another question?"

"Of course, your Majesty?"

"If I needed to get a message from Aurilien to Haizea, what would be the best method?"

"I don't know," Keswick said. "What's the message?"

Elspeth smiled. "That's the question, isn't it?"

She signed where he told her, thanked him again, and headed for the door, where she came up short. She hadn't told the guide to wait, and now she had no idea how to get back to...anywhere, really.

She almost went back to speak to Keswick. Then she stopped. This was ridiculous. It was her palace, for heaven's sake, and she needed to face the fact that she was going to live here for the rest of her life. And she couldn't ever call it home if she was afraid to go anywhere without a minder. She closed the Library door behind her and headed down the long, cold corridor with its dim lights. Past time she took responsibility for herself.

She got lost.

Not very lost—she recognized the halls as ones she'd already passed through. She just couldn't remember how to get from those halls to the north wing. No, that was stupid; she'd told Simkins to send the Magister of the Scholia to meet her in the Library. Easy enough—she'd retrace her steps.

She got lost again.

After ten minutes of wandering without seeing another soul, she leaned against the wall in frustration. Going forward made no sense. Going back made even less, given that she'd already tried retracing her steps and failed. She needed to pause and see if she could make anything of her surroundings.

The halls she currently found herself lost in were wide and painted a dingy white, as was the floor and every door she'd passed. She opened one of those doors out of idle curiosity and peered inside. It wasn't lit, but in the light from the hallway she saw a bed, a dressing table, and an armchair. All of them were covered in dust. Well, the palace was enormous, so it made sense there were areas no one went. What was the point of keeping those areas clean?

She continued to walk down the hall, occasionally peering into rooms and seeing the same things. This must have been a guest wing at some point. The occasional window illuminating the hall showed just how long ago that point was, because in addition to the faded paint, the floors were dull as if they hadn't been polished in forever, and there were faint dark smears across them, like—

Elspeth froze. Like blood.

Slowly, she approached one of the smears like a cat sneaking up on a mouse and knelt beside it. It didn't smell like anything but wood and old paint, and it was so faint she wouldn't have noticed it if she hadn't been searching so hard for a clue that would lead her out of here. But it was clearly a bloodstain. A big one.

The white walls and unused bedrooms didn't seem so harmless anymore. Elspeth walked faster, casting about for an exit. She tried a few more rooms; more bedrooms. The bloodstains were more frequent now, some of them on the walls at shoulder height, most of them covering the floor. Elspeth bit back a shriek and ran.

Ahead, she heard noises, and she ran faster, realizing just as she dove into it that she'd found the Rotunda. She threw herself away from the terrible halls and crouched with her hands on her knees, breathing as heavily as if she'd run a mile without stopping. The palace held horrors she had never guessed at. She knew there had been fighting here over the centuries, but that had been—would have looked like an abattoir when the blood was fresh.

"Your Majesty. Is something wrong?"

Faraday. Elspeth clenched her teeth, took in one last calming breath, and stood. "What is that place?" she demanded. "All that blood."

His eyes widened, and he glanced past her. Then he relaxed. "That was the Ascendants' academy a hundred years ago," he said. "Dozens of would-be Ascendants, along with Ascendant prisoners taken in Willow North's war, were slaughtered there."

"Oh. I didn't know." It was a miracle the place wasn't haunted—or maybe it was. Elspeth was never going back to find out. "It's terrible."

"It is," Faraday said. "It's said Queen Willow ordered the execution of the killers. Strange, considering that she was responsible for the elimination of Ascendants throughout her reign."

"You think she was capable of ordering helpless prisoners murdered?" Elspeth felt unexpectedly defensive of her ancestor.

Faraday's eyes met hers. "No, I don't," he said. "I suppose I mean people aren't ever just one thing."

For a moment, Elspeth felt in harmony with him. "I agree."

Faraday's gaze dropped to the book in her hand. "Decided to become a law-speaker?" he asked, arching one eyebrow.

And just like that, the harmony vanished. "I'm in need of understanding," she snapped, "and since it's clear you resent providing that understanding, I resorted to the Library."

Faraday glared at her. "Believe what you want," he said. "That's the long way around from the Library. Did you get lost?"

It was Elspeth's turn to glare. "I'm learning."

"If you want a guide, I'm sure someone here will assist you." Faraday turned and walked away toward the front door. Elspeth ground her teeth. And to think for a moment she'd thought well of him.

"Excuse me," she said to one of the guards in North blue passing through the Rotunda, "will you escort me to..." Maybe it wasn't too late to catch Simkins. "To the north wing?"

"Your business, miss?" the guard said.

Elspeth almost laughed. "I'm here to see the Queen. I have an appointment," she said after weighing her options and deciding on the easiest one. For a few minutes, she could be anonymous. But the amount of relief she felt on laying down the burden of the Crown for those few minutes disturbed her peace for the rest of the afternoon.

9

———————

hat there was an entire hall within the palace solely to celebrate crowning Tremontane's ruler didn't surprise Elspeth at all. She *had* been surprised by the antechamber to the coronation hall, which was as modern as if it had been designed and decorated yesterday. It had been a surprise because the coronation hall, the antechamber, and the long, long hallway leading to them were in the oldest part of the palace. Walking alone down that seemingly endless hall had felt like stepping back in time, though the Device lamps hanging in sconces on the walls had dispelled that illusion. Then she'd stepped through the pair of small doors and found herself in the antechamber, and was brought back through the centuries with a jerk.

She wandered around the antechamber, whose white plastered walls trimmed with gilt gave the room an open feeling the many mirrors enhanced. The smell of hothouse roses filled the air, sweet and thick and strong and matching her personal scent of cinnamon and roses she'd brought with her from Veribold. The carpet was as white as the walls and as thick as the scent of roses, and she checked to make sure she wasn't leaving footprints. The soles of her green velvet slippers weren't hard enough for that, but she looked anyway.

She stopped to examine her reflection in one of the mirrors. Honey had tamed her hair into several braids she then wove together in a neat knot at the base of Elspeth's neck. Wisps had already started to escape. Elspeth didn't bother trying to fix them. She knew from experience that would only make things worse.

She tugged at the neckline of her gown, the first Tremontanan gown she'd ever worn. The bodice was forest green velvet, her favorite color, fitted snugly through the bust and waist to settle over the green waterfall of silk that was the skirt. Elspeth had seen her mother's court costume, what she wore to official Veriboldan functions, and that had looked nothing like this—but her mother had said hers was in the style of Willow North's court, a century-old style, because Veriboldans liked keeping their neighbors off-balance. "And if they restrict themselves to doing it by making us wear old-fashioned clothes, I'm in favor of that," Fiona North had told her daughter. Elspeth's gown had a slimmer skirt, without all those petticoats, and it didn't require her to be stitched into her sleeves, and forest green made her red hair glow...yes, Elspeth could get used to these Tremontanan fashions.

She ran her fingers over the necklace of silver flowers with diamonds nestled into their centers. The keeper of the royal jewels had imperfectly concealed her horror at learning Elspeth had never worn jewelry in her life if you didn't count the *toan* jade, which neither of them did. Then she'd taken pleasure in bringing out all the jewels for Elspeth to gasp and exclaim over. Whoever had put together the collection had had excellent taste—or was it the work of several hands over the centuries? That made more sense, and made the collection even more remarkable. Like the Library, the jewels were Elspeth's now, though she thought of them more as on permanent loan. And what a loan it was. She touched the flowers once more, then clasped her hands in front of her. Soon, now.

The doors creaked. Elspeth hurried to put herself where Aldous Dane had told her to stand so she would be perfectly silhouetted in the center of the doorway. It was funny to imagine someone working at the door hinges to make them creak and give the monarch-to-be a little warning to get into position. Elspeth controlled a smile and let her hands fall to her side. All that preparation for this moment.

A rustle went up as several hundred people dressed in the finery of four nations turned to look at her. Elspeth held her head high. Being stared at by people had never bothered her, though she avoided looking at the crowd, in case being stared at by hundreds of people made a difference. She paused, counting silently: ...*three, four, five*, and on *six* she took a step onto the carpet unrolling straight as a furrow toward the dais at the far end of the room. Its heavy red velvet was as soft underfoot as the antechamber carpet, and it served as a perfect guide to keep her walking a straight line. Not that she needed it, because the Crown lay on its pedestal up the three steps of the dais, and she felt drawn to it like water flowing downhill.

She kept her eyes fixed on that distant spot. So small, to be the symbol of a nation. She'd tried it on the day before at Dane's request, to make sure it fit and didn't need to be padded. It had slipped down a little over her left ear, so she'd been grateful for Dane's insight. How it would feel when it fit properly, she had no idea.

The room was so still she could almost imagine she and her Aunt Veronica, standing behind the Crown, were the only two people there. Maybe she was more nervous about being stared at than she thought. Tremontanans, Eskandelics, Veriboldans, Ruskalder, all of them come to witness this moment. She should have felt the burden of the Crown more than ever, but instead she felt peaceful, drifting along as if she were watching her body move from the outside. It was an odd feeling, but a pleasant one.

She realized she was at the dais in time to keep from tripping over it. Slowly she ascended the three steps and looked down at the Crown. It was amazingly gaudy and beautiful at the same time, with the huge smooth emeralds the keeper of the jewels had said were cabochon-cut encircling the silver band, the six points tipped with diamonds rising at even intervals around the crown, and tiny diamonds the size of the ones in her necklace ringing the emeralds and sparkling even in the low light of the coronation hall.

People refer to you when they're talking about me, she thought. *The judgment of the Crown, for example. Or the Crown paying for all those books in the Library. They mean my judgment, the Treasury's money, but it's you that's the symbol. And now it's the two of us together. I hope we don't make a mess of this.*

She knelt gracefully before the pedestal and heard the rush of wind that was everyone in the room doing the same. What was that like for the non-Tremontanans? Dane had explained kneeling was a mark of respect, not fealty, and probably all those people knew that, but it still felt strange.

Veronica, the only one in the room still standing, grasped the Crown in her thin fingers and raised it to chest height. "Elspeth North," she said, her pale voice amplified by the exquisite acoustics of the ancient room, "by the grace of heaven, Queen of Tremontane. May your reign be long and just."

She lowered the Crown to rest on Elspeth's head. For a moment, it floated there, feather-light and still supported by Veronica's hands. Then it settled firmly on her head, not slipping at all. It didn't weigh much, and the velvet lining kept the silver from cutting into her scalp, but Elspeth had a feeling it would grow uncomfortable with time. She'd be glad to return it to Dane. For now, though—

She stood and turned around, facing the crowd. *Now* she was intimidated. She hadn't realized just how many people they could pack into the coronation hall. Everyone was still kneeling, and most of them, the Tremontanans anyway, had their heads bowed. Her gaze fell on Dane, who was looking at her with a smile that said everything was perfect. "Three cheers for the Queen," he shouted in that resonant voice. "*Huzzah! Huzzah! Huzzah!*"

The room echoed with shouts. A smile, unexpected and bright, touched Elspeth's lips. "Rise," she said. The wind went ragged as people rose, some with the help of their neighbors. "I never expected to be Queen," she said when the noise died down. "It will be the greatest challenge of my life. But I swear to fulfil my duties as Queen of Tremontane to the best of my abilities, and serve my people with justice and honor."

More cheering followed, this time spontaneous and natural-sounding, and Elspeth felt she might float away on it. It didn't mean the end of her challenges, but at least for now, she had the support of a nation.

She descended the dais and walked at a slightly faster pace back to the antechamber. When the doors were safely shut behind her, she looked at herself in the mirror. The Crown looked smaller than it felt. She gingerly reached up and removed it, holding it in both hands and examining the silver for smudges. Not a scratch. Dane would have nothing to complain of.

The outer door, the one leading to the ancient hallway, opened. "Congratulations, your Majesty," Dane said.

"Thank you. It feels so odd, all that planning and work for something I wear for a minute."

"It is a minute that will go down in history," Dane said with a smile. He held out his hand. "I'll return this to the treasury—and may it be many a year before it's needed again."

Elspeth handed the Crown over. "Isn't it used for other times than coronations?"

"A few. Certain state functions. Formal recognition of other heads of state. I suppose you'll wear it on your wedding day, to symbolize that your spouse is also your Consort."

Elspeth shuddered. "I don't want to think about that today. The reception is bad enough." She might not mind being stared at, but having to make polite conversation for hours filled her with dread.

"Don't put it off too long," Dane warned. "A strong monarch needs a strong Consort as his, or her, support. And a marriage bond is a blessing to anyone, Queen or no." He nodded and carried the Crown away.

Elspeth ran her fingers over her head. She could still feel the Crown pressing into her skull. That wasn't going away any time soon.

THE GRAND BALLROOM, WITH ITS MURALS AND LOW-HANGING chandeliers, was warmer than the coronation hall and more brightly lit, but Elspeth found herself wishing to be back in the drafty chamber. She drifted through the ballroom, greeting strangers Lord Harrington introduced to her. The head of Foreign Affairs knew everyone, and was good at guiding Elspeth toward people she might enjoy speaking to even if she wasn't the newly-crowned Queen. It felt like drifting through a sea filled with floating corks that spoke, a mad comparison, but it had been a long day and Elspeth felt oddly giddy. She wasn't sure how long she had to stay, but surely she could get away before midnight?

Someone put a hand on her waist, an intimate gesture that startled her. The brief thought *No one's touched me for almost two weeks* shot through her, and then the knowledge that she was the Queen and nobody had better dare touch her without her permission stopped her in her tracks and spun her around. "How dare—"

The tall, handsome man standing behind her grinned down at her. "*Playing dress-up, Elspeth?*" he said in Veriboldan.

Elspeth gasped. "*Mihn,*" she gasped, and flung herself at him, not caring what it looked like. "*Sweet heaven, it's so good to see you!*"

"*And you, best of friends,*" Mihn replied. He held her at arm's length and said, "*You look good dressed in your native clothes. I wish Daoine could see you. She'd be incandescent with jealousy.*"

"*Past time for that. I was always jealous of the way she fit into formal robes.*" Elspeth looked around. The circle of guests immediately surrounding them didn't even pretend not to be watching this reunion. Elspeth willed herself not to blush and said, in Tremontanese, "Welcome to Tremontane, Bakarne of the Arhainen. Is your respected father here?"

"He is here somewhere," Mihn said. His Tremontanese was stilted, but not heavily accented, but then he'd practiced with Elspeth for twenty years. "He will be most pleased to meet you in your new role."

"Lord Harrington, do you know where the Proxy is? I would like to greet him," Elspeth said.

Harrington's face was carefully blank, and it made Elspeth nervous. She'd completely forgotten herself in her joy at seeing her best friend, and how terrible must that have looked to her guests? *You're the Queen, they won't dare criticize,* she told herself, and held her head high as Harrington led her across the ballroom to a spot along the wall some twenty feet from the foot of the stairs.

Several ornate chairs padded with red velvet stood there, at careful distances from one another. Two of them were occupied. One of the men sitting there was the Ruskalder chief whose name Elspeth had already forgotten despite having been introduced to him only half an hour earlier. He was the Ruskalder ambassador to Tremontane and had made no secret of the fact that he felt the position was beneath him. Elspeth was just as happy to forget who he was.

The other man sat erect in his chair as if it were a throne. He wore a rose-colored silk robe embroidered with leaping golden fish over black silk trousers and shirt, and his toes, the nails lacquered bronze, peeped out from beneath his trouser hems. His shaved head gleamed in the bright light of the chandeliers, which turned his dark skin a warm brown. Elspeth, who knew he shaved his head because he was going bald, was not overwhelmed by his magnificence.

"My lord Elizdo, welcome to Tremontane," she said, bowing.

Harrington sucked in a breath. Instantly Elspeth knew her mistake. She'd bowed to Elizdo the way she always had when she encountered him in Veribold, showing respect to him as patriarch of the Arhainen family. But what was common courtesy in Elspeth North was a serious breach of protocol in the Queen of Tremontane. She'd just implied she owed Elizdo something. And nobody was going to overlook that.

There was only one thing to do: brazen it out. "It's good to see you," she said cheerfully. "Lord Harrington, is one of these chairs mine? I'd like to have a few moments with my father's old friend."

Elizdo's face tightened minutely. Describing him as her father's friend wasn't so much an exaggeration as a flat-out lie, given that Sebastian North thought Elizdo was a leech on society and Elizdo thought Sebastian was a useless, extraneous royal prince. But he wouldn't call her on it in public.

Harrington, for his part, behaved like the perfect political animal he was. "You are welcome to sit here, your Majesty," he said. "Feel free to mingle as you choose. I have others I must speak to."

Elspeth hoped that was code for *I am going to clean up your mess* and nodded politely as he turned away. "*Elizdo, how do you like Tremontane? You've been here for two years, yes?*"

"*Two years, three months, thirteen days.*" Elizdo glowered at her. "*A Queen should not bow to anyone. Even a foolish girl like you should know that.*"

"*I forgot myself in the joy of seeing you and Bakarne. And I can either be a foolish girl, or I can be Queen, as far as how you address me. You and I both know which of those it's to be.*"

Elizdo's glare could have stripped the paint from the walls. "*I will not have you influencing my son. He is already too fond of Tremontane as it is.*"

Mihn, at Elspeth's left elbow, said, "*Father, liking Tremontane does not make me less Veriboldan, and you know that. Besides, Elspeth can't show me favoritism, so you don't need to worry about her influencing me. It's not as if we're getting married.*"

Elspeth surreptitiously jabbed Mihn with her elbow. They'd never been anything but best friends, but Elizdo persisted in believing Elspeth intended to entrap his son even after Mihn had announced his betrothal to someone else. That didn't stop Mihn from teasing his father, something that usually meant trouble not for Mihn, but for Elspeth.

Elizdo's dark face grew darker. "*Impudent boy! Come. It is past time we left.*"

"Oh!" Elspeth exclaimed, her heart sinking. "*But I've only just seen you!*"

"*Another time,*" Elizdo said with a smirk. "*Bakarne. Now.*"

Mihn shot Elspeth a meaningful look. "I will see you later, El," he said, squeezing her hand so quickly Elspeth didn't think anyone noticed. She smiled and waved, but aside from that one look, Mihn didn't look back.

She sagged into her chair and sighed. All her earlier pleasure evaporated. So being Queen meant she had to conceal or discard her oldest friendship, just because it would look bad for her to be too friendly with the Veriboldan ambassador's son. Heaven certainly was playing a cruel joke on her.

She glared at the Ruskalder ambassador, who turned away as if she'd slapped him. Good. She was in a bad mood, and she intended to spread it around.

She watched the crowds. Nobody seemed inclined to visit her, which was fortunate. There was Lady Serena d'Arden, laughing over something one of the Eskandelic ambassador's harem wives had said. Elspeth couldn't remember the last time she'd laughed so unrestrainedly. One more thing the Queen was deprived of, casual jokes. Casual jokes, a friendly touch, the ability to do what she liked without her every move being scrutinized—

"Your Majesty."

Elspeth managed not to groan. Faraday again. How the man managed to intrude on her at her lowest moments was a mystery. Or maybe his intrusion turned every moment into her lowest one. "Yes, Mister Faraday?"

"There are things I need to discuss with you tomorrow. Is three o'clock acceptable?"

Elspeth sighed. "Mister Faraday, you know better than I do that I have no control over my schedule. See Miss Simkins if you want a moment of my time."

She wasn't looking at him, but she heard him take a deep breath as if summoning patience. "I thought," he said in a level voice that said an eruption was around the corner, "you wanted to control your own life. Do you want Miss Simkins constantly telling you what to do?"

Stung, Elspeth sat upright and glared at him. His familiar scowl annoyed and reassured her, and that feeling of reassurance made her angry. She had no intention of taking comfort from him, even inadvertent comfort. "I thought *you* wanted to control my life. Tell me what to do, what to say, what to think. At this point I don't really give a damn which of you does it. Just pick a puppet master and leave me in peace."

"That's fine language for a priestess. Did they teach you that at the temple?"

She sucked in a startled breath. His insult was so unexpected, so perfectly aimed at a spot she hadn't thought to defend, that tears came to her eyes. "You have no idea what it means to be a priestess of the Irantzen Temple," she whispered. "Get out of my sight immediately."

Faraday's jaw clenched. "Your Majesty," he said, and withdrew. He didn't bow.

Elspeth stared straight ahead at a spot on the wall, just below the ceiling mural, until her eyes stopped stinging. Then she rose from her chair and made her way through the crowds, smiling and nodding but not engaging in conversation. Nobody tried to stop her leaving. She was all the way to the east wing doors before she realized she'd found the path herself. It felt like hollow victory.

Honey helped her take off her gown, which except for all the buttons down her spine she might have removed herself. Elspeth put on her nightdress and let Honey unbraid her hair, which rippled around her face in neat waves that would be frizzy by morning. She declined the offer of hot chocolate and climbed into bed, turning off the light and curling into a warm ball around one of her pillows. In the darkness, she counted to herself, *one, two, three*, and made it all the way to seventeen before crying overcame her, and she wept herself to sleep.

10

*E*lspeth wasn't last to the Council chamber this time, knowing in advance what day the meeting was and guessing it would be at the same time as the last one. The few councilors there ahead of her sat in the same places they had before. Assigned seating. Was that by habit, by tradition, or something Francis or Landon had insisted on? Whatever the reason, it helped Elspeth remember their names.

She'd had supper with Lady Beaumont and Caxton the night before her coronation, and with Lady Wilde and General Beckett last night. The meal with Lady Beaumont and Caxton had been extremely uncomfortable, with neither of her guests being willing to speak and Elspeth having no idea what to say to them. She'd finally hit on the fortunate topic of horses, and Lady Beaumont had taken that line of conversation and run away with it. Since she was the sort of person who delighted in showing off her knowledge at the expense of her listeners, it only made the evening louder, not better.

Lady Wilde and General Beckett had been better dining companions, though Beckett started out as taciturn as Caxton had been. Lady Wilde, on the other hand, was clever and amusing, a wellspring of humorous stories, and Elspeth had laughed for the first time in...it couldn't have been forever, but it certainly felt like it. Lady Wilde's easy good manners had broken through Beckett's reserve, and he'd turned out to know some excellent stories himself. Elspeth had shared a few stories of being an aspirant at the Temple, and had ended the evening feeling that someday Lady Wilde and Beckett might become her friends.

Today, though, their reserve was back, and both greeted Elspeth formally as if the evening hadn't happened. Elspeth concealed her disappointment and sat in her not-a-throne, half-listening to the conversations around her and running over what she intended to say. It would almost certainly cause an uproar, but she was in the right, and this was something she not only wanted, but felt confident was the best decision for the Council.

She ignored Faraday when he entered and took his seat beyond the Countess of Waxwold. Lady Quinn wasn't big enough to block Elspeth's view of her nemesis, but she provided enough of a barrier that not looking at Faraday was easy. They hadn't spoken since the night of the coronation; Elspeth had declined his request for an audience twice, and he hadn't asked a third time. She felt a little guilty about this, because he *was* the head of Internal Affairs and no doubt had important business, but she couldn't forget what he'd said to her, those horrible, smug, dismissive words denigrating her most sacred experiences. The likelihood of her being able to speak to him without screaming felt vanishingly small. She would eventually be able to bear it, but not now. She refused to consider that she was acting like a petulant child instead of a Queen.

She realized Julius Caxton had sat down beside her and realized further he'd been the last arrival. "Ladies and gentlemen, thank you for coming," she said. "Today we have a number of items of business, including a vote on some financial matters. However, the first thing I'd like to address is naming a new head of Transportation."

Everyone was listening politely. She had a feeling that wouldn't last.

"Miss Hardison presented me with a list of candidates, and I interviewed each. They were all well qualified to take responsibility for managing the Crown's transportation, maintaining the roads, et cetera. However, none of them struck me as well suited to serve on this Council. They all lacked the insight and flexibility of thought I believe a councilor needs."

They'd started murmuring midway through that speech, glancing at each other with the expressions of people who'd been tossed overboard and weren't sure they could swim. "Your Majesty," Lady Wilde said, "are you saying you've rejected *all* the candidates?"

"All the proposed candidates, yes," Elspeth said. "But I wouldn't come before you without an alternative solution. The new head of Transportation is Master Martin Keswick. He is a graduate of the Scholia, currently assistant librarian in the Royal Library, and he has extensive experience with the post runner routes. I believe he will serve admirably."

The muttering grew louder. "Your Majesty," Faraday said, "the Council has to approve new councilors. You have to put your...candidate...forward for ratification."

Elspeth's heart beat faster, and she managed not to smile, because it would surely come off as smug. "Actually, I don't," she said cheerfully. "I've been reading the laws pertaining to my responsibilities as Queen, things I have to do and things that are only tradition. It seems the idea of the Council ratifying the monarch's choices for Council members is a relatively recent one that my Uncle Landon instituted, or agreed to—I don't know if it was his idea or someone else's. It was never made into law. It's a nice idea, but I believe it overly complicates what should be a simple matter. So—Master Keswick it is. I hope you will all make him feel welcome when he joins us next week."

Faraday stood. "Your Majesty," he said, "the policy of voting on new Council members is sound practice maintained by most of the Guilds. I think—"

"We're not a Guild, Mister Faraday, we are the ruling monarch and her Council." Elspeth found the sight of his scowling face even more cheering. "But I can understand your reluctance to let go of the policy. Let me reassure you I have given this great thought, and I'm convinced I've made the right decision." She wanted to stick her tongue out at him and say *Tough luck losing some of your power,* but she wasn't juvenile.

"I asked each candidate a question," she went on, not giving Faraday room to override her. "I asked them to tell me the best way to send a message from one city to another. A simple question, and all of them were factually correct in their answers, but none of them understood what I was really asking. Master Keswick, on the other hand, saw immediately that the real point was not the details of travel between places, but the purpose of making the journey. Some messages are a matter of life and death. Some aren't worth the bother of sending. But it isn't until we ask ourselves why we are doing a thing that we truly know what it will cost us."

Everyone was silent. "You members of the Council who are responsible for the departments need a knowledge of the field you're responsible for," Elspeth said. "But you also are given a measure of power in being allowed to determine government policies and counsel your Queen. I could find a dozen men and women capable of monitoring the post horses. There are far fewer with the insight and understanding this position demands. And as the one who ultimately takes responsibility for the decisions we make, I think it's not unreasonable that I take full responsibility for choosing the individuals who will help make those decisions." She fixed her gaze on Faraday, who was still standing. "If anyone would like to contest that, I'm willing to listen to your arguments. But they had better be good ones."

Faraday glared at her for a moment longer. Then he slowly sat down. "Your Majesty has legal precedent on your side," he said. "I withdraw my objection."

"Thank you, Mister Faraday. Anyone else?" Elspeth looked at each Council member in turn. Most of them seemed stunned. Lady Quinn on Elspeth's right had her hand over her mouth as if concealing a laugh. Faraday's sour expression hadn't changed. Well, she already knew she wouldn't win him over. "Then that's settled. As I said, I've asked Master Keswick to join us next week for his first Council meeting, but his investiture will happen tomorrow morning." She'd wanted it to be yesterday, but she judged the Council would be upset about her, as they saw it, usurping their rights, and she didn't want to push so hard it turned into a real fight.

The rest of the meeting was a discussion about Caxton's financial reports. Elspeth let most of it wash over her. She'd read through the report several times and had never gained any enlightenment. His bookkeeping methods made no sense to her, and learning from showing them to Simkins that the methods were standard financial practice didn't reassure her. She didn't like feeling out of her depth, especially since she was sure Finance was a key department she ought to have some basic understanding of.

She was watching the shouting match between Caxton and Beckett about the Defense budget when she became aware of someone staring at her. She turned in time to see Faraday's gaze flick from her to the argument. He'd been unexpectedly quiet after she'd made him back down, and again a tiny flame of guilt sparked in her heart. He was cruel, and arrogant, and power-hungry, but she hadn't exactly been polite to him—no, it didn't matter, because he didn't deserve any consideration and she shouldn't feel guilty about anything.

Finally, when it was nearly noon, she said, "I think we need to break this discussion down into smaller pieces, because there's a great deal of material here—no, Mister Caxton, that wasn't a criticism. I would like to call an interim meeting—" a term she'd learned from her black leather book— "in three days to discuss the taxation reports, and I want each department to prepare a budget report to be presented at the next regular Council meeting in a week. Does anyone have any other suggestions?"

No one did.

"Then—thank you again, ladies and gentlemen, you're dismissed."

She couldn't tell for sure, but she felt the councilors left with more alacrity than they had the first time. She had no idea if she'd done the right thing, but Hien had always said *When someone makes a demand of you, turn it back on them and you will see how urgent the demand truly is* and Elspeth had decided having the departments spend energy on budgets would at least give her time to come to grips with Caxton's accounting procedures.

She rose from her chair after the rest of them and nearly bumped into Faraday, who alone hadn't moved for the door. Anxiety gripped her heart—if he was going to yell at her, it was going to turn into a shouting match. She knew from her reading she couldn't dismiss a councilor unless he broke the law or all the other councilors agreed, so that shouting match would only make her life harder. "Yes, Mister Faraday?"

"Your Majesty," Faraday said in a low voice, though there was no one nearby to hear, "I realize we have frequently been at odds, but I truly do need to speak with you. If you can overcome your need to disregard everything I say."

Elspeth gaped. "*My* need?" she exclaimed. "Mister Faraday, you have done nothing but criticize and belittle me since the moment we met. You are determined to see me fail, and I'm starting to wonder if I should be watching my back!"

Faraday's jaw tightened. "You dare accuse me of sabotage? Your willful ignorance is going to destroy this country!"

"I am *not* willfully ignorant, you...you insensitive clod! I don't know why you think you can get away with treating me like a child, but so help me, if I could remove you from office, I would!"

Faraday spat a blistering curse that made Elspeth blush. "This is getting us nowhere," he said. "You and I will always be at odds, since you—" He cut his words off and gained control of himself. "What I have to say is important. Can we call a truce long enough to discuss it?" he said, more calmly.

Elspeth made her fists relax. "All right," she said, "truce. What is it?"

"I would prefer to discuss it in private."

"There's no one here. How much more private do you want?"

Faraday scowled, but the expression wasn't as fiercely angry as before. He closed the Council chamber door and came back to where

Elspeth stood. "These financial reports are confusing," he said. "I think that's deliberate."

"Deliberate? You think Mister Caxton did something shady?"

"I can't tell what he's done. But I'm sure he's concealing something. With Finance, that could be serious."

Elspeth nodded. "Mister Faraday, I admit I don't understand the finances at all. How can we prove whether or not Mister Caxton is...I don't know. Could he be stealing from the Crown?"

"That's one possibility. Another is that he's manipulating the budgets to conceal where money is being moved illicitly from one department to another."

"Which would mean the collusion of another department head."

"Almost certainly."

"But Mister Caxton is the one in charge of the finances, and if this were happening in another department, he's the one I'd go to for answers. How do we inspect the one who ought to do the inspection?"

Faraday looked thoughtful. It made him look surprisingly human. "With your permission, I can bring in some Masters from the Scholia to do the analysis. I can vouch for their discretion—if that means anything to you."

Elspeth ground her back teeth. "Mister Faraday," she said, "I don't like you, I don't like how you treat me, but you have never given me any reason to doubt your honor. Don't ascribe worse motives to me than I actually have."

Faraday looked past Elspeth toward one of the banners on the wall. "You're right," he said. "I shouldn't have said that. Will you allow me to contact the Masters?"

"I will. Please ask them to—no." If he could bend, so could she. "Have them report their findings to you, and then I'd like you to let me know the results."

Faraday raised an eyebrow. "I'm surprised you trust me."

"I'm giving you a chance to prove you're not a self-centered, arrogant git, Mister Faraday. Don't disappoint me."

To her utter shock, Faraday smiled. "You assume what you think matters to me, your Majesty."

She was about to slap him when she realized it was a joke. "Then do it for your country," she said, smiling despite herself.

"I think that's a cause we can actually agree on," Faraday said.

It felt so odd not to be fighting with him. "I do want what's best for Tremontane," she said. "I know you don't think I'm qualified, but I'm doing my best."

Faraday nodded. He looked down at the Council table, where Elspeth's hand rested. "I would like to apologize," he said, his voice once again almost too low to hear, "for what I said to you at the reception. It was uncalled for, and I didn't realize what an insult I'd given you until it was too late."

Stunned, Elspeth said, "You...you're right, that was a terrible insult." A shadow of the pain he'd caused her touched her heart and vanished.

Faraday grimaced. "You called me a puppet master. I'm afraid that struck a little too close to home, and I lost my temper. Again, I apologize."

"I accept your apology." Then the import of his words struck her. "What do you mean, too close to home?"

Faraday shook his head. "It's not important."

"It *is* important. Do you mean you really were trying to manipulate me?" Her accord with him dissolved like chalk in rain.

He let out a deep sigh. "Let's say I assumed the worst about you, and did everything I could to keep your inexperience from having lasting effects on this country. In my defense, all anyone knew about you was that you were a timid, sheltered young woman—"

"Excuse me?"

"—who was committed to a foreign religious community and had had no instruction in anything necessary to ruling a country. To say that I was terrified for Tremontane is an understatement of epic proportions."

Irritation rose up within her. "So you made a lot of assumptions and then blamed me for all of them? What is it about this country that everyone assumes religious means sheltered and ignorant? Let me tell you—"

"Please, no," Faraday said. "It may have taken me time, but I realize now I was wrong in what I thought of you, and I apologize for my actions arising from that misunderstanding. It's true, you lack experience, but you've done much to remedy that. Though it didn't help that you ripped up at me every time I tried to give you direction."

"Well, it didn't help that you were committed to giving me direction in the most insulting, dismissive way possible."

"That is *not*—" Faraday pinched the bridge of his nose and squeezed his eyes shut. "We have thoroughly misunderstood each other," he said. "Can we start over? Beginning with each of us assuming the other has good motives, regardless of how our behavior looks?"

Elspeth thought back over her interactions with Faraday. She had to admit she'd been at fault sometimes, too. If she gave Faraday credit for having really wanted her to succeed, even if his methods had been...flawed, she could see how her actions might have looked irresponsible or selfish. And when she thought about the joke he'd just made, she realized it was possible she'd taken at face value words that were meant to be humorous, like that dig about becoming a lawspeaker. "You're right," she said. "If I believe you want what's best for Tremontane, I can look past the things you do that make me react badly. And...I'm sorry. For assuming the worst of you."

"I hope this means we can work together instead of being at odds," Faraday said. "Especially since the documents requiring your signature have piled up in the last three days."

Elspeth swore under her breath. Faraday blinked. "All right," he said, "I hope you won't take this as another insult, but I genuinely didn't believe priestesses used that kind of language."

"I wasn't a priestess, just a priestess in training. But we don't believe heaven is closed to those whose vocabulary is vulgar. And most of those words, I learned from my superiors."

Faraday smiled again. "I'll bring those papers to your office after dinner. And I'll let you know what the Masters find out. If I contact them immediately, they might have an initial assessment before the interim Council meeting." He gestured to her to precede him out the door. "At the risk of disrupting our newfound accord, I have to admit I took those papers so I could be sure the important ones didn't get overlooked. King Francis—" He shut his mouth on more words.

"It's all right. I've already guessed Francis wasn't the King he should have been. But thank you for not wanting to speak ill of my dead."

Faraday stopped. Elspeth, a few steps ahead of him, turned to see what was wrong. There was a peculiar, unreadable expression on his face. "Your Majesty," he said, and bowed. "It will be a pleasure working with you."

Elspeth thought about that. "You know," she said, "I think I feel the same."

11

I won't say everything is better, Elspeth wrote, *but Mister Faraday is less overbearing, and I think I'm less oversensitive. And I realize now that he is good at his job, now that he's no longer trying to do all of mine as well. I feel more secure than I did when I wrote that last letter. Please don't worry about me. I miss you all and hope you can arrange a visit soon.*

She signed the letter and folded it neatly, sealing it with dark blue wax impressed with her personal signet. She never wore the ring, which had been made for a man and would have been far too large even if it had been made for a woman, but carried it with her on a string around her neck and hoped that was secure enough. It sometimes tapped against the *toan* jade, a reminder of how her two worlds were still at odds however much she wished otherwise.

She set the letter aside for Gloria to take to the post and climbed onto her bed to sit cross-legged against the pillows. It was far too soft to be comfortable for meditation, but the floor was too hard and cold and the chairs too angular. Normally, she meditated before sleeping, but the interim Council meeting was scheduled for this afternoon, and after what Faraday's Masters had found, she needed all the inner peace she could get.

The *toan* jade's soapy texture calmed her even before her finger-tips sought out a meditation ritual. The third one, the path of wisdom, called to her today. Maybe this was something she should have been doing all along, seeking for wisdom. She ran her fingers along the deeply carved symbols, words in a language older than either Veriboldan or Tremontanese. *Drink deep, and be filled,* they said, and she exhaled and felt herself fall into the deep contemplative state beyond language.

Her breath sounded like the wind stirring the new leaves, her heartbeat was a drum counting out the moments with its slow, measured beats, her skin tingled as the fine linen of her shirt rubbed over her arms. In these moments of deep contemplation, she felt she floated in the pool deep beneath the Irantzen Temple, as if the soft, skin-temperature water bore her up and washed away all her troubles. She let her mind drift without touching on any of the problems and questions that plagued her waking mind, and reached out to heaven for a solution.

The chime of the mantel clock, sounding the half-hour, brought her gently back to herself. She let out a final calming breath and opened her eyes. Her hands still touched the *toan* jade, but they'd moved without her direction from the third meditation ritual to the fifth. The path of harmony. That seemed unlikely, given that what she intended to do today would create the opposite of harmony.

That which is two becomes one, her fingers read, *but much must be shed to achieve it.* Harmony never came without sacrifice. Maybe that's what she needed to remember—to embrace harmony without fearing the road to it. She kissed the *toan* jade, thought briefly of Hien and what she might be doing now, and uncrossed her legs. It was possible Hien was meditating with Elspeth's medallion right now, but unlikely, given that it was earlier in Veribold than it was in Aurilien and Hien was more likely leading the priestesses in worship. Still, it was a comforting fantasy.

Elspeth tucked the *toan* jade away inside her shirt. Her new wardrobe had grown gradually, appearing piece by piece until the dressing room was half full. Elspeth never saw anyone adding to it, which created the illusion that the wardrobes spontaneously generated clothes. She'd folded away her Veriboldan clothes into a single drawer, not wanting to get rid of them entirely, and hung her formal robe with the rest of the clothes.

She'd taken to wearing warm woolen trousers, a linen shirt, and a loose coat not made to button up the front so it hung open over the shirt. Its shoulders and wide sleeves were decorated with cording that made a pretty abstract pattern Elspeth liked, and it was of twilled cotton heavy enough to feel like wearing flexible armor. She hadn't seen anyone wearing anything like it, but no one had made any critical comments, not even Simkins, and Elspeth had figured if Simkins approved, it must be appropriate garb for a Queen. Elspeth only cared that it was warm. The palace was never warm enough except in her own bedchamber, the east wing drawing room, and Elspeth's office, where she'd insisted someone build up the fire early so the room was roasting when she finally arrived.

Now she shrugged into her coat and combed her hair. She ought to get used to Honey helping her dress, but the idea of someone else putting clothes on her, clothes anyone could manage for themselves, made her uncomfortable. So she had Honey come to her in the evenings when she had to dress for supper and told herself that was good enough.

Simkins waited outside her office when Elspeth arrived. "I have made the arrangements you requested, your Majesty," she said, her lips pursed as if those arrangements included Simkins eating a lemon.

"Thank you, Miss Simkins."

Simkins didn't leave. "There is a...gentleman...requesting audience with you," she went on. "He gave his name as Bakarne of the Arhainen. I thought I should speak with you before making the appointment."

Meaning Simkins didn't think a Veriboldan worthy of speaking with the Queen. "Bakarne of the Arhainen is the son of the Proxy of Veribold and an old friend," Elspeth said, drawing on some of

Simkins' snobbishness to put steel into her words. "He's to be allowed to see me at any time. Wait—do you mean he's here now?"

Simkins nodded, managing to do so while keeping her chin high.

Elspeth checked her watch. "Show him in. I have some time before the Council meeting."

"Yes, your Majesty," Simkins said, her voice as icy as Elspeth's. She turned and walked away.

Elspeth went into her office, shut the door, and said a few words Hien would deny knowing. The more comfortable Elspeth felt in her role, the less happy she was with Simkins' attitude. And yet the woman was extremely competent, and Elspeth quailed at the idea of teaching someone else all the minutiae of Simkins' job, especially when Elspeth didn't know all of it herself. She sighed and crossed the room to stand in front of the blazing fire, warming her hands. Someday she'd be acclimated to Tremontane, but she didn't have to be happy about it.

The door opened. "Bakarne of the Arhainen, your Majesty," Simkins said disapprovingly. Elspeth ignored her and crossed the room to clasp Mihn's hands.

"*I hope they didn't make you wait long,*" she said in Veriboldan. "*They're protective of my time.*"

"*I guess I'm not as well-known as I thought,*" Mihn said. "*They probably would have let my father through, no questions.*"

Elspeth shuddered. "*I ought to leave word for them not to do that. I can't imagine anything more distressing than dealing with Elizdo in my own office.*"

Mihn smiled and released her. "*I came to see if you want to get away for a while. Go for a ride in the Park.*"

The Park. Who had suggested she take a look at it? Veronica, right. "*I don't know if my schedule's free. But I'd love to. I haven't been outside in two weeks.*"

"*El, you have to take time for yourself. You're going to go mad otherwise. That's my considered opinion and not just me selfishly wanting to spend time with my best friend.*" Mihn wandered over to the fireplace and winced. "*Aren't you roasting in here? It's like a furnace.*"

"I'm always cold." Elspeth joined him. They stood side by side, watching the flames.

"What's it like? Being Queen?" Mihn finally said.

"There's nothing to compare it to. Nobody ever says my name, did you know? It's always 'your Majesty.' My aunt rarely calls me anything. And they respect me, but it's like I'm wearing a mask, and the mask is really what they respect. I don't know that anyone except you sees Elspeth North beneath the royal mask."

"I'm sorry. I know it's not what you wanted. Daoine said she missed you at the final feast of the Festival."

"I missed her, too. Is she ever coming for a visit?"

Mihn shrugged. *"You know what her parents are like. They think Tremontane is full of uncouth upstarts who wouldn't know real culture if it bit them in the ass."*

"That must be hard."

"We'll be married the month Father's term is up, and then we'll both be free. I can be patient."

The door opened. Simkins said, "Your Majesty, it's time."

Elspeth looked up at her tall friend. *"I'll send word if I can get away this afternoon,"* she said. *"It's so good to see you."*

"Hang in there, El," Mihn said. He squeezed her shoulder and let himself out, passing Simkins, who barely moved to let him by.

"Your Majesty," Simkins began.

"Just a minute, Miss Simkins," Elspeth said. Mihn's gentle touch had struck her to the heart, and she blinked away tears. "That man is not only the son of the Proxy of Veribold, he is my oldest friend and someone I care very much about. If you can't show him the respect due all of that, I will have to consider whether I'm well served by your continued presence in the palace. Do we have an understanding?"

Simkins' eyes widened. "Your Majesty," she repeated, swallowed, and said, "I understand. I apologize—I didn't realize—"

"That's all right, Miss Simkins, just so you realize now," Elspeth said. "Did you send the soldiers to their position?"

"Yes, your Majesty, but I think I will better be able to serve you if you would explain what you need them for."

"I hope *not* to need them," Elspeth said, and left the office.

Lady Quinn, General Beckett, and Lord Harrington were all in the Council chamber when she arrived. They bowed to her, but didn't interrupt the low-voiced conversation they were having. Elspeth, relieved at not being required to make small talk, took her seat and played with the *toan* jade. It calmed her enough that when Julius Caxton entered, she could greet him without any of her inner turmoil showing. He grunted an acknowledgement as he took his seat beside her.

Faraday was the last to arrive. He nodded politely, but his hard gaze told her everything she needed to know. Her heart sank. This was not a meeting she wanted to have.

"Ladies and gentlemen, thank you for coming," she said, stilling the remaining conversations. "This meeting is to address the taxation reports prepared by Mister Caxton. There was some confusion in our last meeting over the distribution of taxes by province. Mister Caxton, would you care to summarize?"

Caxton stood. "It's as I said before," he began. "Provincial taxes..."

Elspeth let him speak for a while. This time, she could admire, in a despairing way, how he deftly managed to speak without saying anything of importance. "...which is why taxes are collected to the Royal Treasury and monies disbursed from the general fund instead of taxes staying within the provinces," Caxton finally said, and sat.

"Thank you, Mister Caxton." Elspeth sat up straighter in her chair. "Is that all?"

Caxton nodded. "I think I've been clear."

"So you're willing to stand by what you've said? You take responsibility for the system you've laid out?"

Caxton's eyes went shifty. "I...yes, your Majesty."

Elspeth stared him down. "Mister Caxton, what you've laid out for us is extremely complex, and no one would fault you for getting a few details wrong. Is there anything you'd like to add?"

The room was as still as if the air had frozen. Caxton swallowed. Elspeth could tell the moment he decided to brazen it out because his eyes hardened, and he licked his lips. "No, your Majesty."

Elspeth turned to Faraday. "Mister Faraday?"

Faraday stood. His eyes were even harder and colder than Caxton's, and Elspeth reflected on how glad she was they weren't enemies anymore. "I took Mister Caxton's financial report to independent auditors," he said. "They reviewed the material and determined that funds were being diverted from the Treasury to certain projects. Some of these were projects the Crown had chosen not to support. A few of them appear to have been created solely as receiving entities to conceal the origin of the money passed along to other recipients. The auditors concluded that this was deliberate and that it had been going on for at least two years." He sat, interlacing his fingers and resting his hands on the table.

"Mister Caxton," Elspeth said, "you have taken responsibility for this malfeasance before your fellow councilors and before your Queen. Do you have anything to say in your defense?"

Caxton licked his lips again. "Everything I did was in service to the Crown," he said. "I never took a single brass drab for my own use. Those were projects—you don't understand what it was like under King Francis. He didn't understand anything about government, or about how you need to spend money to make money. I was correcting injustice, helping people who didn't deserve to have their livelihood yanked out from under them just because Francis wanted to build another folly in his garden." He was breathing heavily, and beads of sweat stood out on his brow.

Elspeth stood. "You meant well," she said, "but that's not how the law works. You can't make things right by doing something wrong, because that wrong will always spread until you're putting out fires you didn't start."

She walked to the door in the far wall, the large one no one ever used, and opened it, revealing four soldiers in brown and green. "Take Mister Caxton into custody pending trial," she said.

Caxton didn't resist when the guards hauled him out of his chair. "I did what was right for the country," he said. "I stand by that."

"And you'll be given the opportunity to say so at your trial," Elspeth said. "I'm sorry, Mister Caxton."

The guards escorted him out through the main door, which swung shut behind them. The instant it closed, the room erupted into shouts and demands for an explanation. Elspeth sank into her seat and looked Faraday's way. His expression was hard and closed-off, but Elspeth understood now that he looked that way when he was controlling a strong emotion. She was sure she looked the same.

"Enough," she said when she judged the outrage had gone on long enough. The noise died down. "Even if Mister Caxton doesn't serve a prison term for what he's done, he can't be allowed to serve in his position any longer. Mister Faraday, is it possible one of your Scholia Masters is capable of taking his place?"

"I can make a recommendation for your Majesty to review," Faraday said.

"Thank you. I'll expect that recommendation in two days, if possible. I'd like to be able to present the new head of Finance at our next regular meeting."

"I'll take care of it."

Elspeth stood, prompting the others to rise. "I think that's more than enough for one meeting. Thank you for your service, and I'll see you in three days, unless something else comes up." She hoped nothing else would come up.

She walked back to her office alone, feeling as if she was dragging a thousand-pound weight behind her. The problem was, she sympathized with Caxton. The more she learned about her role, the more convinced she was that Francis had been a terrible king. No wonder Caxton had broken the law. No wonder Faraday had wanted to usurp some of the King's responsibilities. But there was no end to that line of thinking. Good intentions weren't enough to excuse taking the law into your own hands.

She sat at her desk, toying with a pen, drawing circles all over the handwritten daily schedule she'd insisted Simkins produce. She had nothing to do but sit for her stupid portrait in two hours...

Frustration filled her, turned into impatience. She pulled the bell rope and waited. When Simkins arrived, she said, "Cancel all my afternoon appointments. I'm going out."

"Going out? Where? Your Majesty—"

"I'm going for a ride in the Park with Mihn—Bakarne of the Arhainen. The portrait sitting can wait." Despite her acquisition of Tremontanan clothes, Elspeth still didn't have the artist's approval, and today the thought of facing the woman and her criticisms wearied her.

"Very well, your Majesty."

Simkins' acquiescence surprised Elspeth into giving the woman a long, hard look. She didn't look disapproving or angry, just respectful. Maybe all Elspeth had ever had to do to control Simkins was stand up to her. Some people were like that.

She sent a runner to the Veriboldan embassy to tell Mihn the new plan and hurried off to her chambers to change. When she got there, however, she looked at herself in the mirror and decided she looked just fine for an afternoon outing with a friend. Her heart already felt lighter than it had in days.

The messenger came for her just as she was dithering over where she should go—have someone take her to the Veriboldan embassy? Wait on the steps of the palace like an eloping maiden?—and brought her through back ways to the stables. The furtive way they went excited Elspeth, as if she were doing something forbidden that someone like Faraday would be furious about. But the stables hummed along busily, and the stable hands bowed to her as if she were expected, and she buried her disappointment and walked to where Mihn waited atop a high-sprung carriage, his hands on the reins of a beautifully matched pair of black horses.

"*Let me take you away from all this, my lady,*" Mihn declaimed, bowing as gracefully as anyone could from a seated position. Elspeth laughed and, with some assistance, climbed onto the seat beside him.

"*We're just waiting on your escort,*" he went on. "*You've outpaced them.*"

Elspeth grimaced. "*Let's just go. It's not like you don't know where the Park is.*"

"*Queens don't travel unescorted, El. Get used to it.*"

A couple of guards in North blue trotted up to the carriage, followed by another pair. "Your Majesty," the lieutenant on the white horse said, "where do you intend to go today?"

"We're going to the Park. And could you please...I don't know. Not be obtrusive? I'd like to pretend for an hour or so that I'm not the Queen."

The woman smiled sympathetically. "We'll be discreet, your Majesty."

Elspeth had never spent much time in Aurilien and had never wanted to. Now, the knowledge that it was in a sense her city, her possession, gave it a sense of wonder she hadn't felt before. It reminded her a little of the east side of Haizea, where the common folk lived; that was also a place she hadn't gone often, but that feeling of closeness, of a place lived in for centuries, made her feel at home.

Aurilien's buildings were taller than Haizea's and blander, without the bright colors of ceramic and tile that made Haizea look like a pile of jewels snugged up against the Kepa's banks. But they were beautiful in their own way, with the older buildings' exposed beams stained dark brown or black and making a stark contrast to the plaster and limewash of the walls between them, white or pale blue or even pink. She knew these were older buildings because Francis had said something once about parts of the city looking just as they did when Willow hadn't yet become Queen. That fact had stuck with Elspeth, making her feel a connection to her ancestor and the city she'd loved.

Newer buildings stood cheek-by-jowl with the old ones, not something she'd ever seen in Haizea, where changes in architecture were subtle so the city would retain its uniform beauty. Brick façades, red or yellow or gray, were splashes of color that gave Aurilien a patchy look—and yet it was a look that suited it, made it seem young and vibrant. It was a city that didn't give a damn what anyone thought of it, and it charmed Elspeth.

The day was surprisingly warm for late winter, and Elspeth tossed her unnecessary cloak into the back of the carriage. She turned her face to the sun and closed her eyes until a change in the bumping of the carriage brought her back to now. When she opened her eyes, she gasped in astonishment. The city had disappeared, and lawns and trees and low, rolling hills surrounded her. "This *is the Park?*" she exclaimed.

"*Remarkable, isn't it? I heard your Uncle Landon is the one who built it.*"

Elspeth looked around. The guards kept pace with the carriage, two behind and two to the sides. The grass was winter-pale and yellow, but she could imagine how it would look in full summer, how all these flowerbeds would bloom with color. There were winter plants growing already, crocuses and snow drops and holly bushes, vibrant with color that no amount of snow could completely hide. Even the bare trees had a stark majesty to them, stretching their limbs to the sky as if praying to ungoverned heaven.

Men and women, mostly pedestrians, but a few on horseback and one brightly-painted carriage well ahead of them, thronged the paths that led through the flowerbeds and disappeared into the distant trees. They gaped in awe at the carriage, which wasn't obviously royal, but the guards in North colors made it clear who drove past that afternoon. The horse riders made way for them, bowing and doffing hats, and then they were past and headed away from the gates.

The path took them out of the lawns and into a more densely forested area, this one with pine trees intermingled with bare oaks and maples. Elspeth knew nothing about the flora of Tremontane, but this seemed so unusual she half-stood to get a better look and had to be pulled back into her seat by Mihn. As they came out of the forest, Elspeth said, "*Do I hear running water?*"

"*Look that way,*" Mihn said, pointing.

They came around a low hill, and Elspeth gasped again. A low waterfall, no more than seven or eight feet tall, cascaded over a rocky hill that had to be manmade and into a lake that glimmered in the afternoon sunlight. A pair of swans glided past, apparently unaware of how cliché an image they made. Elspeth didn't care. She'd never seen anything so perfect.

"*This is all outstanding. And anyone can come here?*" she asked.

"*Anyone. It's free to the public and open until sunset every day.*" Mihn steered them around a few more low rises until they once again approached the flowerbeds and the Park entrance.

"*That's—*" Elspeth's eyes narrowed. "*Uncle Landon did this?*"

"*So I hear. It was built about fifteen years ago, so that's all I know.*"

Elspeth glanced back at the guards. They didn't look bored. Well, this was their job, keeping an eye on their Queen. "*Take us round the circuit again,*" she told Mihn.

This time, she counted paces until the number got too high. She kept an eye out for the boundary fence, which came and went in glimpses as they drove. The path had clearly been laid out so as to keep Aurilien from intruding on anyone traveling it. She eyed the swans, which now struck her as twee—just two swans? No ducks?

When they reached the entrance again, Elspeth said, "*I've seen enough. Thank you, Mihn. I feel so much more relaxed.*"

Mihn gave her a skeptical look. "*You sound like you've got something on your mind.*"

"*I do, but it's nothing you need to worry about.*" She rested her head on his shoulder. "*I'm lucky—*"

Something went *pop* in the distance, and a bee whined past Elspeth's ear. She turned to watch it go and saw the guards all lash their horses into a canter, surrounding the carriage. Another *pop*, and pain creased Elspeth's right arm just below the shoulder. She clutched her arm, and then a guard tackled her, dragging her not at all gently off the carriage seat and to the ground, covering her with his body. She struggled, cried out for help, but he didn't move.

"Somebody send to the palace," she heard the guard lieutenant say. "The Queen has been shot."

1 2

*E*lspeth wormed her left arm free and looked at her hand. Blood stained her palm, not much of it, but enough to make her mind a white blank. Someone had shot at her. Actually hit her. She thought of the bee whizzing past her ear, and then she was shaking and couldn't stop.

"It's all right, your Majesty, they can't get at you," the guard atop her said. Elspeth nodded. Her teeth were chattering as if she were freezing cold, which she almost was; the hard ground felt like ice seeping through her thick wool trousers and the heavy coat.

"Please let me sit," she whispered.

"Get her into the carriage," the leader said. The guard's heavy body shifted, and someone gave her a hand up. She wobbled up the steps of the carriage and inside it, where she slumped so no one could see her.

The door opened again, and Mihn climbed in. He put his arms around Elspeth and held her tight. "It is all right," he said in his stilted Tremontanese. "You are not hurt. It is all right."

"My arm—"

Mihn looked at the bloodstain spreading across the sleeve of her coat and swore in Veriboldan. "It is not much," he said. "Let me help."

He carefully eased her out of the coat, but moving her arm hurt nevertheless.

"Why are you speaking Tremontanese?" she whispered. It felt like all she was capable of.

"These guards do not speak Veriboldan," Mihn said, "and they seem very nervous. I think it is good not to give them more to be nervous about."

Elspeth nodded. "That's wise."

Mihn pulled out his belt knife and cut a length of fabric from the hem of his shirt. He used it to bind her wound, and the bandaging made Elspeth feel better. She leaned against him until the sound of many horses made her sit up and look cautiously out the carriage window. More guards, these in Tremontane colors, surrounded the carriage. One of them dismounted and had a low-voiced conversation with the leader of the North guards. It ended with the man climbing up to the carriage seat and cracking the reins over the horses' ears. The carriage jerked into motion.

Mihn's arm tightened around Elspeth, holding her steady. "That is dramatic," he said.

Elspeth choked on a hysterical laugh. "Almost the stuff of melodrama," she said, and burst into tears.

She cried until her throat hurt and her sobs dwindled to sniffs, then sat up and away from Mihn. "I'm sorry, that was...I was overwhelmed."

"With good reason," Mihn said. "You do not need to apologize."

Elspeth wiped her eyes and looked out of the carriage window. They were approaching the stables, where quite a few people had gathered, including someone all too familiar. Her heart sank. "You should go home. None of this was your fault."

"I will not leave you until you are safe, El." Mihn took her hand and squeezed it. "You are not dead. That is reason to be happy."

The carriage came to a halt, and a guard in North blue opened the door and extended her hand to Elspeth. Wincing, Elspeth descended the steps and went forward to where Faraday stood at the head of far too many people. He looked ready to explode.

"What in the *hell* were you thinking?" he shouted. "Driving around in the open, risking your life—"

"Nobody told me that was dangerous!" Elspeth shouted back.

"Nobody should have to, your Majesty!" He invested *your Majesty* with razor-sharp sarcasm. "You have no concern for your safety, no concern for the fates of the guards—what do you think will happen to them if you're killed on their watch?"

"There must have been fifteen people who knew I was going for a drive and not one of them stopped me. If you knew this was a possibility, why didn't you tell someone?"

Faraday looked away, his jaw set in a familiar expression. His eye fell on her bandaged arm, and he closed his eyes as if controlling another outburst. "It wasn't," he ground out. "But the last thing Internal Affairs wants is to find out someone wants the Queen dead only after the killer has already succeeded."

Elspeth took a mental step back and examined Faraday again. Underneath his anger was a current of fear that made her heart ache. "Mister Faraday, I can't apologize when I did nothing wrong," she said, "but I understand your position. Am I right that no one in your department suspected an assassination attempt?"

"That's true. I apologize for failing you, your Majesty." He once again looked at her bandaged arm, and a rush of sympathy for her one-time enemy surprised her.

"I accept your apology, Mister Faraday, and I'd like us to move on." Elspeth stood straighter, even though the cold once more threatened to overwhelm her. "I have faith that you will find out who was behind this."

His lips quirked in a sardonic smile. "That is kinder than I deserve, your Majesty."

"Don't." Elspeth reached out to him, but let her hand fall before it could touch his wrist. "If all you intend to do is berate yourself for failing, you might as well resign right now. I need someone who will protect me more than I need a morose, self-indulgent child."

His eyes, once more fierce, fixed on hers. "You," he began angrily, then to her surprise he laughed. "Very well, your Majesty. I will begin the investigation immediately."

"Thank you. And I expect to see you at supper tonight, along with Lady Quinn. Don't be late."

Faraday bowed, amusement lighting his dark blue eyes. "You have my word, your Majesty." His gaze fell on Mihn, standing at Elspeth's left elbow, and the amusement faltered slightly. Elspeth took Mihn's arm and let him support her into the palace.

Elspeth leaned on him more heavily the farther they went, until when they reached the east wing, she almost couldn't stand unsupported. "He's with me," she told the guards, and they let them pass with no comment. In the drawing room, Mihn helped Elspeth sit, then said, *"I should find a doctor. Or a healer. I think there's a palace healer."*

"No, sit with me, I'll send someone," Elspeth replied, but she didn't move. Moving now that she was seated in a soft, comfortable chair seemed impossible. Mihn scowled and stood, walking away down one of the halls. Elspeth let him go. Her arm hurt, she was exhausted, and she wished she hadn't reminded Faraday of their supper appointment, because all she wanted was supper in bed and an early bedtime.

Mihn came back and sat beside her. *"One of the servants is going to fetch Dr. Ambrose."*

"I don't know who that is, but all right." Elspeth closed her eyes and basked in the warmth of the fire.

She woke, startled, when she heard Mihn say, "Doctor. It is not much of a wound, but she is...I do not know the word in your language."

"In shock," a woman said. Elspeth opened her eyes and saw a young woman, maybe Honey's age, setting a worn leather satchel on the floor near the hearth. "I'm Dr. Ambrose. Your Majesty, how do you feel?"

"Very tired. And cold," Elspeth said, though in truth the warmth of the fire had soaked into her bones and made her feel so relaxed she couldn't be afraid. What a wonderful fire.

"Nice bandaging. Very well done," the doctor said. She leaned over Elspeth and said, "I'm going to remove it now—it shouldn't hurt much."

It didn't hurt much, even when Dr. Ambrose cut away Elspeth's sleeve and touched the wound. Elspeth craned her neck to see it; it was a long, shallow crease along her upper arm that had bled profusely. "It's not deep," the doctor said. "I think I can heal it without hurting you."

"You have inherent magic," Elspeth said.

"I do. Is that a problem, your Majesty? I'll be happy to call a regular doctor if you'd prefer." Dr. Ambrose didn't sound offended.

"I was raised in Veribold, doctor. Inherent magic doesn't scare me."

Dr. Ambrose smiled. "Hold your friend's hand, and we'll take this slowly."

Mihn took her hand. He'd been silent the whole time, for which Elspeth was grateful. She didn't feel up to conversation, even with her oldest friend.

A gentle lassitude swept over her, more relaxing even than the fire's warmth. A tingle began in her upper arm, a tingle that soon became a burning sensation. The burning spread, not quite painful, not entirely pleasant, until her arm ached with it. Then it dissipated as gradually as it had spread until she felt nothing except that relaxed state.

Dr. Ambrose rose and picked up one of the vases on a nearby table. She removed the winter lilies from it and poured some of the water onto a cloth, which she used to wash Elspeth's arm. It was now unmarked as if nothing had ever happened to it. "You're good as new, your Majesty," the doctor said, replacing the lilies. "I'm glad I could help."

"Thank you, doctor," Elspeth said. She twisted her arm; no pain. "Your gift is remarkable."

"There are people in Tremontane who don't think so." Dr. Ambrose smiled, a reflective expression. "I'm glad you're not one of them."

She rose, and Elspeth stood as well. "How can I pay you?"

"The government pays me a retainer to work for the Crown," Dr. Ambrose said. "Call on me anytime."

"I hope it won't be necessary. Thank you again."

Mihn turned to go when the doctor did. Elspeth protested, "*Stay for supper at least.*"

"*Some other time, El. You don't need a Veriboldan eating supper with you and your councilors. That's official business.*"

She wanted to protest further, but Mihn had a better grasp of social niceties than she did. "*All right. I'll see you later, though?*"

"*Count on it, El.*"

Elspeth walked to her rooms and stripped off her ruined shirt. She hugged it close to her chest, feeling too weary to put on a new one. Finally, she tossed it in a corner of the dressing room and pulled one of her old Veriboldan shirts on, the kind that wrapped around and fastened on the side with tapes. She needed comfort, even if this felt like the forbidden kind. She could be Tremontanan again at supper, but for now she was just Elspeth whom no stranger wanted dead. She wished she could be her all the time.

SHE LET HONEY CHOOSE HER GOWN FOR SUPPER, A PALE BLUE SATIN that to Elspeth's surprise looked good against her red hair. Again deferring to her maid, she left her hair down, having brushed it until the thick curls shone. It was the most comfortable she'd ever felt in Tremontanan formal wear.

Veronica and her two councilors rose when she entered the drawing room. Lady Quinn looked much as she always did, but Faraday looked very strange in formal knee breeches and a satin coat, like an actor dressed for a part. He didn't behave as if he wanted to abase himself and beg her forgiveness again, and she relaxed. She could deal with an angry, frustrated, or scowling Faraday far more easily than a remorseful one.

By now, she was accustomed to taking the seat at the head of the table. Faraday held her chair for her and then seated himself to her left. "I understand Dr. Ambrose tended to you," he said.

"Yes, I'm entirely healed."

"I wish I could make this problem go away as easily. We have no idea who might want you dead. Your guards rightly put keeping you safe above searching for the one who shot you."

Lady Quinn flinched at his choice of words. Elspeth, watching her sympathetically, said, "It's only been a couple of hours, Mister Faraday. I didn't expect you to round up the assassin immediately."

"No, but we should be able to analyze what we *do* know and make some initial conclusions." Faraday attacked his soup like a general going to war, though without spilling a drop.

"Well, who would benefit?"

Faraday glanced at her. "That was the first question we asked. The answer is, nobody and everybody. Your heirs are all underage, so killing you—" Lady Quinn winced again "—would put the country in serious turmoil, as the provincial lords and a handful of noble families went to war over who would control the new King or Queen. Destroying the country benefits no one. But of those willing to go to war to claim the Crown, some might think they would have advantage enough to make it worth the risk. Knowing in advance that the Queen would die—"

"Mister Faraday," Lady Quinn said in her quiet voice, "could we discuss something else? My soup is near curdled with all this horrid talk."

Elspeth laughed. "I apologize, Lady Quinn. I'm afraid it doesn't disturb me, so I hadn't considered anyone else might be upset. Mister Faraday, the Countess is right, this is a discussion for my office tomorrow."

Faraday nodded. "My apologies, Lady Quinn."

"Thank you, Mister Faraday. Your Majesty, who was that young man I saw you with earlier, that Veriboldan man?"

"That's Bakarne of the Arhainen, son of the Proxy of Veribold." She hoped Mihn wasn't upset about what had happened. He was too pragmatic to blame himself for her being shot, but he hated when his friends were injured physically or emotionally.

"I heard you call him something else. Mean?"

"Mihn. It's...well, the Arhainen house totem is the swordfish, and 'mihn' means 'little fish' in Veriboldan. Because he's the oldest scion of the Arhainen, you see. I've known Mihn since we were children." She ought to ask him to take her somewhere else, to the opera or something. Someplace an assassin would have trouble reaching.

"You must be close friends," Faraday said. "Your relationship seems rather informal."

"Well, we did grow up together. He's my best friend, and my oldest friend."

"So you're not betrothed?" Lady Quinn asked.

Elspeth laughed. "To Mihn? Excuse me, Lady Quinn, I didn't mean to be rude. But...no. For one thing, we don't feel that way about each other, and for another, he's betrothed to a lady back in Veribold. Also a very good friend of mine, as it happens. But even if neither of those things were true, there's no way a Veriboldan noble of a landed house would marry a foreigner. They take their honor far too seriously, and foreigners are considered..." How to explain something she'd grown up taking for granted?

"Veriboldans don't believe foreigners are capable of carrying on the traditions of their people. I grew up in Veribold, I understand the culture as well as any Veriboldan, but I'm still considered an outsider. Mihn takes his heritage far too seriously to marry anyone not a noble Veriboldan, even if he were in love with her. It would be like a Tremontanan marrying someone without being sworn and sealed."

"I almost feel I should be insulted on Tremontane's behalf," Lady Quinn said with a smile. "Given that Tremontanans care more about the family bond than the nationality of those who are part of it."

"Veriboldans *really* don't understand about family bonds." Elspeth sipped the last of her soup and pushed her bowl away. "Which I find odd, considering that they're sort of obsessive about tracking genealogy. But Veribold isn't rich in source the way Tremontane is, so to them, the family bond is...the landholders almost think of it as a mythical thing, though they're generally polite enough to behave as though our delusion is real."

Faraday chuckled. "I didn't think Veriboldan landholders knew what 'polite' meant. The ones I interact with behave as if they're doing everyone a favor just by breathing the same air."

"That's true. Politeness means something different to them. For one thing, it's polite behavior among nobles in Veribold—I mean nobles of all nationalities when they're interacting with Veriboldan landholders—it's considered polite to speak one's mind, to the point of what we'd call rudeness."

"That reminds me of my Great-Aunt Roberta," Faraday said. "She's one of those people who likes to be cruel under the guise of speaking truth."

"Veriboldans wouldn't do that either. It's like—imagine you're at a party and one of the guests asks for your honest opinion of her new gown, which you think is hideous. A Tremontanan might speak a little white lie to avoid giving offense. I assume your great-aunt would delight in telling the person how ugly her gown is and then praise herself for speaking plainly."

"You assume correctly."

"A Veriboldan either wouldn't say anything, or would say something like 'that's not what I would have chosen' or 'I find your appearance unpleasing.' And the person wouldn't take offense. The idea is that you honor the person you're speaking to by assuming they deserve honesty. And they won't challenge a lie to your face, they'll just shun you until you make amends for lying."

"That doesn't sound so bad," Veronica said. "More honest, maybe."

"Except they use it as a weapon. If two houses fight, and one of them shuns the other, the rest of the houses might assume the one being shunned deserves it on no more evidence than that. I've seen minor houses destroyed that way. On purpose." Elspeth smiled. "It keeps me from being complacent about the country of my childhood being perfect. There are many ways in which Tremontane is superior."

"And those are?" Faraday prompted.

She'd spoken without thinking, and his words gave her pause. "I prefer the openness of Tremontanans," she said slowly, working out truths she'd never articulated before. "And how much less rigid our class system is. There's a hard divide between Veriboldan landholders and the common folk that makes it almost as if there are two Veribolds."

"And yet it's not as if a commoner can become a noble in Tremontane," Lady Quinn said.

"That's not entirely true," Faraday pointed out. "A ruling lord might marry anyone she chooses and elevate that person. And the awarding of noble titles by the Queen or King isn't all that rare."

"All right," Lady Quinn said, "it can happen. But it's not common."

"You're both right. My own mother was an ordinary tradeswoman when she married my father," Elspeth said, "and it's also true that such elevations are rare. But it would be unheard of in Veribold. If it ever did happen, which it won't, the person who was elevated would be utterly shunned by both classes. So Tremontane has an edge in that respect."

"I'm not sure why you call it an edge," Faraday said. He leaned back for the servants to set a plate of roasted quail in front of him. "I would hardly call this a contest."

"I'm not really sure," Elspeth said, "except I can't help but feel a country is stronger when all its people are working toward its prosperity in the same way. Veribold always felt torn in two directions, to me. As if the landholders want one thing and the commoners want something else. And that, to me, is a weakness."

"But the nobles of Tremontane often have concerns that have nothing to do with what commoners need, or want," Faraday said. "Isn't it the same?"

"The existence of the family bond means there's one way in which all Tremontanans are the same," Elspeth countered. "The bond isn't any stronger if you're noble. That's a unifying thing Veriboldans find completely alien."

Faraday nodded. "You have a point."

They were having a normal conversation. It was surreal. "Though you're right about Tremontanan nobles sometimes," she began, then shot a glance at Veronica, placidly eating her quail. She didn't want to bring up her suspicions about her uncle in front of his widow.

"I beg your pardon, your Majesty?" Lady Quinn said.

Veronica looked up and caught Elspeth's eye. "You saw the Park," she said. Her quiet voice was dull and emotionless.

"I did," Elspeth said. "It's beautiful."

"And is that all you thought?" Veronica asked.

Faraday was eyeing the two of them as if he could tell the conversation ran deeper than mere words. Elspeth gave up. "It's very large," she said. "What was it before it became the Park?"

Faraday turned his attention on Elspeth. "Many things," he said. "Slums. A culling ground. A few estates. Some very expensive land. All razed to make room for the Crown's pleasure."

"And then?"

Faraday glanced at Veronica. "A hunting preserve for King Landon, until he turned it over to the Crown for public use."

"It was a generous gesture," Lady Quinn said.

Now Elspeth and Faraday looked at each other. Faraday looked sour, but this time it was an inward-turned look, as if he were contemplating some terrible inner vision. "Was it?" Elspeth asked.

Faraday's expression grew even more sour. Into the silence, Veronica said, "Landon always loved to hunt." Her quiet voice sounded like bell chimes.

"And he would have wanted to bring the hunt to himself," Elspeth said, her own voice quiet. "A hunting preserve, right in the heart of the city. Why didn't it stay that way?"

Lady Quinn looked confused. Faraday said, "Public outrage, and the complaints of the noble lords, most of whom were simply jealous King Landon had tried something they wished they could get away with."

"And yet everyone remembers Uncle Landon as a kind philanthropist," Elspeth said. Her meal had gone sour. "He made a literal land grab at the heart of Aurilien and everyone praises him for it."

"What's past is past," Faraday said. "Those who suffered because of the King's greed have forgotten their grievances because the Park is something everyone loves. Does it matter what kind of man the King was, or what he intended?"

Elspeth picked at the quail's bones. "It matters to me," she said.

"I told you to look because I wanted you to know the truth," Veronica said suddenly. "You have a chance to be better than they were. But it won't happen if you take it for granted that all kings and queens are the same. That they all have the same noble intentions."

Elspeth looked at her. "I understand. Thank you. It can't...can't be easy, knowing that about your family."

"Mister Faraday is right. The past is past," Veronica said. She smiled. "And I choose to look to the future. As you should."

Elspeth thought of that first circuit of the Park, how innocently beautiful she'd found it. It wasn't any less beautiful now that she knew its origins. "I'll try," she said. "But I think I won't be able to face the future if I forget the past."

Lady Quinn still looked confused, but Faraday saluted her with his wine glass. "I don't think you're in any danger of that, your Majesty."

Elspeth didn't know what he meant by that, but it was the first compliment he'd given her, and she decided not to examine it too closely. It might fly away if she did.

13

$\mathcal{E}$lspeth sat very still with her hands folded in her lap and her chin unnaturally high. It was a pose the artist had insisted on, and Elspeth wondered if the woman's dislike of her subject would translate into making her look stupid for posterity. It was unlikely, given how the woman respected Elspeth's role more than Elspeth did, but Elspeth's neck and back hurt and at this point she was willing to assume the worst.

"I didn't realize our relationship with Ruskald had deteriorated so much," she said. The artist grunted in disapproval. Elspeth ignored her. So long as Elspeth didn't flap her arms or nod her head, the artist could do her job.

"It's because the new King of the Ruskalder is testing to see how far he can push us," Lord Harrington said. "That long arm of Ruskald that extends through the Riverlands near Daxtry and Avory has always been a national security nightmare. The only thing that prevents Ruskald from pushing east is how few settlements there are in that area. That, and they don't want to start a war they can't be sure they'd win."

Elspeth reviewed her mental map of the area. "I don't know much about Veribold's international policies, but I think they would prefer

to have us for a neighbor. I mean, if it came to war. We're not plan
ning on starting a war either, right?"

"No, your Majesty. If we were to fight Ruskald to take that territory, it would leave us vulnerable to attack by Veribold."

"I don't think Veribold is interested in attacking us."

Lord Harrington bowed. "With all due respect, your Majesty, your
affection for your adopted country should not blind you to political
realities. Veribold fears us because we have superior military forces,
even in peacetime, and they believe we want an extended coastline,
which we would get if we conquered them. If they thought we were
weakened by war with Ruskald, it's not impossible that they might
seize the opportunity."

Elspeth blushed. "You're right, there's a lot I don't know. I can only
speak to my experiences with meeting the Veriboldan landholders at
embassy gatherings. It's not likely they would have come out and said
they wanted to conquer Tremontane, particularly to the Tremontanan ambassador's daughter."

"Don't worry, your Majesty, this will all become natural in time."

Elspeth suppressed her annoyance at his patronizing tone. She
still did have a lot to learn. "So what do we need to do? About
Ruskald, I mean."

"I'll draft a letter to King Osjan for you to sign. Depending on his
response, we may need to move troops into Daxtry and Avory, but
that will require great care. And you should reach out to the
Ruskalder ambassador, Larssin. Make it clear that Tremontane is
interested in remaining cordial with its northern neighbor, but that if
they want to start a war, we will most certainly finish it."

"I'm not sure how capable I am of conveying that, but I'll do my
best."

Lord Harrington smiled. "I have no worries about that, your
Majesty. Just pretend he's your Council."

Elspeth controlled a laugh that would have earned her a
reproachful hiss from the artist. "Is that a compliment?"

"You've proven capable of keeping them under control. It's not
what anyone expected."

Elspeth's watch chimed the hour. "Mistress Bennegret, it's time," she said.

The artist made a few more strokes, then laid down her brush. "If your Majesty were more patient, this would be done already."

"I have many responsibilities, Mistress Bennegret." Elspeth was never so grateful for those responsibilities as when the artist's hour was up. She stood, stretched, and worked her jaw until it wasn't so tense. "Thank you for *your* patience."

Elspeth and Lord Harrington walked through the corridors back to the north wing. Elspeth was almost certain she could find the way herself, but she was grateful for Lord Harrington's company. He'd proved much more cordial now that she was the Queen instead of Sebastian North's daughter. "Are you looking forward to this evening?" he asked.

Elspeth shrugged. "I don't know how to dance most Tremontanan dances, and I understand it's the Queen's duty to ask for the pleasure, so for me the Spring Ball is more an opportunity to talk to people. Since I see most of them every day, I can't imagine it will be that exciting."

"That's unfortunate. I would think this would be an excellent opportunity for you to meet potential Consorts. Dancing is the first stage in the courtship ritual, after all."

Elspeth's heart gave a startled sideways lurch. "Oh. I...hadn't considered that." Over three weeks had passed since her coronation and Dane's comments on the need for her to marry, and she'd been busy enough she hadn't thought of them since. *Be honest, Elspeth.* She hadn't *wanted* to think about Dane's comments. Meeting men, especially when those men would know she was looking for a husband...it was awkward, and embarrassing, and not something Elspeth was good at. "Is that...will people think it's something I should do?"

"This is the first royal ball since your coronation, your Majesty. I imagine the speculation as to whom you will single out is running high."

She'd never blushed so hard in her life. "But I really don't know how to dance, Lord Harrington! And I didn't realize I'd be expected to. Why didn't anyone tell me?"

Lord Harrington put a hand on her shoulder, a paternal gesture. "You're an attractive young woman as well as being Queen. I don't think it occurred to anyone that you aren't a veteran of years of these social events, or that you might not be enthusiastic about the Spring Ball."

"I suppose my dressmaker might have said one or two things along those lines." She'd put up with the fittings for her new gown because she liked Catherine Elwes, but dressing up wasn't something she loved. "I'll do my best."

Alone in her office, she sat at her well-organized desk and propped her chin in her hands. Dancing. It wasn't that she hated dancing, it was that Veriboldan dances were all variations on the same four movements, and mastering those was simple. Tremontane, on the other hand, had as many dances as it did songs, most of them complicated, all of them demanding the dancers' attention. There was no way she could fake her way through a Tremontanan dance. At least she wouldn't embarrass anyone by turning down a dance request, because no one would dare ask the Queen to stand up with him. She felt unexpectedly guilty about it, as if she'd let her country down.

A knock sounded on her door. "Mister Faraday," Simkins said, opening the door to let Faraday in. Elspeth sat up straight.

"Mister Faraday, do you have news?" she asked.

Faraday looked grim. "I'm forced to admit defeat," he said. "We have been unable to track anyone who might have been in a position to shoot at you. Furthermore, I have no evidence that any of my suspects engineered the attempt."

"What does that mean in terms of possible future attacks?"

The grim look turned sour, which told Elspeth Faraday's frustration was growing. "It means we can't know whether this was a one-time attack, or whether we have to be on guard against someone trying again. We also don't know if it was opportunistic or planned. Since you left the palace without telling anyone—"

"I told plenty of people!"

"I beg your pardon. That wasn't a criticism. I meant that your excursion wasn't on your schedule for an assassin to learn about it and set up that attack. At any rate, I'm inclined to think someone saw an opportunity and took it, except there is always a measure of planning when it comes to assassination. So what I think happened is that someone wanted you dead and was willing to pay an assassin to follow you, looking for his or her moment."

His straightforward words sent a chill through Elspeth. "That means someone with resources, doesn't it? Someone wealthy?"

"Or a secret organization interested in destroying the monarchy. I've come up with half a dozen possibilities, all of them with more possibilities branching off the original ones until I can't see anything clearly. I apologize."

"You've done everything anyone could expect of you, Mister Faraday." Elspeth sighed. "Don't any of your suspects stand out?"

"Some of them. A person who knew in advance you would die could put their resources into position to immediately take advantage of that, getting a head start on their competitors, so to speak. There aren't many nobles or landed gentry or even wealthy commoners who have those kinds of resources. But there are still too many of them to single one out, and at this point, it's not sensible to watch all of them."

"Maybe we just have to wait until they try again."

"*That is not funny,*" Faraday shouted. He turned his head away, struggling for control. "I apologize. Internal Affairs doesn't play games with the Queen's life."

Elspeth nodded. "It was a poor joke. I don't think I could bear walking around wondering if this would be the day they tried again, and succeeded."

"It won't come to that."

Elspeth nodded again. "Maybe they won't try again. Maybe it was a warning."

"A warning against what?"

"I don't know. I was trying to be optimistic."

The corners of Faraday's mouth twitched. "You have hundreds of men and women dedicated to keeping you safe, your Majesty. Let that fill you with optimism."

It actually made Elspeth uncomfortable. All those people who might die to prevent her death...maybe the Queen was worth that sacrifice, but Elspeth North wasn't sure about herself. "That's comforting," she lied.

"I'll let you know if we learn anything new," Faraday said. "Are you looking forward to the Spring Ball?"

Elspeth shuddered. "Not now that I know everyone will be watching my every move, wondering if I'll spontaneously propose marriage to some young noble itching for the chance to become Consort. And I don't know how to dance."

"You shouldn't feel obligated to dance. Walk around. Converse. You have plenty of time to choose a Consort."

"That's not what Lord Harrington said. And Aldous Dane made it sound like it was dereliction of duty that I'm not already married and pregnant."

Faraday chuckled. "Better you choose the right man than that you leap into marriage out of duty."

"Can I quote you on that?"

Faraday just smiled and closed the door behind him.

TRADITION SAID THE QUEEN OR KING WORE PALE GREEN TO THE SPRING Ball, and Elspeth didn't care enough to fight tradition. Besides, green of any shade complemented her red hair. Honey pinned her curls back from her face to cascade down her back "in honor of new beginnings," as she put it. Elspeth wasn't sure what unbound hair had to do with new beginnings, but she liked the look.

She wore a necklace of square-cut emeralds and a coronet that matched it. The coronet itched, and was likely to become uncomfortable over time, but it was so pretty she was willing to put up with some discomfort. Dressed, groomed, and shod in silver low-heeled shoes she could have danced in if she knew how, she checked her reflection one last time and sighed. At least she looked like royalty.

This time, a squad of North guards waited for her outside the east wing doors. She knew she was supposed to have an escort to the ball, but she sensed Faraday's hand in its size. She let them surround her and tried not to see herself as a prisoner being led off to execution.

The route to the ballroom led in and out of places she was already familiar with, giving her the oddest sense of being led through patches of light and darkness. She made herself pay attention to the turnings as a distraction from her anxiety. She was the Queen; no one would criticize her missteps; but she couldn't help feeling, as she had earlier, that she was letting her country down by being unable to participate fully in its rituals.

The guards stopped her around the corner from the long, straight hallway that led to the ballroom stairs. "One moment, your Majesty," the guard lieutenant, the same woman who'd led her escort on that disastrous expedition to the Park, said. Two women peeled off from the formation and disappeared around the corner. Elspeth waited. She had no idea what she was waiting for—they might be checking for hidden assassins, or they might just be clearing the stairs for her grand entrance—but eventually the two guards returned and took their positions. "Now, your Majesty," the lieutenant said, and they all marched forward and up the gentle slope of the corridor toward a bright opening at its far end.

As they approached the doorway, music became audible, and the low murmur of conversation. Elspeth quickened her steps and then had to slow as the lieutenant gave her a warning look. She wasn't so much excited as anticipatory. *Let's get this over with.*

The doors to the ballroom stood wide open, creating an arched opening through which bright light poured. She'd entered here once before, at the reception following her coronation, but that had been almost informal after the rigid ceremony of being crowned Queen. The guards spread out to either side of the landing beyond the doors, the trumpets sounded—Elspeth had trouble not laughing at that, it was so much like a story—and Elspeth stepped through the doors and stood silhouetted against them at the top of the stairs.

"Her Majesty Elspeth North, Queen of Tremontane," the herald said. He spoke into the wide end of a bell-shaped trumpet, and his voice boomed out of the Device to fill the room. Elspeth carefully lifted her skirts and made her way down the steps to the sound of enthusiastic applause. It still didn't bother her, being stared at, but the applause made her nervous, and she didn't know why. Maybe because it was the sort of thing one did at an artistic performance, and Elspeth didn't like the feeling that her rule was some kind of opera. Or worse, penny theater.

She reached the bottom of the steps and raised a hand to acknowledge the applause, then made her way to her seat. She might need to wander and talk to people, but better she let the excitement die down a bit first.

None of the ambassadors had arrived yet, so Elspeth sat alone and surveyed the crowd. Brightly-dressed people thronged the ballroom, sipping from tall glasses brought to them by uniformed servants. The orchestra struck up a new song, with a dance she didn't know, and she watched the couples sway through the steps and felt a pang of loneliness. Maybe she needed Simkins to put dance lessons on her schedule.

The field of pastel dresses and coats and knee breeches looked like pale wildflowers blowing in the breeze. Springtide was a lesser celebration, when the lines of power ebbed for the equinox, but this was a beautiful display. If she were in Veribold, she and her family wouldn't celebrate the holiday, but they might have a nice meal and talk about the families they'd left behind. Father would tell stories of his Great-Uncle Sebastian, last of Willow North's children, and Mother would talk about her parents, dead before any of the children were born. The memory made Elspeth's heart ache.

She straightened in her seat as the Ruskalder ambassador, Larssin, stumped toward her and flung himself into his chair. "Good evening, Larssin," she said. "Welcome to my court."

Larssin glared at her. "Good evening, your Majesty." His gruff, heavily accented Tremontanese made his words sound like a challenge to duel.

"Do your people celebrate Springtide?" she asked, determined on politeness unless he forced the issue.

"We do not have heathen holiday," Larssin growled. "The gods speak at all times, not bound by time of year."

"That's what they teach in Veribold, too. Though of course they believe in ungoverned heaven as the Tremontanans do."

"Heathen," Larssin said. "I see the sanctuary—you say bethel. With the statues. You mock the gods."

He was really pushing the boundaries of good manners. "We respect the lost gods, Larssin," Elspeth said in a level voice. "And it's rude to comment on other people's religious faith. Even the Ruskalder know that."

Larssin grunted, but said nothing more. Elspeth stood. "Please excuse me, but I should speak to my guests," she said. Getting away from him trumped her desire to avoid looking like she was trolling for a Consort.

She moved through the crowd, nodding politely to people who bowed or curtseyed but not stopping to talk. It occurred to her that she didn't know anyone who was a potential Consort, and tradition if not outright law dictated that she not introduce herself to anyone. She felt mingled guilt and sorrow at the thought.

Maybe she did want a Consort. Granted that marrying had never been part of her plan, but it wasn't like she was opposed to marriage. And having someone she could talk to, someone who wouldn't call her Majesty all the time—that was something worth having. Even better if it was someone she could love, someone who loved her...yes, having a Consort was a good idea. So what if people stared and speculated? It would be worth it in the end.

Having firmed her resolve, she set out looking for someone who might make introductions. Almost immediately, she saw Lord Harrington conversing with Lady d'Arden. Perfect. She hurried toward the pair, waited for them to bow and curtsey, and said, "Lord Harrington, I've thought about what you said, and I would like to get to know some of these men. Can you make introductions for me?"

Lord Harrington's eyebrows went up. "Certainly, your Majesty. Though Lady d'Arden is far more socially adept than I."

"I know someone you really must meet," Lady d'Arden said with a smile. "Come with me, your Majesty."

Lady d'Arden wandered through the crowd like a toy boat bouncing off the sides of a bath, finally coming to a stop before a trio of young men. Their conversation ended as each became aware of who stood before them. "Your Majesty, may I introduce to you Mister Gould, Lord Erickson, and Lord Folsom?"

The three men bowed, more deeply than Elspeth thought was warranted. "It's an honor, your Majesty," Lord Erickson said. His blond hair shone in the lights of all the chandeliers. Gould and Lord Folsom, both darker-complected, nodded in agreement.

"Mister Gould owns the company that is contracted with the palace for all its buildings," Lady d'Arden said, "and Lord Erickson is a well-known poet. Lord Folsom, of course, is of the Sandringham Folsoms."

Elspeth didn't know who the Sandringham Folsoms were, but she smiled at Lord Folsom, who was extremely handsome with his dark hair and bright blue eyes that were such an attractive contrast. They were all three of them handsome, and Elspeth's heart lightened. "It's very nice to meet you all," she said. "Mister Gould, what does it mean that your company manages all the palace's buildings?"

Gould smiled as if he'd won a prize by being singled out. "We're the builders for the palace. Any new construction is designed and completed by us."

"Then you're responsible for the pavilion King Francis ordered for the royal gardens." Elspeth wasn't sure she wanted to be friendly with him, given that she'd almost decided to cancel the project, but he likely wasn't directly responsible for the pavilion.

"We are, yes. I hope you like it. I designed the structure myself."

"Did you? That's...very nice." Elspeth swiftly transferred her attention to Lord Erickson. "I don't think I've ever met a poet before. Have you written anything I might have heard of?"

It was Lord Erickson's turn to be smugly proud. "My most famous epic is *The Stolen Heart*."

She hadn't heard of it. Damn. "You must be so proud that so many people want to read your writing."

"It's gratifying, yes. Might I have the pleasure of sending you a copy, your Majesty?"

"I would like that, Lord Erickson." Disaster averted. But now they were all watching her avidly, as if they...yes, as if they were waiting for her to ask one of them to dance. And here was a new tune starting up.

She made a rapid decision. "I beg your pardon, gentlemen, I would ask one of you to dance, but I'm afraid I don't know many Tremontanan dances."

"I would be happy to teach you, your Majesty," Lord Folsom said, cutting off the other two, who'd been too slow off the mark. "It isn't difficult."

She made another rapid decision. "Thank you, Lord Folsom, I would appreciate that. Mister Gould, Lord Erickson, perhaps we might speak again later?"

The two bowed politely, though the glares they directed at Lord Folsom might have cut steel. Lord Folsom offered Elspeth his arm and guided her well away from the other dancers. Elspeth's estimation of his character rose a few notches.

"We join hands, like this," Lord Folsom said, taking Elspeth's hands, "and then it's two short hops, forward and back—you do it the opposite of me, your Majesty, or we'd run into each other!—then step side to side, and then promenade." He released her left hand and guided her into a long, gliding walk that ended with them on the outskirts of the dancing crowd. Elspeth repeated the movements and once more glided along on his arm. He was right, it was easy, and it was even fun.

She watched the dancers around her and, daring, tried a variation on the steps that Lord Folsom easily matched. Nobody seemed to be watching her, no one had made her feel foolish, and she began to wonder if her fears had been unjustified.

When the music came to an end, she was laughing and too-warm. She fanned herself with her hand and said, "Lord Folsom, thank you. That was enjoyable."

"I'm glad to hear it, your Majesty. Shall we find you a cool drink?"

Elspeth nodded and took his arm again. It seemed all the uniformed servants bearing drinks had disappeared. Lord Folsom didn't seem bothered by this. He kept up a steady stream of conversation as they walked, conversation that bored Elspeth as she didn't know any of the people he talked about. She began to regret the impulse that had led her to single out the most handsome of the trio. The other two probably had more interesting conversation. How foolish of her to forget good looks were no guarantee of a handsome spirit.

A small door opened nearly in front of them, a door that had been invisible before now, and a servant emerged, bearing a tray with a few empty glasses and one full one. "Ah, there we are," Lord Folsom said, gesturing to the man. He took the glass of wine and handed it to Elspeth. The servant bowed and walked away.

"But shouldn't you have something?" Elspeth said.

"It's the gentleman's duty to ensure the lady's comfort, particularly if the lady in question is his Queen," Lord Folsom said.

Elspeth took a small sip. It was a rich red wine that made her lips tingle unpleasantly. "I actually don't care much for wine," she said. "Please, take this. I'll find someone to fetch me something else."

"I couldn't possibly."

"I don't want it to go to waste." Elspeth pressed the glass into his hand.

"Very well—if you'll walk with me while I drink it," Lord Folsom said with a smile. It was a pity he was so boring, because he really was very handsome.

They strolled off around the circumference of the ballroom. Lord Folsom gestured at the chandeliers with his wine glass. "King Francis ordered them replaced with Device lights, just a year ago," he said.

"Are they brighter now, then? There aren't many Devices in Veribold."

"Much brighter, and the light is steadier." Lord Folsom drank half the glass in one gulp. "It makes the murals that much—"

He stopped mid-sentence and swayed where he stood. "Lord Folsom?" Elspeth said, gripping his arm to steady him.

Lord Folsom's face looked gray in the brilliant light of the Devices, and his lips were tinged blue. He dropped his wine glass to shatter on the floor and groped at his throat, his mouth opening and closing like a fish. "Can't...breathe..." he gasped.

"Lord Folsom!" Elspeth screamed as his knees bent and he collapsed. She crouched beside him and loosened his cravat, hoping to stop the wheezing sound he was making. His face grew grayer and he convulsed, knocking Elspeth over.

"Excuse me, your Majesty." It was, to Elspeth's surprise, Dr. Ambrose, dressed in a buttercup-yellow gown with her auburn hair piled high on her head. She snatched off her glove and laid a hand gently along Lord Folsom's cheek, almost a lover's caress. Elspeth scooted farther away, her breathing coming rapidly as if she might through some sympathetic magic help Lord Folsom to breathe. She became aware of the crowd surrounding her, pressing in on all sides, and she welcomed their presence even as she wished she could shoo them all away and give Dr. Ambrose room to work.

Dr. Ambrose's eyes were closed, and her chest rose and fell with her deep, rapid breathing. Suddenly Lord Folsom sucked in a deep breath and coughed, a great, hacking, wet sound. The color returned to his face. Dr. Ambrose sat back and wiped sweat from her forehead. "He'll live," she said. "No thanks to whoever poisoned him."

"*P*oison?" Elspeth stared at Lord Folsom's mottled, gasping face. "The wine," she said, pointing at the dark red puddle, the dripping shards of glass. "The wine—I drank some of it."

Dr. Ambrose swiftly grabbed Elspeth's hand and closed her eyes. A dull ache began in Elspeth's stomach and spread rapidly up her chest and into her throat. Then it vanished as rapidly as it had begun. Dr. Ambrose released her. "There's no poison in your system. How much did you drink?"

Elspeth shook her head. "Just a sip. Barely enough to wet my lips."

"You're in no danger. How did you know not to drink?"

"I didn't. I don't like wine. I—" Her hands began to shake. "I made him take it. It's my fault he nearly died."

A murmur rose from the watching crowd that rose as someone shoved his way to the front. "What—" Faraday began. He fell silent when he saw Lord Folsom lying on the ground, limp and unmoving. "What happened?" he demanded.

Elspeth stared at him. She'd nearly killed a man—this was all her fault—

"Poison," Dr. Ambrose said, standing. "Meant for the Queen."

Faraday's gaze came to rest on Elspeth. His eyes blazed with fury, and his lips were pressed tightly against what was sure to be a spectacular explosion. "Get her Majesty to safety. Now," he said to the guard who'd followed at his elbow. The guard helped Elspeth to her feet, but gingerly, as if he was nervous of laying hands on his Queen. He led her past dozens of people, all of whom backed away to avoid touching her, to join the same squad that had escorted her to the ballroom.

This time, they hurried through the corridors, up ramps and stairs until they reached the east wing doors. The guard lieutenant saluted the guards at the doors and said, "Has anyone approached you tonight?"

"No one's been here since you left," the female door guard said, "and the Dowager Consort hasn't gone anywhere. It's been quiet."

The lieutenant nodded and gestured for them to open the doors. Elspeth hurried through and was surprised when the squad followed her. "Into the drawing room, your Majesty, while we search the east wing," the lieutenant said.

"For what?" Elspeth said, then felt stupid. For more assassins. It hadn't even occurred to her. But the east wing was secure, there was only the one set of doors...and all those windows, big and wide and leading to empty suites no one ever looked in. The tremor in her hands spread to all of her. She crouched in front of the fireplace and shook and shook and felt she might never be warm again.

Lord Folsom's distorted face rose up in memory. She'd pressed that wine on him and he had nearly died, would have died if not for Dr. Ambrose. As she would have died if she were a typical Tremontanan noble. She closed her eyes and tried to remember the servant's face, but it was a blank. He had worn servant's clothes just like every other man and woman serving drinks in the ballroom, and she hadn't looked further than that. He'd be long gone by now, so it didn't matter, but she felt even more stupid and guilty than she had before.

Distantly, the door opened, then closed with a bang, and rapid footsteps hurried along the hall. She turned to see Faraday enter the drawing room. He stopped when she looked up, and she cringed at how angry he looked. "I don't know how I could have predicted this, so think about that before you shout at me," she said, as firmly as she could manage while she was still shaking.

"It's not your fault, your Majesty, it's mine. I was complacent, and a man was nearly killed. I came to tender my resignation."

"What?" Elspeth sat up. "We both decided there was no way to know if it would happen again. Am I supposed to resign as Queen?"

Faraday's grim expression softened slightly. "Internal Affairs is meant to protect you. This is twice, now, that I've failed to do that."

"Or our clever plan succeeded. Remember how we were going to wait for them to try again?" Elspeth shook her head. "I reject your resignation, Mister Faraday. I've had to replace two Council members in the last month and I'm not going to replace a third. It's tedious. So stop wallowing in your supposed failure and start thinking like a...I don't know what kind of thinking it takes to catch an assassin, but I have no doubt you're capable of it."

Faraday didn't smile. "Your Majesty," he said, "your faith is touching, but it's misapplied. I can't in good conscience continue as head of this department when your safety is at stake."

"You can, and you will." It was the height of absurdity that she was trying to convince this man not to leave. Two weeks ago she would have rejoiced at an opportunity to be rid of him, but now... "You've already eliminated several possibilities in your initial investigation. Do you believe the same person or people are behind this attack?"

"Your Majesty—" Faraday lowered his head. "Are you really determined not to allow me to resign?"

"Look at this face, Mister Faraday. This is the face of someone who could have died tonight. No, look at me." Elspeth waited until he looked her in the eye. "The fact that you want to resign tells me more than anything that you're the man for this job. Please, Mister Faraday. I'm counting on you."

The grim look fell away. Faraday sighed. "I think it's a mistake," he said, "but I will do everything in my power to protect you."

"At least now we know someone is serious." Elspeth gestured to a nearby chair, and Faraday sat. "It's not two people behind it, right? Because then I would lock myself in my bedroom and push orders under my door."

Faraday managed a smile. "It could be two people, but I believe we're dealing with only one. The attacks are similar in approach—careless, opportunistic, with just enough planning that the assassins could escape. Do you remember the person who gave you the wine?"

"I'm ashamed to say I didn't look closely at him because he was a servant. He was average in height, with dark hair about the same color as yours, clean-shaven—male, obviously—and his uniform looked just like everyone else's. He didn't have any distinctive features or scars. I think he was waiting for me, because he came out of the closest door, and there was only one full wine glass on his tray."

"So they weren't taking any chances on you getting the wrong glass," Faraday said, "and they weren't willing to poison two glasses and kill the wrong target. And it was someone who didn't know you don't drink wine."

"I don't suppose that narrows it down at all?"

"Unfortunately, no. But I'm going to look more closely at my suspects, and damn the expense." The grim look was back.

"My father said there were three families willing to go to war to take the Crown if I abdicated. I don't suppose you know who they are?"

Faraday shook his head. "I can guess who he was thinking of. But of those families, the Montgomerys wouldn't take the direct route of eliminating you, and the d'Ardens have been supporters of the Norths for a century. If they tried to claim the Crown, it would be in honor of the North family."

"D'Arden. Is that Serena d'Arden's family?"

"She's the heir to Patrick d'Arden, head of the family. She's also your second cousin."

"She is? I had no idea!"

"Genevieve North's Consort, your grandfather, was James d'Arden. That should give you both something to talk about when Council meetings lag."

Elspeth realized she'd stopped shaking. "The guards are searching the east wing," she said. "I didn't think...but anyone could hide in an empty room, and sneak out—"

Faraday swore under his breath. "Lieutenant Anselm is bright," he said. "I didn't think of that either. I'll post guards on the roof and outside. It helps that the east wing is three stories off the ground, and there's no way up its sides that can't be seen, but I'm not inclined to take chances anymore."

"I agree."

Faraday rose. "We haven't stopped searching for the 'servant,' just in case, but don't expect a miracle. I'll meet with you in the morning and let you know where we stand."

"Thank you."

"Thank *you* for having unwarranted faith in me," Faraday said with a bow, and left the room.

Elspeth waited in front of the fireplace until the guards returned. The lieutenant, Anselm, saluted her and said, "There's no one here who shouldn't be, your Majesty, but I think you should move to an interior suite, just in case."

That made her even more nervous, but she said, "All right," and had Honey and Shirley, the night maid, transfer some of her things to the room across the hall. It had no windows, and Elspeth felt instantly more secure as well as mildly claustrophobic. She put on her nightgown and climbed into bed. It was lower than the bed in her own suite and not quite as soft, and Elspeth liked it better.

In the darkness, she waited for the shakes to return, but even the memory of how Lord Folsom had looked, convulsing on the floor, didn't do more than bring tears to her eyes. Now that the initial shock had passed, she could think more clearly. It wasn't her fault Lord Folsom had nearly died; it was the fault of the assassin, whoever he or she was. Didn't they say poison was a woman's weapon? That wasn't a good assumption to make, not when they knew so little about her enemy. At any rate, she had nearly been the hands of an assassin that night. And Elspeth would make the person responsible for that pay.

SHE WASN'T SURPRISED TO FIND A SQUAD OF GUARDS, LED BY THE efficient Lieutenant Anselm, waiting outside the east wing the following morning. They formed up around her, not so close as to be uncomfortable, but clearly in position to protect her from any attack. Elspeth didn't fight them. She didn't think an assassin could get at her in the palace, but given the poison attempt the previous night, maybe she was wrong. And if she was going to trust Faraday to protect her, she shouldn't second-guess him. She laughed, and shook her head when one of the guards looked inquisitively at her. Trust Faraday. The world was upside down.

The guards left her at the north wing, but dispersed in a way that suggested they would be there at dinnertime. She let herself into her office and settled in to the inevitable Papers. New financial reports, these easier to understand. An invitation from the Magister of the Scholia to be present at the official opening of the new location in about a month. A letter to the King of Ruskald, written by Lord Harrington for her signature. She settled in to read that one. Lord Harrington was good at threatening action without being aggressive. He came close to accusing the Ruskald King of encroaching on Tremontanan territory without ever hinting at the word "war." Elspeth set the letter aside to discuss with Harrington later. It was diplomatic, but it left her with questions about their relationship with that country she wanted answered before that letter went out with her name on it.

Simkins' knock sounded, and the secretary poked her head inside. "Your schedule, your Majesty," she said.

"Come in, Miss Simkins," Elspeth said. Simkins' attitude had mellowed since the afternoon Elspeth had implied she would fire her. Since her attention to detail and meticulous politeness hadn't changed, Elspeth had gradually become more comfortable around her. "Please have a seat."

Simkins sat—and that was another change; two weeks ago she would have refused the chair as too informal for their working relationship—and steadied her spectacles on her nose. "The final sitting for your portrait is this morning at nine. At ten o'clock you have high court—"

Elspeth made a cranky noise. Simkins actually smiled—not a broad smile, barely touching her lips, but a smile—and went on, "Dinner is at noon in the east wing, as usual. At one o'clock representatives from the Scholia have a presentation and a request—"

"What's it about?"

"I don't know, your Majesty." Simkins' scowl told Elspeth she had pressed for this information and been denied. "They claimed it was a complex matter they would rather put before you in its entirety. I would have refused them, but you did say you wanted to meet with any Scholia masters requesting an appointment."

"I did. The more of them I meet, the more impressed I am by the quality of their education. I'd like to see more Scholia masters in government positions."

"Very wise, your Majesty. My nephew is a Scholia master, so I may be biased."

"I didn't realize you had family. In the Scholia, I mean." Elspeth had sort of assumed Simkins had sprung fully-formed from the earth itself, spectacles and circle skirt and all.

"Yes. We are all very proud of him."

"You should be. I hope he's successful."

"So do we." Simkins cleared her throat before bringing the conversation back to the present. "At two o'clock, you have yet another meeting with the architects. Your Majesty, forgive me for saying, but you cannot keep putting them off."

"I know, Miss Simkins, but I'm reluctant to tell them all their work was for nothing. Even if we pay them for their time, it must still be a blow."

"You don't want a pavilion in the royal gardens, your Majesty. They deserve to know that."

Elspeth let out a deep sigh. "You're right. I'll tell them today."

"And—if I might make a suggestion?" Elspeth nodded. "It would be a bad idea to engage them for a different building project simply to assuage your feelings of guilt."

Elspeth had been considering just that. "I—yes, Miss Simkins, that's very wise."

Simkins nodded. "At two-thirty you have, as requested, a garden party in the aforementioned royal gardens. The guest list is on your desk for your convenience."

Elspeth shuffled papers until she found it. "Thank you. I'll still have to match names to faces, but this will give me a place to start from."

"Then I wish your Majesty luck."

"Luck? For what?"

Simkins gave her an arch look. "Are you not interested in finding a Consort?"

Elspeth blushed and turned the paper upside down. "I...well, I want to get to know people, and make friends, and...if I meet young men and one of them is appropriate, I don't see what's wrong with that."

"Nothing, your Majesty. But—"

"Yes, Miss Simkins?"

Simkins removed her spectacles and looked long and hard at Elspeth. "I never married, and I have never felt the lack of a wife. But it is my understanding that marriage is more successful if it is based on something other than 'appropriate.'"

Elspeth felt her face might burst into flame. "I've never been in love," she confessed. "I didn't think I'd get married. Priestesses of the Irantzen Temple don't. So the truth is, I don't even know what I'm looking for."

"When the right person comes along, you'll know," Simkins said. "Ahem. The garden party is to last until five-thirty, and you have nothing scheduled between—"

Another knock sounded on the door. "Come in," Elspeth said, but Faraday had already entered.

"Your Majesty," he said, "I have information on the attempted assassination last night."

She'd almost forgotten about it thanks to the mundanity of Simkins' schedule. "Thank you. Miss Simkins, is that all?"

"Yes, your Majesty. But may I suggest you take your meeting with Mister Faraday as you go to your portrait sitting? It is in seven minutes."

Elspeth made a face. "The *final* sitting, your Majesty," Simkins said with a straight face.

"All right. Mister Faraday, will you walk with me?"

"Certainly, your Majesty, but I would prefer not to discuss this in front of Mistress Bennegret."

"The sitting won't take long. Will you join me for high court? We could finish our discussion on the way to the Justiciary." She looked around for her guards, but saw no one. Faraday must consider himself protection enough.

Faraday nodded. "There's not much to tell, actually. My people interviewed the service staff last night and this morning. No one was missing, and the servants matching your description could all account for their whereabouts during the time of the poisoning. That means the assassin was not a real servant, suborned or bribed by your enemy, but someone who infiltrated the palace. I think he might have hidden himself where he could approach you rather than pretending to be an actual servant. The service staff isn't so large that the servants don't know each other, and a stranger would have stood out to someone."

Elspeth nodded. "How hard would it be for someone to do that?"

Faraday's familiar scowl inexplicably cheered her. It was something in her world she could count on. "Too easy," he said. "There are closets full of unused uniforms, and the kitchens and wine cellars are always bustling at these events. A stranger might be noticed, but the other servants would be busy enough not to have time or inclination to do anything about it. And all it would take would be for the assassin to come early enough to steal a tray and glasses and conceal himself in one of those retiring rooms, waiting for you to approach."

"That seems...careless, maybe? They couldn't guarantee I'd even leave my seat all night."

"No, but if you didn't, it wouldn't be much riskier for the assassin to come to you. So gracious, thinking of his Queen's need for refreshment."

"That's a disturbing thought."

They entered the bare little room Mistress Bennegret had commandeered for the sitting to find the artist there already. "Your Majesty," she said. "We should finish today." Her scowl rivaled Faraday's usual one in fierceness and the ability to convey the scowler's profound annoyance with the world and everyone in it.

"Thank you, Mistress Bennegret, I'm sure we'll both be satisfied with the results. Mister Faraday, you don't need to wait."

"You have no guard," Faraday pointed out. "I'll wait."

The sitting passed in silence. Elspeth was painfully aware of Faraday's looming presence, watching her as closely as the artist did. They still weren't friends, for all they weren't at each other's throats anymore, and despite their mutual resolve not to assume the worst of each other, Elspeth couldn't help feeling he was still waiting for her to slip up. It made for an uncomfortable relationship.

Finally, Mistress Bennegret laid down her brush. "That's all, your Majesty. I'll complete the painting by next week sometime."

"It's not done now?" The idea of more sittings loomed up before her.

"Background, your Majesty. Your part is finished. And don't look, please. I don't like criticism before a portrait is finished."

Elspeth wouldn't have criticized—that might mean starting the whole damn process over again—but she nodded and stood, stretching out her legs. Faraday stirred from where he'd been leaning against the wall. He wasn't scowling anymore, but he still looked like a thundercloud on legs.

He took her to the Justiciary by corridors she'd never seen before, making her the most lost she'd ever been in the palace. The thought occurred to her that if he was behind the assassins, her body might never be found. Of course, if he'd been behind the assassins, she'd probably be dead.

"Should I be worried?" she asked.

He glanced at her. "Worried about what?"

"You look like you're ready to disembowel someone and it might be me. Was there more I need to know about the assassin?"

To her surprise, he smiled. It made him look surprisingly pleasant. "I apologize," he said. "I was lost in thought. I think I told you I don't know nearly enough. One thing I did learn is that the poison wasn't lethal. You weren't meant to die."

"But Lord Folsom—he was suffocating."

"Dr. Ambrose assures me the effect would have passed in a minute or so. Not long enough to suffocate someone, or to cause permanent injury."

Elspeth came to a stop. "Then what was the point? Doesn't that change everything?"

"It does, but more importantly, it confuses matters. If we're dealing with a single enemy, and other clues indicate this is still true, those shots in the Park weren't meant to kill you either. Which means someone either wants you temporarily out of the way, or intends to warn you off something. Or wants you frightened. But in every case, there's nothing eliminating you would change. You're too new to your role to have made enemies." He scowled again. "And worst of all, there are hints that whoever is behind this is not Tremontanan. That we're looking at a foreign entity, either some other government or a faction within a government. Or it could just be disgruntled foreigners living in Aurilien. I just don't *know* enough, damn it."

"Maybe someone is afraid of what I represent," Elspeth said. "I was raised Veriboldan—what if someone thinks I'm not Tremontanan enough? That I might give preference to Veribold?"

"That's possible, too," Faraday admitted. He steered her down a long, slanting hall she recognized as the path to the Judiciary. "We're following up on every hint. One of them has to lead somewhere."

Elspeth saw her usual trio of guards waiting for her at the bottom of the hall. "I hope that's true," she said.

15

*E*lspeth examined the gown Honey held up for her inspection. "I'll freeze," she said.

"It's a beautiful day, your Majesty, and this is the perfect weight for early spring," Honey pleaded. "And it's so pretty."

The dress was white muslin embroidered with yellow daisies, with a wide scoop neck, a high waist, and a narrow skirt that would swirl around Elspeth's ankles. It was also thin enough to require a full-length silk slip for modesty's sake. Just looking at it made Elspeth shiver. "Can't I wear a coat or something?"

"And cover up the dress? No, your Majesty. You said you'd take my word on what was appropriate clothes for things, and this is a garden party dress." Honey brandished the gown like she was shaking it out of winter wraps. "There's a scarf goes with it," she said as if offering a wonderful treat.

It *was* beautiful. Elspeth realized she was tired of heavy clothing. So what if she froze her nose off? "All right," she said, removing her accustomed jacket. "I certainly don't want to stand out as odd."

"You will stand out as beautiful, your Majesty," Honey said.

The muslin gown was comfortable as well as being pretty. Elspeth sat while Honey did her hair in a roll low on her neck, deliberately encouraging wisps of it to fly free around her face. Elspeth had to agree it was a nice effect. She wound the scarf, made of the same filmy muslin, twice around her neck and tossed the ends over her shoulder to trail down her back. Honey clapped with excitement. "You look so pretty, your Majesty! I wish you'd let me dress you like this every day. You shouldn't wear those dull trousers and plain shirts all the time."

"Those are more comfortable for what I do every day. But...maybe you're right." Nobody really cared if the Queen was pretty, but if she wanted to attract a Consort, maybe *she* needed to care about that.

Her guards formed up around her as she left the east wing and proceeded down a spiraling ramp to ground level, three stories below. Elspeth didn't know what lay beneath the east wing and was mildly curious about it. That was a lot of empty space, if it really was empty space and not solid rock. Whatever it was, it wasn't a danger to her or Faraday would have done something about it.

The small door at the foot of the ramp was pretty and delicate like nothing Elspeth had seen in the rest of the palace. Lieutenant Anselm opened it, straining as if it weighed a ton, and Elspeth, looking closer, realized the door was solid metal three inches thick. So much for it being a security weakness.

The lieutenant gestured to the others to wait. Elspeth craned her neck to look outside, but saw only masses of green that could have been anything from bushes to a painted wall. The smell, though... that could only be a garden, fresh and cool and damp even at this hour of the afternoon.

Lieutenant Anselm returned. "We've checked the whole garden, your Majesty, earlier today, and your guests won't be permitted to carry weapons."

"Thank you, lieutenant. Your thoroughness comforts me."

The lieutenant smiled. "Enjoy your afternoon, your Majesty." It was a smile that reminded Elspeth that the lieutenant—all the guards, really—weren't much older than her.

She stepped through the door and into a living tunnel. Budding vines wove through tall iron hoops that in full summer would create a thick wall of greenery. Even at this early season, the effect was stunning. Elspeth walked forward, head tilted back to appreciate the fragments of blue sky peeping between the vines. They filled the air with an unexpectedly tangy scent Elspeth enjoyed.

Past the arched tunnel, the garden opened up into a broad lawn whose grass had begun to green, giving the sweep of lawn a fresh, new look. It ended at stone walls about eight feet tall, topped with iron spikes, that were far enough apart to keep the garden from feeling closed in. Deadheaded rosebushes, spiky and bare, lined the walls; one more deterrent to any intruder. The spikes gave Elspeth a perverse desire to climb the wall and see what lay beyond it. She'd have to settle for asking someone.

The air was filled with the sound of birds chirping and the elusive tangy scent. Something else she would need to ask about. There was also a low murmuring sound she identified as conversation, quiet except for an occasional high-pitched laugh. A breeze ruffled her skirts and made her scarf flutter and the wisps of hair tickle her face. It was chilly, but not as cold as she feared, and the feel of the air against her skin invigorated her.

The lawn sloped gently downward to an enormous stone fountain topped with brass fish. Elspeth walked down to it, the soft grass putting a spring in her step, and discovered it wasn't running. She ran her fingers over the slightly rough surface of the stone and imagined the cool spray from the fountain in the heart of an Aurilien summer.

She came around the fountain and discovered the source of the murmuring: dozens of people, standing and chatting. Some of them glanced her way and stared. Elspeth blushed. It was her party, and she had no need to be embarrassed, but she felt unexpectedly exposed in the pretty dress.

She put on a smile and walked forward. This couldn't be very different from parties in Veribold—might be better, as the only parties she was used to were Veriboldan landholder gatherings and ambassadorial events. The first were never the kind of fun that let you relax, as she'd always had to be on alert for Veriboldans who felt it acceptable to snub the foreigner, and the second had always required her to be on her best behavior as a representative of Tremontane. Here, she was the Queen. Nobody would snub her. And in a sense, whatever she did was considered best behavior.

"Good afternoon, and welcome," she said, causing a few more faces to turn her way. "I hope it's not too early in the year for a garden party, but I wanted an excuse to finally see my garden." A riffle of laughter passed over the crowd. "I look forward to getting to know you. Enjoy the garden, and the food, and...everything."

The murmur grew louder, and the rustle of fabric as everyone bowed or curtseyed temporarily drowned out the singing of the birds. Elspeth found a servant at her elbow, someone she recognized from suppers in the east wing dining room, offering her a tall glass of dark red liquid with tiny bubbles clinging to its curves. Hesitantly, she took it, sniffed, and discovered it was cranberry juice mixed with sparkling water that smelled faintly of apples. Relieved, she sipped, and relaxed when nothing bad happened.

Two people approached her, one of them blessedly familiar. "Thank you for the invitation, your Majesty," Serena d'Arden said. "May I introduce Michael Argent? Of the Minsonal Argents?"

"It's nice to meet you," Elspeth said, remembering not to offer her hand to shake—Miss Jones White's instructions again. Argent bowed. "Welcome to my party."

"It's a pleasure," Argent said. He had an unexpectedly deep voice for not being a very large man, and his golden curls and bright blue eyes made him look even more like someone who should sing tenor in one of the more epic Eskandelic operas. "Thank you for the invitation. I'd hoped to meet you ever since I heard you had intended to become an Irantzen priestess. My sister has attended the festival every year for the last three years."

"Oh!" Excitement fizzed through Elspeth. "I might have met her —we don't use last names during the Festival—what is her given name?"

"Charlotte. She looks like me, only prettier, of course." Argent smiled, making the corners of his eyes crinkle merrily.

Elspeth cast her mind back. "I think...I remember a young

woman in my meditation group named Charlotte, two years ago. She had very blonde hair I was jealous of—so curly, but so easily managed. Not at all like my mane." She touched her hair lightly and smiled. "Does your sister have a habit of raising one eyebrow when she's curious?"

"That's Charlotte!" Argent laughed. "May I remember you to her? She would be so thrilled to know she has a connection to the Queen."

"Of course." Elspeth became aware that Lady d'Arden had drifted away. "She isn't here?"

"She had a prior engagement. Betrothal matters—she's to be married in two weeks."

"How lovely. Please give her my best wishes."

"I will. But tell me, what's it like? The Festival, I mean. Charlotte won't talk about it—or does that mean it's too private to discuss?"

Elspeth took another drink of her juice. "Not the way you probably think. So much of what we do is personal, it doesn't mean much to anyone who hasn't gone through it. But there's meditation, and fasting, and a lot of discussion so we can help each other understand the visions we see—"

"Visions?"

"That's also hard to explain. We're given something that allows our unconscious minds to communicate with us, and that takes the form of a waking dream, but clearer and more coherent than a dream. We share those visions with the other women at the Festival, and their insights help us understand." She thought back to the vision of the palace, and for the first time since leaving the Temple, she didn't feel resentful.

"So why aren't men allowed?" Argent asked.

"The Festival celebrates Haran's discovery that the gods had abandoned heaven, or been driven out—there's so much speculation on that question. Anyway, Haran's revelations were at first only believed by women, who founded the first religious communities, and the Festival honors that. But Veriboldan men are allowed in the Temple at other times, for instruction and counsel."

"*Veriboldan* men? I'm feeling increasingly excluded," Argent said with another smile.

"Well, it is a Veriboldan temple, and it's in the Jaixante, which is for the most part forbidden to non-Veriboldans. Aside from certain events like the Election. The only non-Veriboldans allowed to live in the Jaixante are sworn servants to the rulers of Veribold and priestesses of the Irantzen Temple. But there are other religious communities in Veribold that are open to men. Other temples."

"Fascinating," Argent said, sipping his straw-pale wine. "I shouldn't monopolize your time, your Majesty, but I hope to speak with you again. You've lived such an interesting life."

"It's not as interesting as you think—but I'd like that, Mister Argent."

Argent bowed again and turned away, leaving Elspeth feeling strangely adrift. She searched the crowd for someone she knew—how ridiculous if she threw a party and custom prevented her from talking to her guests!

Across the lawn, she saw the Countess of Waxwold conversing with a man dressed very finely in sharply creased trousers, a well-fitted spring coat, and a cravat that pushed his chin unnaturally high. She walked in their direction. Lady Quinn saw her first, and a surprisingly unpleasant look crossed her face, swiftly enough that Elspeth almost doubted having seen it. From someone who'd always been pleasant to her, whom Elspeth had hoped someday to call friend, it was like a slap to the face.

The man turned to see who Lady Quinn was looking at. His expression became frankly assessing, admiring Elspeth in a way she found profoundly uncomfortable, as if he could see through her clothes to her skin. Between the two, Elspeth regretted approaching them, but it was too late to turn away now.

"Good afternoon, Lady Quinn," she said with a smile. "I'm so glad to see you. I still know so few people, I'm grateful for the guests I can speak to."

A confused look touched Lady Quinn's eyes briefly, and she shot a glance at her companion. "Good afternoon, your Majesty," she said.

Elspeth detected hostility beneath her polite tone of voice. "May I introduce Lord Randolph Chadwick, third son of the Count of Harroden."

"Good afternoon, your Majesty," Lord Chadwick said, bowing. To Elspeth's surprise and discomfort, he took her hand and brought it swiftly to his lips before releasing her. "I am *most* pleased to make your acquaintance."

"I...it's nice to meet you," Elspeth said. "I didn't mean to interrupt your conversation."

"It was nothing," Lady Quinn said in a tone of voice that said it absolutely was not nothing. "Simply discussing plans for my birthday celebration in ten days."

"Ten days?" Astonishment drove her embarrassment out of her head. "My birthday is ten days from now."

Lady Quinn's expression grew pinched. "Is it," she said flatly.

"Yes. I'll be twenty-three."

The pinched expression went even more sour. "So will I. What a coincidence."

Elspeth sensed she had made a mistake. It seemed the Queen would overshadow the Countess on her own special day. "How do you intend to celebrate?"

"Well, of course we'll attend the Queen's birthday celebration," Lord Chadwick said with a smile not nearly as pleasant as Argent's had been.

"That seems like a dreadful way to celebrate your own birthday," Elspeth said. "Surely you've made plans of your own?"

Lady Quinn eyed Elspeth, looking for hidden motives. Elspeth put on her most sincere smile. "Lord Chadwick has agreed to escort me to the opera," Lady Quinn said.

Elspeth mentally kicked herself. Interfered in the woman's courtship, ruined her birthday... "That sounds much more fun," she said. "I've never been to a Tremontanan opera. You'll have to tell me all about it later."

"Perhaps you—" Lord Chadwick began.

"Oh, I see someone I must speak to," Elspeth said. "Please

continue your conversation, and forgive my interruption!" She turned and hurried off toward a knot of guests before Lord Chadwick could be stupid enough to invite her along on the opera outing. Lady Quinn couldn't possibly be interested in a man who'd flirt with another woman in front of her. Or maybe she was in love, and it had blinded her to Lord Chadwick's true nature. In either case, Elspeth was glad to be out of it.

She found Lady d'Arden again and squeezed a few more introductions out of her, some of them women, mostly men. Lord Erickson from the previous evening was in attendance, and she chatted with him, finding him an entertaining partner even with the awkwardness of her never having read his poetry between them. She nibbled cakes and accepted a second glass of juice, and by the time five-thirty arrived, she'd enjoyed herself enough that she felt disappointed that the party had to end.

She waited near the arch to say goodbye to her guests, wondering idly how they exited the palace. Of course there wasn't an outer gate to the garden, that would be insecure, but people couldn't be allowed to wander the palace unescorted, could they?

"Thank you again, your Majesty, I enjoyed our conversation," Michael Argent said with a bow. Elspeth looked him over, remembered how she'd enjoyed speaking with him, and made a decision.

"Mister Argent," she said, "do you like opera?"

He looked startled, but concealed it quickly. "I do, your Majesty."

"I've only ever been to Veriboldan operas, and I'd like to experience a Tremontanan one. Would you care to accompany me some evening?"

His carefully concealed astonishment gave way to a delighted smile. "I'd be honored, your Majesty."

"My secretary will contact you with the details," Elspeth said, feeling giddy at having Simkins she could pass all this off to, "but shall we say in three or four days?"

"I'm at your service, your Majesty." Argent bowed again and disappeared through the arch.

When the last guest was gone, Elspeth joined her guards for the long walk back up the spiral ramp to the east wing. She felt tired, but it was the kind of tired that came from pleasant exertion. Michael Argent was pleasant to talk to, and had a nice smile, and was hand-some...she wasn't sure she felt the kind of excitement she'd always believed was part of falling in love, but maybe she was wrong about that being necessary. Anyway, it was just one evening.

Supper was just her and Veronica. They ate mostly in silence, Elspeth because she was tired of conversation, Veronica because she was Veronica. When dessert was served, Veronica said, "Did you enjoy your party?"

"Yes, it was very nice. I met some interesting people. It's getting easier to be the Queen now that I know more of my peers. Are they still peers if I'm the Queen and outrank them? But you know what I mean."

"I do." Veronica took another bite of the decadently rich choco-late cake, with the center that oozed dark chocolate pudding. "You're looking for a Consort, aren't you."

Elspeth nearly choked on her mouthful of cake. Veronica hadn't sounded judgmental, but her words, so matter-of-fact instead of questioning, had felt like a judgment nonetheless. "I wouldn't put it that way," she said when her mouth wasn't so full. "I want to meet people, and if one of them turns out to be someone I could love, then that's good, isn't it?"

"Landon and I met before he was King," Veronica said. She set her dessert fork down with a *tink* against the china. "He wasn't what I thought I wanted in a husband. He was loud, and boisterous, and he enjoyed a good story that ended in a good laugh. And I didn't think I was what he wanted in a wife. I never have understood why he pursued me. So many women wanted to marry the Crown Prince." She smiled, memory lighting her eyes. "Some of them wanted to bear his child, legitimate or not. He was very handsome—those blue eyes with that black hair..."

Elspeth held her breath, hoping not to distract Veronica from her reminiscences.

"And he wasn't who I thought he was," Veronica went on. "He was so much like a little boy, afraid of doing or saying the wrong thing, and that came out as brashness as he tried to hide how much he disliked being laughed at. His mother..." Veronica's eyes hardened. "What a bitch."

Elspeth had never heard Veronica use coarse language before. It was like hearing a nightingale swear. "She tried to control that family —succeeded, for the most part. Marrying me was the most rebellion Landon ever managed. Genevieve wanted him to marry a d'Arden cousin, keep the families tied. And don't think I don't know she drove your parents out of the country entirely. I don't know why she wanted Sebastian disinherited, but it wouldn't surprise me if it had something to do with Fiona. She'd have burst a vein if Emily had tried to adopt out while she was still alive."

Her eyes suddenly focused on Elspeth. "But that doesn't matter anymore. I was talking about Landon. I did love him, you know. He had his faults, but that's true of anyone. And he was a bad King, but he was a good husband. He should have divorced me when I couldn't have children after Francis, but...you know, it was the one time I saw him angry, the night I suggested it. He said he could face the country with only one heir, but he couldn't face heaven if I couldn't be with him." She wiped her eyes. "It was terrible, and beautiful, because before that night I hadn't believed he really, truly loved me."

Elspeth couldn't think of anything to say. Her memories of her brash, outspoken uncle whom she'd disliked were turning somersaults in her head.

"I'm sorry," Veronica said. "I didn't mean—anyway. Elspeth, you'll meet so many men who want to be the Consort. They'll act like they love you, but they won't even see you. But among those men will be the ones who would want to marry you if you were a road-sweeper's daughter. If you can't marry one of those, better you stay single, because you might be the Queen in this life, but you'll be Elspeth North forever."

Elspeth let out a breath. "How do I know? I never imagined marrying, let alone falling in love. I don't even know what that feels like."

"I wish I could tell you." Veronica nudged her fork until it lay at a tangent to the curve of the plate. "I knew because there was a day I woke up and couldn't imagine not spending it with Landon. That might not matter to you. You'll have to work it out for yourself." She smiled. "Pray about it, maybe. I've never been able to guess at what heaven will care about, when it comes to human needs."

"I will," Elspeth said, catching hold of something she could understand. "Thank you, Aunt Veronica."

"If you can learn from my experience, that makes me doubly blessed," Veronica said. She pushed back her chair. "Good night."

"Good night," Elspeth said.

Back in her new suite, filled with her things thanks to Honey and Gloria's efforts, she undressed and climbed into bed, but didn't turn down the covers. Instead, she sat cross-legged atop the counterpane and clasped the *toan* jade in both hands. Her fingers found the fourth meditation ritual, the path of understanding. The deeply incised words read *that all may have place on earth and under heaven.* She might have followed the path of awareness, to guide her in discovering her heart, or the path of harmony, to make herself in tune with heaven's desires, but after Veronica's revelations, she found she craved understanding.

She relaxed into a meditative state and let her fingers trace the carved words. The principle of understanding as taught by the Irantzen priestesses was of finding how things fit into the world around them. Sela, whom Elspeth didn't like, had nevertheless put it in a way Elspeth understood: *a bird's wings make sense when you see it in the sky.* So how did that apply to Elspeth?

The more she thought about it, the more she wanted a Consort, someone to share her burdens and support her in ways her staff and councilors and even her family could not. Maybe that was a longing for love, too. She knew so little of romantic love, she couldn't tell if that were true. But that longing meant she needed to find the right person, not just someone who liked the idea of being Consort and was maybe fond of the Queen as well.

She considered what she knew of love from watching her parents.

She knew they had overcome great obstacles to be together, which told her love meant a willingness to face hard things without giving up. They clearly desired each other—they were never shy about holding hands or kissing in front of their children—so love meant physical affection and desire as well. And they were always one when it came to making decisions for the family, which suggested two people in love ought to share the same goals and principles. Persistence, desire, unity. Those were ideals she could found her search on.

She removed the *toan* jade from around her neck and laid it on the bedside table. Someone she would be willing to fight for. Someone who wanted the same things she did. And someone whose touch she longed for. That last made her uncomfortable, because she'd never met anyone who aroused her physically. Maybe there was something wrong with her.

She shook her head to make that thought fly away and tunneled under the blankets. In a few days, she would go to the opera with Argent, and get to know him better. And maybe he would turn out to be the right kind of man. *What would be the odds,* she chastised herself, and settled in to sleep.

16

_E_lspeth gazed at the lavender and green banner representing Huddersfield. The colors were so delicate it was hard to imagine them marching before an army. No enemy would be able to take them seriously. Though it had been generations since Huddersfield had sent men and women to war. Just over a hundred years, in fact, when they'd supported Willow North in her fight against the pretender Terence Valant. Elspeth knew this because the Count of Huddersfield always found a way to drop this fact into ordinary conversations.

The sound of the conversation going on now suggested it was winding down. She brought her attention back to the present. "I think we understand the new tax rates on Devisery," she said. "Thank you, Lady Wilde, for your explanation. Mistress Withers, how does this affect tax collection?"

The Scholia Master stood. "It means we'll assess taxes on finished Devices when they're sold instead of when they're created. Essentially, we'll be collecting taxes as if they're any other merchandise. This will ease the burden on Devisers and Devisery workshops."

"Very well. Is anyone opposed to this change? No? Thank you, ladies and gentlemen." Elspeth didn't like the informality of voting openly. Suppose the vote were on something sensitive, where someone might be persecuted for voting "wrongly"? Or suppose someone might be influenced to change their vote by not wanting to be in the minority? There had to be a better alternative.

"Finally—Mister Faraday. You have a report to make?"

Faraday stood. "Your Majesty asked me to present my findings on the assassination attempt to the Council," he said. "Though my department was unable to track down the assassin, we found evidence that the attempted poisoning was not meant to be fatal. Someone wanted her Majesty incapacitated or at the very least frightened, but not dead. We also found evidence suggesting that the poisoning and the attempted shooting had a single person or group behind them, and that those responsible might not be Tremontanan. We're continuing to follow up on this clue, investigating foreigners with some reason to want Tremontane's government destabilized."

"Thank you, Mister Faraday," Elspeth said as he resumed his seat. "I wanted all of you to know the state Internal Affairs' investigation is in. I have faith in Mister Faraday's efforts, but if any of you can think of anything that might help, any insights you might have, I welcome them."

Nobody spoke. A couple of people shifted uncomfortably. "Well, your Majesty," Lord Heath said, scratching his nearly bald head, "the fact that they didn't want you dead is curious. It means they wanted the government in turmoil. But with your heirs being underage, killing you—I beg your pardon, but I believe you wanted frankness— killing you would introduce exactly that kind of turmoil."

"That's true," Master Keswick said. The new head of Transportation had proved exactly as insightful and helpful as Elspeth had hoped. "On the other hand, an underage King would have a regent, and I believe you've designated one already, is that right?"

"Yes. Lord Harrington would become regent on my brother James's behalf." Elspeth had been leery of choosing Lord Harrington, but she couldn't name her father, the one person she did trust, and she had to admit her reluctance came more from how Lord Harrington still spoke to her like she was a child and not because she was afraid of him abusing that power. "And that would happen right away, so Lord Harrington would have the power to act immediately if an enemy tried to take advantage of the disruption."

"Whereas if you were incapacitated, there are things that couldn't be done because the Council doesn't have the power to act on them," Keswick continued. "Ratifying laws, awarding titles, deciding certain legal matters. Going to war."

"That last is what occurred to me, your Majesty," Lord Harrington said. "A foreign country who wanted to attack Tremontane could take advantage of your not being in a position to declare war to make a preemptive attack. And Ruskald is poised to do just that."

Elspeth glanced at Faraday. "There's no conclusive evidence that Ruskald was behind the assassination attempts," he said. "That doesn't rule them out, either."

"Lord Harrington, didn't you tell me Ruskald is unwilling to attack us because they aren't sure they'd win?" Elspeth asked. "I understand we've made enough of a show of force to keep them off our borders."

"Unwilling, yes, but if they could tip that balance of power in their favor, I have no doubt they'd push to conquer the rest of the Riverlands," Lord Harrington said. "They don't like that we control both banks of the Snow River."

"I see," Elspeth said. "Mister Faraday, I would like your department to concentrate on proving whether or not the Ruskalder are behind the attempts on my life. Lord Harrington, what should be our next step, assuming the Ruskalder are preparing for war?"

"We can't send more troops into the Riverlands without prompting them to escalate," Lord Harrington said. "But we can continue to watch their troop movements and be prepared to act if anything changes."

"General Beckett," Elspeth said, turning to the gruff, silent figure seated next to Faraday, "what is the Army's status?"

Beckett shifted his weight. "We've moved more troops to strategic locations in Baronies Daxtry and Avory," he said in his deep, gravelly voice. "We've made it look like they're on maneuvers—training exercises. Nothing the Ruskalder can object to. But each of those 'training grounds' are within a day's march of the border. We're prepared for whatever comes next."

"Thank you, General. I hope it doesn't come to war, but I'm reassured that we'd be ready for it if it did." Elspeth stood, prompting the others to rise. "That's all for today, ladies and gentlemen. Thank you again."

Faraday hovered by the door as the others left. Elspeth hung back. "Was there something else, Mister Faraday?" she asked when the room was empty except for the two of them.

"You intend to go to the opera in two days," he said.

"I do?" She hadn't realized Simkins had already made the arrangements. "That is—yes. Miss Simkins hasn't told me the actual date yet."

"I wish you'd reconsider. Security will be difficult to manage in such a public place. We will have to disrupt the performance to an extent, you will need guards inside and out of the building...and that doesn't take into account examining the performers and the staff to rule out anyone who might be bribed or threatened into helping an assassin reach you."

"Do you really think that's possible? That someone in the opera house might want me dead? Because I'm sure Miss Simkins has kept this trip confidential. She didn't even tell me, after all. So it's unlikely an assassin would have time to suborn anyone."

Faraday let out a frustrated breath. "I'm not taking chances. Will you at least cooperate with your guard?"

"Of course. I'm not taking chances either. I just don't want you to drive yourself mad trying to cover even the remotest possibilities."

"It's too late for that." Faraday's smile was humorless.

"I can't stay locked in the palace forever, Mister Faraday. I'm looking forward to an evening with an interesting man, and I appreciate your efforts to keep me safe." A terrible thought occurred to her. "You didn't investigate Mister Argent, did you?"

Faraday's expression went perfectly bland. "You're as suspicious as I am."

"Did you?"

"Of course I did. He's completely unobjectionable. I hope that comforts you."

"Not if 'unobjectionable' is the same as 'boring.'"

"I prefer 'boring' in your companions. They're unlikely to want to see you dead." Faraday's bland expression gave way to a scowl. "All right. If you're not going to give up this mad plan, I'll have your escort ready at the appropriate time."

"Thank you, Mister Faraday. I'm sure everything will be fine."

"I'm not," Faraday said with a rueful smile, "but I've given up trying to control what you do."

APPROPRIATE GARB FOR THE OPERA, ACCORDING TO HONEY, FELL somewhere between the garden party dress and Elspeth's coronation gown. It was designed along the same lines as the muslin gown, with a low neckline and a high waist, but was of heavy cream-colored satin with a thin, gauzy blue overdress whose long sleeves made Elspeth want to scratch. Honey piled her curls high on her head, where they would eventually become painfully heavy just before sliding down the back of her head, but Elspeth would be home long before that happened.

Home. She thought about that as she clasped a choker of white gold leaves studded with sapphires around her neck. Did she actually think of the palace as home, or was that just a casual turn of phrase? *Home*, to her, was still the embassy in Veribold, where her family was. During the day, she was too busy to dwell on what she'd lost, but at night she struggled to keep the tears at bay. Weeping would do nothing but leave her miserable and headachy the next day. It certainly wouldn't change anything, wouldn't magically transport her back to Veribold or bring Francis back to life.

And she had to admit to herself, if no one else, that she was growing accustomed to this new role. She felt more confident about giving orders, was less embarrassed by the deference everyone showed her—everyone but Faraday—and had begun to understand how her government worked. Maybe Veronica was right, and this was something she could be good at.

Her guards came to attention when she stepped out of the east wing, and Lieutenant Anselm gave her a smile that said she knew this evening was different. "Your Majesty," she said as their procession headed off down the long hall, "Corporal Higgins and I will accompany you into the royal box, and we will remain there throughout the evening. Mister Faraday's orders."

"I understand. Thank you, lieutenant."

Anselm's smile broadened. "We're sorry for the intrusion."

"I...yes, I suppose that couldn't be helped." Anselm's expression confused her. It looked as if the lieutenant thought her presence and that of Corporal Higgins might affect Elspeth's enjoyment of the performance. "I'm sure you'll be discreet."

"Naturally," Anselm said. Now she sounded like they'd had a conversation with multiple meanings. Elspeth gave up. Whatever Anselm was hinting at couldn't be vital, or she'd be forthright.

This time, the guards took her down familiar paths to the Rotunda and then through the antechamber to the front door. The North carriage was pulled up at the foot of the steps, and Michael Argent waited by its door. He looked very good in a burgundy satin coat and matching knee breeches, though his calves in their silk stockings looked odd. Elspeth didn't have time to examine them closely before the guards spread out before her and she descended the stairs to join him.

"Your Majesty," Argent said. "You look lovely." His smile, genuine as Lord Chadwick's had not been, charmed her.

"Thank you," she said, accepting his hand to help her into the carriage. He held her hand a moment longer than necessary, and the warm feeling his regard had filled her with went flustered. Panic set in. This was courtship, wasn't it? Or the next thing to courtship. She didn't know the rules, didn't know what she was supposed to do or what he expected—

"I hope you will enjoy the performance," Argent said. He seated himself opposite her on the rear-facing seat and made no move to touch her again. "I'm afraid this isn't like Veribold, where they have several opera houses giving performances at once. There's just the one opera house, and they put on one opera at a time. But *Estella in Eskandel* is one of Lady Yvenna Verden's most popular compositions."

The panic subsided. "I'm mostly interested in how Tremontanan opera compares to Veriboldan," Elspeth said. There was no need to worry. Argent was polite, and interesting, and unlikely to press intimacies upon her in the royal box, particularly if her guards were—*oh.* Suddenly Elspeth understood what Anselm had been hinting at. Was that something courting couples did, use the private boxes for intimate relations? She willed herself not to blush.

They chatted all the way to the opera house, and by the time they arrived, Elspeth had relaxed enough to enjoy herself. Argent was just as funny and interesting as she remembered, gave her greetings from his sister, and drew Elspeth out to the point that she could share stories of her own. When he helped her down from the carriage, she dared give his hand a little squeeze and felt a frisson of excitement when that made him smile.

The opera house was as much a monstrosity as the palace, though in a completely different way. It was clearly the work of a single hand, and that hand had belonged to a madman who believed no amount of gilt was too much, that blood red was a charming color to paint a three-story-tall building occupying most of a city block, and that if one Device lamp was a good idea, a roof covered with Device lamps enough to blind the eye was even better. Elspeth shielded her eyes and surveyed the lower levels. "It's...dramatic, isn't it?"

"I take it opera houses in Veribold don't look like this," Argent said. He waited for the guards to form up around them while a pair of guards assessed the opera house entry before gesturing to Elspeth to walk with him. Elspeth had expected him to offer her his arm and was disappointed when he didn't. Surely even the Queen could be allowed to accept a traditional escort?

"They're built under the supervision of the Taixen—it's a sort of board of approval for certain classes of business," she said. "They determine what kinds of businesses can be constructed where, and what they will look like, and how tall they can be, all the way down to number of windows and color of paint. It keeps Haizea from looking as patchwork as Aurilien does."

The guards held both doors open for Elspeth and Argent. "You must think Aurilien ugly by comparison," Argent said.

Elspeth remembered what she'd thought on that ride to the Park. "Not anymore," she said. "It has a different kind of beauty."

The foyer of the opera house was more beautiful than its exterior, though the smell of hundreds of warm bodies mixed with a thick rose attar made Elspeth want to sneeze. Walls covered in red and gold brocade muted the sounds of patrons walking across the plush gold carpet, though at the moment, there were very few people in the foyer with them. Everyone had stopped to bow or curtsey to their Queen. That no longer embarrassed Elspeth as it once had, though she did feel awkward at having interrupted whatever they were doing. She raised a hand to acknowledge their bows, a nice noncommittal gesture she felt didn't make her look like a total fool, and followed the guards across the foyer to a set of shallow stairs. Double doors at the top of the stairs were flung open, revealing rows of chairs in a downward-sloping room.

"This way, your Majesty," Lieutenant Anselm said. Elspeth dragged her gaze away from the vast open space and saw Anselm waiting for her at the foot of more stairs, well to the left of the doors. These were much steeper than the others and ascended out of Elspeth's sight. Elspeth glanced at Argent, who looked as if he were waiting for her to take the lead. Once again, he didn't offer her his arm. Elspeth suppressed a sigh and climbed the stairs, letting her gloved hand rest gently on the rail. Her soft shoes made no noise on the carpet, which felt a little slippery underfoot as if it had been worn down by thousands of opera-goers.

At the top of the stairs, the lieutenant turned right, and Elspeth followed her down a curving hallway to an ordinary wooden door stained dark in contrast with the golden brocade covering the walls.

Anselm opened the door and held up a hand. "Corporal Higgins first, your Majesty."

Elspeth waited for Corporal Higgins, who was a stocky man in his early thirties, to enter the room before following. The room was small and dark, but Higgins pulled aside heavy red velvet drapes to illuminate two rows of three chairs, each with an overstuffed cushion in the same red velvet. Elspeth's attention, though, was all on the auditorium below, filled with chairs arranged to leave aisles down which dozens, maybe hundreds of people made their way. The stage was shrouded in a red velvet curtain similar to the one surrounding the royal box, and light Devices, the largest Elspeth had ever seen, lined the proscenium.

"How does it compare?" Argent asked. He stood close beside her, close enough that the warmth of his body was like a little fire next to her.

"They use lamps in Veribold," Elspeth said, gesturing to the Devices. "I know those are Devices because the smell is different—in Veribold the opera houses all smell of hot paraffin and fire. And most Veriboldan opera houses are smaller than this one, not by much, but smaller." She turned to face Argent. "We have an excellent view."

"I can't imagine the Queen sitting anywhere but the best seat in the house," Argent said, bowing. He said it with a smile, but his words made Elspeth uncomfortable, as if he were drawing attention to the privileges she always had. It wasn't as if she'd asked for this box.

She took her seat and leaned out over the edge of the box until she saw how tense it made the lieutenant. Then she sat back and watched the crowd, what she could see of it. Everyone seemed to be dressed as nicely as she and Argent were. She'd wondered if opera in Tremontane was as exclusive as opera in Veribold. Or maybe these were poorer people who cared enough about the arts to spend their hard-earned money on the right clothing. Again she felt oddly guilty. It wasn't as if it were her fault opera was expensive. Had she paid for these tickets, or had Simkins exercised royal prerogative on her behalf?

The lights dimmed. Unseen violins played a note that thrilled through Elspeth and were joined by cellos, viols, woodwinds, and a deep-voiced drum that made the box vibrate. Then the curtains opened, and performers streamed onto the stage, adding their voices to the orchestra. Elspeth lost herself in the performance, forgetting the guards and the box and even her companion. In Veribold, opera was intentionally elevated to distance the story from the viewers; here, she felt as if the singers were addressing her directly. It was an extraordinary experience.

When the lights came up, her chest ached as if she'd been holding her breath. "That was marvelous," she breathed, turning to Argent. He had a peculiar look on his face, and instinctively she felt he'd been watching her instead of the performance.

"Marvelous," he agreed. "Would you care to refresh yourself before the second act?"

"I will, yes," she said. She hoped the guards wouldn't insist on going into the water closet with her.

But it turned out they were satisfied with clearing the refreshing room and waiting outside for her. Again, she felt odd at how all these people went out of their way to accede to her wishes. She'd never felt more like the Queen than at that moment, as if Elspeth North didn't exist.

Argent waited in the box for her, as if he hadn't moved. "So," he said cheerfully, "what did you think?"

"It's not over yet," she said with a smile.

"Well said." Argent turned his attention to the stage as the lights once more dimmed and the music came up. Elspeth watched the performance, but with only half her attention. The rest was reserved for the man sitting next to her. It was true, he did occasionally fix his gaze on her rather than on the performers. She wasn't sure how she felt about that. He was nice, and clever, but she couldn't tell if he liked her—or, rather, if he liked her more than just as a casual acquaintance. And she didn't know if she wanted him to. Or if she was expecting too much from a first social outing.

Face it, she told herself, *he's not the one.* How she could tell this from only a couple of hours' interaction, most of it spent sitting in silence watching the opera, she didn't know. But much as he was interesting and clever, when she contemplated seeing him again, it was with a feeling of indifference. That surely couldn't bode well for a romance.

She applauded when the performance came to an end, but the lieutenant gestured to her to wait when she would have risen. "We'll let the crowds clear a bit, your Majesty," she said. Elspeth agreed. Even without Faraday's concerns about her safety, she didn't like the idea of pressing through all those crowds, or of making her guards shove people out of the way.

Argent was an excellent conversationalist, and she enjoyed talking about the opera until it was time to leave. "I do regret that there's only one opera company in Aurilien," she said as they descended the stairs together. "It would be so enjoyable to see another."

"I wish I could arrange it for you, your Majesty," Argent said with a smile Elspeth had no trouble reading. Her heart sank. It looked like Argent thought they'd made more of a connection than Elspeth felt. She'd never been so glad that custom dictated the Queen had to ask for the pleasure of someone's company.

The ride back to the palace was quiet, now that Elspeth was nervous about encouraging Argent. She couldn't tell if she was sending the right signals or just being rude. "Should we...take you home?" she asked nervously. What if he expected her to invite him to another social event? Or, heaven forbid, back to the east wing for more conversation?

"That would be welcome, your Majesty," Argent said. "I was instructed to attend on you at the palace rather than have your Majesty come to my home, so I took a hackney. This would save me having to hail another."

He hadn't sounded put out. Good. "I appreciate your willingness to accommodate my security."

"It's no problem. Anything for your Majesty."

There was the smile again. Oh, this was awkward, though apparently only for Elspeth.

Argent gave the driver directions, and soon they rattled to a stop in front of one of the great stone mansions on the hill overlooking Aurilien. "Thank you again for the pleasure of your company," Elspeth said.

"I look forward to seeing you again, your Majesty, perhaps at your birthday gala? If you're willing to save a dance for me."

Elspeth blushed at the thought. She'd been learning to dance, but this felt more intimate than a simple waltz or gavotte. "I...suppose so," she said.

"Then...good night, your Majesty," Argent said, and *now* he took her gloved hand and squeezed it lightly. He was gone before she could react.

She leaned back on the cushions and tried to calm her rapidly beating heart. She was more convinced than ever that Argent wasn't the man for her, but...was this her fault? She'd spoken freely, she'd held his hand—for a second or two, but still—had she accidentally encouraged him? She groaned and covered her face with her hands. She was almost certain she wasn't obligated to continue the relation- ship, even if she *had* encouraged him, but she didn't know any graceful way of telling him she wasn't interested, and he didn't deserve to be threatened by her guards.

Those guards escorted her in silence to the east wing, which was normal—she suspected they had instructions not to be distracted from their duties by conversation—but tonight their silence felt different. Lieutenant Anselm in particular Elspeth suspected of wanting to interrogate her about Argent.

It hadn't occurred to her until that moment that the reason everyone in Tremontane might feel entitled to pry into her personal life was that her personal life, so far as it extended to her choice of Consort, affected them. She knew from reading the black leather book that a Consort had certain government responsibilities beyond just breeding, if she could be indelicate about it, and of course a Consort would have influence on the Queen. So she not only had a duty to herself to choose the right man, she had a duty to her country as well. Her discomfort increased until by the time they reached the east wing, she was ready to run to her room and hide.

Veronica had already gone to bed, thank heaven, so Elspeth hurried through the drawing room to her suite and shut the door behind her as if closing the gates against the barbarian Ruskalder horde. She closed her eyes and tried to calm herself. This wasn't a disaster. She'd figured out how to manage her Council, and how to control Simkins; she could figure out how to convey the message that she wasn't interested to one man.

She pulled the bell rope and kicked off her shoes. They were more comfortable than any of her others. Maybe she needed to plan her wardrobe around them. That reminded her that she would need yet another new gown for her birthday gala. She wondered if the day would ever come that her wardrobe was complete. Probably not in her lifetime.

The suite door opened, and Honey entered. "Your Majesty, did you have a good time? Here, let me help you. Was he handsome? I wish I could have seen him!"

"He was handsome," Elspeth admitted, "but I don't think I'll see him again."

Honey's hands, busy unbuttoning the dress, stilled. "You don't mean he rejected you, your Majesty? He couldn't possibly!"

"No, Honey, I mean I didn't feel...I don't know. He was very nice, but I'm not interested."

Honey finished with the buttons and helped Elspeth slide the dress off over her head. "You mean there wasn't a spark," she said.

"That's a very good way to put it. No spark." Elspeth shrugged into her night gown and sighed. "I thought...he really is very handsome, and nice, and I like talking to him, but...I don't think I should encourage him when there's no chance he's the right one."

"You shouldn't feel obligated to like anyone, your Majesty." Honey carried the dress into the wardrobe to hang it up. "That's true even for girls who aren't Queens."

"I feel awful for encouraging him, but I really didn't mean to." Elspeth climbed into bed. It was so much nicer not to need the little stepstool. "And I think I promised to dance with him at the gala. Oh, Honey, I feel so muddled."

"Dancing's not so bad, your Majesty," Honey said. She gathered up Elspeth's shoes, but stood there holding them. "Dancing's as much politeness as anything else. Except for dancing twice with the same man."

"Why is that?"

"Hasn't anyone told you the two-dance rule?" Honey bent to pick up the pouf of gauze that was Elspeth's overdress. "You only dance once with a person, because two dances says you're interested in him. And two dances in a row is how you say you're courting or even betrothed."

"I'm so glad you told me that!" That would be a mistake nobody would forget. "But I still don't know many dances, so I'm not likely to do that."

"There are so many men who'd like to be Consort, your Majesty," Honey said. She went into the dressing room with the shoes and the overdress. "One of them is bound to be perfect for you," she added, her voice muffled.

"That's what I'm afraid of," Elspeth murmured. Suppose she got tired, someday, of waiting for the right man, and settled for someone good enough? She mentally slapped herself. This was one man, one event, and she'd known going in that there was a chance he wasn't the one. She needed to stop thinking of this as a race, start enjoying herself, and take some time to learn what she wanted from a romance.

Honey said goodnight and left. Elspeth rang the other bell, and soon Shirley appeared with a pot of chocolate and cream. Elspeth drank happily, then settled into her pillows while Shirley put out the light. It occurred to her that she must be settling in to her role as Queen if she could spare mental energy enough to fret over finding a Consort. Cheered by that thought, she drifted off to sleep.

17

*E*lspeth stood at the end of the Long Gallery, gazing at her portrait, and wondered if Queens could arrange to have artists assassinated. Her chin, despite her fears, wasn't held too high, her hands looked natural clasped in her lap, she looked like herself— if herself was haughty, vain, arrogant, and convinced she ruled more of the world than Tremontane. The artist had given her a gleam in her eyes that followed the viewer, demanding they stop and pay homage to her. It was the worst painting she'd ever seen.

"You see why it's unacceptable," she told Faraday, who stood beside her, his hands clasped loosely behind his back. "It looks nothing like me."

"It looks exactly like you," Faraday said. "I'm not sure what the problem is."

"Are you saying I routinely look like I'm about to order a mass execution? Because if that's the case, then yes, it looks like me."

Faraday turned to examine Elspeth's face. Then he went back to looking at the painting. "You get that look," he said, "when you're tired of listening to your councilors debate and wish you were elsewhere. You also frequently turn that look on me when I've told you something perfectly reasonable you don't like. Just because you don't have a mirror handy on those occasions doesn't make it any less true."

Elspeth scowled. "I do not," she said, but weakly. "Besides, my point is that this is how I'm going to be immortalized, and I don't think it's a fair representation. I want a different artist. This one had it in for me."

"If your Majesty demands another sitting, of course we will arrange it."

"Stop that. I'm not being unreasonable."

"I didn't say you were."

"No, but you only call me Your Majesty when you're ready for a fight."

Faraday closed his eyes and tilted his head back, clearly praying for patience. "It's up to you if you want to spend another several weeks sitting for a portrait, which I know you love," he said. "But you asked for my honest opinion, and I've given it to you. Mistress Bennegret captured your spirit, and I think you know that and you're a little embarrassed at being exposed to the world."

Elspeth turned her attention back to the painting and cursed Faraday silently for being right. "Fine," she said. "But I'm never looking at this thing again."

"That's your prerogative. Now, can we return to the north wing? I do have other duties."

"I'm sorry. You're the first person I saw I could count on to give me an honest reaction. Everyone else who saw it just gushed about how the artist made my hair glow." Elspeth tugged on a lock of said hair, which felt particularly unmanageable that day.

"Mistress Bennegret does have a way with light," Faraday agreed. "Would you like me to bring the final birthday gala guest list for your approval this afternoon?"

"I'm not sure why. I don't know more than a fraction of the names on it. What's the purpose of me approving it? I mean in terms of tradition, or law, or whatever it is that says I should."

"The purpose is to make sure nobody is invited whom the Queen would rather not encounter on her special day."

"Oh. That actually makes sense."

Faraday gave a little half-smile. "Surprisingly, most of our traditions have their beginnings in common sense."

"Really? What's the common sense that says the Queen has to declare her interest in someone, and not the other way around? That one's enshrined in law."

"It protects the Queen, or King, from being overwhelmed by suitors. It also allows the Queen to control whom she chooses to bestow her affections on. You can't tell me you don't appreciate that."

Elspeth glanced at him; he was still smiling that crooked half-smile. "You're right. That does make sense. But it seems pretty hard on the Queen, in a culture where it's expected the man will make the advances. What happens if there's someone who'd be perfect for the Queen if only she knew he was interested?"

They rounded a corner and approached the steps to the north wing. "That would be difficult," Faraday agreed. "His only recourse would be to wait, and hope she noticed him."

"Which might never happen." Elspeth sighed. "And now I'm discouraged."

"You have plenty of time to find a Consort," Faraday said. "Don't think of it as a duty. Courtship is supposed to be fun."

"Maybe for you," Elspeth said. "You don't have a whole country speculating on what it means that you chose to dance with Mister Somebody and not Lord Somebody Else."

"True." Faraday stopped outside his office. "I can only suggest you not listen to the rumors. And don't let it make you impatient to choose a husband just to get them to stop."

"You're very sensible."

Elspeth continued down the hall to her own office. As she neared the door, Simkins stepped out of her office, the one immediately across the hall from Elspeth's, and stood waiting. "Your Majesty, Lord Harrington is here. He has no appointment, but you have some time before your one o'clock appointment."

"That's fine. I—where is he?"

"In your office."

Elspeth regarded the closed door. "I think," she said reflectively, "in future you shouldn't allow anyone to wait for me unattended in my office. I trust Lord Harrington, but doesn't it allow for the possibility of abuse?"

Simkins flushed. "I beg your pardon, your Majesty, of course it does. I thought—but you're right, even if Lord Harrington is above reproach, we cannot say the same of everyone."

"That was my thought exactly. It's all right, Miss Simkins, we both should have thought of it. So, going forward—"

"No one is to wait in your office unattended," Simkins agreed. She opened the door for Elspeth.

Lord Harrington was looking out the window toward the east wing, just visible to the extreme right. Despite what she'd said to Simkins, Elspeth cast a quick eye over her desk. Nothing appeared to be out of place. "Thank you for waiting, Lord Harrington," she said. "What can I do for you?"

"May I sit?" Lord Harrington said.

Elspeth took her seat and indicated Lord Harrington should do the same.

"I have bad news," he said. "My agents in Ruskald have been silent for over two weeks. Normally, this wouldn't be a concern, as it takes almost that much time for messages to arrive from Ranstjad. But during times of heightened international tension, they communicate more frequently. It wasn't until today that I finally heard from one of them. And the message was the worst possible news: an agent has disappeared, presumably because King Osjan discovered his existence and had him killed."

Elspeth drew in a startled breath. "Can he do that?"

Lord Harrington smiled. "My agents operate without government acknowledgement, which means without government protection. If Osjan identifies one of them, he can't make a stink about it because we'll deny the agent belongs to us, but in return, we can't make our own stink if he tortures or kills the agent, because he isn't officially ours."

"But Osjan wouldn't do that unless he believed the agent really did belong to us, right? And now he knows we're watching him."

"He knew that already. We have confidential agents in every country, just as they all have agents here. What we have to assume is that he knows everything the agent knew."

Elspeth's hand closed on a letter opener as if it could defend her. "Which is...what?"

Lord Harrington looked grim. "This particular agent fortunately didn't know any of our plans to mount a defense against a Ruskalder attack. But he was aware that the plans exist—specifically, that we know what the Ruskalder intend. That will almost certainly push Osjan into aggressing on us."

"You mean war."

He shook his head. "Not yet. Osjan won't move troops into our territory. He'll just fill that empty territory in the Riverlands with his forces, waiting for us to falter. And if we do, then..." He spread his hands wide, indicating the obvious conclusion.

"Then...am I right that we need to move our own troops into position in Barony Daxtry and Barony Avory? Matching what they're doing, essentially?"

"That's exactly what I was going to suggest. The point is—well, mainly we need to have troops in place to fight off the Ruskalder if it comes to war. But the other thing this accomplishes is to show King Osjan how good our intelligence is. If we move troops now, before his are in place, that tells him we have more agents reporting on his actions, and he might think twice before trying to surprise us."

That made sense. "All right," Elspeth said, "I—you need me to authorize moving the troops, yes? Or is that something General Beckett can do?"

"We only need your authorization to wage war. General Beckett is free to move troops through Tremontane as needed. But I thought you should be aware of what's going on."

"Thank you, Lord Harrington. I'm beginning to understand the politics of international relations, and I owe that to you."

"You've done well for someone who's been Queen for barely a

month," Lord Harrington said with a smile that for once wasn't patronizing. "I hope your reign doesn't have to begin with a war."

Elspeth controlled a shudder. "I hope that as well." She stood. "I have to go. My one o'clock appointment is crucial to the state of the nation."

"It is?" Lord Harrington looked as if he wanted to know why he hadn't been invited to such an important meeting. "What is the subject?"

This time, Elspeth didn't try to hide her shudder. "Dancing lessons."

IT TURNED OUT THERE WAS ONE TRADITION THAT ALLOWED MEN TO make advances to the Queen without breaking the law. Elspeth stood in the gold receiving room and stared in dismay at the piles of presents, brightly wrapped in colored cloth or painted wooden crates. "But," she exclaimed, "isn't this *worse* than them asking me for a dance?"

"You're free to acknowledge or ignore whatever gifts you want," Faraday said. "After they've been opened and examined by Internal Affairs. For security reasons."

Elspeth distractedly flapped a hand at him. "I understand the need for that. There's just *so many*. It's ridiculous."

"Not all of them are from single men," Veronica said in her quiet voice. "Many people like to wish the Queen a happy birthday. Of course, most of them do it for selfish reasons. They hope you'll think well of them if they give you something nice, and then when they ask for a favor, you'll be more likely to grant it."

"If I can remember them in all this...this..."

"Extravaganza?" Faraday suggested.

"I was thinking 'absurdity,' but your word works too." Elspeth sighed. "I suppose you should keep track of who gives me what, so I can have Miss Simkins write thank-you notes."

"That's not necessary," Veronica said. "Or, rather, you only need to acknowledge the ones you intend to reciprocate in some way. Anyone who receives a thank you will assume a personal interest."

"I suppose that saves Miss Simkins some time."

A uniformed servant in Tremontane colors entered, bearing a stack of wrapped gifts. Elspeth groaned. "I'm going to dress for the gala now," she said. "Is it bad that I'm actually grateful for Internal Affairs' security obsession? I don't want to see those things again until they've been unwrapped and the awful ones burned."

"Don't be so discouraged," Faraday said with a smile. "You might like some of them."

"I suppose it's possible." She'd always liked receiving gifts. She'd just never received so many all at once, nor so many that came with obligations attached.

Her gown for the birthday gala was the same old-fashioned style as her coronation gown. She'd expressed a desire to wear that gown, in fact, but Catherine Elwes had said that would make her seem common, as if she were forced to use the same gown because she wasn't wealthy enough for a new one. Elspeth had grumbled—privately; she didn't want to insult Catherine—but in the end had settled on rose-colored satin over a froth of petticoats, with a fitted waist and bodice whose neckline curved lower than she was used to. It was beautiful, but Elspeth had to stop herself hitching the neckline up to cover herself.

The *toan* jade would have made the perfect complement, green like leaves next to the rosy-pink satin, but it wasn't something you wore as jewelry. So Elspeth had selected a simple gold chain from which hung a gilded maple leaf. The keeper of the jewels had told Elspeth it was actually a real leaf that had been dipped in gold, a gift to a long-ago Queen from Barony Steepridge, and the thought had charmed Elspeth so much she often chose it over more ornate jewels.

For this occasion, she went to the ballroom early, before guests arrived, so they could be announced and introduced to her. Elspeth wasn't sure about this, given that any other Queen would have both seen the guest list and known everyone on it, but she chose to be grateful that she got even as much help remembering people as that.

Her usual chair had been moved to the end of the ballroom opposite the stairs and placed upon a low dais erected for the occasion. She sat and looked around. The decorators had outdone themselves; fluttering, cascading lengths of white or pink gauze draped the walls, giving the vast room a surprisingly intimate feeling. The chandeliers had been lowered, brightening the room and making the floor with its gradient pattern of light to dark woods seem to flow underfoot. That was a strange sensation, and Elspeth hoped it wouldn't make dancing difficult. It was already going to be hard enough.

She'd mastered six dances and was adequate in two more, which ought to be enough so long as she chose the right partners. She reminded herself of what Faraday had said and resolved to take his advice. Courtship should be fun, and she intended to have fun. Besides, she was the Queen, and this was her birthday. Nobody had better criticize her on her day.

That thought made her remember Lady Quinn, who was celebrating her birthday as well. She'd been on the guest list, but Elspeth hoped she didn't feel obligated to attend the gala. Sharing a birthday with the Queen must be something like having a Wintersmeet birthday. You'd always be lost in the celebrations. Elspeth also hoped this wasn't the end of any chance of her becoming friends with Lady Quinn. The Countess of Waxwold was shy and quiet, but Elspeth had seen her laugh and concluded there was someone worth knowing inside that shy cocoon.

The trumpets rang out a fanfare, more to alert the Queen to her guests' arrival than anything else, she thought. A couple appeared at the top of the steps and made their way down to the ballroom floor. Elspeth sat up straight. The page in North blue who stood beside her came to attention as well. "Lord and Lady Harrington, your Majesty," she said as the couple drew closer.

"Lord Harrington, it's good to see you," Elspeth said. "And Lady Harrington. It's been a while."

"It has, your Majesty." Lady Alice Harrington curtseyed to Elspeth exactly as if she respected her, which Elspeth knew she didn't. Lady Harrington didn't like any of Prince Sebastian's children, though it was hardly as if she'd seen them often enough to make that decision. It didn't help that the children, when much younger, had played a trick on Lady Harrington that she had never forgotten or forgiven, or that Elspeth had never groveled sufficiently for forgiveness, as far as Lady Harrington was concerned. Elspeth smiled, and nurtured her satisfaction at seeing Lady Harrington abase herself close to her heart.

"Our best wishes for your happiness on this day," Lord Harrington said. "I assume your parents have sent their greetings?"

She wished he hadn't said that. "Of course," she said around the sudden lump in her throat. "It's too bad they couldn't be here."

"Soon enough, I imagine. Midsummer, perhaps?"

"I hope so." Elspeth managed a smile. "Please enjoy your evening."

The two bowed again, and the page stepped up to announce the next guest, a tall, attractive man who was unfortunately too old for her. She smiled, and said meaningless pleasantries, and was relieved when he moved on.

The introductions soon became a blur. She tried to hold on to the names of the young men, at least, but there were so many, and none of them were more than a name and a face and perhaps a pair of well-turned legs. She had to admit the fashion for knee breeches suited almost all her male guests. Too bad Mihn wouldn't be there; he looked simultaneously handsome and ridiculous in Tremontanan men's fashion. But his father had required his presence for some diplomatic function. Elspeth suspected Elizdo had exaggerated his need for his son's attendance out of spite.

"Mister Duncan Faraday," the page said, and Elspeth sat up from where she'd been slouching a bit.

"You're not here to tell me there's some Internal Affairs crisis only I can resolve, are you?" she asked eagerly.

Faraday smiled and swept her a completely unironic bow. He had very nice legs, too, she noticed. "Unfortunately for you, no," he said. "I am here to wish you a happy birthday and remind you that you are supposed to be enjoying yourself."

"I will be once the introductions are over," she said. "I'm actually looking forward to dancing, isn't that strange?"

"Not strange at all." Faraday glanced behind himself. "And I believe the last of the guests are arriving."

"Then I can endure a few more minutes."

Faraday nodded and strolled off. Elspeth looked toward the top of the stairs—yes, there didn't appear to be anyone else entering, and maybe now she could get up and stretch discreetly. She glanced around before the next guests approached. How under heaven was she to locate the men she wanted to dance with? The room was thronged with people.

As the page announced Mister Gould, and Elspeth pretended not to remember him—it was rude, but she didn't want to fall into a conversation about her rejecting his pavilion design—an idea struck her. It might be unusual, but she was sure it didn't break tradition, and it would ease her burden considerably. After the page had announced the last guests, an elderly couple who seemed to see the event as a social nicety rather than anything they personally cared about, Elspeth said to the young woman, "You know all these people, yes? I mean, you didn't have some kind of secret list up your sleeve?"

"No, your Majesty. I memorized the guest list, and I know almost everyone here," the page said.

"Then I want you to help me," Elspeth said.

She sent the page on her way and waited for the dance music to begin. The musicians playing quiet, nondescript tunes sat on a balcony above and behind her, which made it impossible for her to watch them from her seat without looking foolish, so instead she listened. The hum of conversation swept over her, with the soft background music threading through it. The ballroom still felt cool, though that wouldn't last long as the heat from nearly a hundred bodies filled it. Dancing would only make her warmer, and she briefly regretted that formal fashion didn't mean the muslin garden party dress. But her gown was beautiful, and so was she, and she intended to enjoy herself.

The musicians struck a loud, melodic chord, and the movement of the crowd became more intentional as men and women sought each other out for the first dance. As Faraday had promised, it was one she knew. Elspeth sat up straight and scanned the crowd. There was the page, returning, with—

"Lord Erickson," she said, stepping down from the dais. "Thank you for accepting my invitation."

"It's my pleasure," the young man said. He didn't look at all upset about having been asked to dance by proxy, and Elspeth relaxed further. He offered her his hand and escorted her to where the couples were forming up. To her relief, Elspeth discovered Faraday had been right about something else: no one seemed inclined to make a fuss about the Queen joining the company, or to make everyone move so she could be at the center of the ballroom.

The dance wasn't one that allowed for conversation, so afterward Elspeth drew Lord Erickson away with her in search of a drink and kept him chatting for the course of the next dance. It was enough time for the page to secure Elspeth another dance partner, who also didn't mind being asked indirectly. Elspeth danced, and drank punch —it was *her* party, damn it, and if she didn't want wine she wasn't going to have it—and danced again. The gentlemen were friendly, and most of them were interesting, and even the ones who weren't made her feel comfortable—

The doors at the top of the stairs slammed open. "You—you *tjorben!*" shouted the Ruskalder ambassador, Larssin. He scanned the crowd until he saw Elspeth. Roaring incoherently in fury, he ran down the stairs. Guards who'd been standing unobtrusively throughout the ballroom leapt into motion, bringing him to the ground at the foot of the stairs. Larssin screamed something else in Ruskalder.

Elspeth walked toward the ambassador, mesmerized by his fury. Then Faraday was in front of her, putting her well behind him. "Don't," he said. "He's dangerous. The guards will remove him."

"What is a *tjorben?*"

"I don't know. Please, your Majesty, stay back."

Elspeth came to a halt. "Get him up," she said.

The guards looked to Faraday for instruction. He hesitated, then nodded curtly. The guards hauled Larssin to his feet.

"Excuse me, your Majesty," Lord Harrington said. "Let me—"

"Ambassador Larssin has something on his mind," Elspeth said. "I want to know what it is."

Larssin strained briefly against the guards' hold, then subsided. "You bring war to our country," he snarled. "You attack us. We say you *tjorben.*"

"It means 'traitor,'" Lord Harrington murmured. "More or less."

"That's so much better than what I thought," Elspeth said. "Ambassador, you accuse us of pursuing war when your country moved its troops first. We are simply prepared to defend ourselves."

"*That is lie,*" Larssin shouted. "We have move nothing. You want our land. I say you make war."

"Ambassador," Lord Harrington said, "you have no proof. We, on the other hand, have been aware of your preparations for some time now. We will not start a war, but we will finish one."

Larssin spat on the ground near Elspeth's feet, causing a commotion among the nearby guests. "You want war, we give you war," he said.

"Enough," Elspeth said. "We can go around pointing fingers all night. We know the truth, ambassador, and I suggest perhaps you should return to your King and tell him so."

The murmur grew louder. "Is that wise, your Majesty?" Lord Harrington said. "Expelling an ambassador can have serious consequences."

"What? I didn't—oh, that's not what I meant." Elspeth faced Larssin directly, though his maddened eyes and straining muscles frightened her. It wouldn't matter if her guards killed him if he got a lucky blow in on her first. "Tremontane does not wish war with Ruskald. We invite you to send word to your King to that effect. But if you burst in on the Queen's presence again, we will take that as an act of war. You can tell King Osjan that, too."

Larssin wrestled free of the guards, though several of them and Faraday stood between him and Elspeth. "I tell him truth," Larssin snarled. "Tremontane lies. We stand ready to fight." He turned and stumped back up the stairs and out the door, slamming one of them behind him.

Faraday turned on the guard captain who'd been the first to tackle Larssin. "Explain to me," he said in a low voice that could have cut steel, "how you let a threat to her Majesty make it far enough that *I* was her last line of defense!"

"I take responsibility, sir," the captain said, drawing himself up without a hint of fear. "The ambassador was on the guest list, and we believed him to be a late arrival. He didn't show aggression until he entered the room."

"It's true, he was on the list," Elspeth said. "I remember feeling grateful that he'd decided not to come. And I don't think he was armed just now."

"Being unarmed doesn't make someone harmless," Faraday said to Elspeth, his eyes never leaving the captain's face. "See me in the morning, captain. I'll take your explanation into account."

Elspeth let out a long, calming breath. "Well, that was exciting," she said loudly. A ragged laugh went around the room, the sound of nervous people realizing the danger was over. "I think we need an exciting dance. Mister Faraday, would you care to dance with me?"

Faraday jerked in surprise. "I—" he said. For the first time since Elspeth had known him, he looked uncertain.

"We need to talk," Elspeth said under her breath.

Faraday nodded. He made his bow, and Elspeth curtseyed in return, reflecting how grateful she was that this was a dance she knew, if imperfectly. They clasped hands, he put his other hand on her waist, and they spun off into the steps of the dance.

"I almost accidentally sent the Ruskalder ambassador home," Elspeth said. "I must be more shaken than I thought."

"You were in no danger," Faraday said. "But I admit to being shaken myself. If the Ruskalder really were behind the assassination attempts—"

"You don't believe that, do you? It seems a little obvious."

"No, I don't. But if they wanted you dead, a direct attack seems more typically their style."

"That's what I wanted to discuss. Why would Larssin burst in like that and accuse *us* of aggressing when they're the ones who started it?"

Faraday looked over Elspeth's shoulder. "Isn't that something you should ask Lord Harrington?"

"I don't want to dance with him. Besides, his wife would have me assassinated if I did, and then we wouldn't have to worry about the Ruskalder."

"You don't mean she's jealous of you? Because the idea of you being interested in Lord Harrington—"

"Ew, no. She just hates me."

"Lady Harrington? I didn't think she hated anyone."

Elspeth snorted, a quiet but indelicate sound of mirth. "My brother and I might have been responsible for her having to shave her head and wear a wig about six years ago."

Faraday's eyes went wide. Then amusement lit his eyes, transforming his whole face. Elspeth had never seen him so close to bursting out laughing. "That was *you*?" he said. His jaw was tight, not from anger, but from his efforts to contain himself. "Sweet heaven. I would never have guessed. Please tell me this is something the priestesses taught you."

"No, it was Mihn. And you shouldn't laugh and encourage me. Who knows where I might strike next?"

Faraday shook his head. "That was an excellent distraction, but I think we should stay on task. You're right that it's odd, Larssin accusing us of warmongering. It's more likely, if they found out about our preparations for defense, that they'd keep quiet and advance *their* preparations."

"That's what I thought. So what does it mean?"

"I don't know. That really is something to discuss with Lord Harrington."

"Or with the Council. I'll call an emergency session for tomorrow.

If Ruskalder is more on the verge of war than we thought, we need to be prepared."

"Good idea." Faraday swung her around as the music came to an end. "I'm afraid that wasn't a very enjoyable dance. I've robbed you of the opportunity to audition a suitor."

Elspeth made a face that dissolved into laughter. "That is *not*...all right, it is, a bit."

Faraday bowed. "Thank you, your Majesty, for your generosity in sharing your time with me."

Elspeth curtseyed. "Thank *you*, Mister Faraday, for generously not complaining when I stepped on your toes."

"I consider it a sacrifice for the good of the country," Faraday said, and smiled.

18

"*I*n conclusion," Lord Harrington said, leaning forward to rest his hands on the ancient round table, "we must assume that Ambassador Larssin's outburst was meant to garner international sympathy. He claims we are the aggressors, so when his country attacks Tremontane, Eskandel and Veribold will support Ruskald's action." He sat and interlaced his fingers in front of him.

"Thank you, Lord Harrington," Elspeth said. "Ladies and gentlemen, any comments?"

Master Keswick rose. "Ruskald honors bold action," he said. "King Osjan's actions in moving his troops secretly must go against his instincts. It may be that the ambassador's verbal assault was also intended to give Ruskald a pretext for moving openly."

Elspeth glanced at Lord Harrington, who nodded once. "Thank you, Master Keswick, that is a valuable insight. Anyone else?"

Lady Wilde rose as Master Keswick sat down. "We should approach this problem from the direction we intend to take. We want to avoid war. What actions will help us do that?"

"If Ruskald is intent on war, we have to respond to that," General Beckett said. "We can't let them walk over us."

"True," said Lady Wilde, "but I assume that will be our last resort.

What I'm asking is, is there anything we can do to minimize the chance of Ruskald attacking?"

"Not much," Lord Harrington said. "If we show even the slightest weakness, they'll see that as an opportunity. Even withdrawing our forces at this point might be what sets them off."

"But there has to be something we can do," Elspeth said. "What would they accept as a peace offering? Something they wouldn't see as a weakness?"

Lord Harrington shook his head. "I can't think of anything. We're at an impasse."

"Maybe not," Master Keswick said. He pressed his fingers to his lips thoughtfully. "There's an old tradition among the Ruskalder people, dating from when the clans weren't so interconnected. They were more like independent tribes back then. Anyway, when one tribe wanted to show respect to another, as a precursor to joining more closely—like in marriage or adoption—it would send a token of its respect. The token would be something very important to the donor tribe, and giving it to the second tribe was a gesture of trust. A way of saying they respected the second tribe and believed them worthy guardians of the token."

Elspeth sat up straighter. "And it wasn't seen as weakness?"

"No, quite the opposite. The strength of the donor tribe was implicit in the token they gave. Meaning that the tribe had to be strong to even make the offering. Kind of like how a rich man doesn't miss the two guilders he gives to a beggar."

Elspeth turned to Lord Harrington again. "What do you think?"

"I've never heard of that," Lord Harrington said. "Are you sure it's not such an old tradition it's been forgotten, Master Keswick?"

"Fairly sure. Nowadays it's associated with marriage settlements, but any Ruskalder would know the significance if it came from a rival clan or, as in our case, a foreign country."

"And it's something they would recognize as showing we intend no malice," Elspeth said. "Thank you, Master Keswick. Do you think you could come up with a suitable, um, token?"

"I do, if you think you can part with Jeramen's Bequest," Master Keswick said.

"What?" exclaimed Lord Harrington.

Elspeth eyed him in concern. "I don't know what that is."

"It's a priceless relic of Tremontanan history," Lord Harrington said. "It's impossible."

"It's a wooden shield carved with a map of Tremontane, and it's ideal," Master Keswick said. "The symbolism is potent—handing over Tremontane, so to speak, and therefore putting its safety in Ruskalder hands. It would suggest strongly that Ruskald going to war against Tremontane is a breach of honor."

"Jeramen's Bequest is four hundred and sixty-two years old," Lord Harrington said. "It was carved after the Battle of Aurilien to symbolize how no one would fight over the city again."

"Until Willow North did three hundred and fifty-seven years later," Elspeth said. "If it can prevent an actual war, I think it's worth the sacrifice. Master Keswick, I'll need your help drafting a letter."

"Of course, your Majesty."

Lord Harrington still looked stunned. "It's all right, Lord Harrington," Elspeth said comfortingly, "just think of the stories our children will tell about how we used history to make history. Ladies and gentlemen, that's all. We'll have our regular weekly meeting in five days. Thank you."

She sat, waiting, until the room cleared and she and Lord Harrington were alone. "I'm sorry to overrule you, Lord Harrington, but I really believe that relic is best used in this manner."

"I understand, your Majesty. That's not what concerns me."

Elspeth gestured for him to sit. He pushed out Lady Quinn's empty chair and lowered himself heavily into it, as if his joints pained him. Since he was normally very hale for his sixty years, Elspeth felt uneasy.

"Master Keswick's solution is ingenious," he said, "but it will only work if Ruskald is not intent on waging war. If they are, no number of ingenious solutions will help us. I believe we still need to be prepared for an attack."

"I agree with you," Elspeth said, "which is why I haven't asked General Beckett to withdraw the troops from Daxtry and Avory. I don't think we should be careless. But I also don't want to appear so aggressive the Ruskalder feel compelled to attack us to protect their honor. So we're going to stand down. Keep the troops in place where they are, but minimize our martial actions."

Lord Harrington shook his head. "I'm not sure that's wise."

"I know, but I think it's a fair compromise. I have faith in your agents and their ability to keep us informed in a timely fashion." Elspeth smiled. "Weren't you impressed with Master Keswick's solution? I really do feel encouraging Masters from the Scholia to take part in our government is a good idea."

"I admit I wouldn't have thought of that," Lord Harrington said. "Very well. I'll pass on the word that the troops are to stand down— without looking like they're turning tail."

"Perfect," Elspeth said. "I'm off to dinner. Please give my regards to Lady Harrington." She managed to say it with a straight face. Lady Harrington had never given her husband any indication of her animosity toward Sebastian North's children, and Elspeth didn't intend to enlighten him.

She hurried back to the east wing, hunger putting a spring in her step. It had been a long morning, and would be a long afternoon, especially if she had to make time for writing an appeasing but firm letter to Larssin. Maybe she could do that after she ate—no, it wasn't fair to make Master Keswick miss his dinner just to make her life easier.

She hurried into the drawing room and came to a dead stop. "Oh, my," she said, involuntarily covering her mouth as if to hold back a stronger exclamation.

The round table that normally stood beneath the northern windows had been pulled away from the wall, and heaps of packages, small boxes, books, and folded piles of fabric lay upon it. Larger items sat on the floor nearby, including an ivory statue of a collie, sitting alertly upright, and a rotating book stand with ornate metal grilles on two of its four faces.

Elspeth's earlier objections to the gifts evaporated. She approached the pile with something like awe. So much—and all of it for her—it was incredible. She sank to her knees and pushed on the book stand to make it spin slowly. It was just the right height to go next to the armchair in her sitting room. She eyed the ivory statue with skepticism—attractive, but for a specialized taste, and she liked cats better than dogs—and tried to think where she might put it.

"It's dizzying, isn't it," Veronica said, startling Elspeth. "I remember Landon's first birthday as King. We had such fun deciding what to do with all the gifts he didn't intend to keep. It's a challenge, because you can't just give them away, but you aren't obligated to keep them...anyway."

"Let's eat quickly," Elspeth said, "and you can help me. It sounds like a fun game."

She'd never eaten dinner so quickly, feeling the pull of the pile of gifts like a hook embedded in her flesh, but gentle rather than sharp. When she finally returned to the drawing room, though, she stood in front of the table, unable to decide where to begin.

"The fabric," Veronica suggested. "Some of it may even fit."

Only one of the folded piles of fabric turned out to be a gown, far too large for Elspeth, and she set it aside quickly. The others were shawls, scarves, and even unfinished lengths of cloth, some of them exotic, one of them a Veriboldan silk that brought tears to Elspeth's eyes. Each item came with a card upon which was written the giver's name and a description of the gift. Elspeth sorted the fabric into two piles and gave Veronica the cards of the items she intended to keep. Veronica was right, this was fun.

It turned out the book stand was a gift from Lord Erickson. Delighted, Elspeth added his card to the "keep" pile. Tucked inside one of the grilles was a bound copy of Lord Erickson's most famous poem, signed by the poet. Elspeth made a mental note to thank him for that as well. The young lord moved to the top of the list Elspeth wasn't quite prepared to admit she had.

Some of the packages had been opened and re-wrapped, for which Elspeth thanked Faraday or his helpful assistants. Opening presents was much more fun than simply being handed a gift. About half the items were unsuitable in some way: the wrong size, an unattractive color, too intimate, *far* too intimate—she and Veronica laughed over the silk undergarments from a young man Elspeth remembered as examining her as if he wanted to use his hands rather than his eyes. Some of them were just odd, like the mounted fish skeleton and the lump of glass whose purpose even Faraday's people hadn't been able to divine; they'd just marked the card with a ?

But the remaining half were splendid: new books with the pages uncut, old books that smelled deliciously of worn leather and sharp ink, an elegant necklace from Eskandel of polished jasper and onyx, a pen set with a crystal jar of bright blue ink, Devices that did everything from shedding a warm light to playing music with a touch, and pragmatic things like a set of silver soup spoons impressed with the North sign and shield or a pair of opera glasses similarly marked. They were things that said the giver had given some serious thought to what Elspeth North might like, and it warmed her heart even as her head reminded her that all of this had a mercenary motive as well.

She picked up a cubical box about four inches on a side and shook it gently, hearing something rattle dully inside. "I know I should stay at least a little cynical, but if these men intend me to think better of them because of their gifts, I have to admit the ploy works. That book stand is lovely."

Veronica squared up her stack of cards and tapped them against her palm. "If they choose the right gifts, that already is a mark in their favor."

"That's what I thought." The cubical box came in two parts. She worked the top off and set it aside, then looked into the box, and froze.

"Ohhhh," she breathed, lifting out the bracelet inside. It was a bangle of creamy jade the width of her first two fingers and the exact color of her medallion, delicately carved and smooth as soap. Elspeth slipped it over her wrist and ran her fingers over its surface, and received another shock. "It's the fifth meditation ritual," she said.

"The path of harmony." She touched the deep carvings again: *that which is two becomes one, but much must be shed to reach it.* How had *anyone* in Tremontane known to give her this?

"Where's the card that came with this?" she demanded.

"I didn't see one," Veronica said. "Why?"

"It must be from Mihn," Elspeth said, sitting back on her heels and turning the bracelet one way and the other. Mihn would know whom to buy from in Veribold, and the bracelets weren't uncommon there. The trouble was, Mihn also knew enough not to buy a bracelet engraved with the path of harmony for a woman he wasn't in love with. *That which is two becomes one*...even Elspeth knew that for a declaration of love. She couldn't accept this. She *wanted* to accept this. The bracelet spoke to her on a level she never knew was part of her.

She went through the rest of the gifts, but some of the wonder had worn off, supplanted by her curiosity about the bracelet. No extra cards turned up at the end. None of the cards mentioned a bracelet at all.

Finally, Elspeth sat back and examined the much diminished pile. "I know I said I would let Miss Simkins write the thank-you notes," she said, "but so many of them are personal, I feel I want to do it myself."

"Landon always let his secretary write them," Veronica said. "But his handwriting was awful, so there's that."

Elspeth idly spun the bracelet on her wrist. It had grown warm from her body heat. "And then there's this," she said, tapping it. "I shouldn't accept a gift if I don't know who sent it. Who knows what kind of message that would send?"

Veronica regarded it. "It's beautiful, and it's clearly perfect for you. Whoever sent it put a lot of thought into choosing it. Why not wear it, and show it matters to you?"

"And suppose the card was just lost, and I'm inadvertently telling the giver I'm in love with him? I can't risk it. Especially if I don't know the person. What if it's someone horrible like Mister Gibbons, or boring like Lord Folsom?" She gasped. "What if it's someone who paid someone else to figure out what I'd like?"

"Now you're just working yourself up over nothing," Veronica said. She handed Elspeth the stack of cards. "Wear it, or don't. But definitely keep it."

Nothing could compel Elspeth to get rid of it. She slipped it off her wrist and put it back into its box and closed the lid securely. After summoning Gloria and giving her instructions about the disposition of the gifts, she took the little box into her bedroom and set it on her bedside table. It sat there quietly, not at all like it contained something precious. Twice she reached out for it, twice she withdrew her hand before she could touch it. Finally, she turned and ran from the room.

She set the stack of cards on the table in her sitting room along with the pen set, promising herself she would write messages to each gift-giver after supper. Then she turned and looked back at her bedroom door. If she wore it...maybe the mystery giver didn't know the significance. Maybe he thought it was just a pretty gift suitable for someone who'd almost been an Irantzen priestess. Maybe it wasn't a "he" at all. It could be a woman who wanted to be friends, or an older couple honoring Elspeth's faith. But if it wasn't...

She left her suite and headed back to the north wing. Somebody in Faraday's department must know more.

"I didn't open the gifts, your Majesty, but I can send you the ones who did," said Miss Chisholm, Faraday's liaison with the palace's Army detachment and security supervisor. "Were you not pleased with them?"

"Some of them were wonderful," Elspeth said. "I just had a question about one or two."

She walked slowly to her office, her mind still caught up in thinking about the bracelet. If it *was* from a young man, and it *was* a declaration of love, why wouldn't he have signed his name? It would be an easy way around the law that said she had to speak first. Except...it couldn't possibly be love, given that she barely knew anyone in Aurilien. It must be a mistake. The giver had picked it not understanding its true significance.

She sat in her office, going over a series of reports Master Keswick had produced about improving the post horse routes without really reading them, until a knock on the door preceded a couple of people in Tremontane colors. They were a middle-aged man and an elderly woman, and they looked around curiously as if they'd always wondered what the Queen's office looked like. "You sent for us, your Majesty?" the man said. "Something about your gifts?"

"Yes," Elspeth said. "There was a box with no card. Did either of you see that?"

They exchanged glances. "I don't...actually, yes, your Majesty," the woman said. "It was a jade bracelet, as I recall. There was no name attached when we received it. It might have fallen off—the gifts are delivered to the front door, and taken from there to the gold receiving room, and then they're collected by Internal Affairs and taken to where they can be examined. You can see how that might make for something going missing."

"So you don't have any idea who sent it?"

"I'm afraid not, your Majesty," the man said. "Mister Faraday approved everything we examined, so he must have thought it didn't matter if the gift-giver's name was missing."

"We might be able to find out, if it's important," the woman said, examining Elspeth's face closely.

"Could you?" Elspeth asked, hope surging up inside her.

"Well, it's possible," the woman said. "But it wouldn't be private. We'd have to make some kind of announcement."

"Oh," Elspeth said, feeling deflated. She definitely didn't want to make this public, like some kind of newspaper advertisement: WANTED—Young man, single, hopefully handsome, knows how to pick the perfect gift. "No, that's all right. Thank you."

"We hope your birthday was lovely," the woman said, and the two bowed themselves out.

Elspeth sank back into her chair and propped her chin in her hand, sighing. The perfect gift, and she didn't dare wear it. How depressing.

She felt flat the whole rest of the day, her mind circling around the possibilities and continually coming to the same conclusion: she couldn't wear someone's declaration of love if she didn't know who'd sent it. She gave only half her attention to Keswick's instructions about the letter to send with the token to the Ruskalder embassy, enough to feel confident it said the right thing. Even in her depressed state, she admired what an ideal solution Keswick had come up with.

That evening, she dressed for a diplomatic reception at the Eskandelic embassy. It wasn't until she was looking at herself in the dressing room mirror that she realized she'd unconsciously chosen a pale green silk evening gown with a cloth-of-gold cape and shoes to match. Colors the jade bracelet was a perfect match for.

She removed it from its box and slipped it over her wrist. Its cool, smooth texture felt wonderful under her fingers, which sought out the meditation ritual instinctively: *that which is two becomes one, but much must be shed to reach it.* Ordinarily, that would take her back in memory to the temple. Tonight it only made her wonder who had reached out to her in such an extraordinary fashion.

She removed the bracelet and spun it around one finger. Honey, entering the dressing room bearing Elspeth's wrap, necessary on these chilly early spring nights, saw it and exclaimed, "Oh, that's beautiful! Wherever did you get it?"

"I don't know. It was an anonymous gift." Elspeth stopped its spinning and held it close to her heart. Then, with a muttered curse, she slid it on. She was tired of letting fear and uncertainty rule her. The person who'd chosen the bracelet, whoever that was, was someone she wanted to know better. If she was wrong, and wearing it encouraged the wrong person, she'd just have to deal with that. Because if she was right...that was an outcome worth the risk.

The Eskandelic embassy was an unusually short stone mansion, only two stories tall, that its neighbors dwarfed. A man and a woman in traditional Eskandelic formal wear, a deeply pleated skirt and a cropped jacket open over bare skin, greeted Elspeth and Lord

Harrington as they entered. Elspeth always wondered if the women disliked being virtually naked in that getup. Surely the fabric must chafe sensitive skin. And suppose a wind came up and blew the jacket open? She fingered her cloth-of-gold cape. The Eskandelics probably thought her native clothing was strange and uncomfortable, too.

The embassy front door led directly to an atrium, open to the night sky and lit by torches that flickered in the light evening breeze. Its floor was a mosaic of tiny tiles that must have taken months to assemble. Elspeth couldn't tell what it depicted, not in the torchlight, so she found a passing servant and asked. "It a circle of moons is, Majesty," the man said. "The phases of the moon symbolic to Eskandel are, that rulers come and go but Eskandel in unity is."

That sounded lovely. She accepted a glass of wine she had no intention of drinking from the servant, and with Harrington close behind her, moved off through the crowd, though there really weren't enough people to call it a crowd. It seemed most of the guests had passed through the atrium into the garden. Elspeth followed them through the giant stained glass arch that caught the torchlight and fractured it into colored swatches that stained the great flag-stones of the garden path. *This* was how she wished her garden looked, none of those pavilion monstrosities. She resolved to tackle the ambassador, Torossian Enzesh, and find out who'd designed the embassy.

The path led through a series of low hedges defining spaces containing round tables and tall stools, at which sat guests conversing in low voices. More guests drifted along the path, which disappeared into a much taller arrangement of hedge walls. A maze. Fascinated, Elspeth walked faster, leaving Lord Harrington behind, and soon was swallowed up by the hedges.

More torches lit the living walls at intervals, creating flickering shadows that made strange shapes on the stone path and the narrow strips of grass that grew on either side. It was hard to tell where the walls began and ended, and Elspeth more than once came up short against a hedge wall that turned sharply to the left. Before long, she was pleasantly lost, with the sound of people laughing and talking the only evidence that she wasn't alone in the maze.

She came to an open area containing a statue of a nude woman, her back arched painfully, thrusting her hips and breasts to the sky. It had such pent-up power Elspeth set her glass down at its base and looked at it for a while, thinking about the artist and what she or he had felt in creating something so beautiful.

She heard someone emerge from the maze and turned, wanting to share her thoughts with the newcomer. The man was Ruskalder, dressed neatly in the suede shirt and trousers Elspeth now recognized as Ruskalder formal wear. His flat, emotionless demeanor sent a shiver of fear through her that she dismissed. Just because the Ruskalder ambassador was angry with her and with Tremontane didn't mean every Ruskalder she encountered would be hostile.

She summoned up a smile, and said, "This isn't the kind of art Tremontane goes in for, but it's beautiful, don't you think?"

The Ruskalder smiled back at her. His smile wasn't nearly so nice. One of his teeth was gold, and it glinted in the torchlight. Then he brought his right hand out from behind his back, and to the glint of gold was added the gleam of silver as the torchlight illuminated a long, wicked knife.

19

_E_lspeth screamed and ran. There were four exits from the maze center, and she took the nearest one. It wasn't the one she'd entered by—that was blocked by the assassin—but the one next to it. She had no idea where it went, or even if the random turns she took were bringing her closer to the exit. All she could think was a mind-numbing chorus screaming _run, run,_ and her feet thudding out a bass counterpoint to that melody.

She heard someone coming after her, close enough that she could hear his heavy breathing, and she screamed again. Surely someone would come to her rescue. Her pursuer grabbed her cloth-of-gold cape and dragged her backward, choking her. Desperately, she fumbled with the pins and freed one of them, allowing her to tear free of the assassin's grasp before his knife could fall.

She ran again, her breath sobbing out of her, and crashed into a wall. She couldn't help it; she turned to see how close the assassin was, and screamed again at the sight of him rounding a corner, far too close. Where the _hell_ was everyone? She could still hear laughter nearby, as if her screams meant nothing. She pushed off from the wall and ran.

She stumbled around yet another corner and tripped over the

edge of a flagstone that was slightly tipped out of true. This time, voices exclaimed, and hands supported her to a standing position. She wrenched free and staggered away from the maze. That assassin might not care about bystanders, if all he needed was for her to be dead.

Then there were screams, and Elspeth turned to see the assassin silhouetted against the opening to the maze, his knife held high. He surveyed the crowd, then fixed his gaze on Elspeth and snarled. She recoiled. The man turned and bolted back into the maze.

"Follow him!" someone shouted, and servants ran after the fleeing assassin. Someone new came to stand by her side. "They will catch him," Torossian Enzesh said. He laid a reassuring hand on her shoulder. "You shaking are," he went on. "Please, sit. Bring wine for her Majesty."

Elspeth realized he was right, and she was shaking hard enough that her knees couldn't support her. She sank into a chair the ambassador pulled out for her and accepted the glass he pressed into her hand. Without thinking, she drank, and barely managed not to make a face at the taste of the alcohol. But it warmed her all the way to her core, and she found the shaking had diminished. She set the glass aside and said, "I'm all right. He didn't hurt me."

"I apologize, your Majesty. I cannot express how devastated I am, that an attacker here in my own embassy able you to attack was." Torossian's normally tan face was pale, and he wrung his hands like a fainting maiden in a melodrama. "We will find him. And the Ruskalder ambassador will explain himself to you personally."

Elspeth really didn't want to face Larssin, but this wasn't something she should pass off on Lord Harrington, wherever he was. She looked around at the gathered crowd, most of whom looked as if they thought this was great entertainment. Anger surged through her, and she stood. "I am not here for your entertainment," she said. "Where is Ambassador Larssin? I insist on speaking with him immediately."

A murmur went up as the crowd tried to shuffle away. In the distance, Elspeth heard shouting in Ruskeldin. Two voices. That might be Lord Harrington, berating the ambassador. She walked in that direction, the crowd parting for her like the sea in the wake of a battleship, and soon saw Lord Harrington and Larssin facing each other, shouting over one another so none of their words were intelligible.

As she drew near, Larssin shook his fist in Lord Harrington's face and shouted, "Is not true! Ruskald does not want Queen dead!"

"Ruskald would benefit if Tremontane were in turmoil—or do you still deny you are poised to attack the Riverlands?" Lord Harrington shouted back.

"No proof that assassin was Ruskalder. Lies!"

"I saw him myself, Ambassador Larssin," Elspeth said coldly. She didn't raise her voice, but it cut across the argument and silenced both men. "He was one of your men."

Larssin's eyes widened. "You lie."

"I nearly *died*, ambassador!" Elspeth shouted, feeling the shakes return at the thought. "I know what I saw. A Ruskalder tried to kill me. Don't you *dare* try to weasel out of this."

Larssin looked confused. Possibly he didn't understand the expression. "I swear on my life," he said, breathing heavily, "we do not do this thing. If it is Ruskalder, is not mine."

"When we catch him, we'll see," Elspeth said. "But I say you're the one who's lying."

A commotion from the direction of the hedge maze drew Elspeth's attention from the ambassador. Eskandelic servants rushed past her through the atrium and out the front door. "Your Majesty," Torossian said. "They have found the man. He dead is."

"Dead? They killed him?" Elspeth felt irritated. Faraday needed to interrogate him.

Torossian turned to one of the servants—no, he was an armed guard—and spoke to him in liquid Eskandelic that sounded like rainfall. The guard responded with a few words. "He says the man fell from the wall and broke his neck," Torossian went on. "They will bring him, but your Majesty should return to the palace. It not a good thing is, death to witness."

Elspeth wanted to protest, but her knees were still weak and the shaking was getting worse. "I want to know everything you learn," she told Lord Harrington. "Get Mister Faraday down here immediately. And *you*—" she pointed at Larssin, who took a startled step back— "if I hear one word out of you, I'm sending you back to Ranstjad, and damn the consequences." She strode rapidly through the atrium, hoping momentum would carry her to her carriage without letting her fall.

Safely inside her carriage, surrounded by guards, she curled up in a corner and hugged herself. The guards on the carriage had stayed with it because it would have been an insult to her Eskandelic hosts to bring them inside, implying she believed she wasn't safe there. Well, she clearly hadn't been safe. Faraday would be furious when he found out she'd been unattended, even though it was standard procedure. And it wasn't Eskandel's fault if a member of the Ruskalder diplomatic party, one who hadn't been obviously armed, had turned out to be an assassin.

Though...Elspeth remembered how Larssin had looked, fighting with Lord Harrington. That had been fear, not just anger. And Larssin might be many things, but stupid wasn't one of them. So why had he arranged such an obvious attack? Even the Ruskalder national trait of boldness couldn't excuse that.

She let her guards escort her to the east wing, where Honey helped her undress. Honey exclaimed over the ruined cape and listened in horror to her mistress's story. "Your Majesty," she said, "if they'd killed you—"

"We wouldn't be having this conversation," Elspeth said wearily. "It's all right, Honey. I wasn't even hurt, and I'm not scared anymore." This was true. She wasn't scared; she was angry. Angry with the Ruskalder for being so obsessed with war, angry with herself for her carelessness, angry with Francis for dropping dead and mixing her up in this mess.

She put on her nightgown and then her dressing gown, and put the bracelet away in its box. She'd almost forgotten she was wearing it in the terror of the attack. Funny how your priorities changed when you were running for your life.

She declined Shirley's offer of chocolate or herbal tea or even water. Her stomach still churned with agitation even though the shakes had stopped. She walked on steady feet to the drawing room, pulled a chair closer to the fire, and waited. She'd never seen the fire be put out, though surely they must extinguish it during summer. Though this room might be cool even on Midsummer. If she managed not to be assassinated, she would find out. She laughed, realized she sounded hysterical, and made herself stop.

Eventually, she heard the east wing door slam, and someone hurried down the hall, someone whose heavy footsteps sounded as if he wanted to trample his enemies under his feet. She continued to face the fireplace. When she heard the footsteps stop, she held up a hand and said, "I didn't take guards because that would have insulted Ambassador Torossian, so if you want to shout at someone, he's your man."

"I have already shouted at Torossian Enzesh, who was gracious enough not to make it an international incident," Faraday said. He came forward to stand next to her chair. "And I agree that no one could have prevented Ambassador Larssin from bringing the assassin as part of his entourage short of insulting Larssin with the implication that he was not trusted."

"Except we *didn't* trust him, and ignored that, and look where it got us," Elspeth said bitterly. "Ruskald is doing everything they can to incite a war except actually sending troops. Do they have some reason to want us to act first? Or is King Osjan just a madman, and nobody knows it?"

"I agree it makes no sense," Faraday said. "Again, the actions of this assassin as they were described to me indicate that he intended to make you afraid or injured, not kill you. Whoever is behind this, your being incapacitated is key to his plan."

She looked up at him. He was staring into the fire as if he could read the answers to the mystery there. "It all seems too easy. Assassination attempts that aren't. A would-be killer who happens to fall and break his neck trying to get away. Ruskald moving troops in just the right way to force us to retaliate. I don't understand any of it."

"Neither do I," Faraday said. "But there are really only two possibilities. Either Ruskald is so desperate for war they have become stupid, or someone wants us to believe Ruskald is behind the assassination attempts when they are not."

Elspeth sat up. "Is that possible?"

"It fits all the facts. Particularly the attempt tonight. All we know about the assassin, thanks to his broken neck, is that he was blond and blue-eyed and wore traditional Ruskalder garb. That does not make him Ruskalder any more than it would make Master Keswick Veriboldan to put him in a silk robe and lacquer his toenails."

"But that's even more confusing. Why would someone want to frame Ruskald for my death?"

Faraday shrugged. "Someone who wanted you dead and realized they could use the tensions between Tremontane and Ruskald to conceal their involvement. There are families who might not care about civil war if it meant the chance of gaining the Crown. Or it might be an anti-government group who wants to sow discord. Or you might have made a personal enemy."

"I don't think Lady Harrington would bother with such a convoluted plan if she decided she'd finally had enough of me. And I don't know enough people here to have made any other enemies."

"You'd be surprised at how quickly people in the capital develop animosities for real or even imagined slights. It could be someone you don't remember meeting." Faraday sighed and lowered his head. "And I'm back to having too many suspects."

"That makes me wonder," Elspeth said. "Could one of those families, the ones who want the Crown, think starting a war with Ruskald would destabilize Tremontane enough to give them an advantage in taking it? That ties up all our loose ends neatly. I don't know. Maybe it's too neat."

"No," Faraday said, his voice distant as if he were thinking hard, "no, that's actually an intriguing possibility. And it narrows my list of suspects to those who would have the resources to pull it off. I think you may be on to something."

"Which means we have to prevent war at all costs," Elspeth said, "because whoever it is is sure to be prepared to act as soon as we're committed to fighting Ruskald. Which further means—"

"You need to negotiate with Larssin," Faraday said. "You have an advantage in that he's probably tearing his hair out trying to find out which of his people attacked you tonight. And when he finds that no one is missing, he'll be even more confused."

Elspeth stood. "I'll send a message asking him for a meeting first thing in the morning. Send the message, that is. I'm not sure I can stomach facing him early in the morning."

Faraday smiled. "The things you do for your country."

"Indeed." She yawned and covered her mouth with one hand. "So —meeting with Larssin, emergency meeting with the Council...am I forgetting anything?"

"If you are, it can wait. You look exhausted."

"So do you." Faraday did look dead on his feet, with dark circles under his eyes and his hair disordered. "Thank you for coming to me immediately. I don't think I could have slept, not knowing what you'd learned."

"I know." He bowed and walked off toward the door. As soon as she heard it shut behind him, she wearily crossed the drawing room and trudged off toward her suite.

But sleep didn't immediately come. She lay on her back staring at the invisible ceiling. Someone trying to start a war. How unbelievably selfish and arrogant. Her unknown enemy would throw the country into turmoil and disaster just to make themselves King, or Queen. It infuriated Elspeth. Finally, she clasped the *toan* jade to her chest and traced the meditation rituals, from the first to the fifth, then counted knots in the cord until she fell asleep.

ELSPETH SAT IN HER NOT-A-THRONE AND WAITED FOR THE FUROR TO DIE off somewhat. Then she stood, placing her palms flat on the reassuring smooth solidity of the table, and said, "Ladies and gentlemen, your anger and confusion are reasonable. However, Mister Faraday's investigation makes it clear that more is going on than the simple matter of imminent war. If he is correct, we are looking for someone who would benefit from that war. However angry we are with Ruskald right now, it doesn't benefit anyone for us to act on that anger. I will be meeting with Ambassador Larssin later today in the hope that I can ease tensions and prevent war."

"I hope you didn't imply that you were a petitioner in requesting his presence," Lord Harrington said.

"No, Lord Harrington, as far as Larssin is concerned, we still believe his man tried to assassinate me, and that puts him in a subordinate position." Elspeth turned to Master Keswick. "Did we send Jeramen's Bequest yet?"

"Not yet, your Majesty."

"Then I'll take that with me. It may still work. Mister Faraday, you had some remarks?"

"Thank you, your Majesty." Faraday stood. "As her Majesty suggests, we now believe some unknown person or organization is interested in pitting Tremontane against Ruskald. It seems this entity wants war as cover for some other action, possibly making a play for the Crown. If that's the case, they will have plans already in place that will take effect as soon as war is declared. I believe some of those plans may affect your departments, and might be something you're aware of. I'm asking each of you to evaluate your departments with this in mind. Large deposits being withdrawn from the Bank of Aurilien, excessive movement along the post roads, even unscheduled slaughters of farm animals might be the sign someone is preparing to move. Anything you notice, even if you think it's nothing, bring it to my department's attention." He sat down.

"Thank you, Mister Faraday," Elspeth said. "Does anyone have anything else to add?"

"I believe we should still maintain readiness along the border, without doing anything to antagonize the Ruskalder," Lord Harrington said. "I would like to send agents into the area to gather intelligence. They will be very discreet," he hurried to add as Elspeth opened her mouth to object.

"That's a good idea, Lord Harrington. It's still possible none of this will matter, and we'll be fighting a war anyway, so we need to be prepared for that outcome as well." Elspeth rose once again. "Thank you, ladies and gentlemen. I'll let you know what comes of the meeting with Ambassador Larssin."

She found herself next to Lady Quinn as they left the Council chamber. "Did you enjoy your birthday outing?" she asked impulsively. It might be a mistake, but she wanted this woman for a friend.

Lady Quinn smiled, a rueful expression. "I think I owe you thanks, and an apology," she said. "I believed Randolph—Lord Chadwick—cared for me, but it seems he was only interested in the prestige of escorting the Countess of Waxwold in public. We argued, he left, and I returned home, much relieved. I wish I'd attended your gala instead."

"No! You really should have your own celebration. Though mine was quite exciting enough, what with Ambassador Larssin bursting in like he wanted to tear the room apart." They turned the corner at the bottom of the ramp. Elspeth realized Faraday was right behind her, and wondered if she should move to make way for his longer stride.

Lady Quinn sighed. "The nicest part was the gift my mother gave me—a cocker spaniel puppy. I do love dogs, don't you?"

Elspeth thought of the ivory collie dog. "I like other people's dogs. I would be a terrible dog owner, though."

"Oh, but you must have received so many wonderful gifts!" Lady Quinn's smile grew mischievous. "From so many attractive men, yes?"

"Yes, but I confess to being frustrated about the best one. Someone picked the perfect gift for me and then didn't sign his name! How am I supposed to know which young man to single out if the one I'm most interested in is...I don't know if he's shy, or just wants to drive me mad."

"What is it?"

"A bracelet. A jade bracelet." Her previous resolve had failed her this morning, and she hadn't worn it, once more fearing the worst.

"And I can't wear it because suppose it was a gift from someone hideous? That would be so awkward."

"If it's perfect, you should wear it anyway, and never mind the consequences," Lady Quinn said. They stopped outside Lady Quinn's office and made way for Faraday, who brushed past without acknowledging either of them.

"That's what I told myself yesterday, but this morning I was a coward," Elspeth said with a laugh.

Lady Quinn laughed with her. "Well, stop being a coward. If it came from someone wonderful, how sorry you would be to miss out on that!"

Elspeth thought about that all the way to her office. Lady Quinn's words, so closely matching her own thoughts, gave her new resolve. She would wear the perfect gift, and not worry about what message it sent.

At ten o'clock she went with her guards to the gold receiving room, her favorite of the many rooms intended for the Queen to greet supplicants or royal messengers...or ambassadors. It was called the gold receiving room because the carpet and the furnishings were all colored goldenrod, and gilding lined the moldings and made thin stripes over the white and goldenrod wallpaper. The chair in the center of the room looked even more like a throne than her Council chamber seat did. After a moment's thought, she had the guards drag two of the chairs lining the walls to a spot just inside the door, facing each other.

She sat in the one of those two farthest from the door and folded her hands in her lap, waiting. The guards ranged themselves around the room, with the one holding Jeramen's Bequest standing immediately behind her. Time passed. The ambassador was late. Elspeth judged this was the only way he could legitimately show defiance and keep his self-respect, at least as he thought of it. She was willing to allow him that much.

The door opened, revealing the North guard who'd been standing outside, a couple of men in Ruskalder furs bearing the long- and shortswords that were traditional for Ruskalder warriors, and Ambassador Larssin, looking belligerent. He looked around the room before entering, followed by his warriors. "They stay by the door," Elspeth said.

"I do not go without them," Larssin said, stopping a few feet from the empty chair.

"I know. They can come in. But they don't get any closer to me than that. One of your men nearly assassinated me last night."

"That is *not*—" Larssin bellowed. The North guards twitched, hands going for their swords. He subsided, though he still looked furious.

"Sit, and we'll talk about it," Elspeth said.

Larssin glared at her a moment longer. Then he sat, his legs spread wide as if he wanted to take up as much space as possible.

"Who was the assassin?" Elspeth said, keeping the deception going a little longer.

"We not know," Larssin ground out, "because is not mine. I tell you this. I tell your dog this. Not ours."

Elspeth considered telling Faraday Larssin thought he was her dog and concluded he wouldn't find it as funny as she did. "Are you sure? How else would he have gotten in?"

Larssin shrugged. "I have many men. Do not count."

"Sloppy. But," Elspeth held up a hand, forestalling an explosion, "it turns out you're right. That assassin wasn't your man. We're not even sure he was Ruskalder."

Astonishment made Larssin's face a series of circles, round eyes, round mouth, round face. "But...I do not understand."

"Neither do we. We think someone wants to put our governments at odds, and made it look like Ruskald tried to have me killed."

Larssin's wide eyes narrowed. "Who would do this?"

Elspeth shook her head. "We're still trying to figure that out."

"I kill," Larssin said. "They make us fight, they die."

"I'm angry about it too. About being used. But one thing I do know is there's no reason for our countries to fight." Elspeth gestured to the guard behind her to come forward. "Tremontane would like to show its respect for its northern neighbor by giving you...this. In the rite of the *tjorak*."

Stunned, Larssin didn't resist when the guard handed him Jeramen's Bequest and laid Elspeth's letter atop it. "The formalities are all there," Elspeth said, "but I hope Ruskald understands Tremontane intends to deal forthrightly with its people."

Larssin looked at the wooden shield, then back at Elspeth. "I must see it," he said. "To accept or not. But I say...it is a good step."

"I'm glad to hear that, Larssin." Elspeth rose. Larssin stood half a breath behind her. "And if we find out who is behind this plot, we will be sure to tell you. *After* Tremontanan justice has been served," she said, warning him when his eyes lit with an unholy fury. Larssin still looked angry, but he nodded.

Elspeth waited for him to precede her out of the room, then gestured to her guards to form up. They watched Larssin until he disappeared around a corner, escorted by more Tremontanan guards, and then Elspeth and her squad went the other way.

The north wing was busier than usual when she returned. She dismissed her guards and walked down the hall toward her office, surprised when people ran past her without acknowledging her. Ahead, a knot of people hovered at Branton's desk, all of them talking loudly enough that their words were a tangle of sound she didn't understand.

Her steps slowed as she approached Branton's desk. Lord Harrington stood there, arguing with Branton, who looked as if he'd rather be anywhere but there but was holding his own against the Council lord. Lady d'Arden stood nearby, looking terribly conflicted. And Master Erica Withers of the Finance department, leaning on Branton's desk, kept trying to interrupt the argument with no success.

"Excuse me," Elspeth said, "but what is going on?"

The argument stopped. "Your Majesty—" Lord Harrington began.

"Your Majesty, I have been *trying* to explain that no one is allowed in your office when you aren't there!" Branton exclaimed. He sounded so frustrated Elspeth's heart went out to him.

"You're right, Mister Branton. Ladies and gentlemen, if you were trying to persuade Mister Branton to let you into my office, you were wasting your breath."

"Your Majesty," Lord Harrington said in a calmer voice, "it is essential that we enter your office to retrieve a key piece of information."

"That doesn't change what I said, Lord Harrington. You can wait for me to accompany you. What information are we talking about?"

"It's—" Lord Harrington looked past Elspeth down the hall. "Mister Faraday."

Elspeth turned. Faraday strode toward them, his eyes on Elspeth. "Your Majesty, I need to talk to you," he said.

"It sounds like you will have to form a queue," Elspeth said lightly. "Lord Harrington, you were saying?"

Lord Harrington drew himself up to his full impressive height. "Your Majesty," he said, "I accuse Duncan Faraday of high treason against the Crown."

20

"*What?*" Elspeth exclaimed, whipping around to stare at Faraday. He looked utterly astonished, staring at Lord Harrington as if he'd had all the wind knocked out of him. "Treason? Mister Faraday?"

"We have evidence," Lord Harrington said. "If you'd allow us into your office?"

Elspeth cast one last look at Faraday. The astonished look had disappeared, replaced with an impassivity that frightened Elspeth more than anger would have. She led the way down the hall and opened the office door. "Inside. Everyone."

Once inside, Elspeth sat in her chair and watched the others mill about. Nobody took the other chair. Harrington strode up to the desk and put his hands behind his back as if he were a Scholia Master prepared to lecture a class. "Mister Faraday himself asked us to investigate our departments for signs of someone preparing to move against the Crown," he said. "Lady d'Arden, please tell her Majesty what you told me."

Lady d'Arden still looked horribly conflicted. She shot a glance at Faraday, who ignored her. "Your Majesty," she said, "did you mean to sell off The Junipers?"

"I...what is The Junipers?" Elspeth asked, feeling increasingly confused.

"A royal residence in Barony Marandis," Lord Harrington said. "It is very valuable property, used by the Crown as a summer retreat."

"Well, I've never heard of it, so it's unlikely I'd sell it off," Elspeth said.

"But you did, your Majesty," Lady d'Arden said. She produced a sheet of paper and handed it to Elspeth. Elspeth examined it. It was a deed of sale, and The Junipers was described in it. The amount— Elspeth swallowed. *Very* valuable property. The signature at the bottom...

Elspeth looked up. "This isn't my signature."

Master Withers tensed. Lord Harrington exchanged glances with Lady d'Arden. "It appears to be your signature."

"I realize that, but I recognize my signature. This is close, but it's not the same. This is a forgery."

"That confirms my suspicions," Lord Harrington said. "I accuse Mister Faraday of forging your signature and pocketing the money from the sale of The Junipers."

"That is a lie," Faraday said.

Elspeth's heart sank. His voice was emotionless, his face a blank, and she'd never heard anyone sound more guilty of anything in her life.

"There's nothing here that condemns Mister Faraday," she said, hoping she was right. "Why him?"

Lord Harrington turned to Master Withers. Master Withers cleared her throat and said, "I've been monitoring certain holding accounts associated with each department. They're used for...it doesn't matter. A large influx of cash matching the amount listed on that bill of sale was deposited into the Internal Affairs account in the Bank of Aurilien two days ago, and a banker's draft for the same amount written on that account only a few hours later. It would have gone unnoticed if Finance hadn't been undergoing an internal audit —that's why the monitoring."

"I see," said Elspeth. She felt sick. "Who has access to that account?"

"For sums that large, only Mister Faraday can authorize access," Master Withers said. She looked like she felt as sick as Elspeth did. Elspeth couldn't bring herself to look at Faraday. This was all a nightmare she would wake from soon.

"Mister Faraday himself said we should examine our departments for unusual activity that could be a sign of the traitors preparing to take the Crown," Lord Harrington said. "I'm sure he didn't believe he would be the one caught."

She heard herself say, "This could be a coincidence."

"That's why we wanted access to your office," Lord Harrington said. "This bill of sale might itself be a forgery, The Junipers not actually sold, and the funds transfer initiated to throw suspicion on Mister Faraday. But everything you sign, your Majesty, is in duplicate. The relevant department, Commerce in this case, holds a copy...and you hold the original. If this bill of sale is legitimate, it's recent enough that it will be in your desk, filed by you."

Elspeth stared at him. Her chest ached with a numb pain that had begun to spread to the rest of her. "Commerce?" she asked. She wished she dared pinch herself awake. Faraday looked like he'd turned to stone.

Lady d'Arden nodded. Elspeth opened the relevant drawer. Her fingers riffled through the pages, looking for the right one. As she neared the back of the drawer without finding it, the fist around her heart relaxed. Of course it wasn't true. Faraday wanted to root out the traitor, not commit treason himself.

Then two words caught her eye—The Junipers. Elspeth slowly withdrew the paper and spread it on her desk. The signature really was very close. Anyone might have mistaken it for hers—anyone but she.

She held out her hand for Lady d'Arden's copy and laid it beside the original. "I see," she said.

"Your Majesty," Lord Harrington said, "I must ask that Mister

Faraday be taken into custody while we investigate. It might all still turn out to be false."

Elspeth nodded. The nightmare wouldn't end. She looked at Faraday, who refused to meet her eyes. "Mister Faraday," she said, her chest aching once more, "do you have anything to say in your defense?"

Faraday still wouldn't look at her. "I deny these charges," he said.

"Can you prove your innocence?" A spark of hope eased the pain in her chest.

He shook his head minutely. "I have only my word, and my exemplary record, as my defense."

The spark died. "Call the guards," Elspeth said. "Have them...take him into custody."

She didn't watch as the guards took him away.

"I'll keep these," she said when Lady d'Arden reached for her copy. "They're evidence. Master Withers, I'll need the records of the bank transactions as well. And then—" Her head of Internal Affairs had been arrested. He was the one she always turned to in situations like this. Who else was there? Just she. "Then I'll send to the Justiciary and appoint Mister Faraday a law-speaker. Unless he wants to act on his own behalf. Except I don't think he can gather evidence while he's in custody." She realized she was babbling and shut up.

"I'm sure there's an explanation, your Majesty," Master Withers said. She didn't sound certain. Elspeth nodded in acknowledgement.

"Thank you for bringing this to my attention," she said. "Please excuse me. I have work to do."

When they were gone, she put her face in her hands and let her breathing become slow and regular. It had to be false. There had to be an explanation. If Faraday—she realized her breathing had sped up and calmed herself again. Why would Faraday have pointed her, have pointed all of them, in a direction that would reveal his crimes? It was impossible. And yet she had an abundance of evidence that said it wasn't.

She moved things around idly on her desk until it was time for dinner, but her stomach still felt sick enough not to be tempted by the delicious-smelling meal the cook had prepared. She ate alone, grateful that Veronica wasn't there, then went to her bedroom and lay on the bed fully-clothed, clutching the *toan* jade but unable to meditate. Her thoughts whirled around, swirling like cream in chocolate, until with an oath she sat up and set the medallion on her bedside table. It struck something hard that moved a fraction of an inch. The bracelet's box.

She stared at the box for a moment. Then she removed the bracelet and put it on. Once more she traced the ritual, the path of harmony. It soothed her as the *toan* jade had not. She settled the bracelet more firmly on her wrist, brushed her hair, and left her room. She could not believe Faraday guilty, and it was her duty to see that he received justice.

By the end of the day, she was thoroughly discouraged. Faraday had refused the law-speaker she'd sent him, who returned to Elspeth with the report that Faraday had viciously sworn at him and told him not to come back. A messenger from Master Withers' office had appeared around three o'clock with the evidence about the bank deposits. Even Elspeth with her limited knowledge of finances could understand the little handwritten notes. All the figures matched. Only Faraday could have done it.

She ate supper with as little enthusiasm as she'd tackled dinner, to the point that Veronica said, "Is something wrong?"

"Yes. But I don't know what, or how to prove it." Faraday had to be innocent. Everything said he was guilty. Elspeth's chest ached again, and her stomach felt as if everything she put into it turned to acid.

"Sometimes proving something is the wrong approach," Veronica said. "We can find evidence for anything we like, because we're rational creatures and we like believing that the world is rational. But it isn't. And neither are people."

"Unfortunately, the world doesn't know it's irrational," Elspeth said. She took a final bite of the cook's special mashed potatoes, rich with cream, butter, and cheese. They tasted like sand. "I'm going to bed early, and I hope everything makes sense when I wake up."

"I hope so too," Veronica said. "Good luck."

Elspeth lay in her bed and willed sleep to come. She tried every trick she knew to fall asleep. She called for a pot of chocolate, which only made her feel sick. She read the most boring book she could find. Her body stayed resolutely awake.

Finally, she threw off the bedcovers and dressed in comfortable old trousers and a shirt soft from much washing. She pulled on socks and ankle boots that didn't match her clothes but were also comfortable. After a moment's thought, she put on the jade bracelet and ran her fingers over the carvings. She'd never needed harmony more than now, even if it was only harmony with herself.

The guards at the east wing were surprised to see her—well, it was nearly ten o'clock at night. "We should accompany you, your Majesty," the male guard said, but tentatively.

"It's all right. I'm going to the Justiciary, and there are plenty of guards there." She trotted away before the guards could stop her.

It occurred to her, as she made her way to the north wing, that she hadn't gotten lost in the palace in days. She hadn't even realized that fact to reflect on how strange it was. Maybe that was just because she only ever went to the same four places, and if she tried to go elsewhere she'd be as lost as before, but she didn't think so. Even the thought of getting lost again didn't fill her with dread anymore.

The long, sloping hall that led deep underground to the Justiciary branched off before entering those familiar corridors. Elspeth knew the branching led to the holding cells, but she'd never been there. Now she turned left and walked the few short feet to where a pair of armed guards in Tremontane colors stood, watching her suspiciously. "I would like to see one of the prisoners," she said.

The guards glanced at each other. One chuckled. "Sweetheart, aren't you up past your bedtime?" he asked.

Elspeth regarded him steadily. "I can see how you might think that," she said, reaching beneath the neck of her shirt. "Does this clarify matters any?"

The guards leaned forward to peer at the North signet ring. Elspeth's aching chest felt a little better the moment they realized who they were talking to. Both men jerked to attention. "Your Majesty," the first one said. "I beg your pardon for my ignorance."

"That's all right, you weren't to know," Elspeth said. "What do I need to do to see a prisoner?"

"Show the next guard your ring and tell them the name of who you want to see," the second guard said. "But you ought to have an escort, your Majesty."

"Why is that?"

The guards exchanged glances again. "Well...some of these prisoners, they aren't the nicest people. That's why they're locked up," the first guard said.

"I'm not afraid of the man I'm here to see," Elspeth said. "Please open the door now."

The guard nodded and pulled out a ring of keys. He unlocked the door and pulled it open with some effort. It looked like it might weigh as much as he did. "Good luck, your Majesty," he said.

Elspeth passed through into a narrow corridor. The outer hall was wide and well-lit and looked fairly new. This one might well have been as old as the palace. Ancient lamps burned dimly on the side walls, making the tiny space smell of burned oil and smoke. Smoky marks on the walls behind them showed how long lanterns had been used there, probably long enough that they'd been torches originally. The walls were concrete blocks that had once been painted white, but age and wear had chipped the paint away until the walls looked leprous and scabby. The floor was one solid stone slab, and unlike the rest of the room, it seemed untouched by time, with no grooves worn into it by generations of prisoners' feet. Elspeth calmed her breathing. She'd never been anywhere that felt so much like a trap.

There was no one inside. She knocked on the second door, which had a small rectangular window near its top, filled with iron bars as thick as her thumb. Light coming from the other side of the door grew brighter. "What?" an irritated voice growled.

Elspeth said nothing, just held the signet where it could be seen. A key grated in the lock, and soon the door swung open. "Sorry about that, your Majesty, it's late and I ain't slept well in weeks," the guard said. He was tall and pot-bellied and wore his greasy hair long around his face. Elspeth clenched her nose against the whiff of body odor, like old cheese, that rose off him.

"I would like to see Duncan Faraday," she said.

"It's after ten. The prisoners is asleep," the guard said.

Elspeth looked straight at him, wishing she knew Faraday's trick of arching one eyebrow. The guard fidgeted. Elspeth stared. Finally, the guard said, "All right, but that one's got a wicked temper, ain't sure I'd be happy 'bout being roused near the ass-crack of midnight—begging your pardon, your Majesty, I ain't good at watching my language."

"Just open the door," Elspeth said.

The wide hall beyond the door was plain, its walls made of the same flaking white concrete as the trap and its floor the same stone slab. Four doors lined the walls on each side, with plenty of space between them. Each door had a small barred window near its top and what looked like a sliding door only three inches high set in its base. There was a small cot set up near the exit, over which hung a lantern that burned low at the moment. The dim light put the farthest reaches of the room in shadow.

The guard took a second, unlit lantern from a peg on the other side of the door and lit it, swearing when the match burned his fingers. He turned the flame to full and handed the lantern to Elspeth. "He's down here," he said, limping to the last door on the left. He unlocked the door and banged on it. An incoherent shout that made Elspeth jump emerged from within. The guard grinned and swung the door open. "Told you he's got a terrible temper."

"I know," Elspeth said, and stepped inside.

The little cell was surprisingly clean and orderly, despite its size. There was a sink with a tap for running water, and a cot, and a small chest at the foot of the cot. A whiff of ammonia rose from the bucket in the corner, but it was stale and not fresh. It wasn't at all what Elspeth had imagined.

Faraday was sitting up from where he'd been lying on the cot. His frock coat and waistcoat were gone, and he'd unbuttoned the first few buttons of his shirt and removed his boots. His hair was a mess and stubble covered his chin and cheeks. It was the most unkempt Elspeth had ever seen him, and that startled her even more than the cell had. "You look terrible," she impulsively said. Terrible, and yet the look suited him somehow, as if it revealed the man beneath his carefully controlled demeanor. Elspeth's heart ached again to see him so exposed.

Faraday gave her a look that could have stripped more paint from the scabrous walls. "I apologize for offending your Majesty's tender sensibilities," he drawled.

Elspeth blushed. "Don't," she said.

"Don't what? Be sarcastic? I'm in jail, your Majesty. It's the only weapon left to me."

Elspeth came more fully into the cell and shut the door, making Faraday sit up and give her a sharp, non-sarcastic look. "You shouldn't do that," he said.

"Why not? You're not going to attack me."

"You don't know that."

Elspeth rolled her eyes. "If you haven't attacked me on all the many occasions I gave you opportunity, you're not going to do it now. Is it all right if I sit?"

Faraday's eyes widened with surprise. Then he shrugged. "If you don't mind the sag in the cot. It's not comfortable."

Elspeth sat beside him. The cot did sag, and it was uncomfortable. "It's all right," she lied. "I didn't expect much."

Faraday clasped his hands together and stared at the floor. "Why did you disturb my sleep, your Majesty?"

"I couldn't sleep."

"That's not an excuse for you to spread your sleeplessness around. I was sleeping like a baby before you showed up."

Elspeth eyed him. "That's not true."

He shrugged again. "You're right. I was awake. But that doesn't explain why you're here."

Elspeth let out a deep breath. "I don't know. Because none of this feels right. Because it doesn't make sense."

"What is there to make sense? I'm a criminal. Didn't you hear Lord Harrington?"

"Yes. And I don't believe it."

"You shouldn't. I'm not guilty. I was framed as surely as that so-called Ruskalder assassin."

"Then prove it. Please. You must have some evidence that it wasn't you."

He looked away. "I don't. There's nothing to say those bills of sale and those bank transactions are false."

"Then how am I to know it wasn't you?" Elspeth exclaimed.

Faraday turned to look at her. His dark blue eyes were lighter in the lamplight. "Because," he said, "I swear on my life I will never betray you. Hold to that, whatever you learn, whatever evidence mounts against me. I would never do anything to put you in jeopardy, not for any reward. Believe that, or not, but I swear it's true."

Elspeth realized she was holding her breath and let it out slowly. "I see," she said. "So what you're saying is that you have no evidence you didn't forge my signature, sell my valuable property, and steal the proceeds, possibly so you could fund an organization that wants to steal my Crown, and you expect me to believe you didn't solely based on your word?"

Faraday bent his head and stared at his hands again. "Yes," he said.

Elspeth stood. "All right. Let's go."

His head came up fast. "Go where? I'm a prisoner."

"Not anymore," Elspeth said.

Faraday shot to his feet. "No, your Majesty," he said, taking hold of her shoulder and stopping her when she would have gone for the door. "I can't."

"Of course you can. My word is law. If I say so, they have to let you out."

Faraday released her. "I mean," he said, "if I'm free, whoever framed me will know you don't believe the story, and will have me killed to prevent the truth coming out."

"Oh," Elspeth said. She sank back onto the cot. "But what do we do? The evidence against you is so strong."

"We have to discover who's behind the plot to discredit me, and why." Faraday sat down beside her. "'Why' may be easier than 'who.'"

Elspeth suddenly felt sick again. "You were convinced the Ruskalder involvement was a ruse, and you told everyone we were looking for a Tremontanan person, or group, interested in taking the Crown. And then this comes up, and we have our traitor. But more than that, we'll stop looking for traitors not only because you're guilty, but because you're the one doing the investigating. If anyone else had been framed, you wouldn't have stopped trying to find their accomplices, or where they'd strike next...or anything."

Faraday looked grim. "I think you've already seen the implications."

"Someone in my government is the traitor," Elspeth said.

21

"I can't believe it," Elspeth said. She buried her face in her hands. "Someone who...but everyone's been so supportive and helpful! And one of them has been lying to me the whole time."

"At least one," Faraday said. "They might be working together."

"Thank you, Mister Faraday, that is not the kind of reminder I need right now."

"Stop feeling sorry for yourself," Faraday snapped. "The Queen can't afford such indulgences."

"You're right." Elspeth rubbed her eyes until she saw spots, then rested her hands on her knees. "I don't know what to do."

"Use your head," Faraday said. "Our unknown enemy discredited me to prevent me unmasking him or her—"

"Or them."

"Or them," Faraday agreed. "That means I was close, or he believed I was. The only way to reinstate me is to discover the true traitor. If you follow the path I was headed down, you should be able to do that."

"Me? You're the one who knows about plots and the like. How am I supposed to do that?"

Faraday shot to his feet and paced angrily across the room. "At the risk of sounding weak, I have to point out that you are now my only hope," he said. "As well as the only possibility for saving Tremontane from war and chaos. Whining about what you don't know will get both of us killed."

"I was *not* whining!"

Faraday shot her an ironic glare. Elspeth sighed. "All right, I was, and I'm stopping now," she said. "But it's still true I don't know how to proceed. I need your help."

Faraday paced across the cell once more, three long steps in each direction. "The most likely possibility is that the traitor is one of the three involved in framing me," he said. "The other two would be innocents brought in by the traitor to give plausibility to his or her accusations. It's much less likely that someone else came up with the plot, and those three just happened to discover it, but there's still a chance. So your first act must be to investigate those three."

"Which starts with working out if any of them has an obvious reason to plot against Tremontane," Elspeth said. "Serena d'Arden is at the top of my list. You said her family was one of those who would fight to take the Crown."

"Only if the Norths had been destroyed by someone else," Faraday pointed out.

"Maybe. Families aren't always unified. Maybe Lady d'Arden thinks I'm unfit to wear the Crown and would be doing Tremontane a service by eliminating me. It might not have anything to do with the rest of the d'Ardens."

"All right, that's a valid point. I'm less sure about Master Withers. She's on the Council because I brought her to your attention, which means if she had a long-term plan to take the Crown, or to help some group take the Crown, that plan was based on improbabilities. She couldn't have known you would make her head of Finance. But if she was approached later by some outside group...how sure are you that the Scholia's reputation is impeccable?"

Elspeth thought about it. "I don't think any group is uniformly honorable. It's like with families—there might be individuals who want to see Tremontane destabilized so they can put someone who will elevate them into power. But it seems the Scholia already has power and respect. So if it *is* Master Withers, and she *is* working on behalf of another group, that group is probably not the Scholia. Which means it might be impossible to discover who they are."

"I agree. And in truth, Master Withers doesn't strike me as vulnerable to recruitment by a group of traitors."

"Which leaves us with Lord Harrington. He spearheaded the accusations against you."

"But Lord Harrington's power comes primarily from his association with you," Faraday said. "Throwing that over for the chance of power in some other regime would be hazardous."

"I know he thought I was too Veriboldan when I arrived," Elspeth said. "I dressed Veriboldan, I'm friends with Mihn, I bowed to the Proxy in public...he might believe he needs to save Tremontane from my foreign influence."

"You haven't done anything overtly Veriboldan in weeks, though." Faraday stopped pacing and pinched the bridge of his nose. "But there are other reasons Lord Harrington might want you out of the way. He might not like your policies with regard to other countries. Particularly Ruskald. He's never trusted the Ruskalder and I don't think it sits well with him for us to approach them in supplication."

"I haven't done that."

"Any kind of peace overture could be read as supplication, particularly by the Ruskalder. And of the three suspects, Lord Harrington has the best resources for making it look like the Ruskalder tried to assassinate you."

The idea of Lord Harrington turning on her chilled Elspeth. He wasn't a friend, necessarily, but he'd always supported her, he'd been honest with her...unless that had been a lie, too. "All right. So at least two of the three are strong possibilities, and Master Withers might have connections we don't know about. What's the next step?"

"Proving or disproving those suppositions." Faraday came back to sit beside her. "Overthrowing a government, as I've said, isn't something anyone can do alone, or without leaving traces. You will need to investigate each of the three to see if you can find those traces.

Connections to disaffected groups, income from hidden sources, links to Ruskalder—not the ambassador—who might be able to make it look like Ruskald wants war."

Despair crept over Elspeth. She didn't want to complain and risk being accused of whining again, but these were all things Faraday did as naturally as breathing, and none of them were things that came naturally to Elspeth North. "I can't do that personally," she said instead. "And I know you didn't either. Who can I trust to find those things out?"

"My secretary, Miss Ravenscourt," Faraday said. "She will know which of my agents to involve. And Miss Simkins is a valuable resource."

Elspeth felt cold again. "But Lord Harrington arranged for Miss Simkins to be my secretary. If he's the one, mightn't he have put her there as his secret agent? She could even have planted that bill of sale in my desk—she's in and out of my office all the time!"

Faraday cursed. "You have to establish her innocence," he said. "Miss Simkins knows too much about your affairs. She could be dangerous to you."

"I know. And I have an idea for testing her loyalties."

"What's that?"

Elspeth shook her head. "If I tell you, you'll just shout at me. You have to trust me."

Faraday's lips quirked in his familiar half-smile. "I suppose I do."

Elspeth sighed. "I wish you weren't locked up. You're better at this than I am."

"I'd rather be locked up than dead," Faraday said.

"That's true." Elspeth stood. "Can I do anything for you? Have someone bring you a change of clothes, or shaving tackle...?"

"They wouldn't let me have anything remotely considered a weapon, and a change of clothes would just get dirty. But...thank you."

"I'll come back tomorrow night with news."

"Your Majesty, that's not safe for you," Faraday said, sounding alarmed. "Anyone involved in this plot won't stop at killing you to preserve the secret."

"This plot is meant to end with my death, Mister Faraday. I don't think I'm in any less danger just because I visit you." Saying it so casually didn't make her feel as afraid as she expected. "I'll be back. And we'll solve this."

Faraday saluted her without rising. "I'll hold you to that."

Elspeth opened the door—that guard probably should have locked her in, for security—and shut it behind her. Security. *Now* she felt chilled.

She walked to where the guard sat on his cot, cleaning his fingernails with a sliver of wood. "Excuse me," she said, "what's your name?"

The guard peered up at her. "Travis, your Majesty."

First name, or last? It didn't matter. "Travis, I have some instructions about Mister Faraday. The prisoner I was just here to see? No one is to speak to him or enter his cell unless it's me or someone carrying this signet. Do you understand?" She held up the ring so its silver caught the lamplight.

Travis nodded dully. Despair flooded through her. That had not been the nod of someone who was paying attention or who intended to follow through on her orders.

"Stand up, Travis," she said, grabbing his collar and hauling on it. He was far too heavy for her to lift, but surprise carried him to his feet. "Now, *pay attention*. No harm had better come to Mister Faraday while he's here, understood? That is why no one is to enter his cell or speak to him or even remove him from this place unless...what? Do you remember?"

Travis nodded. "Unless it's you or someone bearing your ring, your Majesty."

"Right. And you will communicate those orders to the day shift, yes?"

He nodded again.

"And this is the important part. If anything *does* happen to Mister Faraday, if he so much as stubs a toe while he's in custody, I will make sure none of the guards responsible for his well-being ever work again. That might be because all of you have been executed. Do I make myself clear?"

Travis's eyes were so wide the irises were entirely ringed with white. "Yes, your Majesty," he whispered. "What about the food?"

"What about it?"

Travis swallowed. "I mean, you're worried somebody might want the prisoner dead, right? The food all comes from the commissary kitchen, but it's all different servants what we don't usually know. If one o' them wanted to poison the prisoner—"

Travis wasn't as stupid as she'd thought. It frightened her to think how close she'd come to missing something vital. "I'll send my own people with his meals, and a note signed with my seal. Thank you, Travis. I won't forget that."

Travis relaxed. "I wouldn't never hurt a prisoner," he said. "Seen too many of 'em turn out to go free, and the powerful ones, they don't forget if a guard puts the boot in. Ain't smart."

"You're very wise. And one last thing. Don't explain those orders. If someone comes asking to see Mister Faraday, or wants to take him somewhere, you refer them to me and that's all."

"I got it, your Majesty." Travis slouched to attention and saluted her as sharply as he was able, which wasn't very. Elspeth nodded and handed him the lantern.

At the outer doors, she asked the guards a few questions about their job, and established that guard duty for the outer doors was on a weekly rotation. That meant it was unlikely she could contact every guard who might be on watch outside the cells. Well, she'd done what she could to protect Faraday. Now she needed to work on protecting herself.

SHE ROSE LATE AFTER A RESTLESS NIGHT AND DRESSED RAPIDLY, THEN ate a few bites of food, all her stomach could bear. Without even a second thought, she put on the jade bracelet and spun it around her wrist twice. It no longer mattered who'd given it to her, and she almost hoped no one claimed responsibility for the gift. It was her talisman, and it would give her strength.

"I would like to see Miss Ravenscourt in my office immediately," she told Simkins, overriding Simkins' usual greeting. "You may bring my schedule afterward."

Miss Ravenscourt turned out to be unexpectedly young and very attractive, which surprised Elspeth. She'd expected someone more like Simkins, who'd shown the woman in without a hint of complaint. Ravenscourt looked tense and afraid, her eyes red-rimmed as if she'd been crying, her lips thin with the effort of not looking tense and afraid. She didn't take the seat Elspeth offered.

"Miss Ravenscourt," Elspeth began, "you work closely with Mister Faraday, am I right?"

Ravenscourt nodded. Now she looked thoroughly afraid.

"You know the accusations leveled against your superior," Elspeth went on. "I happen to know those accusations are false. I think you do, too."

The fear left Ravenscourt's face, replaced by wary uncertainty. "I don't know anything," she said in a faint voice.

Understanding struck Elspeth. "Miss Ravenscourt," she said, leaning forward, "I'm quite serious. I think Mister Faraday has been framed. And even if he hadn't been, I wouldn't assume you were also responsible. But I need your help. Mister Faraday assures me you are capable of investigating certain people, or at least of knowing which of his agents to use. Is this true?"

Ravenscourt nodded. She let out a deep breath. "I thought you were going to imprison me, too," she said, her voice growing stronger. "You mean he didn't do those things?"

"Didn't you believe he was innocent?"

"I...didn't know. I believed I would have known it if he was plotting treason. But he's very good. If he wanted it kept a secret, he might have been able to."

That was both good news and bad. Elspeth clung to the good. "So you didn't see any evidence of the things he was accused of?"

"No, your Majesty." Ravenscourt hesitated, then said, "Maybe I shouldn't say this. I don't know if it makes him look more guilty, or less. But..."

"What is it?"

Ravenscourt ducked her head. "A month ago, when your Majesty was first here...Mister Faraday thought about forging your signature. Not seriously! He was concerned you might..."

"I understand. He told me what he feared about me and my inexperience." That conversation felt so far in the past it was like it had happened to two other people. "But we can't bring that up. It would only make everyone convinced of his guilt."

"No, your Majesty. My point is that he made an exact copy of your signature. I couldn't tell the difference, and I'm trained in handwriting analysis. If he forged that bill of sale, nobody would know it wasn't you. Including you."

It lightened a load she hadn't known she was carrying. Trusting Faraday was one thing, but being able to prove it... "Miss Ravenscourt, we'll keep that information in reserve. It might make a difference. For now, it reassures me, so I appreciate you mentioning it. Now, here's what I want you to do..."

Ten minutes later, she let Ravenscourt out and said, "Miss Simkins, thank you for your patience. Please come in."

Simkins entered and laid the schedule on Elspeth's desk. "Lord Harrington asked that you call an emergency Council meeting at ten o'clock," she said. "If you wish to do so, I can move your ten-thirty and eleven o'clock meetings to the afternoon. If not, this afternoon you are scheduled to meet with Mistress Alderly for your monthly report on the palace staff at one-thirty, and with General Beckett at three o'clock."

General Beckett? That one was unexpected. She ignored it for the moment. "I would like to meet with the Council at ten, yes," she said, "but not for the reasons you think. I intend to arrest Lord Harrington for collusion with Mister Faraday at 9:45 this morning."

Simkins gasped and touched her throat as if the gasp had surprised her. "Lord Harrington? Your Majesty, surely not!"

"I'm afraid so, Miss Simkins. Please don't tell anyone. I don't want Lord Harrington learning of the arrest and fleeing. You can see why secrecy is important."

"Of course, your Majesty." Simkins' voice was faint and breathy. "I'll just...inform the Council of the ten o'clock meeting, then."

"Thank you."

When Simkins was gone, Elspeth leaned back in her chair and let out a long, deep breath. Then she got up and left her office. If she was wrong, she'd just lost her secretary and might have alienated one of her most powerful supports. But she had an instinct she was right.

She wandered the north wing for half an hour, startling people with requests for instant updates on whatever they were doing. The responses were so gratifying she resolved to do it again, sometime when she wasn't just killing time. At 9:38 she returned to her office, but left the door open a crack. Miss Simkins returned at 9:40 and went into her own office, shutting the door. Elspeth didn't know what to make of that. Was she, or was she not, a weak link?

At 9:43 Elspeth again left her office and strolled down the corridor to Harrington's office, and knocked on his door. At his muffled invitation, she entered. Harrington looked up, surprised.

"Is there something I can help you with, your Majesty?" he asked.

"I've just been thinking about Mister Faraday's plot," she said. "Do you think it extended to him orchestrating those assassination attempts?"

"It would almost have to," Harrington said. "It's unlikely there was more than one plot against you. I'm sorry you were so disappointed in him. It was despicable of him to use those assassination attempts to work his way into your confidence."

"I agree," Elspeth said, filing that comment away for later consideration. "I'll see you at ten."

She wandered back to her office and rapped on Simkins' door. "Please join me in my office," she said when the door opened.

Elspeth sat in her chair and waved to Simkins to take the other chair. "Congratulations," she said. "You passed."

"I...I'm not sure I follow, your Majesty," Simkins said.

"I'm not arresting Lord Harrington. That was a story I made up to test you. I needed to confirm that you were more loyal to me than to your former superior. If you'd warned him about the imminent arrest, I would have known you weren't."

Simkins' mouth dropped open. Elspeth had never seen her look so flabbergasted. "Test me? Your Majesty, have I given you reason to doubt my fidelity?"

"You haven't," Elspeth said. "But I can't take any chances, because more than my life is at stake. Miss Simkins, there is a traitor on the Council, and I need your help to discover who it is."

To her surprise, Simkins didn't look alarmed at this. "You mean someone other than Mister Faraday," she said. "I suspected as much."

"You did? Why is that?"

Simkins adjusted her spectacles. "Mister Faraday is many things, but disloyal is not one of them. I have observed him over the months I have been in the north wing, first as King Francis's secretary and then as yours, and his devotion to his job and to the Crown has always been clear. He is also extremely competent. I have no doubt that if he were a traitor, no one would know it until it was too late. And—but that's unimportant now. My point is that I believed there was something not right about the accusation that landed Mister Faraday in custody."

"You're right. I've discussed the situation with him, and we agree that it is likely one of the three people who accused him."

"It's not Master Withers," Simkins said promptly. "She lives like an ascetic and has no connections with any group who might be capable of overthrowing the government. Even her links to the Scholia are dormant now that she is a Council member. This may be only temporary, but at least for now, her life is completely absorbed by her work in the Finance department."

Elspeth blinked. "How do you know all that?"

Simkins didn't flinch. "One of my duties is knowing whether those close to your Majesty might be vulnerable to undue influence by outside parties. I had Internal Affairs investigate both Master

Keswick and Master Withers when they were appointed to the Council. I apologize if I have overstepped my bounds."

"No, not at all. That's the sort of thing I want to know." Hope sprang up in Elspeth's heart, tentative but determined. "What do you know about Lord Harrington and Lady d'Arden? Have either of them done anything suspicious?"

Simkins shook her head. "I'm afraid I don't continue to watch Council members once they've passed the initial vetting."

Elspeth swore. Simkins raised an eyebrow, but said nothing. "All right," Elspeth said. "It's not Master Withers. She was always last on my list, anyway."

"If I may," Simkins said, "I have recently had great difficulty finding Lady d'Arden to pass on requests or announcements of meetings. She is frequently not in her office, and some discreet inquiries led to the information that she leaves the office for unknown assignations, is gone for some time, and tells no one, even her staff, where she has gone."

"That doesn't have to be suspicious. It could be an affair. She strikes me as a very private person."

Simkins shrugged. "That is possible. However, we should consider every likelihood, and one of those is that she is involved with our group of traitors. She is, after all, the one who discovered the forged bill of sale."

"You're right. I'll keep that in mind." Elspeth pushed away from her desk and stood. "I'll go straight from the Council meeting to dinner, and then I'll be back here for the afternoon meetings. If Miss Ravenscourt wants to see me, make room for her on the schedule."

"Of course." Simkins made her curtsey and left.

Elspeth ran her fingers through her hair until she was sure it was standing on end, then vainly combed it back into place. As she walked to the Council chamber, she couldn't help thinking about the possibility that Lord Harrington or Lady d'Arden were traitors. Or both, she realized. Both didn't bear thinking about—but she had to, didn't she? As dramatic as it was, the fate of the country hung on it.

22

Faraday looked even more disheveled that night than he had the previous day. With his unshaven face and unbuttoned collar, he looked even more like the disreputable type of gentleman pirate that was a danger to ladies everywhere. Elspeth concealed a grin at the thought.

"Lord Harrington didn't do or say anything at the Council meeting to suggest he is our traitor," she said. "Though there was something earlier today...he said it was unfortunate that you'd faked those assassination attempts to worm your way into my confidence."

Faraday looked up at her where she paced across the cell. For her, it was four steps across and back. "Is that odd?"

"Just that it felt like he wanted to make me trust you even less. Like he didn't think the accusations of treason were enough. Isn't that suspicious?"

"He could have been expressing a natural concern. After all, I *did* go out of my way to encourage you to lean on me and my investigation."

"Because you were trustworthy, not because you were some evil genius bent on sabotaging my reign." Elspeth paced some more. "I don't know. I feel I'm grasping at anything that might be evidence."

"Sit," Faraday said. "You're making me dizzy."

Elspeth sat beside him. Her hand came to rest on her bracelet, and she twisted it idly one way and then the other. Faraday watched her restless motion, but said nothing. Finally, she said, "Both Lord Harrington and Lady d'Arden have done suspicious things. Shouldn't we try to force the issue?"

"That could be extremely dangerous for you," Faraday said. "If we guess wrong, the actual traitor will be warned that you are on the right track, and he or she will not hesitate to eliminate you."

"But Lord Harrington, at the Council meeting today, went into detail about how much evidence the investigation against you was turning up. If we don't act soon, you'll face criminal charges in court, and I'm not sure even my word will be enough to protect you."

"The Queen has the power to commute sentences, but no ruler of Tremontane has ever freed someone accused of high treason. It would look strange, at the very least." Faraday grimaced. "It would be better if you let the charges ride. I'm not inexperienced as a questioner, and I can defend myself."

"With no evidence supporting you? I'm not going to let you go to prison for a crime you didn't commit."

The grimace turned into a sour smile. "High treason is a capital offense, your Majesty. I would be executed."

Elspeth shuddered. "That is definitely not going to happen."

"That reassures me, your Majesty."

Elspeth stopped twisting her bracelet and removed it, holding it loosely in one hand and running her fingers across the meditation ritual. The action relaxed her. She traced the letters again and let her shoulders droop.

"What are you doing?" Faraday asked.

She opened her eyes and saw he was looking at the bracelet rather than at her. He sounded curious, less on edge than before, and the sudden, unexpected change in his attitude made her hesitate before answering. "This bracelet is carved with the fifth meditation ritual, the path of harmony. I was practicing a little meditation to calm myself."

"Isn't that what your *toan* jade is for?"

"Yes, but this is..." She felt a little shy explaining it, now that she'd carried the bracelet for a while and felt connected to it. "It's just different," she concluded. "It makes me feel strong in a different way."

"It's certainly beautiful."

She nodded. "I love it."

Faraday stretched and rose from the cot. "I think you're right that we need a different approach. But *not* one that jeopardizes you. We should choose one of our possible traitors and decide what he or she would do if they were the traitor, then watch for those behaviors. Whoever it is has certainly not given up on the treason plot, and might act on it at any time."

"If it's Lady d'Arden, she'll increase her mysterious trips. Can we have someone follow her?"

"Miss Ravenscourt can handle that. What would be even better would be to have Finance investigate her, because this kind of plot requires a lot of money. If you trust Master Withers, that would be another approach."

"I think I do, after what Miss Simkins said. And Lord Harrington...if it's him, he still needs me dead, or at least incapacitated. I could trail around without my bodyguards—"

"That is *not* acceptable," Faraday shouted.

"Calm down. I meant, without obvious bodyguards. It would be perfectly safe."

"Risking yourself like that is the opposite of safe. Promise me you won't do it." His eyes blazed in his haggard face. Elspeth, startled by his vehemence, nodded agreement.

"With Lord Harrington," he said, somewhat more calmly, "the key is Ruskalder involvement. If he makes a move to incite Ruskalder hostilities, that would be the beginning of his push to start a coup."

"He hasn't said anything about Ruskald. He was even cautiously pleased at the embassy's response to our *tjorak*."

"It's been barely two days. Don't become complacent."

"I won't," Elspeth said, stung, "but I don't want to make assumptions and let them lead me to the wrong conclusions."

Faraday sighed. "I'm sorry. I'm on edge and I don't mean to take it out on you."

"I understand. It must be hard being stuck in here with nothing to do."

"'Hard' is an understatement. I sometimes fear I'm going mad. Your arrival was a relief."

Elspeth smiled. "What do you do all day?"

"Think about the possibilities implicit in my being framed. Go over what we know in a futile attempt to come up with some new fact that will reveal the truth. Eat. I didn't realize all I had to do to get the best meals of my life was to be thrown in jail. Are you responsible?"

"Travis the guard gave me the idea. It hadn't even occurred to me that someone might try poisoning you. So I sent what was left after I ate. Cook seems not to believe I'm not five fat men in training for a pie-eating contest."

"I didn't think of poison either. Nor of telling the guards not to let anyone take me away. You're more devious than I originally believed." He sat beside her again. "More devious, and less fragile."

"You really didn't think highly of me at first, did you?" Elspeth put her bracelet back on and resumed twisting it.

"I didn't know you to think anything of you. I based my actions on the information Lord Harrington had, that and my assumptions about someone who would choose a religious life in a foreign country. It still seems odd to me that anyone would do that."

"You don't understand what it's like, living a life devoted to heaven. But most people don't, so I don't hold it against you."

Faraday turned to look at her. "So...what is it like?"

Elspeth puffed out her cheeks and blew a long, slow stream of air. "We meditate to draw closer to heaven," she said, "and that's a feeling like no other, when there's only the faintest veil between us and it. Some of the priestesses claim to have seen people on the other side, but I never have. I don't know that it's necessary, really. Heaven's blessing extends to all of us, now and after we die, and I don't think we have to touch the afterlife to feel it."

"I've never been very religious. That probably seems strange to you."

"Not really. Most people aren't, except maybe at the solstices. But what people forget is that heaven doesn't care if you're religious or not—it's there no matter how you behave or what matters to you. We're all entitled to heaven's touch no matter whether we're priestesses or...or disgraced Internal Affairs heads."

"I admit it's comforting to think of heaven watching out for me at a time like this. What would that look like? Heaven's blessing, in these circumstances?"

"Peace of mind, maybe. Clarity of thought, to help you figure out the truth. Or it's said that sometimes heaven's blessing comes in the form of other people."

Faraday chuckled. "Which in this case would mean you are heaven's agent."

"Well, I *was* going to be a priestess. We're supposed to divine heaven's will. Unfortunately for you, I was never good at that. I was always better at counseling people and working out what they actually wanted."

"A skill that has stood you in good stead in your current role."

Elspeth shrugged. "I'd like to think so." She stood. "I should be going. Tomorrow I'll learn more. Is it reasonable for me to feel urgency?"

"Of course. Just don't let it make you act in haste. That's the sort of thing that means disaster in situations like these."

Elspeth thought about that on the way back to the north wing. Despite what she'd told Faraday, she was tempted to make herself bait, pretend to be helpless and then swoop in on a would-be assassin, interrogate him...it was a pleasant fantasy, but one she wouldn't act on. Not only would Faraday kill her if she did, she couldn't guarantee that an assassin wouldn't get lucky no matter how many hidden guards she had.

She left the north wing and turned left, grateful for the little light Device that glowed pale red and fit into the palm of her hand. It gave her just enough light to make her way through the palace halls, and the light was soothing and didn't blind her when she accidentally looked at it. She was used to the low light enough that when another light sprang up ahead, she blinked and had to turn away.

The light drew nearer. Elspeth ducked into a side corridor and squeezed the light Device off. Nobody ought to be about this late—well, *she* shouldn't be about this late, but it was her palace, and nobody else had that kind of excuse. And while she had a right to demand an explanation of anyone wandering the halls at midnight, her instincts told her it was better for her to conceal herself.

She flattened herself against the wall and waited. Very soon, two guards—no, soldiers, armed soldiers—in Tremontane colors bearing a lantern marched past, followed shortly by another pair of soldiers in green and brown. Elspeth held her breath, though they made enough noise that they wouldn't have heard her breathing. The light, and the sound of their boots, faded into the distance. Elspeth crept out of the hallway and watched them go. They were headed for the north wing, but where had they come from? She conjured a mental map of the area. The most likely possibility was that they'd come from the Rotunda, where the night guard post was. Someone must have sent them on an errand...but to the north wing, which was silent and dark and empty?

No. To the Justiciary.

Dread filled her heart, and she crept after the guards, staying so far back they weren't more than a speck of light in the distance. Her familiarity with the path kept her from tripping in the darkness. They made the turn from the north wing to the long, long sloping path, and then she had to turn on her light when that turn hid their lamp from her view.

She sidled up to the corner and peeked around it. She saw the lamp just at the limits of her vision. The soldiers appeared to be talking to the guards at the cell doors. Then two of the soldiers went through the door to the cells. Elspeth held her breath. How well would Travis bear up against those soldiers, both of whom had looked tougher and meaner than the slovenly prison guard? Or—Elspeth felt faint—she hadn't considered that someone wanting to remove Faraday might take a more direct approach, and damn the consequences.

She watched, unable to move, for what felt like several minutes, but when she looked at her watch had only been about ninety seconds. Then the soldiers emerged from the door, formed up, and proceeded toward the Justiciary.

Elspeth leaned against the wall, breathing heavily, until she felt capable of moving. Then she flew down the hall and arrived somewhat breathlessly in front of the guards. "Who did you just let in?" she demanded.

"Prisoner transfer, your Majesty," the guard said. "But they said they didn't have the proper papers."

Elspeth looked at the door. "Let me through," she said.

Travis opened the inner door at her impatient pounding. "I didn't let them take him," he said. "I swear it, your Majesty."

"Did you let them in to see him?"

"Not that neither. I ain't stupid. Ain't no weapons allowed in the cells."

Elspeth stared at Faraday's door. "You did well. Thank you."

"You want to see he ain't dead? They didn't get even to the door."

Faraday would think she was mad if she burst in on him like that. "No. It's fine. I'll...be back tomorrow night."

She trudged back in the pale red glow of her Device and didn't stop until she was safely in her room. She slid her bracelet off and put it into its box, then sat on the edge of her bed and shook. That had been close. She wished she had some way of knowing who had ordered those guards to...did it matter if they'd been told to kill him in his cell or to take him somewhere else to do the job? Of course not. He'd be dead either way. The urgency she felt now wound her to the breaking point.

She checked her watch. Almost one o'clock. Someone at the guard post would know who'd ordered those soldiers to do that "prisoner transfer." In the morning, she would...but by morning, there'd be new guards, and tracking down who'd been in charge the previous night would be far more difficult and take more time. On the other hand, they would definitely notice the Queen visiting the guard post after midnight, and if the guards had been suborned, they would tell whoever had given those orders. That would both warn her enemy and put her in danger. Maybe it was better to have an underling do it in the morning.

She lay back, fully clothed, and clasped the *toan* jade to her chest, her fingers groping for insight. She sometimes did this, let her instincts choose the path that would help her most in the hope that heaven might guide those instincts. Her fingers settled on the third ritual, the path of wisdom: *drink deep, and be filled.* She surely needed wisdom. What course of action made the most sense?

She ran the tip of her forefinger over the deeply carved words. A memory came to mind, Faraday telling her not to be impatient. She felt impatient, ready to leap from her bed and fly through the halls to the Rotunda and the guard post. She could learn immediately who the traitor was—at the cost of warning her enemy that he had been exposed. Right now, he believed he was safe, that Elspeth wouldn't know he'd made a move until tomorrow, possibly late tomorrow. That meant he wouldn't act in a panic, and that gave Elspeth time.

She sighed. Waiting was so *hard*, but it was the right choice. She wearily undressed and crawled into bed. Her last thought was of Faraday, sleeping on that uneven cot. She wasn't going to let him die, even if that meant looking like a fool for pardoning a traitor. She couldn't believe she'd ever hated him.

SHE ROSE EARLY THE NEXT MORNING AND HURRIED THROUGH DRESSING and eating. She settled the *toan* jade around her neck to rest just above her breasts and slipped the bracelet over her wrist. Doubly armored, she set off for the north wing.

"Lieutenant Anselm, come with me," she told the lieutenant when they reached the steps to the north wing. The lieutenant looked puzzled, but followed Elspeth to her office. "I need you to find something out for me," she said, "and I need you to be discreet."

"Of course, your Majesty. Anything you command."

"Four soldiers tried to remove Mister Faraday from confinement late last night. I need to know who gave that order. And by that, I mean where it ultimately came from, not just the guard captain who sent them. Can you do that?"

"I can, your Majesty. How discreet do I need to be?"

Good question. "It will be hard to conceal my involvement, given that you're a North guard and not a Tremontanan soldier, but if you can misdirect people into believing you're acting on behalf of the Judiciary, that would be best. The Judiciary employs both soldiers and North guards."

Anselm nodded. "I understand, your Majesty. I assume you want this done immediately?"

"Yes. Please. The faster, the better."

Anselm gave her the abbreviated bow the military used and excused herself. As she left, Simkins entered the office. "Is now a good time, your Majesty?"

"I suppose. A good time for what?"

"For your schedule, your Majesty."

She'd been so focused on the problem of treason she'd forgotten she had more mundane responsibilities. "Yes. All right."

She listened with half her brain to Simkins' recitation, the other half running through unanswerable questions. How would her enemy strike? Did he or she believe Elspeth was closer to unmasking them than she was? That ought to make them careless, if they were afraid of being revealed.

"Your Majesty?"

"Yes?" Elspeth dragged herself back to the present.

"If something is distracting you, I can return later."

"I'm sorry, Miss Simkins. I do have other things on my mind, but that's no excuse for rudeness."

"I understand, your Majesty. Is there anything I can do?"

"Not right now, Miss Simkins, but please stay close at hand. Today might be interesting."

Simkins smiled. "Does 'interesting' mean 'full of excitement'?"

"That is exactly what it means."

"Then I await those interesting developments with great anticipation," Simkins said, and let herself out.

Elspeth went through more work, including signing the personal petitions she was so accustomed to Faraday bringing her. It irritated her that her enemy had struck at someone she depended on just to divert attention from his plans. She signed a few more papers, used the signet to seal the ones that needed a more official stamp, and leaned back in her chair to stretch her back out. She checked her watch: it was only 10:27. She had no appointments scheduled for this morning, nothing but a diplomatic reception at the Ruskalder embassy at three o'clock that afternoon. The invitation had indicated it was to reciprocate for the *tjorak*, which intrigued Elspeth. So at least one thing had gone right this week.

Simkins knocked on the door. "Lieutenant Anselm, your Majesty."

Elspeth sat up straight. "Show her in."

Anselm didn't look as if she'd learned anything earthshattering, and Elspeth's eagerness faded slightly. "Well, lieutenant?" she said.

"I think your Majesty should know this was more difficult a task than you probably anticipated," Anselm said. "Certainly more challenging than I thought. Someone wanted this information concealed."

"That is important, lieutenant, thank you. But you did learn it?"

"The captain in command last night, Captain Sommers, gave those orders directly to the soldiers involved. He flatly refused to tell me who had given the orders to him. I tell you this so you'll be warned, your Majesty. I think Captain Sommers is corrupt."

"I agree. Thank you."

"So I went to the soldiers in case one of them might have seen whoever controls Captain Sommers. As I hoped, no one had told the soldiers they weren't to speak of their orders. People in command sometimes don't believe ordinary soldiers are smart enough to have opinions. One of them recognized the person as Lyle Carruthers."

Lieutenant Anselm fell silent. Elspeth waited. Finally, she said, "Should I know who that is?"

Anselm shifted uncomfortably. "I'm sorry, your Majesty, I forgot you're new to Aurilien. Lyle Carruthers was a d'Arden before he adopted out. He's Lady Serena d'Arden's younger brother."

23

---

*L*ady d'Arden. It was a relief to put a face to her nameless enemy. "Thank you, lieutenant," Elspeth said. "You've done excellent work. Who is Captain Sommers' superior officer, and where can I find him or her?"

"Major Ellen Grant," Anselm said. "I think she suspects Captain Sommers of shady dealings, not just this one. You don't get put on night guard duty as an officer unless you're under some kind of condemnation. She would be willing to put pressure on the captain if you asked."

"I will need his testimony eventually. For now—I don't think I have to tell you not to mention this to anyone."

"Of course not, your Majesty." Anselm bowed and let herself out.

Elspeth gripped the edge of her desk and went over her options. She could confront Lady d'Arden directly. She could free Faraday and have him confront Lady d'Arden with her. She could call a Council meeting and denounce Lady d'Arden publicly. She could arrange to have Lady d'Arden followed and discover more of her plot. All of those options had problems.

So, what did she know? Lady d'Arden wanted Faraday eliminated because...why? Almost certainly because she believed he was a danger to her. How, Elspeth didn't know. She set that aside for the moment. Lady d'Arden intended to take the Crown once Elspeth was out of the way. But Elspeth's death wouldn't be that disruptive, because Lord Harrington would be James's regent and could protect his interests from any usurpers. Which meant—

Elspeth sucked in a startled breath. It wasn't just her life in danger. Lady d'Arden would need to eliminate Lord Harrington, too. And it didn't matter whether that was before or after Elspeth was killed, just so long as it meant there was no one minding the store when Lady d'Arden slipped into the Queen's role.

Elspeth ran for the door and burst into Simkins' office. "Miss Simkins, can you find out where Lady d'Arden is? Discreetly?"

"Certainly, your Majesty," Simkins said, not showing any alarm at the Queen bursting into her office like a madwoman.

Elspeth went back to her desk and sat, not behind it, but on top of it, too restless to be confined in a chair. It might not matter, because Lady d'Arden wasn't likely to dirty her own hands with an assassination. But if they could arrest her immediately, they might be able to stop whatever plans she had in motion. She wished she'd thought to ask Simkins to find out where Lord Harrington was. Well, that she could manage herself.

She went down the hall to Lord Harrington's office. His secretary, an elderly man with sharp hazel eyes, told her Lord Harrington was in a meeting with members of his staff. Elspeth declined his offer to interrupt the meeting. That should keep Lord Harrington safe for now.

She returned to her office and met Simkins on the way. "Lady d'Arden is meeting with Guild representatives in the Oak Hall," Simkins said. "I spoke with her secretary, who told me her ladyship intended to go to an early dinner after that meeting."

Elspeth made a decision. "I'm going to speak to Lady d'Arden," she said.

"Your Majesty, is that wise?" Simkins asked.

"Maybe not, but lives are at stake." Elspeth turned on her heel and hurried through the north wing to where her guards waited. She looked them over; they were armed, and there were four of them, which should be enough. "Where's Lieutenant Anselm?" she asked.

"She's not on duty again until after the dinner hour, your Majesty," one of the guards said.

Elspeth would have felt more secure with the confident lieutenant at her elbow, but she wasn't needed for this. "Come with me," she said. "And be prepared to make an arrest."

That startled them. All four moved restlessly, glancing at each other, but none of them said anything. It was nice to have guards loyal to her. She couldn't imagine if she had to depend solely on Tremontanan soldiers, if leaders like Captain Sommers were in a position to give them bad orders.

It was also nice, she reflected ten minutes later, to have guards who knew the palace better than she did. The Oak Hall not only wasn't on her list of places she knew, she'd never even heard of it. But the guards took her around the north wing to the far western side of the palace and into a hallway that was itself wide enough to host a gathering of Guild leaders. It was paved in gray marble streaked with black and lined on both sides with fat ridged columns painted sky blue to match the ceiling. Elspeth took a good look at the ceiling: fluffy white clouds gave the hall the illusion that it was open to the summer sky, though no one would ever believe the effect because the hall smelled not of fresh air, but of old, greasy smoke as if there had been a fire there recently.

Double doors about halfway down the hall, curved at the top and painted blue to match the columns, stood halfway open, and men and women strolled out of the room beyond, chatting quietly in a way that reminded Elspeth of the Temple and how leisurely everyone was leaving an instruction session. These people, though, were dressed in rich robes and coats bearing the insignia of their various Guilds rather than the plain linen trousers and shirts of the priestesses. As they registered Elspeth's presence, they stopped in place and bowed. Most of them clearly wanted to ask what she was doing there, but when Elspeth acknowledged them without a word, they moved on, glancing over their shoulders once or twice.

Elspeth waited for the doorway to clear, then entered. To her surprise, the Oak Hall reminded her even more strongly of the Irantzen Temple than the people had. There was a room in the Temple large enough for all the priestesses and aspirants to gather, filled with wooden benches stained dark and lacquered to a high gloss, with a rostrum at the front where a speaker could stand to address the room. The benches were so smooth someone could take a running start and slide from one end to the other...not that Elspeth would ever do anything so undignified. Of course not.

And here was this high-ceilinged room filled with glossy wooden benches, the windows stained glass creations that would cast colored light across those benches when the afternoon sun struck them, the rostrum where Lady d'Arden stood speaking to one of those women in Guild colors. Both looked up when Elspeth entered. The Guild woman gasped and bowed deeply. Lady d'Arden bowed, not as deeply. Her face was perfectly serene.

"Lady d'Arden, I'd like a word with you," Elspeth said. The Guild woman muttered something about needing to leave and hurried out the door. Lady d'Arden faced Elspeth, still showing no sign of self-consciousness or guilt.

"Yes, your Majesty? I have a dinner appointment in a few minutes," she said. "But of course if this is important, I can move it back."

"This won't take long." Elspeth was growing uncomfortably aware that she hadn't thought past stopping Lady d'Arden from executing her plan. She'd sort of believed Lady d'Arden would collapse when Elspeth appeared, confess her guilt, and offer herself up for arrest. Now that she was here, Elspeth wasn't entirely sure this was something a Queen ought to do. Maybe she should have sent the competent Lieutenant Anselm instead. Well, she was here, and there was nothing for it but to move forward.

"You sent guards to take Mister Faraday out of confinement last night," she said, beginning with the one thing she was certain of.

"I did," Lady d'Arden said coolly.

"And why was that?"

"I believed he was in danger. I didn't want him killed in custody before he could go to trial."

Elspeth blinked. "What gave you the right to do that?"

"I felt it was my duty to a fellow Council member."

"And it wasn't your duty to report your suspicions to me?"

"I believed time was of the essence."

Elspeth felt as if she were trying to wrestle water. Lady d'Arden sounded so sure of herself...and yet Elspeth knew it was a lie. "Your duty to remove him in the dead of night? That doesn't sound like you intended to protect him."

"How do you know what happened, your Majesty?"

Elspeth wished she could wipe her sweaty palms on her trousers without looking uncertain. The room was uncomfortably warm. "I put safeguards in place to protect Mister Faraday against exactly what you claim you were trying to prevent. It's far more likely you wanted him secretly dead than that you were acting out of altruism."

Lady d'Arden shrugged. "Believe what you like. The guards will back up my story."

"Because you told them to." Elspeth drew herself up to her full height, which made her slightly taller than Lady d'Arden, and hoped she looked confident. "Serena d'Arden, I'm taking you into custody."

Lady d'Arden smiled. "On what grounds?"

"High treason."

The smile grew broader. "High treason? Me? You don't have any proof."

"I know you framed Duncan Faraday because he was getting too close to the truth," Elspeth improvised. "You're poised to take over as Queen when I'm assassinated, something else you have planned. I'm sure if Finance digs a little deeper, they'll find the money from the sale of royal property didn't go to Mister Faraday, but to you." Elspeth smiled back. "And you may have forgotten, but I am the Queen of Tremontane. I don't need proof to arrest someone. Now, will you come quietly?"

Lady d'Arden's smile disappeared. "You're making a mistake," she said. "None of what you say is true. You're going to look like a fool, your Majesty."

"Then I'll look like a fool. But I'd rather err on the side of caution, if that means saving Mister Faraday's life, and Lord Harrington's."

A puzzled frown creased Lady d'Arden's brow. "Lord Harrington's?"

"You can't think you'd be able to pull your coup attempt off without getting him out of the way as well? Lord Harrington as regent is a powerful force. He wouldn't let you take over."

"Naturally," Lady d'Arden said, her face smoothing back into that insufferably certain smile. "Well, if you're determined on arresting me, I suppose we should go."

Elspeth eyed her suspiciously. "You seem awfully calm."

"Because I'm innocent."

Elspeth heard running footsteps in the corridor, growing louder and closer. A lot of running footsteps. "Watch her," she told the guards, and stepped into the corridor. Lord Harrington, his clothes and hair in disarray from running, trotted toward her, his pace slowing as he neared.

"Your Majesty," he said. "You're not hurt?"

"Of course not. Why are you here?" She looked past him at a squad of soldiers in Tremontane colors, coming to a halt a few feet away. "And why did you bring soldiers?"

"When I heard you intended to confront Lady d'Arden, I knew you were in danger. You didn't come alone, did you?" Lord Harrington had never sounded so agitated.

"I brought my escort...why did you think I was in danger from Lady d'Arden?"

Lord Harrington glanced back at the soldiers. "Inside," he said, and ushered her back into the Oak Hall.

Lady d'Arden hadn't moved. She still wore that superior smile, but it faded when she saw Lord Harrington. "What are you doing here?" she said.

Lord Harrington ignored her. "Your Majesty," he said, "why did you decide to arrest Lady d'Arden?"

Elspeth took a step back. "How did you learn that?"

Lord Harrington smiled. "My sources are extensive. I try to stay informed about anything that affects the stability of this country. I already know Lady d'Arden—" he flicked a glance at her— "tried to make Mister Faraday disappear last night. What else do you know?"

Elspeth didn't like the way this conversation was headed. Deep inside, a tiny voice was screaming at her to get out—but Lord Harrington wasn't a threat, and Lady d'Arden had no weapon. "Let's go back to the north wing and discuss it," she said.

Lord Harrington didn't move. "Did you learn who her co-conspirators were?"

"I...didn't know she had any," Elspeth said. Lord Harrington, with his intent eyes and the way he leaned over her like a predator, didn't seem nonthreatening anymore.

"Well, we'll interrogate her and find out."

Elspeth risked a glance at Lady d'Arden. She still looked as smug as a cat who's found the creamery. "Then you know Mister Faraday was framed."

"Of course." Lord Harrington smiled, but his eyes were cold. Elspeth took a step back and made herself stop. She did not want to look afraid in front of him.

"Why did you come yourself? You should have sent a detachment of guards," he said.

"It all happened rather fast," Elspeth said. "Shall we go?"

"And you should have informed the Council," Lord Harrington went on as if she hadn't spoken. "Who *did* you tell?"

"Everyone," Elspeth lied. She'd been so stupid. "My secretary, Lieutenant Anselm, Lady Quinn...I made sure everyone knew."

Lord Harrington took a step back. "So you haven't told anyone," he said. "So foolish."

"Lord Harrington," Elspeth said desperately, "Lady d'Arden intends to have you killed so she can become Queen. We need to take her into custody."

Lord Harrington looked at Lady d'Arden, then back at Elspeth.

"Well," he said, "this is awkward. It seems I acted too precipitously. You don't actually know anything, do you?"

"She was throwing a lot of guesses around, Felix," Lady d'Arden said. "But that's all they were."

Elspeth stepped backward again and was suddenly surrounded by her armed guards, all of them with weapons ready. Of course. She hadn't been completely stupid.

"So it's you," she told Lord Harrington. "I can't believe I was worried for your safety."

"Neither can I, but it's nice to know you care," Lord Harrington said. "Serena, what did you tell her?"

"Nothing." Lady d'Arden turned her superior smile on Elspeth. "And nothing has to change."

"So you want her wearing the Crown," Elspeth said. "Why? You already wield tremendous power. Why throw your lot in with someone who might not even win a civil war?"

Harrington ignored her. "Go back to the north wing," he said to Lady d'Arden. "You need to be conspicuously there. I'll handle things here."

Lady d'Arden nodded and let herself out without a backward glance. Lord Harrington examined Elspeth as if her guards weren't there. "She's not completely right. Something does have to change. I was hoping to coerce Ambassador Larssin into killing you, but I'll have to fall back on my first plan."

"I'm leaving," Elspeth said. "Get out of my way, or they'll cut you down."

"I'm sure you thought you were safe, bringing your armed escort," Lord Harrington said. "But I brought soldiers of my own—and you're outnumbered." He clapped twice, sharply, and both doors opened and soldiers streamed through. Elspeth's escort swiftly put her behind them.

"Are we?" Elspeth said. "Soldiers, I order you to stand down."

None of the soldiers in green and brown moved. All of them were poised to attack. "Soldiers," Elspeth said again, cursing how her voice shook. "I am your Queen. Stand down or be executed for treason."

"You're not long for this world, your Majesty," Lord Harrington said. "They're loyal to their new ruler."

"I see. That's you, is it? Or are you willing to let Lady d'Arden rule?"

Lord Harrington laughed. It was a cheerful, completely not sinister sound. "You really don't know anything, do you?" he said. "I don't care who rules Tremontane. I'm only interested in one thing, and that's protecting this country from Ruskalder aggression. You could have worn the Crown for half a century if you'd been willing to start a war. As it is, I need to replace you with someone more...amenable."

Elspeth cast her mind back weeks to an earlier conversation with the Foreign Affairs head. "The Riverlands," she breathed. "You want that piece of land that abuts on Daxtry and Avory. That's what this is all about!"

"I see you're not a complete loss." Lord Harrington took a few steps to put himself clear of the soldiers. "Yes. You'll be found assassinated, this time clearly by Ruskalder hands. I'll be regent and order us to go to war. Your brother will become King, and I'll stand ready to guide him in these troubled times."

"So Lady d'Arden was just a pawn. You don't intend her to be Queen."

"A wealthy, resourceful pawn. How unfortunate she succumbed to greed and abused the power of her office to embezzle Treasury funds." Lord Harrington smiled. "Now. Tell your guards to stand down, and I'll spare their lives."

"They're sworn to protect me. They won't let me be slaughtered."

"I don't intend these soldiers to kill you. I told you, you'll be found dead at the hands of a Ruskalder assassin. Mister Faraday won't be in a position to point out how ludicrous that is. Tell them to stand down."

Elspeth hesitated. One of her guards said, "Your Majesty, we won't let them take you."

"But—" If she ordered them to fight, they'd fight, and they'd all die, and she'd still be Lord Harrington's prisoner. "No. Lay down your weapons. We'll go peacefully."

"Your Majesty—"

"Do as I say. Please."

The guards in North blue slowly laid down their swords. "Good choice," Lord Harrington said. "Come with me, your Majesty."

Elspeth stepped out from behind her guard and went to his side. Lord Harrington gestured for her to precede him out the doors. She thought about running, decided she couldn't outpace the Tremontanan soldiers, hated herself for her cowardice, and walked into the corridor. Lord Harrington walked beside her, not touching her, and she hated herself even more that he'd controlled her without even the hint of violence.

They'd only gone a few steps when a terrible scream rang out through the halls, and there was the sound of fighting, fists meeting flesh, a couple of grunts. Elspeth spun around. Through the open doors, she saw scuffling, and then another scream filled her ears, one that cut off abruptly.

She ran for the room and stopped in the doorway, her heart pounding so hard it hurt. Crumpled bodies in North blue lay beyond a handful of Tremontanan soldiers, one of them cleaning his blade on the North livery. Smears of blood turned the wooden floor scarlet. None of the soldiers looked at her.

She turned on Lord Harrington and flung herself at him. "*You swore!*" she screamed, aiming her fists at his face. She got in one good hit before the soldiers dragged her off him, kicking and shouting and struggling. Then Lord Harrington slapped her, a powerful blow that knocked her head back and set her ears ringing.

"That's enough," Lord Harrington said. "Escort her Majesty, and make sure she doesn't try to run."

Hands gripped her upper arms and dragged her along. It had been so long since anyone had dared touch her, let alone so roughly, that between that and the slap she didn't resist. Then she came to her senses. She was going to die because she didn't have the nerve to fight back. She tried to pull away, tried going limp, but they only held her tighter and dragged her as if she weighed nothing.

The hall they were in was lined with small doors set at regular intervals, all of them painted a bright cherry red that contrasted with the white walls and gave the place the look of a candy manufactory. "Here," Lord Harrington said, and opened a door that looked just like all the others. "Once I've arranged things, I'll be back for you, your Majesty."

Elspeth spat in his face. He jerked, then wiped the spittle away with his sleeve. "Defy me all you want," he said. "It won't change anything."

The soldiers threw Elspeth into the room and slammed the door on her before she could try to escape. She heard the scrape of the key in the lock, and then heavy feet marching away, and then silence.

2 4

The room had no window, and was perfectly black except for the light shining through the keyhole and limning the door. Elspeth stared at the outline until the light was burned into her eyes, then she fumbled in her pocket for her light Device. Its soft red light revealed a room no more than twelve feet on a side, in size uncomfortably like Faraday's cell. It was bare of furnishings, but its floor was completely covered by a plush carpet that ran from wall to wall and extended a little way under the door. The light showed there had once been a window, but it had been boarded up, not haphazardly, but smoothly to make an unbroken wall. Empty sconces on two walls showed where lamps had once hung. Elspeth couldn't begin to guess what the room had once been used for.

She prowled the circumference, looking for anything that might give her an exit. She could fit her fingers beneath the door, but only as far as her palms. So she could wave at anyone who passed by. How cheering. What she needed was a good set of lock picks—except she didn't know how to pick a lock. So, a good set of lock picks and a thief willing to save the life of his Queen. Or a pistol, to shoot the lock out. Or...she stopped daydreaming about wild possibilities. She was trapped.

She sat by the door and ran her fingers through the soft nap of the carpet. She would just have to escape when Lord Harrington came back. Run away—he wouldn't want to kill her too far from the place he'd arranged for her "assassination" to be uncovered, would he? Elspeth closed her eyes and leaned her head against the door. He might. He could probably get away with just about anything so long as Faraday wasn't in a position to challenge him. How long would Faraday be safe once she was dead?

"Your Majesty. Your Majesty!"

Elspeth jumped. The whisper felt like it had entered directly into her skull. She moved her head and saw her ear was level with the keyhole. "Who's out there?" Elspeth said.

"It's Miss Simkins. Your Majesty, did they hurt you?"

Elspeth gingerly touched her cheek, which felt puffy and hot. "Not really. Miss Simkins, how did you find me?"

"You did say to keep close, your Majesty. When I saw Lord Harrington leave the north wing, I followed him. Well behind him, because I didn't like the look of those soldiers. I saw him drag you out of the Oak Hall and bring you here. Your Majesty, what should I do?"

"Go get—" Elspeth silently cursed. A squad of guards, hopefully led by Lieutenant Anselm, could force the door open, but she didn't know how many Tremontanan soldiers Lord Harrington or his stooge Captain Sommers had suborned, and she might only be sending more guards to their deaths. And she needed someone she could trust who could act independently, someone who wouldn't need this whole mess explained to him.

She tucked her *toan* jade inside her shirt, then whipped the signet ring on its cord over her head and crouched low to the ground. Her fingers fit, but would the ring? She poked it into the gap, and it went in a fraction of an inch and stuck. Cursing again, this time aloud, she pressed the ring down into the carpet as hard as she could and felt it move a little farther. Panting, she let go of the ring and examined the door. It was too securely fastened to move back and forth more than a fingernail's paring worth, but it was loose in its hinges, and Elspeth discovered she could lift it straight up so long as she used both hands. It didn't go far, but it might be far enough.

"Miss Simkins, get down low and look where I'm pointing," Elspeth said. She waggled her fingers until she felt Simkins grasp them, then freed her hand and pointed at where the ring was wedged under the door. "When I say pull, grab hold of the ring and pull it free."

Elspeth wormed both fingers beneath the door on either side of the ring and squatted low. "Pull!" she said, and lifted with all her might. Her arms strained against the weight of the door, her shoulders ached—

"I have it, your Majesty!" Simkins exclaimed.

Elspeth let go of the door and collapsed backward in a heap. "Take that ring to the jail cells," she panted. "Show it to the guards and tell them the Queen has ordered Mister Faraday's release. Tell Mister Faraday that Lord Harrington and Lady d'Arden are working together to start a war with Ruskald. And *hurry*."

"I understand. I'll be back, your Majesty." Simkins hurried away without any exclamations of surprise. She really was extraordinary.

Elspeth lay until she wasn't breathing so heavily, then rolled to her knees and stood. That was something, but she wasn't going to sit around here and wait passively for her death to walk through that door.

She decided to take another look at the door. She'd never really looked at a door before, not as anything more than something allowing passage from one room to another, or from outdoors to indoors. The handle was a knob that turned freely, or would do if the door weren't locked. She shone the Device into the keyhole, but didn't see anything but empty space. She already knew she wasn't strong enough to break down the door, and it wasn't loose enough for her to wiggle it free from the latch. But those loose hinges might be something she could use.

There were two of them, both of brass, both hidden away inside the door so all she could see was what looked like metal cylinders wedged between the door and the frame. She was too short to get a good look at the upper one, so she knelt and examined the other. The hinge looked simple enough, just a series of stacked, interleaved metal hoops through which a pin was threaded. She picked at the pin and felt it move not at all. There was enough room for her to fit her fingernails under the knobby head of the pin, but not enough for her to get a good grip.

She let go, frustrated. It was obvious if the pin was removed, the hoops would separate and the door would fall away from the frame. All she needed was some way of removing the pin.

She scoured the room again for something, anything, that was thin and flat and long enough to help her wiggle the pin free. Nothing. Elspeth sat by the door and fell back into despair. If Simkins couldn't get Faraday free in time, if she was gone when they returned...he really was going to kill her. She needed to find a solution.

She leaned back on both hands and bumped against the light Device, knocking it a few inches from where she'd set it on the floor to illuminate the room. She didn't know how long the light would last, but she hoped it would be a good long time. Sitting here in the dark waiting for her doom was too much even for her to bear.

She picked the Device up and examined it. It had three major pieces: its shell, which came in two halves molded to make an easy grip for its user; its light, which was a gleaming glass bead the size of a pea that glowed when you squeezed the case and stopped glowing at a second squeeze; and a piece Elspeth believed told the bead when to glow. That fit between the two halves of the shell and was a long, thin, inflexible piece of metal—

Elspeth gasped. Then she fitted her fingernails into the space between the halves of the case and pulled. It gave, but didn't come apart. Swearing, Elspeth pulled harder, and with a sharp *crack* the case snapped in two and the light went out. Elspeth scrabbled the flat piece of metal free of the case and felt it all over. It was about the length of her palm and fingers and about as wide as her forefinger and middle finger combined, and it was only a little thicker than her fingernails. It radiated a dim purple light, which made her nervous—

suppose the magic leaked out?—but not nervous enough to discard it.

She fitted the strip of metal edge-on to the knob of the hinge pin. It was just thin enough to fit. She slid it so it stuck out from the pin on both sides, then worked at the pin, wiggling the strip of metal while slowly pushing upward on the knob.

At first, nothing happened. Elspeth gritted her teeth and kept at it. She had nothing better to do, and it beat sitting and staring into the darkness. She wiggled the metal until her fingers were sore, then removed it and groped at the pin. She'd moved it! Only about half an inch, but the pin had definitely slid upward.

She attacked the pin with greater energy, and after some time— watches really needed Devices that cast a light on their faces so you could read them in the dark—the hinge pin fell and hit the soft carpet with a barely audible thump.

Elspeth put her fingers under the door again and pulled, this time toward herself. The door separated from the frame and moved toward her at the bottom, but not far—certainly not far enough for her to fit through. The gap lit the room slightly, but Elspeth was too frustrated to care. She let go of the door and let it fall back into place. It wasn't a perfect fit anymore and had obviously been tampered with.

Elspeth took a better look at the top hinge. Pulling on the bottom of the door had twisted the top hinge out of true, and it would now be impossible to lever the pin out the way she had the bottom hinge. She kicked the door, making it shift a few inches forward before settling back into place. There had to be a solution. She kicked the door again, eyeing the broken top hinge. It couldn't be a very strong metal, to twist so easily—

She grabbed hold of the bottom of the door and pulled toward herself as hard as she could. The gap was larger now. And she wasn't all that big. She sat on the floor on the side away from the hinges and pulled again. This time, she wedged her leg into the gap and used her knee to shove it farther open, then got her other knee through the space. Halfway out. She shoved with her hands and knees and scooted more of herself into the gap. Now she was thoroughly stuck.

She twisted and got one shoulder into the space. The top hinge whined at the pressure she was putting on it, her arms were scraped by the edge of the door, but that didn't matter, because she was...almost...*out*.

On that thought, she popped free of the gap and sat, wheezing with exertion, until her heart wasn't beating quite so fast. Then she stood and dusted herself off. She'd freed herself. It felt good.

But...now what? Faraday would come here looking for her, and if she left, he wouldn't know where to find her. On the other hand, she had no idea when Lord Harrington would return, and she absolutely could not be here when he did. Even if she hid in one of the nearby rooms, she couldn't count on him not searching them for her. So she had to leave, and fast.

Elspeth headed off down the hall, hoping she remembered enough of the route they'd taken. This was the western half of the palace, and if she had a compass, she could find her way to the north wing, But she had no compass, she had only her poor memory of how she'd gotten here. She firmed up her resolve and trotted away, determined not to get lost.

In hindsight, she reflected ten minutes later, getting lost was probably a given. What she couldn't understand was how she hadn't seen anyone else. The palace might be large, but it was also full of people. Surely she should have seen some of them by now?

She came around the corner and shrieked in surprise when she nearly ran into someone. The woman was dressed in a servant's uniform—a palace servant, green and brown, not North livery—and was standing on a short stepstool, reaching up to dust a light fixture high on the wall. She looked at Elspeth curiously. "What are you doing here, miss? These halls are off-limits to the public."

Trying to convince this servant she was the Queen would take forever. Elspeth made a lightning-fast decision. "I'm a candidate for the Scholia, and I was told to go there for my examination. But I got lost. Can you tell me which way to go?"

The woman frowned. "You're a long way from the Scholia, miss. And I don't think it's there anymore. They moved quarters."

"Yes, but I'm a...I want to be a librarian, and I was to see Master Coll Trapane about my course of study. Please, can you help me? I'm going to be late, I'm sure."

The woman stepped off the stool and walked toward Elspeth. "Go back the way you came and take the second hall on the right. Follow that hallway past three turnings, left, right, left, and take the next left. That hall ends in stairs. Go up the stairs one flight, take the first right off that landing, and that hall leads to the Royal Library."

"Thank you," Elspeth said, and took off before the woman could ask any more questions.

She recited the directions in her head: second right, third left, up the stairs, right off the first landing. Simple. Even she could do it.

The second hall on the right had a floor of two-foot-wide red tiles, gently pitted with age, and each hall leading off it was flanked by pillars and a carved wooden arch. Elspeth flew past, counting, idly noticing that the carvings were all different animals, a deer, a dog, a badger. The third left was a snake. Elspeth shuddered. Snakes made her uncomfortable. But this was the right turning—

—except the hall kept going and going and there were no stairs in sight. No doors, either. Elspeth came to a halt and cursed. What was wrong with her that she couldn't even follow basic directions? When this was over, she was going out with a guide and a compass and she was going to map the damn palace down to its bones.

Going back didn't make sense, especially since it might arouse the servant's suspicions, and Elspeth wanted to pass through the palace unnoticed. She set off walking again. The hall was as long as the one leading to the Judiciary, but Elspeth thought it sloped gradually upward by the amount of tension in her calves.

She needed a better plan. Ideally, she needed to get to the north wing, have someone call out all the North guards, and set Lieutenant Anselm to summoning the Tremontanan captains who could be trusted. Then they could work on finding Lord Harrington and Lady d'Arden and arresting them and all the traitorous guards working for them. Elspeth's chest ached at the memory of those slain North guards. They would receive justice, she promised.

Finally, Elspeth saw stairs in the distance. The servant just hadn't been specific as to how far apart everything was. With renewed hope, she ran for the stairs and clattered up them. They were an iron spiral, very tight, and Elspeth was dizzy when she arrived at the first landing. She stood still with her eyes closed for a moment, gripping the *toan* jade through her shirt. Then she drew a deep breath and made for the first right.

The servant hadn't been completely accurate; the first right actually led to a short, tunnel-like hall that let out on the freezing ancient corridor that only went to the Library and, past that, a little door opening on the palace grounds. And just like that, Elspeth's sense of where she was snapped into place. She turned and ran for the north wing.

She started to see people, mostly servants, a few green and brown soldiers she avoided. Almost there. Nobody hailed her or tried to stop her. Up one more ramp, and around the corner, and then she'd see the short flight of stairs leading up to the halls of the North wing.

She came around the corner and froze. A knot of green and brown soldiers stood only two feet away from her, completely filling the corridor. They came to attention immediately. Just like they'd been waiting for her.

Elspeth turned to run and heard the unmistakable sound of a pistol being cocked. "Don't move," a woman said. "I will shoot."

25

*E*lspeth slowly turned around. The corridor was empty of everyone but her and the soldiers. She opened her mouth to scream, and found the pistol's barrel suddenly inches from her face. "Start walking," the woman said. "Just act like nothing's wrong. I'll tell you where to go."

Elspeth took a step backward. She should run anyway. The woman might not hit anything vital—those pistols were notoriously inaccurate...over long distances. Not at point-blank range. Where in the *hell* were all those people who were in and out of the north wing all day? "Put that pistol down," she said, and this time her voice was steady. "This is your one chance. Put it down, let me go, and you won't be executed for treason. I won't make this offer again."

The woman smiled, but her gun didn't waver. "You won't be Queen much longer, and it won't matter," she said. "Walk. Now. Or I'll shoot you in the leg and we'll carry you."

Getting shot would make escaping impossible. Elspeth turned and walked. "Straight ahead, not around the corner," the soldier said. Elspeth, cursing inwardly, did as she was told.

They took her through semi-familiar halls to a door she recognized as leading outside—to the stables, in fact. Elspeth couldn't believe no one they passed thought anything was wrong with that picture. Well, if the woman concealed her pistol, it looked just like the Queen being escorted somewhere by her guards, and what was wrong with that?

The stables were as busy as ever. Elspeth looked once over her shoulder and discovered there weren't as many soldiers in her "guard" as before. It didn't matter. There were still enough of them to force her to go where they wanted. She'd been so stupid. Lord Harrington had known she'd make for the north wing and all he'd had to do was set soldiers to watch every approach. It was a risk, but a calculated one, because her lack of knowledge of the palace meant she was unlikely to beat his men there. Stupid.

"A carriage for her Majesty. She's going for a ride in the Park," the woman soldier said. Elspeth watched the carriage they brought for her. It had doors on both sides—she could get in and make a dash for the other door, get away far enough to start screaming. She tensed herself to run.

Something cold and hard pressed into her side. "Don't even think about it, *your Majesty*," the woman said in a low voice. Elspeth hated her as she'd never hated anyone in her life.

She climbed gingerly into the carriage, the gun's barrel never shifting more than an inch away from her side. The woman soldier followed her, along with two other guards, and more of the green and brown soldiers climbed onto the seat and roof. With a jerk, the horses set off out of the stable yard and onto the long curving gravel path that circled the palace to the front courtyard. Elspeth looked out the window, hoping to see someone who would know she was in danger. Servants bobbed and curtseyed as she passed, but no one raised a cry. Elspeth's chest ached with numb terror. She'd run out of ideas.

The journey through the city to the Park passed in silence. Elspeth thought about pleading with her captors and decided that was pointless. Girls in epic adventures always had a ready quip when they were in danger, but Elspeth couldn't think of anything clever to say. She kept a close eye on the pistol, determined to leap from the carriage if it ever wavered, but it continued to point steadily at her. Her hand closed on the window ledge. The woman soldier smiled as if she knew what Elspeth was thinking. The pistol twitched. Elspeth folded her hands in her lap. All that was left to her was to die fighting.

The carriage rattled through the massive ironwork gates of the Park and took the road to the left, the one that led to the tiny forest in the minuscule hills. How much of this had Landon designed? A hunting preserve wouldn't need flowerbeds. But the hills—Elspeth could imagine he would have enjoyed chasing foxes over those hills. She didn't know how to ride, so the idea didn't appeal to her, and at the moment it just seemed stupid.

The walls of the Park disappeared, and soon they were deep within the range of hills. The carriage came to a stop. "Out," the woman said, gesturing with the pistol, and Elspeth climbed out. The other soldiers had already leaped from the carriage and surrounded her. "We're going for a little walk," the woman said.

Elspeth didn't move. "If you're going to shoot me, I'm not going to make it easy on you," she said.

The woman took a step closer. "If I have to shoot you here, I'll also have to kill everyone close enough to be a witness. Is that what you want?"

Elspeth saw a couple of riders on horseback approaching, too far away to be of any use to her. "Damn you," she said in a low, terrible voice.

"You'd know, wouldn't you? Being a priestess and all," the woman said, unmoved. "Start walking. That way."

Elspeth's heart was pounding so hard she was surprised no one else seemed to hear it. She headed off across the hills, climbing the shallow incline until she reached the top. Even from that vantage point, the walls weren't visible. She descended the far side, then up another small hill, up and down until the woman said, "Here is fine."

Elspeth turned and faced her. "Do it," she said. "I'm not afraid of you."

The woman smiled. "We're waiting for someone."

Elspeth looked around. The area was as remote as she imagined was perfect for a murder. "What, you don't feel up to killing your Queen?"

The woman said nothing, just scanned the close horizon. "I can't believe so many of you were willing to betray me," Elspeth said. "How many was it? Or was Captain Sommers the only one, and you are his underlings?"

"Captain Sommers is a fool, but he knows which way the wind blows," the woman said. "Talk all you want. I don't mind."

This made Elspeth decide to shut up. She was shivering in the light breeze, though it wasn't all that cold, and she hugged herself and felt the cool touch of the bracelet against her other wrist. Now she would never know for certain who her mystery man was. And there would never be a chance to learn if he was someone she could love.

She ran her fingers over the meditation ritual and drew in a deep, calming breath. At least she wasn't afraid of reaching heaven, though she wasn't thrilled about the prospect of meeting her grandmother Genevieve. But maybe she and Landon had more in common than she'd believed.

Footsteps rustled the winter-dry grass, and Elspeth looked up to see Lord Harrington descending the slope. He, too, carried a pistol which he held loosely in one hand. "Is everything in order?" he asked the woman.

"We have witnesses to swear the Queen was taken from the road by Ruskalder," the woman soldier said. "They'll find her body and the 'Ruskald warrior' who declared his desire to see the traitor Queen dead before he was shot down by her loyal guards." The woman smiled nastily.

"Very good." Lord Harrington approached Elspeth. "It really is unfortunate it had to end this way," he said. "You had the makings of a good Queen. You just didn't know whom you should listen to. But in honor of that, I'll make this quick and as painless as possible." He smiled, as nasty an expression as the soldier's. "Well, that's untrue. It will probably hurt a lot. Just not for very long. I'm afraid that's the best I can do."

Elspeth lowered her arms and stood facing him. "I'm not afraid," she said. "But you should be very worried when it's your turn to die. Heaven isn't gentle with murderers."

"If I shared your faith, I'm sure that would worry me," Lord Harrington said. He raised the pistol. "Goodbye, your Majesty."

A thunderclap shattered the sky. A knife-edged fist punched Elspeth hard in the chest, knocking her backward. She heard a cry of pain and was surprised to discover it hadn't come from her. Then there were dozens more sharp explosions, too high-pitched to be thunder, and shouts, and screams.

She lay on her back and blinked up at the sky. Her chest hurt so badly she could barely breathe. She tried to lift her hand to touch where she'd been shot and found her limbs wouldn't move. Shaking, she tried again, and her left arm twitched and then lay still.

Someone crouched beside her, brushing Elspeth's hair out of her face. "Your Majesty," Simkins said. "Can you move? You've been shot!"

Elspeth worked her lips, ran her tongue over them, and whispered, "It hurts."

"You'll be fine, your Majesty. We'll get you to the palace and Dr. Ambrose will help you." Simkins took Elspeth's hand and patted it. "It's all over."

"What...happened?" Elspeth managed.

"Not right now, your Majesty. You need to lie still. But—" Simkins touched Elspeth's chest right where she'd been shot. A sharp pain shot through Elspeth, making her keen through clenched teeth. "Dear heaven. What is this?"

Elspeth tried again, and this time managed to raise her hand. She lightly touched the remains of the *toan* jade, cracked into half a dozen pieces from what her fingers told her. "Shot...in the chest..." she said. "He didn't...believe...the more...fool...him."

Someone else knelt beside her, casting a large shadow over her that chilled her. "I don't think she should be moved," Faraday said. "Someone bring Dr. Ambrose here. Quickly."

"You...found me..." Elspeth said. She couldn't draw breath deeply enough to speak normally. Anything more than a shallow breath felt like being knifed in the chest.

"I'm sorry, your Majesty, I didn't realize you were conscious," Faraday said. He gripped her hand in his large, warm one, and the shivers stopped. "Just lie still."

"Don't...yell..."

"Not until you're better. I promise to let you have it when you're well enough to fight back."

Elspeth smiled. "What...happened? Talk...keep me...alive."

"You're not going to die."

"Then keep me...being bored."

She opened her eyes to see Faraday and Simkins look at each other over her recumbent body. It was a look that said they weren't at all sure about her prospects. Tears slid down the sides of her face. She couldn't die, not now that Faraday was here—he would never forgive himself.

"Please," she said. "It hurts."

Faraday looked down at her. He looked terrible, between the three days' beard growth and the dark, sleepless circles under his eyes. "Lord Harrington shot you in the chest," he said. "He's a very good shot, fortunately for you. He hit the *toan* jade and the ball ricocheted to hit him in the face. That's what I saw right before I knocked him down and broke his wrist."

"But...so many...soldiers..."

"Perhaps I should explain more thoroughly," Simkins said. "I freed Mister Faraday and we returned to find you gone and the door broken. We guessed it meant you had freed yourself, as the soldiers had the key and would not need to destroy the door to retrieve you. So we went back to the north wing and summoned as many North guards as were on duty. We hoped you would make your way back to us, but I knew we could not trust any Tremontanan soldiers and that you would understand that as well, so as soon as the guards were assembled, we set off in search of you."

"We were lucky," Faraday said. He hadn't let go of Elspeth's hand, and it both comforted her and frightened her, because much as his hand warmed her, it also felt a little like the kind of grip that says someone is close to death. "One of the servants remembered seeing you heading for the stables with a soldiers' escort. And the stable hands told us you'd definitely said you were headed for the Park." He held her hand more tightly. "Just keep breathing, your Majesty. Everything...everything will be fine."

"Might...have been...a diversion..."

"It might have, but we were running out of time and I hoped it meant the enemy was too," Faraday said. "And we were lucky again, because as we entered the Park, Lieutenant Anselm saw a squad of Tremontanan soldiers disappearing into the hills. We chased them... sweet heaven, your Majesty, I am so sorry." Anguish filled Faraday's voice, and his grip on her hand was so painful she let out a squeak he was too far gone to notice.

"Why...sorry? Saved...my life..."

"I was seconds too slow to keep him from shooting you. The only reason you're still alive is that heaven loves you and your unwavering faith. Your Majesty, I insist you let me resign. I can't bear this."

Elspeth blinked up at him. "Give you...different job. Royal...dog catcher."

"I'm serious."

"So...am I...all those dogs...running around loose."

"May I suggest this be a decision for another time?" Simkins said, her voice sharp with fear.

Elspeth heard more voices, one of which was familiar. "Don't leave me," she told Faraday. "He stays," she told Dr. Ambrose.

"As you wish, your Majesty." Elspeth heard cloth tearing, and Faraday looked away. Sharp pains twinged through Elspeth's chest as the doctor plucked the fragments of the *toan* jade from her wound. It still hurt far worse than anything she'd experienced before.

Dr. Ambrose put a warm hand on Elspeth's wrist just above the bracelet. "Your breastbone is cracked, and you have some internal bleeding," she said, "so I'm going to put you to sleep while I heal you. Don't worry. Everything will be fine."

Elspeth looked up at Faraday. "Everything...will be...fine," she said, and slipped into unconsciousness.

26

*S*he woke in her own bedroom and inhaled deeply before remembering she couldn't. Nothing hurt. The smell of cinnamon and roses, her own personal scent, filled the air as it always did. She pushed herself up on her hands and found her body responded just as if she'd never been wounded.

She sat up fully. Someone had removed her clothes and dressed her in her nightgown, no doubt why she felt so comfortable. She plucked at the neck of her nightgown and peered down at her chest. It was smooth and unmarked, with no sign of where the pistol ball had struck her or where the *toan* jade had dug into her chest.

The memory made her heart skip a beat. Her precious medallion, shattered beyond repair. It had saved her life, but she missed it so much she...well, no, she didn't wish she'd been killed, but she was furious with Lord Harrington for destroying something she loved so dearly.

With that thought, she reached for her left wrist and breathed another deep sigh when she found the bracelet. That someone had realized not to remove it warmed her heart. She ran her fingers over its surface until she felt calmer. *Toan* jades, as Hien had often told her, were only special in how they linked someone to heaven, but hers had been given to her by Hien and Elspeth irrationally felt as if she'd let the chief priestess down in letting it be destroyed. Which was foolish, and Hien would probably be the first to point out how direct heaven's intervention had been on Elspeth's behalf.

She looked around for her watch and didn't see it. The clock on the mantel showed 8:17, but in this windowless room Elspeth didn't know if that meant morning or evening. She climbed out of bed and put on her dressing gown. She could ring for a maid, but the quietness had started to get to her, and she felt an urge to go where people were and reassure herself that not everyone in this palace wanted her dead.

Her sitting room was empty and dark. She fumbled her way through it, missing her light Device—something else she owed Lord Harrington a beating for—and opened the door. Everything was dark and quiet, but she saw firelight in the distance, and made her way toward the drawing room until she could see the fireplace fully. The windows were all dark. Veronica sat in a chair before the fireplace, staring into the flames.

She startled when Elspeth entered, then stood swiftly, more swiftly than Elspeth had ever seen her quiet aunt move, and hurried to put her arms around Elspeth and hug her tightly. "I know Dr. Ambrose said you would live," she murmured, "but you looked like death when they brought you home. I am so glad you're well."

Elspeth clung to her aunt and blinked away stupid tears. "It was that bad?"

"The doctor said the internal bleeding was serious, and that your ribs as well as your breastbone had cracked. And that the medallion hurt you badly when the ball impacted on it. But you would have been dead without it, so she said we could call it a miracle. And be grateful Lord Harrington didn't try to shoot you elsewhere." Veronica released her only to hold her by the shoulders at arm's length, examining her closely for hidden wounds. "You aren't still hurt?"

"I feel perfectly healthy and in no pain. Where is everyone? Where is Mister Faraday?"

"Gone," Veronica said, "to arrest everyone who might have been complicit in the attempt on your life. Lord Harrington is in jail. General Beckett locked up all the traitorous soldiers Lord Harrington convinced to follow him. Serena d'Arden is still at large, but I imagine they'll capture her soon. It's over, Elspeth."

"It's over," Elspeth said. That wasn't true. For her, it was just beginning. But it was the end of Lord Harrington's bid for power.

Veronica patted her shoulders. "I'm going to bed now. I only sat up to be sure you were well. You should rest. The doctor said you would feel very tired—that a major healing is like the body healed itself, but at twenty times the normal rate of recovery. Are you hungry?"

"No," Elspeth said, then realized that was a lie. "I'm famished."

Veronica smiled. "I'll have the kitchen bring you a tray. You should sit here and rest. I'm sure Mister Faraday will return eventually. He wanted me to make his apologies to you for leaving."

"He did the right thing," Elspeth said.

She sat in one of the hugely overstuffed chairs and leaned well back, closing her eyes and basking in the heat from the fire. She realized she'd dozed off when Shirley nudged her and settled a tray over the arms of the chair. Elspeth devoured everything they gave her, for once feeling the cook had guessed right: roast chicken and slices of tender beef in gravy and a bowl of buttery new peas and a pile of mashed potatoes as big as her doubled fists. She gulped orange juice straight from the carafe, burped, and felt at peace with herself and the world.

Shirley returned a few minutes after Elspeth had finished and removed the tray. Elspeth went back to reclining in the wonderful chair. She understood now why her aunt was so fond of these Ruskalder furnishings, with their heavy arms and cushions deep enough to swim in. The fire's heat caressed her bare feet, and she dozed again, dreaming of drowning in a sea of cinnamon buttercups.

The sound of the east wing door slamming woke her, frightening her with the thought that they'd missed someone who was now on their way to kill her...no, that was stupid, the North guards wouldn't let anyone like that through. She sat up and turned in time to see

Faraday enter the drawing room and approach slowly, his eyes fixed on her. He still looked terrible, unshaven and his mouth drawn down at the corners, but the sight of him relieved her heart.

"I'm sorry," she said before he could speak.

His mouth tightened. "*You're* sorry? Your Majesty—"

"Mister Faraday, I did everything wrong. I shouldn't have confronted Lady d'Arden directly. I put myself in danger and it's entirely good fortune and heaven's blessing that it all worked out. There are so many things I should have done differently, and because I didn't, I put you in a terrible position. I am so sorry. Please don't blame yourself."

Faraday took a seat beside her. "I was so slow in following you," he said. "And to come over that rise just in time to see him shoot you...it felt like he'd hit me instead."

"I can imagine. But—look. We could go on blaming ourselves all day, and threatening to resign, which you are forbidden to do, by the way—"

"You can only go on refusing my resignation for so long, your Majesty."

"Mister Faraday, I have just lost my Foreign Affairs head, and it sounds like Commerce is gone, too. Have you found Lady d'Arden?"

Faraday nodded. "She was captured boarding the overland express to Belenda in Eskandel. She is locked up, as it happens, in the cell I occupied until a few hours ago." He ran his hands over his scruffy face. "I can't believe it was only a few hours ago."

"I can't afford to lose you, too. I don't have any idea what happens next. Please, advise me. And stop making those absurd noises about resignation. I told you how tedious I find it."

Faraday scowled, an expression that made her heart feel light. "As your Majesty wishes."

"Stop it. I'm not overbearing."

"I would never say that."

"You just did. Maybe not in so many words, but don't think I can't tell what you really meant."

Faraday smiled. "Have I no secrets, then?"

She thought back to sitting next to him in the cell. "Not many. Please, tell me what to do. I have cells full of traitors—when do they go to trial?"

"The trial is a formality. And it's just for your noble prisoners. The soldiers who took up arms against their Queen are guilty under military law and are tried at court-martial, also a formality. They have no defense. Though I imagine some of them will try to claim they were only following orders."

Elspeth's heart hardened, remembering those fallen North guards. "They should have known better than to follow orders like those. Surely even soldiers can decide not to choose evil?"

"Precisely." Faraday looked away toward the windows. "The sentence is handed down immediately, and carried out three days later, by tradition."

Elspeth's anger drained away, leaving her feeling cold. "You mean executions."

Faraday nodded.

Elspeth rose from her chair and walked toward the fire. "You said the Queen can order any sentence commuted."

"But no ruler of Tremontane has ever rescinded a punishment for high treason."

"Maybe that should change."

"Your Majesty—"

"I have seen enough death, Mister Faraday!" Elspeth shouted. "I understand executing those who murdered my guards. But Lord Harrington's plot is over, and he will never have the power to hurt me or mine again. Why can I not exile him, or imprison him for the rest of his life?"

"Because you are not just Elspeth North," Faraday said, rising to tower over her. "You are the Queen of Tremontane, and a threat to you is a threat to this country. You cannot allow traitors to live, because that tells the world that you are weak and vulnerable to the same threat again. Do not show mercy, your Majesty. They would have shown you none."

Elspeth wiped tears from her eyes. "I know," she said. "But I hoped—Mister Faraday, I would have devoted my life to peaceful worship. And now I have to send I don't know how many people to their deaths."

"It's not your fault," Faraday said. "Don't take that guilt on yourself."

"It's not about guilt." Elspeth wiped away more tears. "It's their fault they have to die. They broke the law, and the punishment is clear. But there is still the reality that I am the one who enforces the law. Their lives are in my hand. And that is something I will have to live with forever." She drew in a deep, shuddering breath. "When I think of the men and women who died because of their stupid choices, it becomes easier. But I will never not resent them for what they did in making me complicit in their deaths."

Faraday lifted his hand, but let it fall without touching her. "I think I understand."

"Do you? I'm not sure I ever will." Elspeth turned away. "How soon can they be tried?"

"Two days. Execution happens three days after the verdict is rendered."

"Then in six days, we'll have a Council meeting. I will present the new heads of Foreign Affairs and Commerce, and we'll go over the Magister of the Scholia's request for additional funds."

"Your Majesty," Faraday said, then paused. When he finally spoke, Elspeth could tell it wasn't what he'd originally intended to say. "You will have to preside over the trial."

"But I don't know the law."

"Just preside. I will take care of the actual trial. I would spare you that if I could."

"I know." She looked over her shoulder at him. "And the executions?"

"You don't have to go to those."

She shook her head. "Actually," she said, "I think I must."

~

THE DAY OF THE EXECUTIONS DAWNED COLD AND RAINY. ELSPETH didn't like to see heaven's hand in everything that ever happened, because she believed heaven cared more about people acting of their own free will than in seeing them sheltered and guided every step of the mortal journey, but she couldn't help seeing the weather as an omen.

She dressed for the first time in her formal noble's coat, worn for coronations, royal funerals, certain official functions—and executions. It had been Willow North's coat, dark blue and silver, and Elspeth was startled to discover she and Willow had been the same size. The silver thread was only silver colored, not real silver, which was another surprise, and one she couldn't explain. She buttoned it up to her chin and surveyed herself in the mirror. She didn't look at all like someone who'd spent the morning crying.

The gibbet had been erected on the parade grounds. She hadn't been present earlier for the firing squad that had executed the more than thirty soldiers complicit in Lord Harrington's treachery. She didn't think she could have borne that. She was barely sure she could bear to witness a hanging. When Aldous Dane had suggested that a much older tradition allowed noble traitors to die by beheading, she'd run out of the room and vomited. So hanging it would be.

The parade stand overlooked the parade grounds, which were a vast sweep of packed earth that no amount of rain could churn into mud. Generations of soldiers had drilled there; generations of generals and captains and Kings and Queens had watched them drill. There was a canopy, a heavy fall of canvas, that shielded the parade stand from the light mist that hadn't yet become true rain. Elspeth's guards escorted her to its center, where she was flanked by General Beckett on her right and Faraday on her left. Elspeth had been grateful beyond belief to learn Beckett had been as much Lord Harrington's dupe as she had.

The rest of the Council stood around them, most of them huddled into cloaks. Lady Wilde, Lady Quinn, and Lord Heath were splendid in their own noble's coats, though lavender and pale green didn't suit Lord Heath at all. Elspeth didn't dare look directly at any of them, for fear she'd see condemnation in their eyes. Knowing she was doing the right thing hadn't made it easier.

She made herself look at the gibbet, skeletal and tall over the raised platform with the two trap doors. Two long ropes terminating in nooses dangled loose in the light wind. Her gorge rose again, and she swallowed to quiet her stomach.

More watchers filled the space between the gibbet and the parade stand. Elspeth had made it clear that she would tolerate no one whose sole purpose was to witness something horrible to tell their horrible friends later. There weren't many people. Guard officers. Palace functionaries. The families of the prisoners, which made Elspeth feel sick again. Lady Harrington was not there. She'd screamed threats and accusations at Elspeth when the sentence against her husband was handed down and eventually had fainted and been carried away. Elspeth hadn't seen her since. The memory of the trick she and James had played on the woman felt sour and terrible now.

The d'Ardens, on the other hand, had gone out of their way to assure Elspeth of their continued support. Lyle Carruthers, nearly dead with fear, had begged Elspeth to believe his involvement had been innocent, that he'd believed he was simply playing a joke. Elspeth had examined him closely and decided to believe him. She'd also suggested he take a long trip out of the country. He'd left on the next coach south.

Elspeth still had a hard time facing Serena d'Arden's parents. They'd sounded so timid, like they'd expected her to hold them responsible for their daughter's treason. It made her even angrier with the traitors, who hadn't thought beyond their own selfish needs to the consequences for people they supposedly loved.

Motion below shook Elspeth out of her reverie. Lord Harrington and Lady d'Arden were being led around the crowd to the steps leading up to the platform. They wore plain trousers and shirts and had neither coats nor hats, and the mist beaded on their hair like fine droplets threaded on silk.

Someone touched her left hand, and Elspeth turned her head to see Faraday, who stood next to her, watching the proceedings intently. Though his attention was on the scene below, his hand had reached for hers and now clasped it tightly. The reassuring touch warmed her in a way Willow North's coat couldn't, momentarily easing her pain. Elspeth clung to him, grateful for the reminder that she wasn't evil, that someone believed she'd done the right thing.

She saw the rest of the terrible ceremony in a daze, her eyes unfocused so the traitors were just a couple of white blurs. Lord Harrington shouted something her ears refused to make sense of and was silenced. Someone sobbed, a muffled sound that broke Elspeth's heart. Then there was a snap, a flurry of motion, and the blurs below her were still—far too still.

Elspeth wiped her eyes with her free hand, and Faraday let her other hand go. "Thus perish all who threaten this country," she said as loudly as she could manage. The ritual words released them all to go back to their lives, grateful not to be those still, grotesque bundles that had once been living people.

She let her guards form up around her and escort her back to the east wing, not the north wing, which would be empty today; she'd declared the day, not a holiday, which implied celebration, but a day of reflection and prayer. She spent it in her room, clinging to her new *toan* jade Mihn had given her and trying not to see dangling, twisting dead bodies when she closed her eyes.

27

Faraday came for her that evening while she was sitting in the drawing room, staring blindly into the fire. "Up," he said. "Don't make me carry you."

"I'm fine where I am."

"No, you're not. No more moping. You're coming with me."

Elspeth felt enough curiosity to go along with his demands, though when he told her to bring her cloak, she asked, "Where are we going?"

"You'll see," Faraday said, and refused to speak further.

She had thought they were going to the stables, perhaps for a late ride—not in the Park, that was closed after sunset—but he took her through the halls of the palace and into old stone corridors that looked like the one leading to the Royal Library. He stopped at an ancient wooden door and gestured her through. The chilly room beyond was pitch dark and smelled of wet stone and melted wax. Faraday lit a lamp and lifted it off the wall. "Up," he said.

The room turned out to be narrow, and looked narrower for being very tall. A steep, rickety staircase constrained only by a slim rail filled most of the space. In the lamplight, the black stone walls glittered with specks like gold. Elspeth tilted her head to look up. The staircase spiraled around the shaft's interior and extended well beyond the reach of the lamplight. "What is this place?"

"Start climbing, and you'll see," Faraday said.

"I hate climbing."

"It's worth it, I promise you."

She scowled, but began the ascent.

After about a hundred steps, her legs ached, her chest hurt from breathing so hard, and she didn't know why she'd ever thought the stairs in the Irantzen Temple were a hardship. She stopped, forcing Faraday to stop as well. "This is insane," she gasped. "Why are you torturing me?"

"It's only torture because you don't get enough exercise." Faraday wasn't even a little out of breath. "Does your Majesty need to be carried?"

"Mister Faraday, have we established that I am your sovereign lord and can command you to take a flying leap off this staircase?"

He chuckled. "Just...trust me."

Elspeth drew in another deep breath and pressed on.

She didn't realize the staircase opened to the outdoors until she emerged onto the tower's top to find the sky spread out around her. The morning's storm had passed quickly, and the skies were now clear and spattered with stars. Elspeth took a few more steps out of Faraday's way and turned in a slow circle. All of Aurilien lay before her, from the lights of Lower Town to the hill where the wealthy and noble had their estates. "It's so beautiful," she breathed.

"I told you it was worth it," Faraday said. "But that's not why we're here."

She turned to look at him. He'd set the lantern down by the top of the steps and it cast odd shadows up his legs and across his face. "Come over here," he said, walking away from the edge of the tower where they stood. Curious, Elspeth followed him.

In the center of the tower was a large humped shape on a stone slab that turned out to be an enormous brazier, with a signal fire laid ready in it. Faraday withdrew a matchlighter from within his cloak and clicked it a few times.

"Willow North climbed the outside of this tower to light the fire that brought the troops into Aurilien," he said. "After that, they lit the fire as a symbol of her victory, and now lighting it every night is tradition. Something I know you're fond of," he said with a smile. "They usually light it at sundown, but I told them I knew someone who needed to do it herself tonight." He handed Elspeth the matchlighter. "There's kindling in place already."

Breathless, Elspeth took the matchlighter and stepped up to where she could reach the kindling. The fire caught right away, consuming the wood shavings and twisted papers and licking along the split logs making a pyramid around them. She took a few steps back and admired how the light and smoke rose into the air, like many thin arms reaching to heaven.

Faraday came up behind her, prompting her to turn around. "You did something today no Queen or King should ever be forced to do," he said, his voice nearly lost in the crackle of the flames, "and I know it's eating you up, whatever you might say about knowing it's not your guilt. I wanted to remind you that this, too, is part of who you are. This heritage. And I wish I could tell you this is the last hard thing you'll have to do as Queen, or that it will all be joy and happiness for the rest of your life. All I can tell you is that I have absolute faith that whatever comes, you will face it with strength and honor."

Elspeth's breath caught in her chest. "That's...I don't know if I'm worthy of that."

He smiled, a wry half-smile that made her smile in return. "We all get things we don't deserve. I still say you should let me resign."

"Not a chance. You're my councilor, you should counsel me." She turned away and walked around to the far side of the brazier. "In fact, Mister Faraday, I am in need of your advice as a law-speaker."

"I am yours to command, your Majesty."

She looked up into the starry sky. "I need to know what laws there are concerning my choice of Consort."

He was silent for a moment. "There aren't many laws about that," he said finally. "The ruler of Tremontane is free to marry anyone she chooses and elevate her spouse to the rank of Consort. You could marry a road-sweeper if you wanted. The idea is that anyone capable of ruling a country is assumed capable of choosing an appropriate spouse."

"So it could be anyone? A foreigner?"

"Anyone. Though from what you've said, I imagine it wouldn't be a Veriboldan landholder."

"No, not that." Elspeth turned to face him. He was partially hidden by the growing blaze, only the top of his dark head and the outline of his shoulders visible. "So the only law," she said, "is the one that says I have to be the one to make the proposal."

"That is correct."

She took a few steps toward him, back around the corner of the brazier. "That's a big responsibility. I'm not sure I'm equal to it."

"You don't have to decide immediately, no matter what Aldous Dane says." His smile had vanished, and his expression was completely impassive.

Elspeth controlled her smile. "Tell me something, Mister Faraday," she said, running her fingers along the stone slab. "What qualities should I look for in a Consort?"

He looked in the direction of the fire. "I'm not qualified to make that assessment."

She took a few more steps and stood in front of him, looking up at him through her lashes. "You must have *some* opinion. Please. I need your perspective."

Faraday pursed his lips thoughtfully. "Well, in my opinion, a good Consort should be someone you can trust. Someone who will never betray you."

Elspeth nodded. "And?"

"Ideally, he should be someone who understands what it means that you are Queen, and who understands the decisions you have to make. Someone who knows at least a little about our government. It would be even better if he had experience with the law."

"I suppose you would know, being a law-speaker yourself," Elspeth said. "Those are good qualities. Anything else?"

Faraday made a show of looking into the distance beyond her, searching the stars for wisdom. "He should have a strong personality, be able to stand up to you for your own good, and back down when he's wrong."

"Are you sure? That sounds like we would argue frequently."

"Oh, but you wouldn't mind arguing, because you'd always make up in the end. I understand making up—" His lips quirked in that familiar half-smile— "is an enjoyable part of marriage."

"Hmm. All right. Anything else?"

The smile faded. He looked down at her, his eyes dark and intent on hers. "He should also be a devoted husband," he said, "who loves you more than fire loves air."

She couldn't look away from those eyes. "And you believe there's someone out there who has all these qualities?"

Faraday nodded. "I know there is."

"Someone near to me? Someone I know?"

"I hope so."

"Someone who's bound by law not to tell me how he feels."

Faraday's lips curved in a wry smile again. "Maybe he tried, and heaven intervened. Are you going to let that stop you taking a chance?"

Elspeth couldn't help herself. She looked demurely away, a mischievous smile touching her own lips. "But suppose I ask, and he rejects me? I don't know if I could bear that."

Faraday let out a deep, frustrated breath. "Elspeth," he said, "if you don't ask me to marry you, I will be forced to ask *you* to marry *me*, and then you will have to send me to prison, and that would be a terrible way for our life together to begin. And I really don't want to go back to that cell. So—"

Elspeth put her arms around his neck and pulled him close. "Will you marry me? Or should I spend the rest of my life trying desperately to find someone else I can love as much as I love you?"

He smiled. "Thank heaven it's not to be the cell," he said, and kissed her.

It felt like being struck by white hot lightning, how his kiss shivered through her whole body and left her trembling and desperate for more. "Oh," she gasped when they finally separated, "oh, that is *so* much better than meditation."

He burst out laughing, a merry, unconstrained sound, and drew her closer to him so they were pressed against each other. Even that touch set her heart racing. "You are my dearest love, and everything you do and say delights me," he said, "but I intend to record that sentence in my diary, and bring it out on our wedding night, and we will see if we can raise your standards for pleasure a little higher."

Elspeth blushed. "Kiss me again, then, because I truly didn't know what to expect."

He smiled, and brushed his lips against hers before kissing her more deeply. She responded by slipping her hands from around his neck to his waist, marveling at how strong the muscles of his shoulders and back felt under her hands. The shock of his first kiss had faded into a warm, melting glow that flooded through her. A fleeting thought shot through her mind: *my dearest enemy*, and she smiled against his mouth and pressed herself closer to him. She wondered how it felt to him, if he too wanted it to go on forever.

He withdrew from her, and she made an unhappy noise and reached for him again. He captured both her hands in his large, warm ones and said, "It's getting cold."

"I can't tell."

"Well, I can, and I intend to make sure my bride doesn't freeze to death before we are husband and wife. One of us has to be sensible."

Elspeth lowered her hands and felt her bracelet rattle around her wrist bone. "As sensible as you were?" she said, raising her arm so the bracelet was level with his eyes. "This was your gift, admit it! I guessed it when we were in the cell and you asked me about the meditation ritual—you said it like you already knew the answer. Duncan, why didn't you put your name on this? It would have saved us days of dancing around!"

Faraday grimaced. "I knew I should have put the card inside the box, but I thought that would look like subterfuge, like I needed it kept secret from the world. I didn't know it had fallen off at first. You didn't acknowledge the gift at all, didn't wear it, and I had about a day of black despair thinking you'd rejected me—worse, that you disdained me so much you couldn't even reject me to my face. Then I overheard you telling Lady Quinn about the mystery bracelet with no name, and I went back to where the gifts were examined and found the card on the floor."

"But you could have come to me then. You had to know how I felt."

"By then it was too late—I couldn't tell you the truth without sounding pathetic or maybe even going to jail. I'd made up my mind to tell you anyway, but then I was accused of treason and that was the end of that plan. And when I finally saw you wearing it, we were, as you pointed out, in my cell, and a man doesn't declare love to a woman when he's imprisoned, not if he wants to keep his self-respect."

She thumped him lightly on the chest. "I forgive you because it was the perfect gift, and if I'd been thinking at all, I would have known there was only one man who could have chosen it for me. You know the significance, right?"

He held the bracelet loosely and traced the letters. "*That which is two becomes one, but much must be shed to reach it.* I thought it perfectly symbolized our relationship. We had so many misconceptions to shed."

"Exactly." She put her arms around Faraday and hugged him. "And tomorrow we will see if I can shock Aldous Dane with my request that he plan a royal wedding."

"A fast royal wedding." Faraday put his arms around her and slid his hands beneath her cloak to run his fingers lightly up her spine, making her shiver with pleasure. "I'm not a patient man."

"I know I don't intend to dawdle," Elspeth said. "I've only just discovered kissing. I hear that's just the beginning."

"You hear correctly," Faraday said, and kissed her once more.

28

*E*lspeth had thought, when the Magister of the Scholia had invited her to the opening celebrations, that the new building was just that—one building. She hadn't expected a beautiful, sprawling campus with rolling lawns cut by gravel paths between many buildings, all of them built solidly of stone that looked as if it were intended to last longer than Aurilien. They looked less like houses than bethels, their walls reaching for heaven, pierced by arches and topped by slender spires. Her carriage drove through the arched stone gateway just as the bell in the tallest tower pealed the hour. "Extraordinary," she breathed, leaning out the window not caring if she looked like a gawking country girl.

"It had better be," Duncan said. "I couldn't believe Finance's final report on the Crown's contribution. I hope we can get our money's worth out of them."

"You can't put a price on learning."

"Actually, you can, and that price is 'sweet heaven, they needed how many windows?'"

Elspeth laughed. "They turn out the best educated men and women in the country, and those men and women will come to work for the Crown, and everyone will be satisfied."

Duncan took her hand. "I believe you're right. But the Royal Library isn't being moved?"

"Nobody wanted to take responsibility for hauling that many books fifty miles. Besides, I want it where I can reach it." Master Coll Trapane, the Royal Librarian, had looked relieved when Elspeth had told her the news. "And its current home is just right."

"It will outgrow that room eventually."

"Then eventually we'll move it. You're unusually pessimistic today."

He kissed the back of her hand. "Just thinking practical thoughts. The Magister didn't look happy when you turned down his request for a permanent endowment from the Crown."

"That really would have been a stretch. We may support the Scholia, but they need to be responsible for their own maintenance, which means their own funding. And the Magister will come to terms with that eventually."

Duncan looked out the window past her. "He will. And this place really is beautiful."

The carriage came to a halt outside the largest building, where the Magister, a tall, angular man who resembled Veronica except for his bald head, waited to greet the Queen and her soon-to-be Consort. More carriages bearing the rest of the Council and key government officials drew up behind them. Elspeth climbed out of the carriage without help and cast her eye on the building's stone façade. Two enormous stained glass windows, each depicting men or women engaged in study, drew her eye immediately, and she remembered Duncan's comments and suppressed a giggle.

"Your Majesty, welcome," the Magister said in his light, wispy tenor. "Please allow me to escort you on a tour of the Scholia."

"I'm looking forward to it," Elspeth said.

They'd thought of everything—buildings to house different scholastic disciplines, dormitories for students, housing for instructors, a low-roofed refectory for those who didn't want to go into the nearest town for their meals, and a bethel for worship. The last was the building housing the bell tower. "You see we're prepared to be self-contained," the Magister said.

Elspeth cast her eye over the wide benches that would allow for the entire population of the Scholia to gather, the shallow niches for individual worship, and said, "Do you anticipate the bethel seeing much use?"

"We're not a religious institution, obviously, so its practical purpose is for community gatherings. But we recognize the influence of heaven in bringing all this to pass, and we want to allow for individuals to worship as they please."

Elspeth thought it was more likely he'd recognized the influence of Elspeth North. A shiver of disquiet went through her that the Magister had tried to pander to her, but she suppressed it. If he wanted to honor her by honoring heaven, well, that was the sort of gift that ultimately blessed everyone, however cynical its beginnings might be.

The bethel was the final stop on the tour, and the Magister led Elspeth to a seat at the front of the room, facing the benches. More seats had been arranged in rows beside and behind it, but this one was clearly intended to be permanent. Elspeth guessed it would ordinarily be the Magister's. It was ornately carved, with dark green cushions and arm rests that curved at the end to invite the sitter to curl her hands around them. It was not a furnishing typical of a Tremontanan bethel, and was too fancy to be like similar ones in Veriboldan sanctuaries or even the Irantzen Temple, and Elspeth wondered whose inspiration it had been.

As students and Masters in their black robes and colored stoles filed in and took their seats, Duncan whispered, "This isn't what I expected."

"Me neither," Elspeth replied. "He asked me to say a few words, but I feel like I'm presiding over a religious service."

"I suppose if they want to remember heaven guiding them in their work, that's a good thing."

"I suppose." That was true, but it was also the sort of thing that could lead to hidebound tradition as people forgot the spiritual intent and held onto the trappings of worship. And now she'd been infected by Duncan's pessimism. The Scholia masters had the highest goals for the institution, and she was borrowing trouble.

The Magister waited for everyone to settle in, then walked to a spot between Elspeth and the community. "This is a momentous day," he said, "a day to celebrate the joy of learning and teaching. The Scholia seeks to uphold the traditions brought from Eskandel by Kerish North, but also to reach beyond those traditions to make our Scholia peculiarly Tremontanan. We are capable of reaching those goals primarily because of the support of the Crown. Please rise for her Majesty, Elspeth North."

The assembled men and women stood, the Masters' robes swishing so the air was filled with the sound of a spring breeze. Elspeth stood and walked forward to take the Magister's place. "I recognize the tremendous work you of the Scholia do," she said, "and acknowledge how much my government has been aided by the Masters who fill vital roles within it. I hope the Scholia's continued association with the Crown will benefit both of us."

She looked up at the vaulted ceiling, imagining she could see the bell tower through it. "Today, I invite you to consider the nature of this building. Our bethels reach toward heaven to encourage us to remember the ultimate destination of every man and woman. They are rooted in earth to remind us of our duty to live the best mortal lives we can. You of the Scholia have the opportunity to make tremendous advances in learning that will bless the lives of others, enriching mortality and aspiring to heaven. Please remember this as the Scholia continues to grow. Thank you for your service to Tremontane."

She sat, and the spring wind blew again as everyone resumed their seats. "Thank you, your Majesty, for your inspiring words," the Magister said. "We will now take a moment for silent prayer and thought."

In the Temple, a priestess would have led the prayer. Elspeth touched her *toan* jade through her gown's thin muslin and contemplated how different worship could be even when people shared the same faith. How many of these people were thinking about their dinners rather than heaven? It wasn't any of her business, and she certainly didn't judge; it was just an idle thought that arose out of her reverie. After all, every one of these people, she hoped, was destined for heaven whether they thought about it or not.

The moment ended, she rose from her seat, and everyone else stood as she and Duncan walked down the center aisle, followed by her entourage. She looked ahead to where the grassy green spring lawn was visible through the half-open doors, propped that way to let cool air into the stuffy room, and took Duncan's hand with a smile.

"Ready for another long ride?" he murmured.

She shook her head. "I was anticipating," she said, "another walk just like this one."

The Crown gleamed in the bright lights of the antechamber. Elspeth stood regarding it, once again looking for scratches or smears. It was perfect. She brushed a fingertip over one of the emeralds, whose cool, smooth surface didn't feel anything like the jade bracelet she wore on her left wrist despite its not matching the rest of her attire, which was North blue satin. The bracelet mattered more to her than anything else she wore that day.

She lifted the Crown off its velvet cushion and settled it securely on her head. It fit as perfectly as before, not shifting when she turned her head to one side and then the other. It probably wouldn't survive a vigorous head-shaking, but it would be fine for a walk down the long red velvet carpet and up the three steps of the dais.

The door behind her opened, and she turned. "Well," she said with an appreciative smile, "I'm certainly marrying the handsomest man in Tremontane today."

Duncan came toward her, his smile matching hers. "Just Tremontane?"

"I don't know everyone in the world, my love. But I suppose that's possible." He looked wonderful in the North blue satin coat that matched his eyes and showed off his shoulders—how long it had taken her to realize how broad his shoulders were?—and the matching knee breeches that showed off his excellent legs. Those, she remembered making note of almost immediately. "Let's take a moment to admire how good you look."

"I ought to be offended that you see me as nothing more than a handsome body, but as I was just thinking how much I wanted to hold your beautiful body in my arms, objectify away." He put his words into action, drawing her close for a long, sweet, breathless kiss.

The sound of the double doors creaking open separated them. Duncan took her hand and guided her to the designated spot. "Are you ready, your Majesty?"

"Mister Faraday, I have never been more ready for anything." She paused, framed in the doorway with him, and looked out over the assembled crowd. "And that's the last time I will ever call you that."

They took their first steps together, hand in hand, down the carpet that led straight as an arrow to the dais where their families waited. Elspeth's eagerness propelled her faster until Duncan's hand restrained her. He glanced briefly at her, smiling as if he understood how much she'd anticipated this day. Why he wasn't running with her, she had no idea. Well, one of them needed to have restraint, and it might as well be him.

As they neared the dais, Elspeth watched the people standing there: to the right, Duncan's parents, who still looked utterly shocked that their son was marrying the Queen, and his married sister holding her infant son, with her husband behind them. The baby wasn't crying, though Elspeth felt it would add to the miracle of the proceedings if he did. Duncan's unmarried younger brother stood beside his sister, grinning as foolishly as Elspeth feared she was. He had his brother's dark blue eyes and the same funny half-smile. Elspeth glanced quickly at Duncan; he was smiling too, and her heart gave a little extra thump of excitement.

To the left, her own family: her mother, tears streaming down her smiling face, her sibs, Ian wearing the scowl that said he hated his formal clothing, Sariah bouncing with joy, James overtopping them all. Veronica, looking strangely relieved—she'd lost so many loved ones, that made sense. And in the center, her father, with an expression of pride and happiness so profound Elspeth thought that alone might propel her up the stairs, dragging Duncan with her.

She managed to maintain a respectable pace all the way up the steps and to her designated place to her father's right. She felt her family ranged behind her, and it gave her strength. Duncan, facing her, let go of her hand with a final squeeze. She wanted to laugh at the humor in his eyes. Yes, this was a day no one had expected, least of all her.

Her father cleared his throat, and the room beyond went even stiller. "We are here today," he said, his voice carrying to the far ends of the room, "to witness the joining of Duncan Faraday to the house of North by adoption, and to witness the joining of Elspeth North and Duncan North by oath of marriage. If anyone disputes the right of these people to make oath to each other, speak now."

The pause that followed keyed Elspeth's nerves to the breaking point. If anyone did have the temerity to speak up, she'd probably assault that person with her own hands.

Father shifted. "Duncan Faraday, step forward."

Duncan clasped Father around the right wrist as Father returned the grip. "Duncan Faraday, do you of your own free will relinquish all claim to the name of Faraday, to take the name of North to yourself and to your children?"

"Yes," Duncan said in a voice as ringing and resolute as Father's. His eyes closed briefly, and a smile touched his lips as the new family bond took effect. Elspeth's heart ached with love for him.

"Elspeth North, step forward," Father said.

Duncan opened his eyes, and his smile broadened. Elspeth knew she was supposed to look at her father now, but she couldn't break away from Duncan's gaze, and he looked like he felt the same. What was a little break with tradition on a day like this?

"Clasp left hands," Father instructed. Elspeth took Duncan's left hand and felt his larger one close over hers. "Elspeth North," Father went on, his voice suddenly rough, "do you take Duncan North as your husband and Consort, father of your children and strong left hand for all your days?"

Elspeth wanted to shout her response to the skies, but managed a clear and resonant, "Yes," that still felt as though it rang with everything in her heart.

Distantly, she heard her father say, "Duncan North, do you take Elspeth North as your wife, mother of your children and strong left hand for all your days?"

Duncan looked at her, and his grip tightened. "Yes," he said.

"Then exchange rings," Father said, "and your heart's oaths."

Elspeth fumbled the heavy gold band out of her sleeve and slid it over Duncan's middle finger. "Duncan," she said, and her mind went briefly blank as everything she wanted to say deserted her. "Duncan, you were my strong left hand before I knew it, and I swear to be the strength to your weakness, all the days of my life."

Duncan produced her ring more smoothly. It was cool against her finger, smooth gold set with a North blue sapphire that glittered in the lamplight. "Elspeth, my love," he said with a crooked smile, "you hold my heart in your hands, and I will be strength to your weakness forever."

Father said, "Do you gathered here today bear witness?"

The roar of the crowd nearly deafened Elspeth. She took Duncan's hand in hers, and drew in a steadying breath against what came next.

"Then as patriarch of the house of North," Father shouted over the crowd, "I declare this marriage sworn and sealed!"

They'd told her what to expect. They'd told her to brace herself. But none of that instruction prepared her for the fire that swept over her, rocking her to her core and making her cling to Duncan's hand so she wouldn't fall over from the rush of power that was the marriage bond taking effect. She closed her eyes and sent up a brief prayer, not of thanks nor of supplication, but of joy, and felt an answering joy touch her heart.

Duncan was leaning close, speaking into her ear so she could hear him over the screaming of the crowd. "Are you all right?"

She opened her eyes. "More than all right," she said, put her arm around his neck and kissed him.

~

"DUNCAN?"

"Yes, Queen of my heart?"

"Can we do that again?"

~

MUCH LATER, SHE CURLED UP AGAINST HER HUSBAND'S SIDE AND breathed him in. He usually smelled faintly of woody musk and the clean scent of his soap, but now her smell of cinnamon and roses mingled with his. It felt beautifully symbolic.

"I think," she said, "when I first had the chance to become a priestess, if I'd known you were in the world, and that sex was so wonderful, I'd have had serious trouble deciding which path my life should take."

"I understand from reputable sources," Duncan said, "that it's much better than meditation."

She slugged him lightly on the chest. "Touching the face of heaven is beautiful in its own way. But this—being close to you in every possible way—this is simply miraculous."

"I'm so glad you're not a priestess," Duncan said, turning to put his arms around her. His lips touched hers and she kissed him back, feeling once more as if her heart might crack from joy.

When they separated, Elspeth touched his cheek, making him smile. "Do you remember," she said, "the first thing you ever said to me?"

"Was it 'I want you desperately, o love of my life'?"

"No. It was a somewhat surly introduction, followed by a lecture."

Duncan arched one eyebrow. "If this is meant to be romantic talk, you have some learning to do. Maybe the Scholia offers a class."

She smiled. "It's just that I was thinking you never know how life will turn out. It took me so long to be able to see past those first terrible words."

"I fell in love with you almost immediately. Against my better judgment, even. You were not at all what I'd expected." He ran his fingers lightly over her collarbone. "That first assassination attempt —some damn fool came in shouting that the Queen had been shot, and naturally I thought they meant you were dead, and it hit me like a lead weight to the stomach. I told myself it was just guilt over failing at my duties, but then I saw you in the stable yard, so afraid and yet so mulishly defiant, and all I could think of was taking you in my arms and kissing that look away."

"I don't know at what point I loved you, except that there was a part of me that opened that little box, saw the bracelet, and wished your name was on it." She snuggled into his arms more deeply. "And now, here we are."

"With our whole lives ahead of us. I still think we should take a wedding trip."

Elspeth shuddered. "Think of how the paperwork would pile up. We'd have to take the whole north wing along, and who wants a wedding trip at that cost?"

Duncan kissed her forehead. "You could burn the paperwork. You've set the precedent."

"And you could yell at me for being irresponsible. So long as we're talking about precedent."

He shifted so he could kiss her lips. "You know," he said, "there are better precedents we could set."

"Like the one where you—oh, yes, that one."

"Or the one," Duncan murmured, "where I love you past the telling of it."

"I love that one," Elspeth said. "Let's explore the possibilities."

ABOUT THE AUTHOR

In addition to the Heirs of Willow North series, Melissa McShane is the author of The Extraordinaries series, beginning with BURNING BRIGHT, the Crown of Tremontane series, beginning with SERVANT OF THE CROWN, the Last Oracle series, beginning with THE BOOK OF SECRETS as well as COMPANY OF STRANGERS and many others.

After a childhood spent roaming the United States, she settled in Utah with her husband, four children and a niece, four very needy cats, and a library that continues to grow out of control. She wrote reviews and critical essays for many years before turning to fiction, which is much more fun than anyone ought to be allowed to have.

You can visit her at her website www.melissamcshanewrites.com for more information on other books.

For information on new releases, fun extras, and more, sign up for Melissa's newsletter: http://eepurl.com/brannP

If you enjoyed this book, please consider leaving a review at your favorite online retailer or Goodreads!

The Book of Peril

The Book of Mayhem

The Book of Lies

The Book of Betrayal

The Book of Havoc

The Book of Harmony

The Book of War

The Book of Destiny

COMPANY OF STRANGERS

Company of Strangers

Stone of Inheritance

Mortal Rites

Shifting Loyalties

Sands of Memory

Call of Wizardry

THE CONVERGENCE TRILOGY

The Summoned Mage

The Wandering Mage

The Unconquered Mage

THE BOOKS OF DALANINE

The Smoke-Scented Girl

The God-Touched Man

Emissary

Warts and All: A Fairy Tale Collection

The View from Castle Always